Praise for
The Nightworkers

"A gripping, bighearted thriller about a family of criminals coming apart at the seams. Whip-smart and surprisingly funny, *The Night-workers* is a terrific debut about loyalty and the ties that bind."
—Harlan Coben, author of *The Boy from the Woods*

"Consider this a working-class version of one little pocket of *The Godfather* . . . Like the strongest authors in this genre, Selfon bares the effects of death on each of us. His dialogue is compelling, his plot actions and his images of Brooklyn's underworld unforgettable . . . A few chapters in, there's no chance of putting down this book until the highly satisfying yet unexpected finale."
—Beth Kanell, *New York Journal of Books*

"One of the best novels of the year thus far . . . Remarkable from beginning to end."
—Joe Hartlaub, *Bookreporter*

"Brian Selfon steps firmly into the new genre known as Brooklyn Noir and the result is a twisty crime thriller that will hit home . . . Fans of the crime thriller genre will particularly enjoy the time Selfon has taken to focus on what he knows while creating very believable characters that you will instantly care about."
—Ray Palen, *Criminal Element*

"A dark slice of Brooklyn noir with a family drama at its core . . . It takes a lot to make a NYC noir feel fresh, and this one does . . . Selfon's understanding of how psychogeography shapes criminals is what drives the development of those characters—and the characters are what turn *The Nightworkers* into a great novel . . . The arrival of a promising voice."
—Gabino Iglesias, NPR

"[Selfon] sets this stunning debut in [Brooklyn]—the gritty bits, not the trendy ones . . . Selfon slowly unspools his plot with striking prose and characters whose frailties and strengths take precedence over slam-bang action." —Adam Woog, *The Seattle Times*

"Selfon's experiences as an investigative analyst for the Brooklyn District Attorney's office bring a realistic element to [*The Nightworkers*], weaving truth and fantasy seamlessly to create an exciting look into the city's seedy, treacherous back alley world of drugs, money laundering, and murder." —Carmen Clark, *Library Journal*

"Unearths not just the gritty mechanics of organized crime but the collateral damage it inflicts on perpetrators and victims alike, damage that outlasts the acts for as long as a lifetime . . . Selfon elegantly and eloquently unspools the entire chain of cause and effect . . . Selfon's ability to give each character his or her own perspective, desires and demons makes *The Nightworkers* a resonant work of fiction, one that rises above its crimes to tell bigger truths about family, love and hope." —Paula L. Woods, *Los Angeles Times*

"Page-turning Brooklyn noir meets compellingly complex family drama in Brian Selfon's atmospheric, edgy, and thoroughly modern *The Nightworkers*. You'll enjoy every unexpected page." —Kimberly McCreight, *New York Times* bestselling author of *Reconstructing Amelia* and *A Good Marriage*

"Electric, surprising, and tightly plotted, *The Nightworkers* establishes Selfon as a compelling writer to watch." —Adrienne Westenfeld, *Esquire*

"Selfon's ambitious, character-driven debut tells the interconnected stories of 'a perfectly wonderful, perfectly Brooklyn family of misfits' . . . Selfon fully fleshes out the major characters' backstories, dreams, and disappointments, and even the minor characters get their moment in the sun. Superior prose is a plus . . . Fans of literary crime fiction will be enthralled." —*Publishers Weekly* (starred review)

"Selfon is a major talent with a gift for illuminating an imagined underworld and populating it with a vivid cast of characters."

—Dwyer Murphy, *CrimeReads*

"The poetry-loving, sharply reflective Kerasha alone makes [*The Nightworkers*] worth reading. She deserves a sequel all her own. A sharp, surprisingly affecting debut." —*Kirkus Reviews*

"*The Nightworkers* grabbed me from page one, and led me breathlessly through what I think might be one of the best Brooklyn-set novels I've ever read—because it understands how the people and the place are inextricably linked. An absolutely stunning debut."

—Rob Hart, author of *The Warehouse* and the Ash McKenna series

"*The Nightworkers* is a propulsive thriller that takes you by the throat and doesn't let go. Brian Selfon's riveting story about a Brooklyn money-laundering family shimmers with razor-sharp dialogue and nonstop suspense. Electric and gritty, this stunning debut is not to be missed." —E. G. Scott, author of *In Case of Emergency*

"The murder of a promising young painter lights the fuse for Brian Selfon's deep dive into the wicked stain left by addiction, crime as just another business, and the way families can fall apart as easily as Jenga towers, and then be partially patched back together in the most heartbreaking of ways."

—Jenny Milchman, *USA Today* bestselling author of
Cover of Snow and *The Second Mother*

Laura Utrata Vasilopoulos

brian selfon

the nightworkers

Brian Selfon has worked in criminal justice for nearly twenty years, more than fifteen of them with law enforcement agencies in New York. As the chief investigative analyst for the Brooklyn District Attorney's Office, he handled cases ranging from money laundering to first-degree murder. Selfon now lives with his family in Seattle, where he works as a public defense investigator. *The Nightworkers* is his debut novel.

THE
NIGHTWORKERS

THE NIGHTWORKERS

BRIAN SELFON

MCD PICADOR

FARRAR, STRAUS AND GIROUX NEW YORK

Picador
120 Broadway, New York 10271

Grateful acknowledgment is made for permission to reprint an excerpt from
We're On: A June Jordan Reader, edited by Christoph Keller and Jan Heller Levi,
Alice James Books, 2017, © 2020 June M. Jordan Literary Estate Trust.
Used by permission. www.junejordan.com.

Interior hand-lettering and brushstrokes by Tyler Comrie

The Library of Congress has cataloged the MCD hardcover edition as follows:
Names: Selfon, Brian, 1978– author.
Title: The nightworkers / Brian Selfon.
Description: First edition. | New York : MCD / Farrar, Straus and
    Giroux, 2020.
Identifiers: LCCN 2020013396 | ISBN 9780374222017 (hardcover)
Classification: LCC PS3619.E4629 N54 2020 | DDC 813/.6—dc23
LC record available at https://lccn.loc.gov/2020013396

Picador Paperback ISBN: 978-1-250-80019-0

Designed by Abby Kagan

Our books may be purchased in bulk for promotional, educational, or
business use. Please contact your local bookseller or the Macmillan Corporate and
Premium Sales Department at 1-800-221-7945, extension 5442, or by email
at MacmillanSpecialMarkets@macmillan.com.

For book club information, please visit facebook.com/picadorbookclub
or email marketing@picadorusa.com.

picadorusa.com • instagram.com/picador
twitter.com/picadorusa • facebook.com/picadorusa

1 3 5 7 9 10 8 6 4 2

for my family

part one

the almost family

chapter 1

The first time he meets Emil Scott, he falls in love.

They're at an art opening in Bushwick, the latest neighborhood in Brooklyn to burst with creatives and almosts. For over an hour Henry Vek and Emil Scott have circled each other without realizing it. Then it's like an old rom-com. Their eyes lock across the room. They look away. (They're straight-ish for 2014, and the rule is you have to look away.) Then, oh so casually, they find their way to the same painting. And it's here, standing close to the painting, close to each other, that Emil taps his back left pocket and asks if Henry wants to buy some heroin.

"Jesus fuck, no. Not here." He puts a warning hand to Emil's chest—already they're touching. "Outside. Now."

Five minutes later they're stepping out onto the roof. "Hold the door," Henry says. He walks off, comes back with a loose brick, and props open the door. Light comes up at them from the stairwell. Henry breaks out rolling papers, a bag of kush, and a bottle of Jim Beam and paper cups he swiped from the opening. Then they blaze, and when they exchange names, Henry chokes on his smoke. Emil Scott? Jesus, this guy's got art up at half the coffee shops on Metropolitan. Another detail: he's good.

Henry feels within himself a tremor that could grow into a life-quake.

Emil is tall and long-limbed, like Henry, but without the muscle, and his rounding stomach suggests a habit of late-night pizzas. He's handsome, with his bold nose and his bedroom smile, but what catches Henry's attention now are the paint stains. The yellow on the hands, the purple on his pants—this is a *worker*. A tickle in Henry tells him this is something he can use.

"You've got that big canvas up at the Thirsty Bear," Henry says, handing the joint to Emil. "That purple octopus? With the baby octopus? Blew my fucking mind."

Emil shrugs.

"Nuh-uh. Don't piss on your gift." Henry lowers his voice, leans in. "I paint too, okay? Or I'm trying. Doing it since . . . since my mom died. She was an artist. And she was pretty good, and I fucking suck. But you've got something. Don't act like it doesn't matter. 'Cause let me tell you. It fucking matters."

Henry brings his hands in front of him. Long fingers, flat tips, calloused skin. There are scars on his knuckles, and there's a long, fresh scab on his left palm, as if from a blade badly deflected. And yes, there's paint, just like on Emil's hands.

"I don't know," Henry says. His voice low and fragile. "There's something . . . I can't get it out." A deep sigh, and then a hardening comes over him. He raises his eyes and looks at Emil. "But you're getting it out. And you're connecting to people. Your work sells, right?"

Emil drains his cup, makes a whiskey face. "Sometimes."

"Don't piss on sometimes. You're a real artist." Henry refills Emil's cup. "So the fuck you doing selling heroin?"

Emil has, until this moment, been somewhere between cool and snarky. Now he wilts. "It's fentanyl," he says. "Cut with lactose. It's rent—that's all it is."

"Shit. I get it." Henry is nodding. Side schemes, queasy compromises, backroom handoffs. We all got to eat. Henry's mouth plays a smile as he thinks about the strange kinship he and Emil somehow sniffed out downstairs. If Emil is maybe 90 percent artist and 10 percent criminal, Henry is the same, only with the proportions reversed. And this completes the detail Henry picked up before: Emil's work is up everywhere because he hustles—and he hustles because he needs the money. We can be *useful* to each other, Henry thinks, and if that's not the basis for a connection . . . Henry looks the artist over, confirming to himself that this isn't some specter born of hard liquor and GMO'd weed. No hooves, Henry sees, and no horns. He shakes his head and grins. "My uncle was right."

Emil looks up. "About what?"

"You never know someone till you get your nose up their money."

Henry feels Emil's gaze moving over him, feels the terror and pleasure of being seen. Emil says, "Your uncle?"

"He's got these little gems," Henry says. "He can drop some heavy shit. Sometimes it takes me a week to get my head around it."

Emil puts down his whiskey and takes out a short pencil, a pocket sketchbook. "Tell me about him." His pencil dances all over the page, his gaze returning again and again to Henry.

Who leans back into a shadow. "Whoa. You're not drawing me."

"But you looked so perfect." He smiles at Henry's hesitation. "The way your face changed when you mentioned your uncle." He puts his hands together. "Please? This is just for my sketchbook."

Henry shakes his head no, but then slides out from his shadow. "Are you for real?"

"Of course," Emil says, putting down his pencil at last. "But I'm *my* kind of real."

A profound feeling moves through Henry. It's desire, it's gratitude, it's fear—it's one of those in-between *somethings* he has in him and can't figure out. "Okay, my uncle." Deep breath, a roll of the shoulders. "He's my family. I mean . . . he's all that's left."

Emil takes up his pencil. "Your folks?"

"Gone. Both of them. My mom was an artist, like I said. I mean not *paid*, like you. She was a cashier at Union Market over in Park

Slope. And then the car crash." Henry's looking out at the night now, his voice low. "And my dad went a few years later. Aneurysm. I was ten." More whiskey. He's feeling too much, not getting it right. Emil's attention, though, seems to be on Henry's hands. Detail one, Henry himself notices: they have closed into fists. Detail two: the scars on his knuckles.

Fuck the whiskey. He puts down the drink, lights the joint, pulls hard, and hands it to Emil. A tight moment, then he says, "So Uncle Shecky takes me in, and he teaches me the business. And it doesn't matter that I'm ten, that I'm fifteen, that I'm twenty-two now. It's always the same. He's teaching me."

"Like?"

"Like adjustable-interest loans, interest-only home loans."

"He does mortgages?"

"And LLCs, and PACs, and profitable nonprofits." Henry smiles, picking up steam. "And pass-through accounts, and offshore accounts—all kinds of shit. Whatever the client needs. My uncle's like a secret genius." Henry takes the joint back from Emil. Pinches it out and says, "Uncle Shecky's got this amazing, twisty mind. And there's no show with him. Like he's great and he's different, and he doesn't even know it."

"And I was just thinking the same thing about you," Emil says.

Their eyes meet, then Henry looks away. When he raises his eyes again, there's no break in his voice, and his hands open. "Your turn. Heroin, fentanyl—what's the fucking deal?"

Emil's smile is pained, as if telling a doctor about an embarrassing itch. "Was kind of hoping we'd let that drop." His hand goes into his skinny jeans, and out comes a ziplock bag. Inside: teeny baggies, maybe a dozen. "I buy for ten, sell for twenty." A shrug, like it's no biggie, but his embarrassment is obvious. "Just a supplement."

"Hey, glass houses," Henry says.

"But?"

"Opioids are bad business. They went suburban, and now the

courts are coming down hard. ODs are everywhere—fucking Scarsdale, places where judges live. Hitting home for them. So they're laying down these crazy sentences. Bottom line?" He leans in and puts a heavy hand on Emil's shoulder. Feels a warm charge move into him, spread down through his body. "Not. Fucking. Worth it." He releases his grip. "There's a better way."

Emil's voice goes soft: "I'm open to suggestions."

A predator's smile as Henry gives Emil a soft elbow to the side. "You're going to come work for me."

Next day, a construction site. Henry shields his eyes from the sun. Emil takes out his sketchbook, which, by this light, Henry can see has a floral print cover.

Emil asks, "What am I looking at?"

"A client." Henry waves at one of the workers, who waves back—but slowly, as if confused by Henry's visit. Wary. He watches Henry for some time before getting back to his tools.

"Most of our clients are decent people," Henry says. He takes out a baggie, rolls a joint. "Two-thirds are mom-and-pop shops. Just regular Brooklynites who don't want the IRS in their pockets. So we take their cash and help them load up on Amex cards. Or we pay their bills—big ones, like college tuition—through generous relatives."

"You work with their relatives?"

"They're overseas," Henry says. "Also, they don't exist."

Emil, who has stopped sketching, shakes his head admiringly and gets back to work.

"So that's scenario A, the tax dodge. But sometimes it's the opposite." Henry flicks the lighter, but the wind knocks it out. "They're not avoiding taxes." He flicks it again and gets the joint going. "They *want* them."

Emil again lowers his sketchbook. "They want to pay taxes?"

"Let's pretend we're talking about Mel." Henry indicates the construction worker he waved at before. "Let's say he's a subcontractor, unlicensed, unofficial. And he's been getting paid under the table. So he's living the dream, right? No taxes, no problems. But then he gets shackled." Henry points to his ring finger. "Wife, baby. And they need space. Bank is like, you want a home loan? How about you get some reportable income."

Emil gives up on his sketchbook, puts it in his pocket. Accepts the joint from Henry. "How does that work?"

"Step one is the same. We take the cash. But then we create a big old paper trail." Henry relights the joint for Emil. "Articles of incorporation, certificate of this and that." Pockets the lighter. "Now Mel's got legitimate income. We can print up some pretty-looking tax returns if Mel wants that. And now Mel can go back to the bank and get a loan. Wife's happy, Mel's happy. And that's all we want for our clients."

Nearby: the loud beeps of a truck backing up. They wait it out.

"Okay, so two-thirds of your clients are Mel," Emil says.

"And the mom-and-pop shops."

"Right." Emil's eyes flash mischief. "What about the other third?"

Henry takes the joint back, his face a cold mask now. "Not your problem. Not your business." He's quiet a moment and then says, more gently, "Ignorance is deniability. Uncle Shecky says that. What we're doing here—right now, at this site—you'll never do this again. You'll never *see* a client. Ignorance is *safety*. For them, for you. Listen." He pinches out the joint, pockets it. He takes Emil by the arm and leads him away from the site. "Darkness is your friend. I run the mules in my family, and this is my promise to you." He leans in—his mouth, Emil's ear—and says, "I will keep you in the dark."

The alley is cool and shadowed. Henry brings Emil in deep and stops him at a dumpster. Here is an unexpectedly fresh smell, sawdust, and poking out from the dumpster are broken boards and cracked sheets of plywood.

Emil takes out his sketchbook. "What am I looking at?"

Henry spreads his arms. "Your first workspace."

Emil gives Henry a look—*are you fucking with me?*—and Henry's smiling as he goes to the dumpster, picks up a loose board, uses it to stir what's inside. "Your pickup spots won't usually be this clean, but this is the first part of your job. This is exactly what you'll be doing." He bends over, reaches into the dumpster, and pulls out a garbage bag. Holds it up for Emil. "This is your pickup."

Emil stares at Henry: *the fuck?*

Henry, for the first time with Emil—for the first time in forever, it feels like—bursts out laughing.

A walk, a train, a bus later, they step into a Western Union.

"And this is your drop-off," Henry says, getting in line with Emil. "It's this simple. You pick up, you drop off, and I'll pay you. Easy money. Maybe an hour's work, and you'll get fifty for your everyday bag. A hundred for a big one. You'll work up to that." The line snakes past a table with stacks of wire-transfer slips. Henry takes one, shows it to Emil. "You'll fill this out. You'll have the account number in advance. Same with the routing number. Sometimes you'll have to split it up—multiple accounts. Or you might have to go to different branches, different banks. The post office, drugstores—they all do money orders now. I'll tell you where to go. You'll get very clear, specific instructions."

Emil is, of course, sketching. He hardly glances up long enough to say, "So we're giving clients back their money—"

"So they can actually spend it," Henry says. "Sometimes it goes overseas and back again. Sometimes it's a straight deposit. Like this one." He gives the bag a shake. "This is going into my account. This is my bag. My own money. I put it there. For your lesson."

"Your bag?" Emil lowers his sketchbook. "So that construction worker . . ."

"Random dude." Henry shrugs. "Never seen him before in my life."

Emil looks a little hurt. "You were fucking with me."

"Teaching you."

"But how will I know what's real or not?"

There's a smile and a dare in Henry's eyes. "You'll just have to trust me."

Over the following weeks, Henry teaches Emil code words and best practices for anonymized calls and self-destructing texts. When to use drop boxes or hand-to-hands; how to spot a tail, or lose one. The art of patience. The locations of fallbacks—places you can disappear into, when Plan A goes up in flames.

"I never expected this," Emil says one afternoon, "but I'm having fun." It's May, and Brooklyn is at its most beautiful. Emil is now officially a runner. The work, he tells Henry, has fired up his art: "I'm walking with my eyes open now." Maples and sycamores, plastic bags flapping like flags from their branches. Weeds pushing up full blossom from the broken sidewalk. Girls in skirts, babushkas with blue hair. "I'm starting a new series. Paint here and there, but a lot of charcoal. And no angles. Everything's fluid and dynamic—and everything's from Bushwick."

Henry can't wait to see it. He loves this, the shop talk, being connected to—supporting, in a way—a working artist. He's seen his own work improving under Emil's eye.

In June, Emil is commissioned to complete a mural at the Thirsty Bear, and he takes a hiatus from his work for Henry. He comes back as a runner the next month, though, and from then on it's steady. Weekly meetings. Whiskey. Late-night talk of Twombly, talk of Haring.

"I'm working on something new," Emil announces one night.

"That charcoal series?"

"It evolved." There's a strange gravity in Emil's voice. Shadows under his eyes, a haunted expression. "I'm calling it 'Origins.'"

"Whose?"

No answer.

"You don't know?"

Emil lets this question hang too, and when the meeting ends Henry feels unsettled.

The following day Emil goes out for a cash bag, his first big carry. He doesn't make his checkpoint at the MoneyGram on Jay Street, and by the time Henry gets to him, his body is already cold.

chapter 2

"Now let's see here," says the wig, "you're going to be living with your parents. Is that right?"

It's June, a month before the murder, and Kerasha Brown is sitting across from her probation officer. If this is freedom, Kerasha thinks, I was better off at Franklin. Six dull years there, a quarter of her life, but never once—and this consolation comes too late, as consolation does—never once in the cage did she have to look at this stringy wig. Yuck. The woman fumbles through multicolor folders. Licks her fingers between every turn of the page. "Now let's see here," her verbal tic. This woman won't ever *see here*, Kerasha knows. The highlights, the folders—this wretched creature is blind.

A stray bullet took her father twenty years ago, and Kerasha had hardly set foot in Franklin when Mama put a needle into her last vein. So no, Ms. Wig, you aren't *seeing*, and that's not *right*. But Kerasha says nothing. Silence, she's found, and an idiot's smile, are her best defense against bureaucrats. But her mind rarely slows and never stops, and now she's remembering a line from Paul Laurence Dunbar: *We wear the mask that grins and lies.*

"Now let's—wait, here's your file." The woman flourishes it and beams. Kerasha envies the ease with which stupid people take pride. Hopes the opposite is true, that the misery of her own life signifies intelligence. A paltry compensation, but she's an orphaned ex-con at the mercy of a wig. Paltry will do.

"You're going to stay with your uncle, that's right. And he signed for you as . . ." She mumble-reads her way through the whole file. Kerasha's eyes wander. A born thief, she spots a half-dozen places she could peek into, if she were in the mood. The wig's purse, huge and pink. Unzipped, half open, and within arm's reach. The cream-colored file cabinet behind her, pocked with stickers, most of them fairies or frogs. The lock on this cabinet wouldn't withstand a toothpick. Inside, she knows, are probate files; she watched as her own battered file—her battered *fate*, more like—was taken out from the second-to-bottom drawer. Probate files mean names, dates of birth, and social security numbers. Not only the probates', but those of anyone who paid their bail bonds. The street value of an unredacted probate file is $150. Oh, the things you learn at Franklin.

The wig reads as though words are just sounds. Then she pushes documents at Kerasha. "Sign by the Post-its. I put them there for you." Her smile tells Kerasha to be grateful. Kerasha knows this smile from Sister Xenia, one of the senior nuns at the halfway house where Kerasha has been staying for the last month. The documents are a dull rainbow of carbon paper. They smell like gunpowder.

We wear the mask that grins.

"Those Post-its are so helpful," Kerasha says. "Thank you." She signs the papers. Pushes them back across the desk. The wig reshuffles them, clips some and staples others. Lines them up in three piles. She mumbles something about "conditional discharge" and "reincarceration," and Kerasha wishes she could pay attention. Knows she ought to, but she's distracted, squirming, anxious—and this amazes her—to get back to Sisters of Mercy. Dinner tonight will be gray vegetable soup and butter rolls—that's not the draw. Waiting for her under the half-collapsed mattress she shares with a failed suicide is a gorgeous copy of Saint Augustine's *Confessions*. She liberated it from Sister Xenia's locked library just last night. Stayed up reading about how Augustine monkey-fucked some woman in his church, timed her groans to synchronize with the tolling of the bells. *This* is how to do it, she thinks. If you know you're going to be saved, fall first, and fall all the way down.

Daydreams of her favorite saint break apart when she hears the words "your appointment." *Focus, Kerasha.* There are rules to follow. First, don't get caught. Second, when there's an appointment, show up. Franklin was not hell, far from it. But she robbed the warden on her way out, and every warden is a genius when it comes to revenge. Going back is not an option.

She picks up the appointment slip on her way out. Dr. Andrew Xu, tomorrow at four o'clock. Apparently she needs a physical now, and with *Andrew*—of course it's a guy. His hands will be moist, and they'll be all over her. Then she'll have to decide: report him and be transferred to another pair of moist hands, or snap off his chode and go back into the cage. Fuck you, Andrew Xu. Fuck your moist hands.

Already violated, she begins to plan her retribution.

Andrew Xu turns out to be a slim, balding man with a thin pony-tail down to the small of his back.

Turns out, motherfucker, to be a psychiatrist.

He indicates the couch across from his armchair, his hands small, girlish. Dr. Andrew Xu will be the greatest trial of her life. It comes to her with perfect certainty. It is whispered by Saint Augustine himself.

She thinks of the wig and knows this is her vengeance. Unplanned, yes, but a kind of cosmic justice Kerasha usually doesn't believe in. Payback for what Kerasha took from her. A half block from that beastly, mumbling bureaucrat, Kerasha felt something heavy in her pocket. Reached inside and discovered a stapler. Kerasha hadn't meant to swipe it, hadn't even noticed herself doing it. But sometimes your hands do the work for you.

No doubt Dr. Xu would have something to say about this. If she tells him.

If she lets him in.

chapter 3

Family. Shecky Keenan once thought he'd never have one. But on the day before Emil's murder, he walks into his home, wiping sweat from his face, and here they are, seated in his dining room. The cousins are both orphans, and though everyone in this room is mixed race, Henry and Shecky look white, and Kerasha, black. For Shecky this proves a point. The three of them are the family he glued together, and Shecky wouldn't want any other.

Tall, angular, and sinewy, Henry is the closest thing to a son Shecky will ever get. His mother, Molly, was Shecky's first cousin. A part-time artist and full-time boozer, she drank herself into a car crash when Henry was seven. His father, Alessandro, went down three years later, dying *with* a brain tumor, but technically *from* an aneurysm. Poor bastard. Alessandro spent his last year in the psych ward, the tumor having made a monster of the gentle man.

And how Henry has changed. He was a chubby fifth-grader when he moved into Shecky's house on Hart Street. Couldn't sleep alone. A crier at home but a brawler at school—Shecky shivers now, remembering the stories. The pencil he stabbed into one kid's hand, the combination lock he slammed into the face of another. To his credit, Henry never started fights, and he backed down from fights with smaller kids. Give him a worthy asshole, though, and Henry would get to work. Guidance counselors and teachers all said the same thing: Henry's fights were red and dirty—eye pokes, crotch kicks, quick hits to the throat. Half the fights, though, Shecky never heard a word about. Henry would just come home battered and bandaged. Wouldn't say nothing, had no peaceful way to let out his feelings. A little ball of fury. But look at him now, how he's grown into his anger. A rugged man, broad shoulders, broad chest. Well over six feet tall, and his legs stretch under the table and rest on the opposite chair. You wouldn't guess that Henry and Shecky share any DNA at all. But fuck appearances, the proof is here on the dining room table.

The sketch pad in front of Henry is bigger than a pizza box, and in his hand is a pencil. He picks this stuff up at the art-supply store over on Myrtle Avenue. Wasted beer money, other kids probably think. It's almost a joke: a strong, physical kid like Henry, laboring— and that's the word for it, *laboring*—over sketches. The paintings Henry keeps in the basement, but the sketches Shecky finds every- where around the house. On the back porch he's found sketches of that tabby that hunts and fucks in the alley. In the upstairs office, where Henry is working more and more these days, Shecky finds the desk covered with sketches of the faces and back rooms Henry has gotten to know through the family business. The kid has a red streak, but here he sits, trying to turn that into a kind of beauty. And maybe speaking back to his mom, too.

Shecky loves thinking about this, the artistic spirit in the family. He was a four-year member and two-term treasurer of the drama club at Bushwick High School. (Stole *from* it far less than he stole *for* it, when Jesus knows he could have cleaned the thing out.) Still a thes- pian as recently as last Christmas, when he played the Ghost of Christmas Future in the Watts Community Theater's annual produc- tion. So he understands Henry's need to express something true. Knows the power of the urge, the violence in it, and how when it comes up, you can't fight it. You're the vehicle, and something wicked does the steering.

Henry's been in this house twelve years now—*twelve*—and each year has passed like a breath. Hard to believe. The downside to happy times, what life takes from you in kind, how time can just up and vanish. But Shecky will pay it, pay double if that's the ask. He who grew up amid such squalor and violence, getting passed like a dirty joint among a trio of vicious uncles. Uncle Samuel, who beat him, wrecked his ankles with a pipe. Uncle Joseph, who used Shecky's name and social security number, busted out Shecky's credit for drinking money. Let's not talk about Uncle Tomas.

Henry rotates his sketch pad ninety degrees. Goes at it from another angle. His face is lined with concentration, the palm of his right hand black from the pencil. The kid may brawl again, but at this moment, and Shecky's lonely years taught him to appreciate moments, Henry is an artist.

Shecky's eyes turn to Kerasha, his second charge. The miracle of her arrival last month is still so fresh that sometimes, when he's walking distracted into his own kitchen, he can startle at the sight of her. Or he'll step into the bathroom and wonder at the smell of lavender, and it'll take him a beat to remember that it's her lotion. Her bathroom, for that matter—he and Henry moved their toiletries to the one downstairs. She's beautiful, Kerasha, with sharp eyes, quiet feet, and quick hands. Shecky may be biased, but in *his* opinion, the three of them make a perfectly wonderful, perfectly Brooklyn family of misfits.

"I have an update," Kerasha says. "My little project."

"Let's hold that thought," Shecky says. He tilts his head toward Henry, who, thankfully, hasn't looked up from his sketch pad. Kerasha gives Shecky a coconspirator's tight smile: we'll talk later. Then she turns back to her book.

Give the girl credit, she's been working from the day she moved in. And she didn't bat an eye when he explained that the family business depended on compartmentalization. "I'll trust you just like I trust Henry," he told her. "But you'll have to trust *me* about when to look away."

How at ease, how *in place* she looks now, reclining on that leather armchair Shecky keeps in the corner. Used to be his own favorite seat, when he wasn't at the table eating, but now he wouldn't touch it without permission. And he's glad for this, glad she's claiming her own space here. She has a foot on the windowsill, another swaying to the rhythm of—wait, what's she reading—Jesus fuck, it's Sophocles. No lightweight, this one. But this morning it was a poetry chapbook. Each day means a new book for her, sometimes two, and this worries him.

They're all stolen.

They can put her back.

The cage doesn't care that she mostly grabs paperbacks, which, God knows, are worthless these days. All the cage knows is *predicate felon*—the pharmacy bust, then the escapes.

All the cage knows is, *Welcome back.*

But he won't let it happen.

You mean you won't let it happen *again*, a wicked voice whispers.

A dim memory from his cousin Paulette's filthy apartment, which Shecky visited exactly once: a big-eyed skinny girl, small and quick. And those big eyes had fixed on him, reached into him—and then he'd looked away, and kept on looking away. For years. And then he'd heard she got caught, her sentence maxed, then extended, because of the escapes. And suddenly his half-forgotten visit to Paulette's apartment was all he could think of, his memory of the big-eyed girl never leaving him alone. Her stare was on him again, defiant. Vulnerable.

I'm smarter, I'm faster, she said without saying. You don't know what I can get away with. You don't know what I've done. Her stare had been like a middle finger, but he'd sensed the longing behind it. She knew he couldn't keep up, but she'd wanted so badly for someone to try.

And now, settling into his seat at his dinner table, Shecky finds himself back in the moment he completed the application to be Kerasha's parole sponsor—which he'd signed here, in this very seat. He remembers how he'd turned the pages one last time, double-checking everything he'd written, and how it had dawned on him that he'd hardly had to lie at all. Almost against his principles, to submit a legitimate document like that. At no profit. But he'd felt, and still feels, that this submission was a promise.

You have a home here, he thinks at Kerasha, looking at her across the room. This is your home, and I'll be your family.

As long as you'll have me.

Kerasha, fucking mind reader that she is, sneaks him a melting half smile as she turns a page.

"My home, my family," Shecky says, hearing his voice shake, hoping the kids wouldn't tease him. My family—what's left of it.

Someday he'll tell the kids about Dannie, his big sister. He wants to tell Henry about the girl who, like him, was quick to raise her fists. And Kerasha might be interested to hear that Sophocles ran in the family, Dannie having played the title role in the high school production of *Antigone*. And Kerasha might laugh to hear that when Antigone's suicide was announced in the play, Shecky—just a child then—had screamed so loudly, and so insistently, he'd had to be carried from the theater.

But think about what Dannie would see if she were here. The artist-enforcer, with his sketch pad. The thief and her poetry. And Shecky himself, a grizzled fixer who, following Dannie's lead, dabbles in theater. Yes, if Dannie were here, she'd see a miracle. Home. Family. If there are any holy words left, here they are.

And Jesus fuck, Shecky needs them. Because there are unholy words, too, and the fuckers have been coming at him fast.

From outside: a car ignition. Shecky jumps, goes to the window—just a blur going around the corner, too late to see anything. Unsettled, he returns to the table with a put-on smile.

"Everything okay?" Kerasha's eyes point him back to the window. She obviously wants to talk about her update, but he's not ready, and besides, Henry's here.

"Just a car. Startled me."

But the truth is, Shecky is far past startled, and he has his reasons. The email from Bank of America last Wednesday: *Transfer denied.* Coming at him old school, on Saturday, a paper letter from Chase: *Internal inquiry.* And the Capital One letter in his drugstore PO Box just yesterday: *Account closure.*

Shecky has heard nothing definitive, and he can't investigate when

the accounts aren't in his name. But these notices, when pieced together, form a question that could come only from the devil. And
this question had Shecky springing up in bed at three o'clock this
morning, had him coughing out fear until his eyes were wet.

They're wet again now.

Blearily, then, he looks at Henry, sharpening his pencil. At
Kerasha, turning another page. At the empty chair, where Dannie
will never sit. And Shecky can't ignore it any longer—the question
that's been whispering all this time.

Are they on to me?

Shecky rises and goes into the kitchen. Fires up the oven broiler.
Opens the cabinets, takes down dishes, glasses. Considering, all this
time, how little the kids know—about him, about anything.

Too fucking young.

How could they imagine that you could wake up twenty years old,
and by the time you sit down for lunch, you're fifty-eight. That it's
possible to have no real memories from half your life, that time can
disappear *in* you, and a lonely heart can shrink and turn cold.

But how his races these days, thumping warm, thumping in double time, in *makeup* time, when he steps into a room and sees family. Over twelve years gone now, his cold, lonely quiet. Feels like a
thousand.

Oven ready, apple-chicken sausage inside. Water boiling, rigatoni
added. A dash of salt. In the wok: olive oil, green pepper, red pepper,
sliced eggplant. Shecky, a part-time waiter when he was in his twenties, returns to the dining room with dishes, glasses, and silver. "How
are we today?" he asks, setting the table. "What have we done, who
have we seen?"

Silence, though Kerasha is giving him a loaded smile: Do you
really want to know what I've seen? Now?

When Shecky shakes his head no, Kerasha shrugs and goes back
to Sophocles.

Not like pulling teeth, small talk with these two. Teeth break off sooner than you'd think. More like pulling off hands. But fuck it, he'll love them, he'll be here for them, even after . . . Stop it. Don't think about them leaving. Don't follow that thought, don't even look at it. But the thing about time is, you can turn away from it all you like, it'll wash everything away just the same.

The table is set. Shecky makes a quick visit to the ground-floor bathroom, where he pushes open the frosted-glass window and scans the alley. Inventory: garbage bin, recycling bin. Two rusting bicycles, a cracked plastic snow sled, a pile of loose lumber. No sign of the tabby, no sign of danger—just an ordinary summer evening.

He wants so badly to believe this.

He closes the window. Flushes the toilet and runs the sink, for appearances. Comes out, returns to the dining room, and here they are, both of them at the table now—his kids.

"Guys, come on, I've been looking at spreadsheets all day. Give me something. A grunt. An anything. Kids, please." Desperately: "Are you alive?"

The scratch of Henry's pencil. Kerasha's eye roll, but also the little upturn of her mouth.

Kids, he thinks, shaking his head at himself. Henry is twenty-two, Kerasha twenty-three. They're already grown up, they'll move out and on. It's your core hope for them—it has to be—and when it's fulfilled, you're alone.

Shecky returns to the kitchen. Checks the sausage, turns down the flame under the vegetables. Returns to the dining room with beer bottles for everyone.

Guinness from a bottle—his father would reel, slap, shout. Fucking sacrilege, he'd say, and disown him all over again. But that's fine, Shecky isn't like his father. He's *alive*, for one, and thank Jesus. And second, he's in the one place his father was never to be found: home with his family. Shecky wonders, though, what the racist bastard would make of this pack of mutts.

"Moving past the palaver," Shecky says, as if he weren't the only one talking, "and turning to the business." Business: the word is hardly out and the kids' eyes are up, they're facing him, Henry even putting down his pencil. Money can divide a family, but in this house, there's comfort in shoptalk.

"We've got two heavies tomorrow." He looks to Kerasha to make sure she's following.

She raises an eyebrow: Really, Uncle Shecky, you're testing me?

Shecky smiles an apology, but it was just last week that he began her training. Explaining, as they chopped vegetables together, that a *heavy* was a heap of loose cash, ten thousand or more, which had to be magicked into bank money—clean, respectable, and pseudonymized.

"The first heavy's a rough two-fifty in dirties," Shecky says. "The second heavy is an exact three hundred thousand in crisps." He again looks to Kerasha: You still with me?

Now she raises both eyebrows.

Shecky smiles another apology, but really he's not sorry at all. Can't be too careful. Profit from the two heavies tomorrow means a mortgage payment for the family. So, yes, Kerasha's always watching, always listening, and can take in a room like a police wire. But it's important that she understands how you can tell a client by the kind of cash they bring in: the office jobbers with their "crisp" cash, usually flat and clean. The street clients, whose crumpled, stained bills have to be handled with rubber gloves.

"Big day for the family tomorrow," he says, tapping a spoon against his bottle. Getting the kids to look up at him. "Bag of crisps, bag of dirties. How about a round of Guess the Client? What belongs to who? And the prize will be—"

"Dirties are from Red Dog," Henry interrupts, "crisps are from the Paradise Club." He doesn't give Shecky a chance to confirm he's right—which, of course, he is. "And speaking of Red Dog . . ." Henry looks up with a hesitant smile. "A friend of mine had this idea."

Shecky's body tenses. Ideas from Henry's friends are rarely good, and there's a certain friend—a girl, a lunatic—whom Shecky would be glad to see out of the family picture.

"We were talking about how maybe with Red Dog," Henry says, licking his lips as if readying his mouth for what he'll say next. "Since I brought in the business . . ." He coughs, obviously uncomfortable with what he's saying. As he fucking well should be. Henry forces a smile as he at last gets it out: "Maybe I should get a cut."

Shecky's breath is like a snort. "You were talking to a friend about our work?"

"Nothing specific," Henry says quickly. "Just basic business principles. Like if I'm doing regular work, I get regular pay. I'm staff. But if I'm bringing in clients—especially a big one like Red Dog—doesn't that . . ."

Kerasha completes the trail-off: "Make him a partner."

It's like a wineglass has been dropped: no one moves, the air itself cries danger. Then there's a beep from the kitchen, the timer for the vegetables. "You're getting ahead of yourself," Shecky says to Henry, standing up. His voice is flat, cool, and much stronger than what he's feeling inside. He walks calmly to the kitchen. There, only there, does he allow himself to lean against the counter and feel the full weight of the challenge.

Henry, a partner. Not looking up to Shecky, but standing beside him. Not a child anymore. Not his boy.

How will I protect him?

Eyes dry, hands steady, Shecky returns to the dining room carrying three large serving plates. "And here you go, plenty for everyone." He dishes out the sausage, the veggies, the pasta. He sits, finally. The kids' eyes are on him, waiting for his grace. "Thank you for being here," he says at last. "Thank you for being my family."

The kids say their thank-yous and get to eating.

The silence that begins the meal is awful. They're waiting for an answer.

Shecky keeps his face neutral. Takes a moment to collect himself. A cut for Henry—a personal cut, separate from the family's—what would that mean, and what could that lead to? Henry moving up? Or out? Those empty, quiet nights; those empty, quiet years—Shecky pushes them back and puts on another smile. "Hey. We're all in this house together." The smile feels like it's fighting with his face. "What's ours is all of ours."

"No disrespect," Henry says. "I'm just saying, my role has already changed. So maybe we can acknowledge that." He turns to Kerasha. "You're objective, you've got no stake in this. What do you think?"

Kerasha almost laughs. "Ref *this* fight?" A slow head shake. "First thing you learn in the cage—never take a side till you know who's got the shiv."

Shecky is done with his smile now. Done with this whole fucking conversation. "This isn't rule *by committee*. There's a right way to do this, and it's not everyone for themselves." He's certain this is true. Certain the kids can understand this. Okay, Henry is immature. He has that red streak, and worse, he has *artistic aspirations*. The opposite of good business sense. But at the end of the day, Henry is responsible. More than that—let's face it—he's irreplaceable. His quick temper, the power in his arms and fists, his willingness to start fights—it's *good* for the family business. Competitors back down. Late payments come in. And while violence is never Shecky's first choice, it is, none-theless, always on the table.

"Income is family money," Shecky says. "If you want, we'll go over the numbers, and—"

"Okay, let's do that."

"*After* the two heavies. After we've gotten confirmations that the money went through. Next will be—what, the tenth? That'll make it three full months we've been doing business with Red Dog. A full quarter year. And you're right—he *is* a major client. It's something to celebrate." Shecky goes into the kitchen and comes back with whiskey and three shot glasses. He pours and distributes. "Tomorrow we'll do another clean job for the client. And by the end of the week we'll have a better sense of how much business he means for us." He raises his glass. "Sláinte."

Shecky feels Henry's eyes on him a long time. Then the kid nods and downs his shot, and air comes back into the room. Henry's backed down, remembered his place. Punk. Love him to death.

"Both transfers need to happen tomorrow," Shecky says, after the kids have had a quiet minute with their food. To Kerasha he adds, "Not ideal, but it happens." He asks Henry, "Do you have runners?"

"*A* runner," Henry says. "My Thursday guy."

Shecky lowers his fork. "What happened to your other guys?"

"Well, I used to have Thursday and backup. Then backup was playing games, getting sloppy, a little skimmy, and I had to throw him against a wall." He extends and pulls in his fingers. "His face did something to my hand."

Shecky shrugs. "As long as you can do your job. That's what matters."

"But that's not *all* that matters. Not to me."

And there he goes, looking at his sketch pad again. He's lucky I'm a softy, Shecky thinks. Lucky I love him. Because Jesus fuck, the job isn't just money, it's *us*! These chairs, this table. Your bed, where you bring that girl. Our home, your fucking art supplies. Love has a price tag. Survival has a price tag. How can you live on it, and not understand where it comes from?

Not now, Dannie whispers to him. *Mind your timing.*

Gone for decades, she's still his life's stage manager. Had been an actual stage manager, working for community theater when she died. He sat in at rehearsals, heard her say, "Keep quiet. You'll have your lines, but you have to let the other guy talk."

Shecky gives Henry a moment to feel he's been heard. Then he says, "This isn't about your art. This is about your Thursday guy. He can't do both. We can't put two bags on one guy. We'd risk—"

"I'm sorry, Uncle Shecky," Henry says, "but you've got to let me handle this." When Henry draws himself up straight, his chest seems to grow. His hand grips the pencil, shaking with emotion, and Shecky's eyes fix on that point. "I've been managing the runners since winter," Henry says. "It's my job, I know how to do it."

The focus of the world is that pencil point—all else, a blur.

Timing, Dannie says again. *Wait for your moment. Concede, retreat. The kid is too unsettled, and you're too pissy, to have this conversation tonight.*

"Let Thursday handle the crisps," Shecky says. "We can trust Thursday." Crisps are always tempting, the bills so new and clean. One of Henry's first jobs—years ago now, different protocols—was helping Shecky count money for the Paradise Club. Henry would undoubtedly still recognize the white-and-blue currency bands this client uses, and the neat stacks in their leather briefcases. *Beautiful*—Shecky remembers how taken aback Henry was—how he actually raised a hand, as if to shield his eyes, the first time Shecky opened a Paradise Club briefcase for him. *It's like a box of light.*

"So we're good with the crisps," Shecky says now. "But the dirties need other hands."

Henry scowls, obviously biting his tongue. A moment later, though, he's talking sense—pencil down, thank Jesus—and going through the options. Or lack of. One veteran runner is out of town, another got herself shot in a club, another is—

"So use a pup," Shecky says. But then, seeing the happy surprise on Henry's face, he quickly adds, "Not your buddy, though. Not him."

Henry's smile turns into an angry line. "Why not?"

Because you like him too much.

"Sorry," Shecky says, cutting his sausage with more exasperation than appetite. Henry's frustration is coming at him like a chemical cloud. Shecky remembers hearing about this friend, remembers how Henry's been itching to promote him. And why not? Henry trained this guy months ago, and according to the ledger Shecky keeps in his upstairs office, this pup hasn't lost or pinched a penny. There's nothing unusual in this, Henry's an effective handler. What's unusual is that Henry once asked whether the pup could come over for dinner.

"His name's Emil," Henry had said. "He's different."

Henry doesn't have company over often. Never had many friends—and no, *that girl* doesn't count as a friend. It's the old orphan's curse, how lonely need can scare people off. And so when Henry asked if Emil could come over, Shecky had wanted to say, Of course! How about tonight?

But the rules.

"The rules mean safety," Shecky had said, "and not just for us." The clients depended on it. So did the runners. "Think about *his* safety. Your buddy's." There were lines you couldn't cross with the guy who carried your bag. "You'll do him no favors," Shecky said, "if you bring him in too close."

Henry was disappointed then, but tonight, Shecky can tell, this disappointment is hardening into something else. "I'm trying to tell you something," Henry says. "This friend is important to me. He's more than just a *buddy*. He's teaching me, and—and—you're not even letting me talk!"

Henry's chair scrapes across the floor. He stands and takes up the sketch pad, and at his full height Henry towers over Shecky. Looks down at him. And then he turns, and in four long strides, he's at the basement door. Here he pauses. Looks back.

"If my lives can't fit together here," Henry says, "I can't promise I'll choose this one."

The slam of the basement door. A long echo. The earth has buckled and now it's still, but there's no telling, Shecky knows, whether a bigger quake is yet to come.

Absently rubbing his hands, his chin, Shecky is warmed by the sight of Kerasha, who's waving a forkful of sausage at him. "His loss," she says. "They don't serve this at Franklin."

Affection, gratitude—Shecky takes it in like oxygen. Thank Jesus for this girl, he thinks, picking up his napkin. Wiping his eyes. It's silly, breaking up inside like this—an old underworlder like him, who's seen and heard some bad things. Done some pretty fucking bad things himself, but vulnerability is the price of family. Good riddance, lonely years, but not a day now without a bruise.

It's not the first time Henry's stormed off like this. It kills Shecky every time, though—*slays* him, as Henry said in his more annoying days. The family dinner has always been the supreme house rule. Family of two, now family of three, the rule is the same: together at the table. Guinness for him, whatever for the kids. A fresh loaf from Regina Bakery, the catch of the day from Katti's Fish Market. Or maybe some slab of red, chopped and stewed, or braised and roasted, or maybe just seared under the foot-level blue flame. Roasted veggies and baked potatoes, or yucca and seared sprouts, each meal laid out on the clean-enough tablecloth. The curtains are open as long as there's some orange left in the dusk. And there's no TV, no "background music"—Shecky remembers how Dannie had abhorred noise for the sake of noise. "We need silence," she'd say. "It draws us out."

And you were right, Dannie, look at us. *Listen:* The only sound here is family. Our days, our stories. The putting aside of grievances, the rebraiding of the threads. The sharing of bread. These things matter.

Taking Henry's plate to the kitchen, covering it with foil, and putting it in the refrigerator, Shecky wishes Dannie were here, even as a ghost. Wishes she could see him with the kids, watch the family dinners (not *this* one, obviously), and know how carefully he'd listened to her.

She was a high school actor, then a waitress and a community theater stage manager, and then she was dead, killed on his birthday. That was her whole story, a fucking one act.

But is it really over? All the way over? Isn't *this* her next act—me with the kids? The way she taught me, looked out for me, loved me when no one else did—aren't I doing the same for them, and isn't she alive in this house, as long as they're here?

Shecky closes the refrigerator, makes espressos, and returns with them to the dining room. Two go on the table, the third he brings to Kerasha. She's back on the old armchair, at peace with Sophocles. Henry's seat is empty. Shecky looks to the basement door. He thinks about Henry storming off and remembers how another house had shaken when Dannie walked out of it for the last time. That friend of Uncle Joseph's having come around one too many times, trying to mess with her. And Dannie finally saying to hell with it and going off to live with her boyfriend. Leaving Shecky alone with their uncle.

And this reverberating silence goes on until Kerasha, her eyes still on Sophocles, breaks it—and her uncle—with two soft words.

"It's back."

So this is her update. *It's back*—said simply, as if it didn't matter. But Kerasha must have seen him fidgeting around the room, leaving and coming back. Sneaking looks at her, opening his mouth as if to ask but then closing it again with a quick glance at Henry's empty seat. *He* mustn't know, not until Shecky is ready for him to know.

But the family is in the hands of the devil.

Shecky moves food around his plate. Sausage on fork, sausage off. Pointless. Can't eat. At last, he forces himself to say, "Tell me everything."

"Last time I saw the Chevy," she says, "it was parked on our side of the street. This time he was opposite. Farther away, but at a better angle. No tree in the way."

"At a better angle to see *us*," Shecky says. Part of speaking to Kerasha is filling in the gaps. "It's a guy?"

She's not quite smiling, but there's pride coming off her. "I got a good look."

"Did he look like a cop?"

An eyebrow raise, noncommittal. "Do you want me to bring you his badge?"

"Seriously. Do you think he's a cop?"

A shrug. "Doesn't have to be. Though he's definitely too old to be a straight-up hood." She sips her espresso. "Gray polo shirt, couldn't see his pants. Saw his arms, though—definitely works out. I think he's short. Hard to tell, but something about the way he was sitting." Another sip. "Should I be worried?"

"Yes," Shecky says, getting up. Bringing dishes into the kitchen. He clears the food scraps into the compost bin. Loads the dishes into the sink and turns on the hot tap. Waits for the water to steam, squirts bio-based dish soap into the basin.

Shecky rinses out the beer bottles, pours himself another whiskey. Fuck.

She first told him about the blue Impala a couple of weeks ago. It faces this way or that, she said. Sometimes there's no one inside, and sometimes there's *this guy*. Sometimes in a Nets hat. Different spots, different hours, but always, always in sight of the house. Is he police?

But we've been so careful, Shecky tells Dannie. We have our system, our fallbacks, our double-blinds.

Could he be a hitman? But who would bother? We're just *us*, a nobody fixer and his kids.

Could he be—

Every answer seems wrong, because this *presence* is wrong. Shecky has denied this man, has obsessed over him, has retched up into the toilet at three in the morning because of him. But still this shadow haunts his home.

"Home," Shecky says, more to himself than to his niece—but she is listening, her eyes and ears always open. "Means nothing if you can't keep it safe."

chapter 4

Henry thunders down the stairs, playing the dinner back in his head. "My family," Uncle Shecky had said, "my home"—Henry has heard it all before, but tonight it sounds different. What about *me*?

Henry loves his uncle, knows he owes him everything. But he sometimes gets these flashes of a future he doesn't want. Pictures himself, gray-haired in the little office. Holding the handrail as he walks down the stairs, grumbling about his ankles. Growing old in this house.

Down the last step to concrete. He passes loose boards and plywood, left over from bookshelves he made a couple of months ago. Passes the washing machine and dryer, goes to his draftsman's desk, and tosses his sketch pad on top. Frowns at it, can't get his eyes to focus. Doubles back to the dryer. He empties the clothes into a basket, carries this to a folding table, and sorts everything into three piles. Awkward with Kerasha's underwear. Neat and efficient with his own and his uncle's clothes, which are easy enough to distinguish: Henry is a half foot taller, and all his clothes are new, most either black or bright. His uncle's clothes, when Henry spreads them out and folds them, look tired and sad. He pauses on his uncle's favorite gray pants, the pleated cotton pair he wears for all his meetings with big clients. The fabric is worn smooth, and there's a faint stain above the left knee, and Henry feels shitty—just shitty—about what happened upstairs. He takes down the iron. Ten minutes later, when most of his uncle's clothes are in a neat pile—everything pressed, even the undershirts—Henry hears the *tap-tap*.

The basement has two high windows. If you're outside on the street, one window is at ground level between this two-family house and the one next door. The other window, again at ground level, faces the backyard. And this is where she raps when she comes to visit.

He goes to the window, pushes the folding chair beneath it, and lets her in.

Lipz.

She uses his shoulder, his arm, for support. The contact gets something going in him. Warms her, too, he knows, and now she's on her feet before him. Five foot nothing, weed breath, a general air of crazy. "You look like shit," she says. He follows her eyes as she scans the room, lingering at the laundry area before turning back to him. "The fuck, he makes you iron his undies?"

Henry looks down and sees that he is, in fact, still holding his uncle's boxers.

"Fuck." He throws the boxers over at the laundry area. "We got into a fight."

"Let me guess." She indicates the boxers, now on the floor. "You lost."

"He didn't ask me to wash his . . . Jesus." She's getting on his bed. Taking off her hoodie, and she's got nothing on underneath but a sports bra. He turns away, goes to his draftsman's desk, and comes back with her phone. Tosses it on the bed beside her. Avoids direct skin-to-skin contact.

"You remembered! Is it . . . ?" She powers it on. "You fixed it!"

She catches him looking at her sports bra. He turns away. Lipz is sexy, but in a dirty way. Though a weed and vodka girl now, she has a history with hard drugs. She also has a history of combat with her exes, and a kind of genius for self-destruction.

She shifts on the bed. "So what'd your uncle say?"

He walks a few paces away. Picks up his uncle's boxers, refolds them, puts them in the right pile. "I brought it up. I said maybe I could get a cut, and things kind of spun out."

Lipz lets out a snort-laugh. "The fuck I care about *your* cut?"

"We talked about—"

"*My* cut. That's what we talked about. Me. I hooked you up with Red Dog, I get a piece of that. Listen, I just read this thing by Michael Lewis . . ." She goes off about managed investment funds, alternative portfolios. Finder's fees, basis points. She wants more than a point, she's saying: she wants a point and a half. Henry's not following. Lipz is annoyingly well read for a heroin dealer. But she's low level, and Henry's sense is she may never even have met Red Dog. *He's* never met Red Dog, and her accounts of him are rather spare. But Red Dog is *the* heroin distributor in Bushwick, and he's become a major client for the family. And it's true that she was the one who introduced Henry to Red Dog's lieutenant. She made that connection—she's right, he owes her something. He's reflecting on this when he sees mud on his sheets.

"Lipz, your fucking boots."

She gives him a "Who, me?" look. Then she pivots and hovers a boot over his pillowcase.

"Jesus, can you just . . . Fuck. I told you. I'll give you half my cut—when I get a cut. It'll happen, my uncle told me."

Lipz rolls her eyes. "You're too trusting." She swings her legs around so her feet are off the bed. "And how much laundry are you going to have to do," she says, "before your uncle . . . Fuck it, this isn't even why I came." She takes out a cigarette. "Tiger."

"I thought you broke up."

She blazes, blows out smoke over her shoulder, looks Henry in the eye. "Fucking cuntface took my stash. My whole bag."

Henry watches her smoke, trying to figure out the alarm going off in his head. Tiger is Lipz's mostly-ex. He's a big, rough guy, a low-level slinger like Lipz. Lifts weights all the time—"diesel," as Lipz says, sometimes about Henry himself—and freakishly vain about his hair. Gets minor alterations twice a week: on Monday he gets buzz lines; on Friday he'll go for tints, slants, or dye dots. "My ugly pretty boy," Lipz sometimes calls him. Not today, obviously. The alarm in Henry's head is still going off. Tiger is, or should be, what was it . . .

"I need my stash back," she says. "You're coming with me."

"Says who?"

"Your debt."

Henry blows a sigh. He goes to the laundry area, comes back with the pile of his own clothes, which he folds and sorts on his draftsman's desk. "This is a bad idea."

"It's not an idea. It's a mess you're going to make with me."

"Lipz, you can't go out and get caught up in some shit."

"Says who?"

"Your criminal record."

When Lipz smiles, there's a sinister light in her eyes. "I beat that thing."

"The word *murder* is in your file."

"Indicted but not convicted."

"That's not a win, Lipz. Half a year in the psych ward—"

"And I was laughing every second." Another smoke blow, her expression darkening. Memories obviously coming back to her. "Fucking pedophile. I'd kill him again if I could." It was Lipz's stepdad, and Henry regrets bringing him up. Lipz was still in high school when it happened. The bastard's hands, and then her baseball bat . . .

Change the subject.

"Okay, Tiger's a bitch," Henry says. "But you don't need this. How much is a bag? Three hundred?" He reaches for his wallet. "I've got maybe fifty now, over the next couple of weeks—"

"It's not about the money." Lipz stubs out her cigarette on the sole of her boot. Still looking down: "You ever read the Bible?"

"Jesus."

"No, I'm talking first season. Book of Job. You read that?"

Henry watches her flick her cigarette at the can. A long shot, but it lands. "Not lately."

"So there's this brother called Job. He's a farmer, and his crops die. And he's a husband, and his wife dies. Then his kids. And his house falls down. And he's covered with scabs, and he's all disgusting and shit."

"There are scabs in the Bible?"

"*Everything*'s in the Bible. Nothing new under the sun. Hey!" She snaps her fingers. "Put down your socks. Listen."

Henry looks down at his hands. He has, in fact, taken up his laundry again. "I'm listening. Book of Job. Lot of bad shit happening."

"And the worst of it—the worst thing that happened to him—was he had *no name in the street*." Lipz makes a little kaboom motion with her hands.

And Henry thinks, Really, *that's* the worst? Not the wife, the dead kids?

"No name in the street," Lipz repeats. "Disgrace. And that's what's happening to me. Because of Tiger. And there's more." Her words speed up, and she gets on her feet. Moves her shoulders, her fists, as if revving herself for a fight. "He's talking shit. About me. About *you*. He's saying he owns me, fucking bitch. Who owns me? *I* own me. You taught me that." She's getting worked up, shadowboxing, shuffling her feet to the rhythm of her words. "Take *my* shit? Fuck no. I'm getting it back. But take my *name*? Better believe, Tigey, I'm getting your balls, dropping them in a hot pan with some hot oil—"

"Okay, okay," Henry says, with a shudder. "What's he saying about me?"

"Just the old bullshit," Lipz says, with a what-*evuh* hand flap. "You're a bitch, you're a faggot." Then her expression changes, and she looks at Henry with something close to a *gotcha* smile. "He's saying you hide behind your uncle. *Like a child*. That's what he's telling everyone."

He studies Lipz. Hiding like a child—is this something Tiger really said, and she just remembered it? Or is this something she made up, knowing it would boil his blood?

Either way, he's going to throw someone against a wall.

My name in the street. Faggot. Hiding. Uncle Shecky.

Uncle Shecky who won't give him a cut, won't let him use Emil tomorrow. Won't let him *be*.

"Fuck it," Henry says. "Let's get him."

"Easy, killer." She puts her hand to her head and cracks her neck. "He's up at his aunt's tonight. But he's back tomorrow."

Henry helps Lipz up and out the basement window. He's securing the latch when he hears a buzz. He goes back to the nightstand and picks up his phone. A message from Emil: *Got work?*

Henry lowers his phone. Uncle Shecky said don't use him. But the smoke from Lipz's cigarette is still in the air, and her voice—a part of his life for so long—reminds him that Uncle Shecky doesn't manage the runners anymore.

Henry lifts his phone again. *You're on.*

chapter 5

Late morning the next day, Emil wakes from a dream in which his whole childhood home—the yard, the tiny room his mother kept as a shrine to her long-dead father (photographs, diplomas, medals, and his rifle), the tattered flag over the garage, the bunk beds little Emil shared with the ghost of his stillborn sister—all of it exists impasto. In the dream, the living room is rearranged, all the furniture turned to face the walls, and the shadows they cast sway like gray-black balloons. An unexpected effect. Unexpected *solution*, Emil realizes, now fully awake. His pocket sketchbook and 2B pencil are ready for him on the nightstand. He doesn't even sit up, already working.

The big commission of the summer is a major project—a mural that's to cover the whole back wall of the Thirsty Bear. He'll get eight thousand dollars for it, if he does it right, but there have been shadow problems from the beginning. Even in Emil's head—even as an idea to paint toward—the shadows have been wrong. His first attempt at a fix was to shift the light source, his second to re-center the piece, his third was to . . . But before the dream he never thought to rearrange everything, to spin round all the objects in place. So drastic, so simple. His pencil fills page after page. He has to sharpen it twice.

"It's morning," he hears from Imani, in bed beside him. "Do you have to be so fucking productive?" Imani's a workaholic herself, dreaming up high-concept video games for an unprofitable start-up. He suspects that, on the whole, he's had a bad effect on her creative life. Game ideas used to come from tequila, tequila from misery, but with him—and she tells him this all the time—she's the happiest she's ever been. She's "in a good place."

Emil likes the notion that he's a kind of geography. Idea for a future work, after the Thirsty Bear mural is signed and paid out: part self-portrait, part landscape. Trees and buildings inside, legs and arms as mountains.

The vision fades as Imani removes the sketchbook from his hands. Rolls him onto his back. In the morning Imani does not smell her best, and there's a faint crust under her nostrils, the AC making autumn of the summer nights, but Emil doesn't recoil. The female body with all its funk turns him on. He forgets the pencil. Knows his priorities.

Hours later, outside, he's on his way to the pickup. His first big one—Henry has hyped it up for months. Promised him he'd make extra. Emil checks his latest burner—a new one every couple of weeks—and there's a text from Henry. Arrived last night, just the digit *1*. This is part of the code Henry taught him during his training weeks. The *1* is just a check-in, asking without asking whether he's ready for the job.

More than you know, Henry.

Curbside, a car slows, a black Ford SUV. It idles as if the driver wants directions. The training kicks in: Emil turns away. He takes an imaginary call on his burner, says, "nuh-uh," and "for real?" to the air. The car is gone. It's nothing, of course, but Henry warned him of "blues" and "wolves." The principal breeds of those who would hunt him. And you have paranoia without letting it have you, Henry promised him. It can be a kind of performance, a mime show if you keep your spirit clear. If your luck holds. It's a decent philosophy, Emil supposes, but even Henry isn't faithful to it. Look at how quickly he brought Emil into his family's business. Just as an errand boy, but still, absolute trust from the beginning. Well Emil likes him right back, and he feels bad about missing Henry's text from last night. Henry could well have been pacing and shitting himself. He lives and breathes the street, but he worries like a mom.

Emil texts back *3*, the all-clear code, and then picks up his daily coffee and banana from the Muddy Cup. The coffee shop is new to Bushwick, but they've already put up a couple of his paintings. They'll keep half the money if something sells, and in the meantime he gets his breakfasts comped. It's a fair trade: they don't have his best work.

Back outside, Emil scans the street, looking out for blues and wolves—performing paranoia, as he was taught. Smiling over Henry's lessons.

"Here's rule one about carrying the bag," Henry said to him once, quoting his uncle. "Never forget it could get you killed."

For Emil, training had been more than just safety lessons. Henry opened his eyes to a whole city that lay hidden just below the one he knew. Dumpsters, gym lockers, coffee shop toilet tanks—almost anything, it seemed, could hide a bag of cash. ("Client money," Henry explained. "We don't ask, they don't tell.") Banks that didn't look too hard at IDs, ATMs known to have bad cameras, post offices where money orders were processed like stamp sales. ("I'll give you the names and the numbers," Henry said. "Just get the money in and walk away.") The thermos of coffee Henry brought for them to share, and his endless questions about art. How intently Henry listened. And Emil, too, how scared he'd been on his first runs.

Now he walks with his sketchbook out. Pausing, here and there, to draw.

Storefronts and debris, traffic cones and potted plants, kids and moms and hipsters, and now a Sanitation Department road crew, half lean, half beefy. Details move through his 2B pencil. One of the beefy guys reminds him of his stepdad, himself a foreman, originally from Ronkonkoma. Young Emil had loved hearing that town's name, the syllables at once hard and childish. *Ronkonkoma*: a toy jackhammer of a word. In his memory his stepdad is always lying on the couch, always dozing with the TV on. And Emil is painting at the kitchen table, while Mom scowls, forever cross-armed from the doorway. "Contain your mess," she used to say. No art teacher gave him better advice.

He should reach out to Mom now, he knows, while he remembers. While there's still a breathing Mom he can reach out to—his stepdad's stroke taught him that. But it's a lesson he forgets and forgets, and so he forgets it now. The pickup site has come into view.

Alan's Happy Falafel is on Wyckoff Avenue near Troutman Street. He's already there. To reach its back lot, however, Emil must walk an extra half block to Jefferson Street. "Sharp left," he hears Henry's voice, "then squeeze between the brownstones."

At last he's in the lot where Alan's Happy Falafel keeps its garbage and recycling bins. Everything in place, everything exactly how Henry described it. This can be dangerous work, Emil reminds himself—blues and wolves—but it doesn't feel like it. The sun shines happy over Emil's little corner of Brooklyn; he has never felt more comfortable. And so he pauses at the bins and sketches. Takes a moment to consider, on paper, composition options, different angles and shadows. Those two brownstones, the gap between them, the seeming fakeness of this physical truth—they mean nothing to him, but for his hands nothing else exists.

Then the pencil is back in its case, the sketchbook again in his pocket. The leftmost bin open, he pulls out semitransparent blue bags packed with plastic, glass, and metal. A strange tint, the blue on the white yogurt containers, on the black and brown and green soda bottles, on the crushed metal cans. Another image to lock away. Or maybe to lose.

At the very bottom of the recycling bin is, as promised, a black trash bag. (Henry switches between white and black for the pickup bags, changing every few weeks.) It's packed with cash, Emil knows. He gives it a squeeze, feels the lumps. Dense. Firm.

The bin restocked and closed, trash bag at his feet, Emil feels Henry's smile. Emil's an old hand now, as his stepdad used to say. *Old hand*, a wonderful expression for an artist. Emil sends Henry another all-clear text. Pickup done, easy enough. Bigger bag, much heavier, but otherwise it's just another job. At this moment there's nothing between him and a clean, quick drop.

Nothing, that is, except for a quick stopover. Sorry, Henry. Won't take but a minute. And though he knows he'll feel sorry tonight, he can't let himself dwell on this now. He has work to do.

Back between the brownstones. Out of the shadows, onto Jefferson Street. And just as Emil steps into the sun, a gate creaks open. Windblown, it seems, and it leaves him with a haunted feeling.

Picking up his pace, Emil wonders how he can get this feeling on canvas. He thinks about brush heads and finish, and at one point steps within ten feet of the man who has been following him.

part two

the woman with twisted hands

chapter 6

Nearly thirty years before the murder of Emil Scott, a baby girl—tagged Zera, with no family name—is dropped off at an orphanage in Montenegro. Zera is twelve when a well-dressed bachelor appears at the orphanage and says he's always wanted a daughter. He pays the "administrative fees" in cash, and he will sell her again and again.

In the dark house where she is kept, the other girls tell her to forget everything. Close your eyes, hear nothing, say nothing. Katja, a few months older, is her survival mentor. "Lights off," she says, pointing at her head. Zera keeps her lights on, though, because she can't help herself. "Welcome to the Paradise House," she hears in a dozen languages as the men come in for the girls who are kept in the dark house. She remembers faces, scars, tattoos, and smells. Her mind is always mapping escape routes, and her eyes are always on the doors and windows. Always watching the locks and noting where they keep the keys. The well-dressed bachelor beats her when she breaks free. Beats her more the second time. She is bruised, blistered, scarred, and sometimes infected, but the men still come for her. After they are spent, or before they are up and ready, some talk about their daughters. On August 23, the Sunday before her seventeenth birthday, she breaks several of her fingers to get out of the manacles. Her hands will heal badly, but she is free. She looks at them and thinks of Katja. She remembers the men who bought and sold her.

Then comes the war. Refugees are accepted here and there, far from the Paradise House, and Zera finds herself in the hands of a charity that's actually charitable. An anti–human trafficking non-profit that has a partner organization in New York City. She attends high school in Greenpoint, Brooklyn, then graduates from CUNY with a degree in criminal justice. Not quite eight years out of the Paradise House, Zera Montenegro, as she is now called, sits across a desk from a round-bodied alcoholic in a blue uniform. "Why do you want to join NYPD?" he asks.

To burn down the dark house, she thinks. To cage the well-dressed bachelor.

"Justice," she says, remembering Katja.

The round-bodied alcoholic writes nothing. He is staring at her hands.

chapter 7

It's June, still early in her weeks of living with Uncle Shecky, and Kerasha is sitting on a shabby gray couch. The pillows make her skin crawl. If Satan has a single masterpiece, it must be faux velvet. When Kerasha was little Kerry, she could give herself goose bumps just *thinking* about texture like this, the fibers against her skin like tiny fingers. This talent had impressed Mama, who, before heroin took over, had herself been an imaginative person. Mama won a Burghardt Prize for her poetry while still in high school. Got a scholarship to Barnard, a young white woman determined to study African American literature. She married an older black professor who dropped dead from a heart attack when Kerasha was still young. The transition from struggling widow to full-on junkie seemed as smooth and natural as an ice cube melting.

But early Mama, poet Mama—Kerasha wonders what she would say if she came back today. Heard what was left of that powerful imagination.

We wear the mask that grins and lies . . .

What if Mama could see her clever Kerry now? No quick eyes registering all the stupid around her. No wicked laughter ready on her lips. Instead, there is only this husk. But this is the dull, empty, nonperson Kerasha must become—in miserable fifty-five-minute increments—every time she steps into this room. The whiff of pot-pourri. The little man with the ponytail, that fucking faux velvet. Her brain cries outrage, knocks against her skull, as Dr. Xu packs more and more humiliation into every session. At Franklin she had keepers, and over time her hatred of them evolved into a kind of art. Here the enemy is herself, the idiot she must perform. Empty-headed. Powerless.

Not me.

Dr. Xu and his ponytail have held Kerasha hostage for a half hour now, and Kerasha wonders how many patients have sat in this office, on this very cushion, and breathed the same potpourri. How many have run out midsession to commit suicide.

"Just get through it," Uncle Shecky has told her. Tells her again in her head. "You did six years at Franklin—after seventeen at the Moses Houses. If you had a real lawyer, he would've argued that as time served."

A dangerous feeling, nostalgia for prisons past. But at Franklin and in the Moses Houses, hostility was physical and out in the open. The ugliness was a kind of honesty. With the ponytail, though, hostility masquerades as "treatment." Comes as "betterment questions," each of which is a drizzle of piss on her brain. She is amazed by what she longs for in this space. The morning roll calls at Franklin, the gummy bread, even the punitive room tosses—she *misses* them.

Get through it. Good advice, Uncle Shecky. I'm trying.

Take things one breath at a time. This is from Kerasha's onetime cellie Nicole, a yoga instructor who embezzled some fifty thousand dollars from her aunt's studio. More sage advice. Wisdom everywhere. Mostly reiterations of the code billions of people live by every day. Don't kill yourself. Don't kill your psychiatrist. Simple enough, but Kerasha doesn't know whether she is equal to it.

Still, Kerasha Brown is famous in Bushwick's underworld for a reason, preternaturally gifted in evasion since girlhood. No room she can't get out of, no person she can't get past. Security guards, police. Teachers, social workers—outdumb them, look befuddled, let them talk. Fences can be climbed, shadows can be friends, and so, even here, in this office, she has tactics. Playing the fool, an act this so-called doctor is all too ready to believe. Echoing his questions, stumbling over big words. Pauses, blank stares. All while giving free rein to her fantasies. Like how about we kick over this coffee table. And the glass bowl hits the floor, and she picks up a shard, giving no fucks what it does to her fingers. And her free hand takes hold of that ponytail, and she saws that motherfucker off.

If only.

Kerasha's eyes stay on the glass bowl. It was empty during her first session, she remembers. Today it's filled with marbles.

Count the marbles in your head. Uncle Shecky never said this to her. Couldn't have, she's never shared any details about this room or what happens in it. Nonetheless, it's his voice she hears—it's the spirit of his counsel. *Count slowly.*

The coffee table is enormous and ornate, and it's completely out of place here. Kerasha herself has never lived in a building that had furniture like this, but she's broken into plenty of homes and offices, and she knows the function of this table. It's a show-off piece, something you stick in the middle of a show-off room, and you surround it with paintings and wedding photographs, icons and altars, cheap souvenirs from expensive trips. Coffee tables like this rarely see coffee, and in this room, it sends a clear and specific message: You're a nobody. I know your kind. I've heard all about your weak mothers, your vanished fathers, how it's their fault you shit-wrecked your life—I know your *type*, the coffee table says. You're a—

Full stop. Dr. Xu is looking at her through narrowed eyes, saying something about reincarceration.

Shit, she thinks, I missed something.

"Sorry, doctor," she says, and makes her first truthful and complete statement to the man paid to know what's on her mind: "I kind of tuned out there."

Dr. Xu grins—a first for *him*, the only genuine expression she's seen on his long face. "Part of the court mandate is that your early release is conditional on positive reports from me." He speaks slowly. "The first one is due within ninety days of your release. Part of the write-up is attendance. So far, so good on that front. But then another part of the write-up is participation and progress. And on that front . . ."

The trail-off. What a showman.

Kerasha hates everything about this little man: the way he speaks, the profession he chose, his taste in pillows and coffee tables. She hates his chin, his nose, his eyes, his hair stylist. (Yes, she decides, he has a hair stylist.) But most of all she hates his grin, and the undisguised pleasure he's taking now, turning her freedom over in his hands.

chapter 8

Two big carries tomorrow, and Shecky can't sleep. When he finally does nod off, he dreams of the blue Impala. Of his argument with Henry. Exhausted in the morning, he puts ten one-hundred-dollar bills into a copy of *The Accidental Alchemist*. Bribe money. Seems like yesterday you could buy a police clerk with a fifty.

He closes the book with the money inside, brings it downstairs into the kitchen, and puts it high (for him) atop the china cabinet. Out of sight, for now. Henry's the one with the hookup at the precinct. Henry's the one who can find out exactly how fucked they are. But Henry generally can't be asked to do anything until he gets some food in him.

Breakfast o'clock, Kerasha pads in and yawns. New slippers, he notices, zebra-striped and puffy, swiped from fuck knows where. To risk her freedom for such ridiculous . . . Shecky shakes it off. Doesn't have it in him to lecture her, after all she's been through. "Good morning, Kerry." He touches her shoulder as he passes into the kitchen.

Grill pan: thick-cut maple bacon. Sizzle for five, flip, sizzle again, flame off. Whole-wheat sourdough: slice with a bread knife, drop in the toaster. Pan number two: butter, eggs, a touch of milk. A shake of salt, a shake of pepper, simmer. The percolator rattles as if it wants to topple. Settles. Mug one, for Kerasha: cream and sugar. Two, for Henry: cream. A splash of whiskey goes into his own mug, and minutes later the breakfast table is set.

Kerasha raises the coffee to her nose. Closes her eyes. "The smell of freedom," she says. She opens her eyes, gives her uncle a little smile, and raises her mug to him. "This is how I know I'm out."

Shecky looks away, embarrassed, and his eyes land on Henry's chair.

Empty.

Where is he?

Dinner at eight is the family rule. Breakfast, also at eight, is optional, but Henry rarely misses it. Has even stayed up through the night for it after hard nights out partying. And who fucking knows, it could still happen this morning. Henry staggering in, dropping into his seat, and slopping food into his mouth. His eyes half closed.

Where is he?

Last night, after the argument, Shecky pushed Henry's chair back into place. Or thought he had. It's aslant from the table now, though, as if Henry isn't quite all right with the family anymore. But is he all right, period? And as Shecky hurries to straighten the chair, Kerasha's warning from last night—the Impala—is back on his mind.

The Impala.

The watcher.

Fear comes at him fast. Henry in a dumpster. Henry in handcuffs. Henry tied to a chair, or, frightening in a very different way, Henry peacefully breakfasting elsewhere—by choice. Having taken a last hard look at the family and clicked "unsubscribe."

He'll come back to you, Shecky tells himself. He'll be up from the basement in ten minutes.

But this is a hollow hope. Last night, after all, Shecky went downstairs to make peace. Found the basement empty, a cigarette butt. Shecky had picked it up—couldn't help himself, always tidying—and seen the dark lipstick on the filter.

Shecky checks the time. Just five minutes late. And besides, eight o'clock isn't even a hard start time. Breakfast isn't like dinner, he tells himself again. A no-show means nothing.

Except if it means everything.

Most likely Henry's splayed out on some dirty couch. Dry mouth, dry sweats, still tangled with *that girl*, but so what. The kid needs to let loose from time to time. The thousand ways Shecky pushes him, *tasks* him, it's amazing he doesn't skip more often.

Seven minutes.

Shecky goes to get his laptop. Comes back with it, opens it on the table. "Sorry," he says to Kerasha, "bad manners. Won't be a minute." Log-in. A VPN connection, a spoofed IP, and now he's losing himself in a transaction. The client, whom he met at the Muddy Cup yesterday, lives by cash. Runs a subcontracting business fixing roofs, fixing furnaces, installing water heaters. Would have to lay off half his staff, he once told Shecky, if he did it on the books. But now his daughter's starting at Colgate University, and the tuition is "a fucking heart attack." "So what am I supposed to do," the client asked yesterday, "drive up with a sack full of cash?"

Shecky took a sip of coffee. "You can call Aunt Pitney."

"I don't have an aunt Pitney."

Shecky took another sip of his coffee. Delighting, as Dannie used to, in masterful pauses. Then he smiled and said, "Let me introduce you. Your aunt Pitney lives in Guernsey. She is a widow and the heiress of a small fortune." He picked at his muffin. Continued in a lower voice: "I created your aunt Pitney two years ago. Whatever cash you give me, I'll wire to her. Whatever Colgate needs, she'll wire them. And don't worry—this lady is very real on paper. Colgate will hit her up for contributions to the endowment, and believe me, they will take her money with their eyes wide shut."

As do we all, Shecky thinks now. Feeling wise and philosophical and competent, he powers down the laptop.

Henry is twenty-eight minutes late.

Kerasha is smiling into her book. Shecky raises his mug to whatever sweet devil brought her here. "Hey, kid. How about rosemary chicken tonight?"

She smiles a yes. Turns a page.

Twenty-nine minutes.

Henry must be so angry. Shecky can almost hear himself being trashed, can almost see Henry cutting the air with his big hands, bitching to the dirty girl. My uncle this, my uncle that. No combat pay, no finder's fee for bringing in a new client. But what if it was worse than anger. What if, like last night, Henry was cold about him. Didn't care anymore.

Back in the kitchen, Shecky clears the drying rack. Pours the bacon fat, thickening but still runny, into the grease jar he keeps in the refrigerator. Then he wipes out both pans, drops the soiled paper towels into the compost bin, and washes his hands. Washes berries, too. He brings out three heaping bowls, three little fruit spoons. Kerasha's eyes get big. She even puts down her book. Shecky sits down with his own bowl, but his eyes are on Henry's. How forlorn it looks in front of that empty chair.

Thirty-two minutes. Shecky calls defeat.

"Breakfast was perfect," Kerasha says. "Again."

Her voice sounds different, and he looks up. Her bowl is empty. Her seat is empty. Kerasha is back in the corner, in his old armchair—now hers—and she has her book again. Left leg swaying to the rhythm of whatever she's reading. And yet she's keeping an eye on him, he knows. Kid has eyes all over her body, eyes in every room, it seems. So while her mouth holds a sad-wise line, and her leg sways, and her eyes move across and down the page, a good part of her attention, he knows, is on him. Her warning is in the air again, like a late echo, and he wants to ask, and she's just waiting for him to.

Don't. Let her have her peace. She's been through enough.

Shecky clears their fruit bowls but leaves Henry's next to his plate, which is still heavy with eggs, bacon, and toast. Just in case. In the kitchen Shecky washes the pans, the bowls, the silver. Loads the drying rack. Pours himself more coffee.

Forty.

In his dream the Impala was parked in Henry's basement room. A *thump thump* from the trunk; he knew the kid was inside. Frightened again, like a child, Shecky peeks back into the dining room. Steals a glance at his niece, who's still reading. Reassure me, he wills her. Always serene, his Kerasha. Could be mistaken for innocence, for obliviousness, even. But the thing about Kerasha is her eyes are wide open.

"Henry came home late," she says. "A little after three o'clock."

Shecky lets out his breath. Feels something unknot within himself. He rushes to her and asks, "And the Impala? Have you seen it?" The words are out before he thinks them. "Can you get the license plate for me? Without, you know, being seen?"

Shecky's relief about Henry—it was beautiful, but now other fears come fast at him. Bank of America: *Transfer denied*. Chase: *Internal inquiry*. Capital One: *Account closure*. And the watcher, that fucker in the Nets hat.

"Henry's got that friend at the precinct," Shecky says. His eyes turn automatically to the china cabinet. The mystery novel stuffed with bribe money. "She could run the plate. Tell us who's fucking with us."

The words are hardly out before he regrets them. Henry's friend is a *source*: you can pay her, get the intel, and move on. Kerasha is family. There should be more between them than the ways she can be useful. Her reports on the car—that's all been her initiative, he's never asked. And now he's treating her like—

"Can't get the plate for the Impala," she says. "It's gone."

He stares at her. "You're shitting me. Thank Jesus. Look, I know—I know. A touch of paranoia makes good business sense. But sometimes an Impala is just an Impala." His relief is a firehose. He catches his breath. "It's really gone?"

Kerasha turns a page. "Now it's a green Mustang."

His heart freezes, but the dramaturg inside him is all admiration. *Beautiful deadpan.*

He takes a long time to collect himself. "How do you know?"

She raises her eyes, and for a moment she's the little girl he saw in Paulette's apartment all those years ago. Vulnerable. Playful. Defiant. The sight of this girl in that cockroach nest broke him up, but there was nothing he could do about it then. He had no claim on her. So he went on with his hollow little life, swept her to the back of his mind until he heard about the arrest. Her mother's death, while Kerasha was fresh in jail. Kerasha's multiple escapes from jail, then from prison, and how they caught her again and again, and added years to her sentence.

"Spotted it this morning," she says. "It's the same guy."

"Jesus fuck," Shecky says. "I must've, I don't know . . . how . . ." Fucked us. Somehow. But how? And how now to un-fuck . . .

He goes to a chair. Remains there, a deflated flap of nothing, for several minutes.

Kerasha, meanwhile, turns the pages. Sips her coffee. "Your shirt looks nice," she says at last. "Ironed like that."

Shecky stirs. He looks down at his shirt. Ironed? When the fuck did this happen? He doesn't even remember.

"Listen," he says at last, sitting up, "I don't want you to do anything dangerous, but—"

"I'll get the plate for the Mustang."

He stands. Crosses the room. Gives her a one-armed hug. She doesn't quite reciprocate, but out comes her tiny smile.

Let her stay here always, he thinks. His cousin's daughter, a survivor of a scampering, filthy life—let her ease into something better here. Let her stay.

Footsteps. The moment snaps and the basement door creaks open. Henry blinks and squints as he steps into the light.

Shecky's smile is big and warm and real. "Henry. I'm so glad . . . Your breakfast plate's right over there. And there's plenty more if you finish that. Here, let me make you a new coffee."

And pour myself a whiskey. Jesus fuck, what a morning. Down and up and down again. Two kids here, but also that watcher. And the canceled transaction. And the night he spent in his ledger—he'll need to go back to that. But here's whiskey in his glass, and morning whiskey isn't his habit, but right now it's beautiful. Looks like a glass of magic. He raises the glass. Stops. He's remembering his uncle Joseph, a raw motherfucker who drank straight whiskey every morning. Shecky empties his glass in the sink. Returns to the dining room and puts Henry's coffee in front of him.

"How you feeling?" he asks.

"Eh."

"Listen, about last night. I thought about what you said. And I get the sense that . . . that you don't realize how much I appreciate you. Your work is outstanding. Day in and day out, the bread goes where it's supposed to. And when a dollar's missing, you don't run crying to me. You go out and get the fucking dollar. I'm proud of you. Which is why I'm trusting you with a new project. Time-sensitive like a falling bomb."

He goes to the china cabinet. Brings down the book with the bribe money.

Henry manages a sleepy smile. "Is this the bomb?"

The book, as if in response to the question, flops open. Henry recoils from the lump of cash. Then a hesitant joy begins to light up his face. "My cut?"

"What? No." Shecky slaps the book shut. "That's not for you. That's for your friend at the precinct." He releases the book, which again flops open. "We're going to need her help."

"And what about *my* help?" Henry says. "You said we'd go over the numbers." He nods at the book. "You came up with *this* number fast enough."

"We're going to talk about that."

Henry pushes the book away from him. Crosses his arms. "How about now?"

Shecky goes to him. Places a hand, which may or may not be shaking, on Henry's shoulder. "Hen, listen to me. I'm looking at the ledger. I was up half the night with it. I'll go back to it today, while you're managing the two heavies. And . . ." He freezes, remembering how yesterday's conversation ended. "You got someone else for the dirties, right? Not your friend?"

Shecky's hand is still on Henry, and he feels the shoulder muscles tighten. And is utterly unprepared for the calm.

"Don't worry about anything." Henry puts the money back into the book. Closes the book, pushes it aside, picks up his knife and fork. "I'll take care of everything." And then the food is going into his mouth, and the conversation—for Henry, quite obviously—is over.

Shecky remembers Henry's nine-year-old meltdowns, remembers the teenage indignation. This don't-give-a-fuck-ness is far more unsettling. And Shecky watches as Henry takes up a strip of bacon with his long fingers. Cuts into the flesh with his teeth.

chapter 9

Starr, Henry's friend at the precinct, is a very good friend. And Uncle Shecky remembered right—she's a fan of mysteries. And it's smart to put the bribe money in a book. Henry can't be seen just handing cash over to a police clerk. But this money isn't for Starr, who's not expecting anything. This is for Henry, who's *owed*. So what to do with a thousand dollars?

The day of the murder, Henry swears he won't waste a penny. He's investing—in himself.

9:45 a.m., first stop, the Russian barbershop. They're not Russians, of course, they're Kazakhs—the Russians' *victims*. In Russia they'd be among the unwashed and unwanted, but here in Brooklyn, they've been rebranded. Matt, as the barber calls himself, considers it the quintessential Russian joke: "It is bitter and it is not funny." He talks as he trims Henry's beard. "In America, Russia completes the conquest." Identity crushed, identity overwritten, Henry loves this. Already knows the tip will be forty dollars. Matt has broad shoulders and hairy arms, scars on his face, dark medieval eyes. A part-time barber with rough hands, he cuts Henry's hair better than anyone in Brooklyn. Gives good beard. Rumored to dabble in some serious nightwork himself when the pay is right.

"Same hair," Matt says, "same head." Matt says this every time

Henry sits at his chair. Henry is supposedly a doppelgänger of someone Matt knew in Kazakhstan, a fellow prisoner at the complex where Matt did four years. *Same hair, same head . . .*

"I don't like it," Henry told Emil. A couple of weeks after the opening where they first met, they were at another gallery, sharing another joint in an overlit stairwell. "A copy of *me* out there," Henry said. "What if he's living me better?"

"That's not even the question." Emil tapped his big nose, his crooked mouth always on the edge of laughter. "What if *you're* the copy?"

Henry leaves the barbershop with a snip and beard job he wants Emil to see. Today after the big carry, he thinks. I'll buy him a round after he finishes the job.

Second investment in his best self: a visit to Pauper's Palette, the art-supply store on Myrtle Avenue. Henry already has plenty of supplies, but Emil told him the store is "going gallery." The second floor was being refitted for wine-and-buy evenings. "They're going to put up local art," Emil said. "Might as well be yours."

"I don't know, man," Henry said. Echoing Emil's words and phrases; catching himself, but unable to stop. "Do I have art?" His recent sketches and paintings resemble Emil's, or works by artists Emil has introduced him to. Henry's money, on the other hand, is never derivative. Maybe if he spends big here today, at Pauper's Palette, it could give his art—if that's what he's making—a snowball's chance. He spends with purpose. A new easel, new brushes, new 2B pencils— all Emil's brands. Oops, forgot this, whoops, forgot that—back and back to the checkout line. At last he makes eye contact with the manager. She approaches. "Good to see you again," she says, obviously mistaking him for someone else. Then she mentions artists as though they're discussing mutual family, and he is immediately out of his depth. He nods knowingly, smiles hopelessly, when she jokes about "Cecily Brown's scather at the Maccarone." He's never heard of Cecily Brown, never heard of the Maccarone, can't imagine what *scather* might mean. But he nods and nods, and his desperation is hideous. She sees through him—he knows this. And what was he thinking, coming here? He set to invest a thousand dollars in himself as an *artist*, but here he is—at the fucking art store—hustling.

At the Thirsty Bear the walls are covered with native Bushwick art, and the most prominent of these is Emil's mural in progress. In a corner of the mural is an angry face framed by crude, bright-purple tentacles. Tentacles are a signature detail for Emil, and the whole design here, Henry intuits, is a kind of tribute to Kehinde Wiley, the artist Emil apprenticed under a few years ago.

Kehinde Wiley—Henry flushes. He glances around as if afraid someone overheard his thoughts. Before Emil, Henry had never heard of Kehinde Wiley. Now Henry name-drops the artist at every bar in Bushwick, and he knows he's doing it, and he can't stop.

Henry orders a beer, Belgian and fruity. "Breakfast of champions," the bartender says. Henry knows her. Some months ago they had a long weekend, though since then they've been just awkward-friendly. "New ink?" she asks, indicating his arm. His honey badger tattoo.

"New in two thousand ten," he says.

"Well, I've never seen you with the lights on."

Flirting for tips, everyone a hustler. He puts a twenty on the bar.

It's a little after eleven o'clock. The haddock and chips he orders take ten minutes, and just when he's squeezing a lemon wedge over the fish, his phone beeps. The bartender gives him a respectful nod and moves to the farthest register. He's told her nothing of the family business, but word, it seems, gets around.

The beep, disappointingly, is just an alarm Henry programmed himself. Emil should've checked in by now. Should've gotten the bag to Cha-Ching Money Services, should've put through the first of his money orders. But Emil's not bothering with protocol, it seems. Something small and mean inside Henry clenches up. This isn't the first time Emil's been late. Apparently Henry is someone who can be left waiting. Be forgotten.

The haddock tastes old and wet. He pushes his plate forward.

Gives the bartender the nod. More cash on the bar, he stands. A trip to the bathroom, a face splash. Then he's heading for the exit and can almost hear his uncle's voice.

I told you so.

"Forget likable," Uncle Shecky had said. "What you want is usable." This was back in the winter, when Shecky was readying Henry to take over the runners. "You're hiring someone who picks up and drops off. Right place, right time, with the right stuff—and all of it. They're employees, not friends." Maybe he was right, Henry at last acknowledges. Maybe he shouldn't have given today's job to Emil.

Henry loves his uncle. And fucking hates him for being right.

He texts Emil's drop phone. Silence. Troubled, Henry finds himself taking his uncle's perspective. Discovering in it a second layer of wisdom.

A runner must be dependable, but they should also be expendable.

Running cash is easy—pick up, drop off—but easy isn't the same as safe. Henry considers the size of today's first heavy, a quarter million in dirty bills, and understands fully, for the first time, how it invites disaster. A bold runner will take off, while the gentle runner will be taken out.

He checks his phone yet again. Nothing. Where the *fuck*? Idiot, he thinks at Emil—just follow the fucking rules.

One foot out the door, Henry pauses. Turns. Takes a last look at Emil's unfinished mural. The face encircled by tentacles seems anything but whimsical now, and Henry walks off feeling like he's tossed his friend to all the demons of Bushwick.

He stops at Molasses Books, the best place in the neighborhood for art books. One hundred and eighty dollars from the self-investment fund vanishes. He also picks out something for Kerasha, takes all his new purchases home, then heads over to Maria Hernandez Park, where another $125 gets him a bag of quality kush. He makes sure to set aside a hundred for Lipz, something to tide her over until he works things out with Uncle Shecky. To show some appreciation for a friend who, for all her faults, notwithstanding her history of murder, has never ghosted him.

Minutes pass, hours. At three o'clock Emil still hasn't checked in. Henry stops pretending everything's going to fix itself. He goes home.

A new drop phone from the drawer. A walk around the neighborhood until he finds an unsecured Wi-Fi. He logs in to a throwaway WhatsApp account, which he uses to call—you're welcome, Uncle Shecky—Starr, his friend at the precinct.

"I can't talk," she says. This is how many of their conversations begin: Starr is often mid-emergency.

"Just a quickie," Henry says.

"No, really. The desk sergeant looks pissed. She's walking over. Oh God!"

Henry usually enjoys his conversations with Starr, whose life, by her own retelling, can sound like a grand, blundering farce. But right now he needs an answer.

"Yes or no," Henry says. "Anyone get dropped today?"

"This is Brooklyn, Henry. Someone's always getting—"

"Any bodies?"

"No, but—"

Henry wants details, but he hears someone—the pissed desk sergeant, no doubt—telling Starr to "put down the phone. Are you working here, or are you getting fired?"

An unexpected turn of events: he asks Starr out to dinner.

Early evening, no message from Emil. Henry feels seasick. He regrets the mixture of alcohol and caffeine in his blood, as well as the line of Ritalin he snorted in his room. He can't even think about eating, but here he is at Alan's Happy Falafel. On the table: a basket of pita, bowls of hummus and baba ghanoush. Across it: Starr Richardson. Starr is an adorkable, voluptuous woman who has no idea how sexy she is. He's painted Starr more than once, and from time to time he thinks about how much fun the two of them might have together. Without clothes. Neither has initiated anything, though, and Henry's pretty sure it has something to do with her cat. Her commitment to that animal is formidable.

Also on the table: a strawberry milkshake, a coffee for Henry, a plate of fries between them. Next to the fries: *The Accidental Alchemist*.

Starr was so grateful when he handed it to her, he almost regrets having taken out the money.

Another regret: still nothing from Emil.

"So Banana needs another biopsy," Starr says, "which costs like two-fifty." Banana is the cat. "And the vet lets me pay in installments, but I already owe her . . ."

"Sorry," Henry says, maybe ten minutes into this story. "I need . . ."

Air. He steps outside, takes out his phone.

Purple sky, humid and hazy. The smell of weed. A muscle car on oversize wheels, a muscle man at the wheel, the stereo an eruption—amazingly—of smooth jazz. The muscle man scans the streets, begging to be challenged. Henry turns away. Pockets the phone, walks a block and a half, then pauses. Before him is an alley that passes between two brownstones and leads to the back lot of Alan's Happy Falafel. Henry pictures Emil arriving here for his pickup. Pictures him passing between these brownstones, coming up on the garbage cans, the recycling bins. Scanning the windows, the fire escapes, the rooftops, as he was trained to. As Henry is doing now.

Something went wrong, he thinks. *Something bad happened here.* And maybe it's because Henry already has doubles on his mind (same head, same hair), but even fear today has a second self. Did something bad happen *to* Emil, a wicked voice asks him, or did something bad happen *because of* him?

Henry empties the recycling bins. Empties the garbage cans, just in case. No money, no runner, a silent phone, no messages. Henry stomps a can half-flat. Hurls a metal lid against a wall—no, misses—cracks a window. A scream. It's not Emil's, of course, but to Henry it sounds like a late echo.

Back at the halal diner, Starr holds up a bit of baklava. "I saved you a piece," she says, her fingers honey-wet.

"I need your help," he says.

"You okay, Henry?"

He draws in a slow breath. "I can't find my friend."

Starr lets out a noise. Henry feels himself on the brink of tears, but he clenches his fists. He can't melt. He needs to know where his friend is, needs to know if . . . the money . . .

If Emil took the money and ran.

Fuuuck. If only there were something he could do. To not know like this. Frozen, with movement possible, no *action* . . . He tightens his fists till they're shaking and then gets a text from Lipz:

Tiger back from aunt's. Whupping ass tonight. You in?

Henry feels the rush coming on. Finally, fucking finally, here's something he can do.

chapter 10

Emil smirks, remembering Henry's Super Important Rules.

Don't open it, don't weigh it, don't hold it up to the light.

Christ, Henry takes himself seriously. On the day of his murder, Emil gives the bag a good ass-grab. Hey, Henry, how'd you like *that*? Imani wouldn't like this, Emil taunting and acting lewd. She'd be jealous—yes, even of this bag. So why not go all the way? He could cut a hole in the bag and make love to the money—now *that* would make for a high-concept video game. *Money Ba(n)g*, Imani could call it, and the challenge is to make love to as many dollar bills as you can before the clock runs out.

Running cash. Seemed such scary, serious work the first time. Now he has his fun with it.

Emil stops at a bodega. Doesn't buy anything at first, just studies the candy racks. Revels in the over-bright colors, the hideous contrasts, every wrapper a study in power clash. A packet of Skittles in his pocket, he heads back into the heat. Climbs the steps to the aboveground platform of the M train. Garbage on the tracks, food bags and hats, magazines and paper cups—everything here is filthy and shapeless. Emil has no use for it. Behind the benches, though, movie posters are mounted on the corrugated sheet metal. Imani would know the actors. The video games she works on are cerebral and edgy, but her taste in movies is straight Hollywood. More than once he's snuck up on the house, slipped into their second-floor apartment, heard the big orchestra swell, and peeked in to see her crying over her laptop. Her face electric blue in the monitor light.

The train comes in. The rails shake and whine, then the dirty machine lumbers up, brakes squealing. He catches himself swinging the bag. Realizes he's aroused just thinking about Imani. At ease, soldier, he tells himself. Make your stopover, then finish the drop, *then* you can have your fun.

On the train he holds the bag by its neck with one hand and hugs it with the other. Henry would not be happy with him: train travel is against the rules.

"Blues and wolves are everywhere," Henry had said during training, "but they're not the only danger."

"Cameras?"

"Friends."

But you're trusting *me*, he thinks affectionately now.

"You take the train four times a day for a month," Henry had continued, "and you'll never run into anyone. But the one time you've got a bag, it's your fucking life reunion. Your fourth-grade homeroom teacher. Every ex and her sister. Some old roommate, some aunt you thought was dead—when you're carrying the bag, they're all on your train."

"They'll ask about the bag."

"They'll fuck your brain. They'll make you self-conscious. You'll act suspicious. You'll think *they're* suspicious, and that's the shit part of working street," Henry said. *Working street*—Henry was obviously in one of his grizzled, seen-it-all gangster moods. Jim Beam sometimes does that to him. "It cracks your capacity for trust." Emil likes the accidental poetry that sometimes comes out of Henry. Loves the self-conscious, half-apologetic glances that follow. Imani would adore Henry, Emil knows, but he's been careful to keep the two from meeting. His lives are already entangled enough.

The train doors open, the train doors close. A concept for a new work explodes into life. Henry angular, Henry muscular, Henry a racehorse of a young man. He faces away from an anvil, head in his hands. Farrier tools scattered around his feet. All blacks and grays and browns, but from Henry's eyes, the whites shine. The work could be faux woodcut, Lynd Ward minus the class-struggle allegory, Raymond Pettibon without those fucking text bubbles.

The work turns in his mind, and he's calm until he's jostled. Passengers mass at the doors, which close on someone's rolling suitcase.

Where am I?

A glance at the window plucks him from his vision. This is the Myrtle Avenue stop. Across the platform is the Z train, an express that will shave five minutes off his stopover. If he can make it.

Emil Scott doesn't hurry, that's not his way. But then again he doesn't usually have a bag heavy with cash. Doesn't usually have a secret stopover.

The subway doors bang on the rolling suitcase a few times and then reopen. Emil springs to his feet. A breath later he's on the platform. His express train awaits, its open doors a personal invitation. Emil Scott is not athletic. His heart pounds as he dashes across the platform. Fumbles over a battered wooden bench. Runs at his express train and then skids to a stop. "This is a J train going on the local line," the PA bleats. "For express service on the Z line, please take the M train across the platform to . . ."

The trusty old M train, the one he just left, is still chewing on the rolling suitcase, unable to close its doors. Emil steps over it, squeezes through, despite his little belly. Back on the right train, he catches his breath.

And yet can't get settled.

As the adrenaline burns off, Emil processes something he observed on the platform. For over a decade he's been an around-the-clock artist, his eyes trained to pick up odd movements and details. His pulse responsive to cracks in the humdrum. What just happened?

A shadow raced off the J train. Followed him. And now Emil and this shadow are together on the same train. Am I being followed? The evidence is slim, and yet Emil is "working street," as Henry put it. And Henry's voice calls up from training.

"Trust your body," Henry had said. "It knows danger."

part three

the marked wallet

chapter 11

The day starts well enough. It's June, one month back, about an hour after breakfast, and Kerasha is reading in bed, her door open so the breeze through the window can flow. A soft knock, Henry pokes his head in. "Hey, you seen the old man?"

Kerasha lowers the book. Henry is tall and muscular, good-looking in a rough kind of way, and very, *very* respectful of her privacy. Even now, he's not stepping inside, even though this room was his just this past spring. Even though he's obviously curious. She notes his shy way of scanning the towers of books. She sees him lean in to look first at *Lit*, the top book on the tower to the left, and *Directed by Desire*, the top book on the tower to the right. She likes this, his interest in her, likes that it's not asking for anything.

"Uncle Shecky went out about a half hour ago," she says. "He had the tote bags, so—"

"Farmers market," they both say at the same time. They share a smile.

Then his eyes are again on the stacks of books. He looks like he wants to say something, but he just waves and heads out.

Later that afternoon, Kerasha returns home with a backpack full of new books. There's a different smell in the house: sawdust. Seems to be coming from the basement—that door is open. She can hear

Henry down there—he's on the phone. She's picks up a word or two, but nothing explains the smell.

Until she gets to her room.

Three new bookshelves, her books placed neatly, in roughly the same order they were in when they were stacked as towers. The shelves are huge and a little crude, banged together out of unmatched wood, but when she grabs the nearest shelf and gives it a shake, it's sturdy. She looks at her hands: dust on her fingertips. Being thought of, being a part of a family—this is a new feeling.

It doesn't last.

Some buildings invite break-ins. This one demands it.

Camera out front: mounted low on the wall, pointed down and across the front door. It covers some of the largest ground-floor window, Kerasha figures, but not much.

Camera across the street: covers the far side of the same window.

Look left, look right. Look across, up, down—no peepers. The left window, not covered by cameras, opens up in two minutes—thank you, pick-and-hammer combo. Most of her kit goes untouched, as usual. She's overdressed.

Open, slip in, close.

Kerasha catches her breath. *Listen.* Good habits die hard. This is a nothing job, and it will only get easier. On behalf of her talents, she's insulted.

Smell, the younger Kerasha insists. Take it in.

Kerry the girl thief was more methodical than Kerasha the excon. Thinner, too, no hips.

Listen, she repeats. An AC hums. *Smell.*

Perfume. Febreze. Tobacco.

Perfect. Her own scent masked, she may end up carrying a little of this one away with her—a false trail.

There are no unpeopled rooms for Kerasha Brown. In this one: a female, definitely. A secret smoker, or maybe just permissive with certain visitors. Either way, Kerasha decides, this woman has a soul.

Outside: a truck huffs by—white noise. She moves to the door and unlocks it. Enters a hall, where she wonders if you can judge a head-fucker by the women who work in his building.

Kerasha has a sixth sense for blueprints and layouts, a feel for floors and walls, corridors and closets. Office space, always the same everywhere, navigates itself: left to the staircase, up two flights, first right, and here's the door. His. Just a knob knock, three pick-points. She feels the click even before she's at a full kneel.

Door open, enter, door close. *Breathe.* That's skinny Kerasha again, her younger self just won't shut up. Listen. Smell.

She is alone. The windows, she knows, face an alley, so it should be safe to turn on the lights. Secure the door, skinny Kerasha says. Silly, the idea that at three in the morning, some lonely headfucker is just hanging out in his office. Be humble, skinny Kerasha insists. Or maybe this is Saint Augustine? You just spent six years in the cage, you don't know everything. Definitely Saint Augustine. Broke into a church, had sex to the rhythm of the church bells, got himself canon-ized. Brother played the game—and fucking won it.

She takes off her outer shirt, rolls it tight, and presses it along the bottom of the door. At last she turns on the light. Here we are, Dr. Xu's office, minus Dr. Xu . . . It feels smaller. Sadder, somehow, and less hostile. Consider the coffee table, so loathsome during her ses-sions. Now it's just an ugly, out-of-place thing. A *mistake*, a miserable something she has to check herself from overidentifying with.

Back to business. Young Kerasha is delighted to see that the file cabinet has a real lock. Enjoy, skinny girl, Kerasha says. You know why we're here.

Dr. Xu is, by all evidence, balding self-importance. He doesn't know her, doesn't understand her—and can't. As she's revealed nothing of herself, he has no facts on which to base an understanding. And yet it's *his* opinion—this man whose judgment acquired this coffee table, grew that ponytail—it's *his* report to the probate court that will deter-mine whether she can remain with Uncle Shecky. His report that can put her back in the cage. She and the ponytail have met several times now. Usually his hands are empty, and his fingertips touch as if to form a ball. Every ten or fifteen minutes, though, he nods in response to some silence or evasion from her—nods in deliberate response to *nothing*, it seems—he nods and takes a silver pen out of his hip pocket, and he writes something down. Notes taken with this pen will indicate which way he's leaning, how he's perceiving—to use language from the court order—her "progress and compliance." His notes will decide whether the man needs to be interfered with.

The lock should have yielded already. A little extra pressure should do it—doesn't. She turns harder, jiggles it, and then skinny Kerasha whispers—definitely not Saint Augustine this time—for her to pay attention to her technique. Force it and you'll break the lock or the tool. Pause and listen. Listen, breathe, listen. *Be not impatient*, as Whitman would tell her.

Fucking Whitman.

At Franklin, Kerasha had lived on poetry. Arguably she was born into it, her mother considered the poet laureate of the Moses Houses. Mama always reciting poems, even when her own writing gave way to heroin.

But here's the thing about reciting poems when you're smacked: you don't always get the words right. Here's the other thing: you don't always bother with attributions.

The terrible revelation hit in Franklin's dank library. It was there Kerasha discovered that "The Noiseless Patient Spider"—one of her favorite poems, which she had always thought of as Mama's—had actually been written by a dead white man named Walt. Kerasha hated this man—hated his name, hated his foul-smelling beard. (Yes, it smelled. Look at the picture.)

But it was too late, in that dank library, to unlove the poems.

And Kerasha was too tenderhearted—despite everything—not to feel a new wave of loss. Addiction had taken her mother's present, death her future, and now came Walt, estranging even the past. Goodbye, Mama, whoever you were.

But come on, Kerasha, you remember. The most important fact about Mama, the decision that changed everything, you know in your bones.

The heroin started *after* Kerasha was born.

"After!" It was Mama's last man who broke the news. Smiling, that beast, every time he explained the progression, which she now recites like an epic poem. Stanza one: Complications from Kerasha's birth. Stanza two: Mama's back problems, her painkillers. Stanza three: Smack.

He was clever, for a beast. Knew damn well how little Kerry would put the pieces together. Before me, she was okay. After me . . . *because of* me.

Mama, though, to her credit, never put it like this. "I'm still strong, Kerry, still going up and up and up," she'd say. At Franklin, Kerasha discovered that this was a riff on some lines by Langston Hughes. "You'd better not fall," Mama said. "Look at me, I'm still climbing."

Kerasha still can't make sense of this, how Mama—whom Kerasha saw only in freefall—believed herself climbing. How the woman who became a mother *and then* a junkie could still mumble—aiming at Hughes again—about "going on and on in the dark."

As if Mama ever went anywhere but down.

Look at me, Kerasha thinks, a girl in her psychiatrist's office, thinking the sad-sad about her mama. *Alone* in the office; who needs the doctor?

Kerasha looks down at her hands. They aren't on the cabinet. Aren't even on the pick, which has somehow made its way back into her utility belt. No. Her hands are before her, fingertips touching fingertips. Making a ball.

Apparently the office does his work, creates the doctor in whoever's here. So again, who needs that fucking ponytail?

Well, maybe *she* does. It's three-something in the morning. While Brooklyn sleeps, dreaming of everything but her, she stands alone in her headfucker's office—by choice. Head full of darkness, her heart bleeding June Jordan: *I am the history of the rejection of who I am.*

"You're a rejection," she says to herself.

Quiet, skinny Kerry tells her. Focus.

Before her is a cabinet, unremarkable in every way. She has

unlocked cabinets just like it. But this one defeats her, humiliates her, *endangers* her, prolonging her trespass. Has forced her, by the black magic of association, back into childhood.

Just a cabinet, she thinks. I'm still climbing.

This cabinet is not in control. It was *designed* to be opened. But she's letting it defeat her. Why? The question comes in the doctor's voice, the answer in her own.

Want.

Franklin's library had a half shelf of psychology books, and from them Kerasha learned that every human brain is controlled by a toddler-god called *want*.

Okay, for the sake of sanity, let's take that as truth. Let's think it through.

Kerasha wants the cabinet closed. Why?

She wants this not to be her fault. Why?

The answer takes so long that when it comes, it's like a sucker punch.

She wants it not to be that she's afraid.

Fear. It's that simple—she's afraid of what's in the files. And though she doesn't understand this fear, and can't banish it, somehow, just by owning it, she gets it under control. Still going, still climbing—here comes your girl, Mama—in the dark.

And now it's easy.

She upsizes her pick. Poke, twist, press, and the lock springs, and the drawers open. Ponytail is a careful labeler, well organized, good penmanship. The file for Kerasha J. Brown is right where it ought to be—and then it's not.

"Patient was referred by . . ."

She skips ahead, not caring about the referrer or his bullshit. Needing only Dr. Xu's. Less than five minutes later the notes are back in the file, the file back in the drawer. The drawer is closed, the cabinet locked. Lights off. Shirt out from under the door. Outside, hours till daylight, she puts two pieces of gum in her mouth. The word of the dark morning is *recalcitrant*.

"Recalcitrant and uncooperative, the patient has evinced no interest in her treatment."

She smiles at this, always enjoys good bombast, but her pleasure is hollow. *Recalcitrant*, she knows, means the cage. Her parole is "absolutely conditional"—the court papers, all riddles and legalese, were clear on *that*.

She crosses a street. An ambulance rounds the corner just behind her, lights on, sirens off. She watches it make another turn. Waits to be alone before letting her thoughts back in.

Be not impatient, Walt says again. Saint Augustine whistles Jesus, while Mama and Langston speak of *still climbing*. As for little Kerry, she's with the history of her rejection. And she's afraid.

There are places without light, there are rooms without exit. And then there's that other place Kerasha knows, where once upon a time, a famous girl thief got lost.

chapter 12

July again, unlit stairwell, Moses Houses Tower B. Lipz lights a spice joint and her face glows sinister, glows beautiful. Henry can almost taste her whispers: "Shit's going down."

"What's the plan?"

"Boom the door. Grab my stash."

Henry takes her joint. "Fucking Tiger." Pulls on it, hands it back. Exhales. "Why's he fucking with you? Where's *his* stash?"

"Red Dog won't supply him."

Henry begins to say something. Stops. The faint warning bell he'd heard before—the last time he talked to Lipz about Tiger—now it's ringing loud and clear.

"Don't give me that look," she says.

We're already a bickering couple, he thinks. So why not . . . actually couple? He looks her over, the bright, loony eyes; the barbed wire tattooed around her neck. This ink goes all the way down, he knows—he saw some of it get needled in. And the warmth of her body, and the hot and fetid stairwell, and the bubble-gum smell of her breath, and that I-dare-you look on her face . . . It would be so easy.

"Shut the fuck," she says.

"I didn't say shit."

"You don't have to."

Henry sighs. "Red Dog does smart business. If he won't supply Tiger, he's got a reason."

"Fuck reason."

If Lipz has a credo, this must be it—Henry enjoys hearing it aloud. "Listen," he says, "this is no disrespect to you, okay?" Her body stiffens. She waits like a predator. He puts a hand on her shoulder and lowers his whisper. "Tiger got arrested—you told me that. He got arrested, then they let him go. How did that happen? He's got a record, and he probably has warrants. The only way the cops let him out like that—"

"Fuck you."

"—is if he's working for them."

"Fuck. *You.*" She pushes his chest. She's done with her whispers. "Tiger's not a snitch. He's a bitch, but he's one of us. And that bitch is handing back my stash, or whatever bread he got for it. *Tonight.*"

Henry picks up the joint, which must've fallen when she pushed him. Studies it—bleh—drops it and stomps it out. "Tiger have a gun?"

"He's slow."

"Is that a yes?"

"If he reaches, I'll take it."

"Great plan."

"You don't have to like it," Lipz says. "This doesn't involve you."

Henry wonders if he's just been uninvited to a party he never wanted to go to. He feels a little hurt.

"If you come in with me," Lipz says, "then it's *you* getting my stash. And I'm this weak girl people can take shit from."

"So why the fuck am I here?"

"You're not my bodyguard," she says. "You're my medic. If he kills me, fine. You can whatever. Go out and get fucked. But if he just hurts me, you're taking me to the hospital." She shudders, and Henry remembers that Lipz is afraid of hospitals. Remembers her bout of acute pancreatitis, back before she put a full stop to the hard drugs. Remembers the complications.

He tries to get in a word but she cuts him off with a touch. Just her fingers on his ear, but touch doesn't happen between them without a total body freeze. Is this happening? his body asks. He feels the blood rush. Now? *Here?*

"You came out for me," she whispers. "Thanks." She pulls his face down to her mouth and then vanishes, leaving him with a warm spot on his cheek.

Alone in the dark, Henry tries not to think of Emil, who still hasn't surfaced. Henry hasn't stopped reaching for his phone, feeling phantom buzzes, this whole time. He also bats away his feelings for Lipz, and what went through him when she held him. He's leaning against the cinder-block wall, his hand on his phone again—where *is* he?—when he hears the scream.

chapter 13

Earlier that morning, Shecky goes to the corner bodega and buys a *Daily News*. He takes a reading walk around the neighborhood, peering over the pages, circling and then counter-circling his block. Looking for a green Mustang, for a blue Impala, for *him*, whoever he is—the monstrous cop/assassin who haunts his life. Everyone looks suspicious. And somehow *not* seeing the watcher becomes, as the hours pass, most unsettling of all. The watcher is beyond human, it seems. A spirit of evil.

Around lunchtime he makes his rounds at the "bean banks"—coffee shops, quiet places with Wi-Fi he uses for wire transfers and to open and close accounts. At the Muddy Cup he gets a muffin and, while sipping his first cup of black, moves forty-thousand dollars through Mexico into Russia. At Crespella, as he picks through his usual lunchtime salad—kale and spinach, light on the tuna, heavy on the wasabi peas—he completes a complex restructuring of narco money through legitimish shell companies. He meets a client at Bean Stalk, and when the client asks if Shecky might give him a 2 percent discount—"as a favor"—Shecky annihilates the request with a hard, cold stare. In between his visits to the bean banks, he comes home to walk the block. He scans the curbs, the driveways. The passing traffic, the open garages. He finds nothing; he feels the spirit everywhere.

Afternoons are for clients. Handshakes, PINs, and stored-value cards. Hard drives get swapped. Lefty Franklin talks politics, Jacob Burnside goes on about his ex-wives, and Shecky has a lot to say about the Mets. Business is fine, no new account closures, but hunting his watcher disrupts his day. He's late to several meetings, including the most important one. But at last he's at Maria Hernandez Park, where the client is still waiting on the bench.

Vasya—actual name unknown—is a small, flaky-skinned man who wears neat suits. Gorgeous shoes. A jaunty pin in his lapel, a little white cat face—what's it called?—Hello Kitty. Seeing Shecky, Vasya flicks his cigarette, stands, and extends a hand.

"You need a drink," Vasya says as they begin their walk-and-talk.

"Thank you for taking my call last night," Shecky says.

"How could I not? Your problems are ours." Vasya is Shecky's liaison at the Paradise Club, an early and very important client. Shecky has explained this clearly to the kids: everything done *by* the Paradise Club is none of our business, but everything done *for* the Paradise Club must be done right away. Like get off your ass and go fucking help them right now. Last night, though, it was Shecky asking *them* for help. "And you did the right thing," Vasya says, as if reading Shecky's embarrassment, "calling me. Thank you for your trust."

Shecky shakes his head. "What a mess." The call was miserable and shameful, a new low in an already wretched month—all those banks turning against him, freezing his accounts. But the call was also *necessary*, and he made it just moments after he worked it all up in his ledger. Scheduled out the whole family disaster, transaction by transaction, calculated to the last penny.

"Don't worry, we've all known messes." Vasya speaks with casual conviction. "We'll get it cleaned up together." Slow walking, now, they share a look. We're old-timers, we've seen and done plenty, we'll get through this. Then a hint of mischief comes into Vasya's eyes. "Tell me, though. If it's not too personal. These problems with the accounts, how did they start?" Now the mischief is in his mouth. "Was it your son?"

A punch of mixed emotions. My *son*. If only! But Vasya's insinuation about Henry—it's painful precisely because it echoes Shecky's own thoughts. Henry did nothing wrong *on purpose*, and he's never *lazy*, but sometimes his judgment . . . And now Shecky feels the heat in his face, hears the thud of his heart. "My *nephew*," he says pointedly, "is absolutely responsible." Pause. "No, wait, I didn't mean . . ." Shecky feels worse, now, tricked by his own tongue. An angry ache moves down his shoulders to his fists. Vasya should never have brought up Henry. "All due respect, but we will not discuss him."

"Of course, forgive me." Vasya stops the walk-and-talk. Puts a hand on his shoulder. "You'll come out from this, you understand?" His smell: cigarette smoke, cologne. His eyes: cold. "In the end, every problem is just an expense."

More errands, and Shecky comes home late to dinner.

Late to dinner—him! Jesus fuck, he thinks. These kids are your responsibility. What good are your schemes and your scrambling if, come dinnertime, you're not here for them?

Take it down a few, Dannie scolds him. "You don't have to actually rip your heart out," she said once to an actor. Overacting was a kind of apostasy for her. "This is a five-buck show. No one's expecting warm blood."

He imagines Dannie in his kitchen now, rolling her eyes at him. Telling him not to beat himself up. But she'd be amused, too, because—and this amazes him more and more as the years pass—she actually enjoyed his little quirks. Just liked being around him. And now she'd remind him that he's only a half hour late. She'd indicate Kerasha, whose presence means he hadn't missed the family dinner after all.

Down a few, Shecky. Keep your blood off the floor.

Kerasha is in her usual seat. In her usual pose, too: leg over the arm of the chair, foot on the windowsill, book open on her lap.

"Sorry I'm late, kid," he says. "You must be starving to death."

"I'm not going to let myself die, Uncle Shecky," she says. "Not before dinner."

How does she do it? Decades younger and fresh out of the cage, but she always comes off like she's holding the family wisdom. And who knows, she probably is. She spotted that watcher, after all, credit where due. And speaking of, she must know now—even from the armchair—whether that watcher is close.

But shouldn't *she* come to *him* for help? He is, by some twists of luck and law, her sponsor. Maybe just once in a while?

Earlier in the week he spoke about this with Fat Boris, the family ID doctor. A dad with a daughter.

"Shouldn't she look up to me?"

"How could she? You're, what, five foot four?" Fat Boris smiled as he handed over the passports he'd printed for Shecky. "She tolerates you. Be grateful for that. Start from there."

Tolerant is a good word for Kerasha. *Tranquil. Self-contained.* Whereas he, her de jure guardian, lives from terror to terror.

"Sorry," Shecky says again, a good word for *him*. "We'll get something in your belly right quick." He slices up a dry salami, a garlic pickle, and a cheese wedge, and puts them on a serving plate heaped with crackers. "Get started," he says, hurrying back to the kitchen. He wants to ask Kerasha about the green Mustang. Wants to call Henry to see why he's not here. Ask about the heavies. See whether he's still sore about last night's tiff. But so much of being an uncle-guardian-employer is doing nothing, saying nothing, just abiding. It's not enough for questions to hang unanswered; often they mustn't be asked at all.

"It's bluefish tonight," he tells Kerasha, peeking in on her from the kitchen. She turns a page, which is all his announcement deserves. No doubt she's expected nothing else. Bluefish is all they have, and even with her eyes in her books, she seems to know every inch of the house. Inside, outside, the surrounding streets. The contents of the refrigerator. The presence or absence of a green Mustang.

Down a few, Shecky. Give the girl a proper meal, and she'll talk when she has something she wants you to hear.

He sets the oven to broil. He stretches foil on the pan and lays the bluefish—gutted, but with the head, tail, and fins still on—at the dead center. Salt, pepper, olive oil: it needs nothing else. Wild rice and broccoli rabe, both cooked earlier this week, will do fine for sides. One in the microwave, the other simmering in a pan, he checks the clock. Seven more minutes, then the fish can go in under the flame. The meal has basically made itself. He opens a Guinness.

Fuck the green Mustang. I have a niece and beer.

Life has played me fair.

He brings three loaded plates to the kitchen table. He also has his Guinness and one for each of the kids, including the absent one. Jesus forbid Henry should come home and see there's nothing left out for him. Henry feeling given up on, feeling forgotten—never. He can slam all the doors he wants, but Shecky won't let him down like that.

Plates down. Shecky himself down. There's an empty chair, but fuck it. Grace: "Thank you for being here. Thank you for being my family." Eyes open. A sparkle, a bit of leather, a length of steel, a flash of gold. His bottle hits the table, a clatter, a mess.

"Jesus fuck," Shecky says. "Where did you get that?"

On his kitchen table is a large black pistol. A Glock, he's pretty sure, a 9mm demon—*on his kitchen table*, not twelve inches from his niece.

Next to the pistol is a police badge.

"The plate is K8134M," she says, righting Shecky's bottle. Leaving the table, coming back with a dishrag. Putting it to work. "Not sure we still need to run it."

Shecky's eyes go from gun to badge, and stay there. NYPD, Detective 7229. "This is real?"

"They were in his nightstand," she says. "The lock was pretty good, but the hinges popped right off."

And so ends the non-mystery of the blue Impala and the green Mustang: the watcher is *police*—the obvious answer was the right one. Now before him is the actual mystery: What the fuck are they going to do about it?

"We have to get rid of those," he says, indicating the gun and the badge.

"Do you want me to put them back?"

A pause. The offer, like Kerasha herself, is wild. Audacious.

But also tempting.

The watchers don't have to know *they're* being watched. They can be misdirected. But if this means putting Kerasha back in danger—

"He doesn't even have to know," she says.

He catches the glint in her eye, and all at once he gets it, why she brought the badge and the gun here. *She's having fun.* Of course she is, she was born to this—the silence, the darkness, the score. Even the danger, he supposes, her power to slip through it. But to steal a badge and gun from a cop, to hit him in his own house, and then *to go back*—how could he allow it? But how could he say no when it's so obviously the right move, when it would allow them to stay a step ahead, for once? For a moment he shares in her thrill at what she's done, at what she's proposing to do again.

But then in her eyes he sees the little girl as she was when he visited Paulette's apartment. Just one visit, maybe fifteen years ago, but he still remembers the stank of those rooms. Remembers, with shame, how he'd turned away from his cousin—wretched, practically decomposing. Shecky was disgusted, but he was also powerless, with no custody rights—and he'd run from her scabs and scratching.

And left the girl behind.

Not this time, Shecky thinks. Today I'm the uncle I should have been from the start. And I'm not sending her back to a cop house.

Shecky picks up the badge: 7229, NYPD Detective. "Fuck him," Shecky says. "We give it back and he'll go on with his meddling. We lose it, and they'll put him in the rubber room." He sets the badge back on the table and pushes it next to the gun. "Out of the house, off a cliff. Both of them."

"Gowanus Canal," Kerasha says after another forkful of fish. "Won't be the first time something's disappeared there."

chapter 14

Hours earlier, Emil Scott is on the run. Breathless. He leans against a brick wall, gasping as he counts his options. One, hail a stranger. Maybe this dog lady across the street will do. Rat terrier on one leash, Great Dane on the other, a study in contrasts. Everyone an artist in Brooklyn, even in dog selection. Excuse me, ma'am, he'd say. I'm carrying what I'm pretty sure is drug money, and someone—a man, I think—is chasing me. Do you mind if I use your phone to call . . . What's that? My phone? Funny story . . .

But it's not funny at all, and it's not even a story. His phones—both burner and personal—have vanished.

He at first chalks this up to absentmindedness, a fault he has made no apology for since he sold his first painting. But a shadow has followed him from one end of Bushwick to the other—despite the three fallback hideouts, chosen, Henry said, expressly for him—and as he leans against this brick wall, his heart racing, he cannot turn away from the fact that his phones were plucked from his pockets. He's being hunted, that's certain now. The only question is whether he's already caught.

A parked truck, two men in the bed unloading lumber. Filthy clothes, bright orange hard hats—possible details for an oil painting.

An *oil painting*? Fucking plant your feet, Emil. (He's hearing Henry in his head.) You're holding a bag and you've got a tail. What do you do?

The answer takes a moment, but it comes.

I look for options.

This is no small miracle. In his hour of need, the training is coming back to him.

Okay, options. How about this road crew? May I use your phone? he'll ask. May I borrow your truck, may I wear your clothes? Can you please hold this garbage bag for me—can we swap lives, just for today?

Okay, so you get a phone, he says to himself. Talking himself down, turning the panic into an actionable plan. Who do you call?

A moment passes.

His talk-down has backfired.

Who *would* he call? Not his mother in Woodstock. Not his dead stepdad, obviously. Not Imani, and definitely not Henry—Emil would have to talk circles around his aborted stopover. He'd also have to remember the number. And he can't call the people he was supposed to meet at the stopover—another forgotten number—and you're not calling 911 when you're holding the devil's bag.

Here he is, Emil Scott—the "hipster prince of Bushwick," as Imani sometimes calls him. Never without an opening to attend, always some Facebook friend waving him over, everywhere a girl or boy waiting out Imani. Here he is, the man who always has *someone*—alone.

No, not quite alone. His hunter will be his final companion.

His creative genius is usually playful, but at this moment every vision is a horror. A long coat, a blade visible just beneath it. A child transfixed by a red ball, a dark shadow approaching. A couple sleeps peacefully, while, through the doorframe, tendrils of black smoke . . .

In a dusty bodega he catches his breath. Visible out the windows are the towers of the Moses Houses. The AC in this bodega, mounted just above the front door, rattles while blowing in warm air, yet Emil is chilled and shaking. They must think him a trust-funded addict, he considers, another bohemian visiting the Moses Houses for a hit. And why not. The way he's feeling now, he'd try anything.

He walks along an aisle of detergents. Industrial-strength cleaning sprays fill the top shelves. Then scouring powders, then drain de-cloggers. The colors on these bottles would have lit him up this morning. Now they make him dizzy.

Toss the bag here, he thinks. Just stuff it behind the Windex.

But then he'd answer to Henry, to that uncle he answers to. This isn't his money to lose. Emil hurries out of the bodega, afraid of his own impulses. Emil, who's always trusted himself, now doubting; always one with himself, now divided.

Across the street are teenagers: cigarettes, red bandannas, bare arms. Restless. The mostly white hipster set from Emil's corner of Bushwick—men with mustaches, women with sleeve tattoos—they'd probably avoid these kids. Cross a street to get away from them. For Emil, they are a godsend. Safety in numbers, safety among witnesses—seeing them Emil remembers both the general tactics Henry taught him, and the specific reference to a room in the Moses Houses that could serve as an emergency hiding spot. And so Emil goes to the kids, asks for weed. They blaze together, no one asking for money. No one even looking at the garbage bag packed with cash, which, per training, he's got slung over his shoulder. ("Forget it," Henry said, "don't fucking look at it. People follow eyes.") The bag is still over Emil's shoulder when the kids get bored with him, forget him, and one of them says something about seeing a girl. The bag is still over Emil's shoulder when he follows them into the tower.

Just inside is a busted fire alarm. The kids slap it as they pass, maybe for luck. Emil slaps it, too, after the kids have disappeared around the corner. Why not? And who knows, maybe the luck's already here. He's inside a large complex where it will be easy to get lost. He knows about a hiding spot. For the first time since that odd train transfer at Myrtle Avenue, his whole body relaxes.

Heartened, Emil walks the halls, thinks about Imani, and does not immediately hear the approach of the man who has been following him.

chapter 15

Another scream.

They're killing her. Henry races out of the stairwell, down the hall. Fight time is now, his body knows what to do.

Medic, coroner, avenger—whatever you need, Lipz, I'm here.

Corridor of doors, only one half-open. Only one that's screaming. He barrels toward it, previewing the horror show in his head. Lipz on the floor, Tiger and his boys over her, beating her flat with bats. Or they have knives, they're carving her up. Or it's a chain, a wire—it doesn't matter, he'll go at them, just him and his hands. Whatever she's getting, he wants for himself: she made the mess, but they're in it together.

And so he's unprepared to see Tiger on the floor, Lipz above. Tiger a human X, his limbs tied open with coaxial cables. Lipz's hands wet, her shirt crimson, a glob of something fatty hanging near her mouth. She's hacking at Tiger's head with *keys*, Henry sees, sawing off his beloved hair—his buzz lines, his dye dots—cutting into the scalp. Tiger screams like an animal, and Henry's eyes keep going to the coaxial cables. Tiger's wrists and ankles are tied to a radiator, a bedpost—what Lipz has accomplished is admirable, in a way, but she's a little too psychotic to take advantage of the situation.

"Where's my stash, bitch?" Key cut, scream. "I need my shit!"

Henry grabs her hands. "Let him answer."

Minutes later, Tiger is left whimpering, and Henry and Lipz descend the unlit stairwell. "This country's so fucked," she says. Her stash is long gone, but she has the four hundred dollars Tiger made from it. She also has Tiger's prized wallet, the leather marked as if by claws. "I sell for ten, and everyone says ten is the ask. But now I fucking find out that fucking Tiger gets fucking fifteen? Fucking fifteen to my ten? Fucking disrespect, that's what it is." They step over a wino, and three steps later Lipz's outrage has become *in*-rage. "Fuck me. No name in the motherfucking *street*. I ask for twenty, but then they look at me like I'm nothing. Then I *feel* like I'm nothing. And I cave." They come to a flickering floor light. Henry can see her now, slouch-walking with her eyes on her feet. Her tatted arms crossed over her chest.

"Hey." Henry catches her by the elbow. "Hey. Look at me. You just tossed Tiger on his ass. You got things right with your business." He lowers his voice. "I'm proud of you." Then with a shiver he hurries away, uncomfortable with the moment he's created.

Lipz catches up. "Thanks." She touches his hand and—

He steps on a bottle. Tripping, he bumbles against Lipz and then catches them both against the handrail. They're body-to-body, in the near dark, and he's pressed against her side. He begins to pull back just as she says, "I'll never forgive you."

He doesn't move. Can hear her breathing. "If we do or if we don't?"

He can't see her smile, but he can hear it: "Either way."

A door opens somewhere, and they pull back. Footsteps approach, fade. A haunted feeling. Neither moves back in again.

"Did you hear about the little kid they found?" she asks. "He was stuck in the D Tower stairwell. Couldn't reach the doorknobs, couldn't get out, and no one heard shit, and when they found him . . ."

Or they heard and didn't give a fuck, Henry thinks. For every down-and-outer doing something stupid, there are a hundred middle-income don't-give-a-fuckers, looking away from what's right in front of them.

Henry tells the story of the drooling man they caught in the A Tower's basement. He'd been living down there for years, and whisper was that his family had just offloaded him one day. Threw him down the stairs, slammed the door, and moved the fuck out of town.

"But imagine that little kid," Lipz says. "What if they didn't find him? He'd just walk around crying. And then he'd dry up. And then he'd drop and just lie there till someone gets around to changing these fucking lights."

They arrive at the ground floor. She has led them by touch. Good old Lipz, bashing boyfriends, swimming in vodka. Guiding him through the dark, and then getting him out. The hall lights blind them, and in the hot white Henry thinks about Emil. *He* could have dried up and dropped, *he* could be in some stairwell. Could be in *this* stairwell, even, and we'd never know it. The towers of the Moses Houses are vertical labyrinths: easy to get lost in, a good place to disappear.

A memory stirs. *A good place to disappear* . . . He's heard this before.

No, idiot, you said it. To Emil.

Henry stops. He stands before the door to the Moses Houses Tower B HVAC room. He is afraid to move.

Last month Henry and Emil were in the Moses Houses, stepping out from a rent party. Henry handed his one-hitter to Emil, and as he blazed, Henry noticed the HVAC room.

"This could be a decent fallback," Henry said.

"How's that?"

"Easy to get to, hidden in plain sight."

Henry is always on the lookout for fallbacks—every runner needs their own. On that night Henry made a mental note to come back sober and inspect this site. Look at the lock, he told himself. Don't forget. But then the one-hitter was back in his hands and . . .

He forgot.

And now Emil is missing, and Henry stands before the HVAC door. Wonders if it's possible that Emil's assignment went to shit. That maybe he tried each of his assigned fallbacks and burned every one of them. He must've been desperate, lugging that stash, nowhere to put it. And he lost his phone, or maybe it got ganked. And panic took over, but then—Emil saw the Moses towers. Remembered *this* room, remembered what Henry said about it and hurried over. Found his way inside.

I told him he'd be safe here. He listened. He always did.

The lock is already broken. Henry opens the door.

A blast of cold air. A thing on the floor, a twisted figure, red-white mush where the back of the head should be.

It's a mannequin, Henry thinks. He backs out of the room, his entire body shaking.

Lipz is asking him something.

"But it's not *him*," he says, as if Lipz were arguing with him. "It's not him, it's not." At last he turns and looks her in the eye, a choke on every word: "That thing is not my friend."

part four

the well-placed friend

chapter 16

"Officer Montenegro?"

Zera turns to find a small, muscular man in a Nets hat and a fitted polo shirt. His badge on a neck chain. Lighting everything up with a beautiful smile. He extends a hand. "Detective Fung. Kurt."

She crosses her arms. "Why am I here?"

Kurt lowers his hand, his smile not breaking, just changing its shape. So it's going to be like *that*.

It's two months before the murder, and the officers are in Maria Hernandez Park. It's dusk, and they are in relative seclusion: a patch of trees, the back wall of a public bathroom. A dumpster.

"I got the money memo last week," Kurt says. "Your phone must be ringing off the hook."

She looks over his shoulder at the picnic benches behind him. She sees a figure seated alone, and a second figure standing behind the first. This second figure stands like a cop, and she can almost make out a badge and chain. Zera focuses on the seated figure. She can't tell, from this distance, from her angle, whether he's handcuffed.

"Why am I here?" she says again.

"Because of your memo," Kurt says playfully. "This guy checked all the boxes." Zera and Kurt begin a slow walk toward the picnic benches, Kurt lowering his voice: "Red-code neighborhood, check.

Subject with a bag, check. Subject's movements and demeanor consistent with countersurveillance, check." A pause. "Not very good at it, obviously."

Closer now, Zera can make out a bag not far from the man's feet. She still can't see, from her angle, because of how he's slumped, whether he's sitting on his hands, or whether they're locked behind him.

"The suspect's not in custody," she says. This is somewhere between a question and an accusation. Her money memo, as the detective called it, has been widely distributed but imperfectly read. More than once she's had to arrange for a suspect's release. What this means: a pound of paperwork. What this also means: lost time. This more than infuriates her. It feeds a fear that has her up and working—reviewing bank records, compiling telecommunications data, creating link charts—through many nights. And all for nothing, so far. Her prime targets—Elijah Arep, Shecky Keenan, and Moshe Lefkowitz, names culled from field intelligence reports—have no reason to lose sleep. Her fruitless initiative is a pilot project running on empty. The grant is limited, the funds already low, and she knows the precise date she will have to file her closing memo. Knows, even, the opening words for this memo: *Regretfully, at this time we are not able to provide evidence sufficient to justify, for any of our key targets, the continuance of* . . .

"He's not in custody," Kurt says. "I don't know if *he* understands that, but officially, we're just having a chat. *Beautiful night, how are you, what's in your bag* . . . Friendly."

She stops while still some distance from the picnic table. Examines the suspect. White male. Mid- to late twenties. Button-down short-sleeved shirt, checkered, cargo pants. On the ground: messenger bag, or maybe a softshell briefcase.

"Get in there," Kurt tells her, nodding toward the bag. "Open that bad boy. It'll get you all tingly."

"You don't have a search warrant," Zera says. Another question/accusation, but she can already feel Kurt's big smile.

"I said *pretty please*." A laugh of self-love. "Sometimes that's all it takes."

Back to the suspect. He's watching *her* now, taking out a pocket notebook, a pencil. Then he's writing something, pausing to look up at Zera, his hands moving in a peculiar way—across the page, up and down, rather than left to right.

Not writing, Zera realizes. Drawing. Me.

She goes to him, takes in his long nose, his nervous eyes. His sensuous mouth.

"I'm going to look in your bag," she says, pulling on rubber gloves. "I have your consent, yes?"

A tremor in his voice: "It's not my bag."

Rookie, she thinks. Could be his first job.

Having carried the bag a few yards back from the bench, she takes a mini flashlight off her service belt. Shines it into the bag—leather—and illuminates a fist-size roll of cash held together by rubber bands. She removes the bands and flips through the bills, mostly twenties. Just shy of a thousand.

Okay, so not his first job, but definitely still a rookie.

A change in the air, cinnamon, and Kurt, popping gum, is close. "So . . ." His confidence is against her like a dance-floor erection. "So how'd you get to be the queen of money laundering?"

She puts her back to the detective before recounting the bills. She rolls and bands them. *Shit.* She returns the money roll to the bag. *Shit-shit.* Zera works with her guard up, but somehow the detective's question got through.

How.

The memories are never far from the surface.

A man at the Paradise House unbuckling his belt. In Russian: "You're going to like how this hurts."

The round-bodied alcoholic in a blue uniform: "Why do you want to join NYPD?"

Years later, a windowless interview room. A haggard girl named Sveta Lvov, all makeup and bruises. "They said if I talk to you," the girl told Zera in Polish, "they'll go to my village, they'll take my sister . . ." Zera caught the girl by the wrist. At first the girl was scared, but then she saw Zera's hand, the shape of it. The two shared a look, and the girl extended her arm so Zera could read the tattoo. PROPERTY OF THE PARADISE CLUB. Zera released the girl, withdrew as if from a hot touch. Not the same, Zera told herself. Crossing her arms, tucking in her hands. *Club*, not *House*. America, not Montenegro. Sveta, not Katja. Different girls, different men. And this girl isn't Katja—she's not *me*—but . . .

Another memory, a training room. Uniformed and plainclothes police officers in student seats, the woman at the whiteboard wearing a different kind of badge. A lieutenant, the first woman of this rank Zera had ever seen.

"This is not your grandfather's police initiative," the lieutenant said. "This is a unique partnership between the Financial Crimes Unit and the department's Human Trafficking Task Force. Everyone in this room is a volunteer. So now you get to learn what you signed up for." Muted laughter around the room, but not a peep from Zera. A mask of skepticism and, beneath it, a flickering hope.

"The men who buy girls," the woman said, "make for terrible witnesses. You've seen it, you know the reasons. The johns are ashamed, they'd rather eat a misdemeanor than take the stand. And the girls—think about why they're doing what they do. Trauma, intimidation. Addiction. Immigration issues. Threats to family members—sound familiar?"

The crowd: nods, knowing grins.

Zera: leaning in now. Her mouth open, as if she would drink in the words.

"The old approach has a long history of failure," the lieutenant said. "We're here for something else."

Two months later—the winter before the murder—and it was Zera at a whiteboard. Talking to a different room full of uniformed police officers. "We're here for something else," she said, doing her best to deliver the lieutenant's speech. "We're going after the moneymen."

Zera is not a natural public speaker. Odd pronunciations, awkward pauses. Some unnatural cadences, her discomfort obvious, but she forced herself through it. This matters, she reminded herself. This is what she signed up for.

"Moneymen are essential to the trafficking business," she told the officers. "Every trafficker above a street pimp has one." She went to an officer sleeping in his chair. Fat. Open-mouthed. For a moment she just stood before him, then she kicked a leg of his desk, jerking him awake. Some low laughs but she cut them off: "Some of these moneymen are tax preparers," she continued, beginning a slow walk around the room. "Some are paralegals, some are real lawyers and accountants." She went to two whispering officers and stood directly before them. Resumed after their silence filled the room.

"The moneymen are the bridge between the streets and the banks." She continued her walk. "Many of them have no criminal record. Many have houses, many have families. And what does this mean?" Her walk brought her back to the whiteboard, where she pivoted and faced the room again. "They have something to lose. A reason they'll want to help us, if we can get something on them." Another pivot, back to the whiteboard. She uncapped a dry-erase marker and started writing. Three names: Elijah Arep, Shecky Keenan, Moshe Lefkowitz.

"You may be thinking," she said over her shoulder, aware that at least a third of her audience was lost in their phones, "that prostitution is a victimless crime. The girl gets the money, the guy has his fun, so what's the problem." She kept her back to her audience. Lowered her voice, almost as though speaking to herself. "I'm going to tell you the problem." She drew in her breath, thought of Katja, and now Sveta, and then turned to face the group. "There is no consensual sex between master and slave." All eyes were on her now, and her low voice had power. "Every instance—every sale—is an act of rape."

A moment later she was writing again, the audience uncomfortable, Zera all business. "Indicia of money laundering. One. Multiple money orders, each less than three thousand dollars. Two. Multiple cash deposits, each less than ten thousand dollars. Three . . ."

And now she's at Maria Hernandez Park. Zera has the bag with the cash roll, and Detective Kurt Fung, with his bright, cinnamon-fresh smile, has his question.

She turns away from him. Walks with the bag to the picnic bench, where the young man hurriedly closes his sketchbook. She looks him over. His body, a rounding belly on a slender build. His sideways glances, lazy head tilt, his loose-shouldered slouch. And the fear he breathes out, so obvious, even in this semidarkness.

A child, she thinks.

I can use him.

chapter 17

A noiseless patient spider. Uncle Walt whispers to her night and day. *Launch'd forth filament, filament, filament, out of itself.* If poetry is music, then this is her theme song. *Ever unreeling them, ever tirelessly speeding them.* On the night of the murder, Kerasha wonders if anyone else in the underworld feels poetry the way she does. If anyone else hears lines in their heads, and feels that a lost and frightened part of themselves has been thrust into the light. Made beautiful with words. Made strong.

The spider spins its web, one thread at a time, connecting this to that, never stopping, never doubting. On real jobs, when she is on the high wire, this is Kerasha.

And now she sits atop a three-story apartment complex, looking down at the entrance of the office building across the street. Waiting. A spider with fangs, Kerasha never feels more alive than the moment she sights her prey.

The door at the main entrance of the office building opens. A redhead exits and holds the door. A small man with a ponytail steps out. He says something to the redhead. She throws her head back and shows her teeth. Motherfucker, Kerasha thinks, is he *flirting*? It's painful to imagine Dr. Xu even contemplating romance. And this laughing redhead, is she charmed? If so, she must be a patient. Must be *in crisis*, and have left reality far behind, to be enjoying this company.

The redhead turns left, Dr. Xu walks in the opposite direction. The woman walks only half a block. At a bus stop, waiting, she takes something out of her purse and stares at it. A phone, an e-reader—for a crazy person, she's holding up remarkably well. She's *passing*, the way one of Kerasha's father's great-aunts supposedly did, a light-skinned black woman who one day just disappeared into the white world. Or maybe, and Kerasha is loath to admit this possibility, the redhead isn't a lunatic after all. She's a working, functional anybody, and Dr. Xu just *interacted* with her, no court order required. He can be a person when he chooses to. Why not with me? The spider is out of patience. She will have her revenge.

A few buildings down from his office, Dr. Xu stops at a fence. Unchains a bike. Bad news for the spider. In Brooklyn, bikes are almost unhuntable.

The spider is a blur down the fire escape: hang, drop. Hang, drop. She lands in a blacktop lot and rounds the building, emerging through an alleyway. Across the street Dr. Xu straddles his bike. Snaps on a helmet.

That's right, Dr. Xu, take care of that priceless brain.

First the helmet, now the pant leg—he's rolling it up. This buys her a few more seconds. She goes to the Nissan sedan she spotted when she scoped out the site earlier today. The model is maybe ten years old: she knows the type, has the right tool for the lock. Another for the alarm. Dr. Xu is just blocks away when she catches up with him. He is—and this amazes her—waiting at a red light. You're on a *bike*, she thinks. Are you *trying* to be hunted? What a good citizen you are, Dr. Xu, what an example for your patients.

She lets a Toyota SUV pull out of a driveway so that there will be an extra car between them. She still feels too close. She can see his ankle. It means nothing, she knows, bikers do it everywhere: protecting the pant leg from the chain, the gears; protecting the chain and gears from the pants. But at this moment it seems lurid. She feels uncomfortable, seeing his ankle like this. And then a voice in her head, soft, infuriating—a voice that sounds remarkably like Dr. Xu's—asks her why.

This is the danger of hunting a psychiatrist, she supposes: he hunts you right back. She's followed gunmen and looked out for guns. Followed street girls and looked out for street daddies, followed armored cars and looked out for armored men. With a psychiatrist, she's realizing, the one you look out for is yourself.

A half mile, three-quarters, a mile, another tenth. Dr. Xu dismounts just outside a bike shop. Kerasha ditches the car, leaves it behind a parked city bus with blinking hazards, then doubles back to catch up with her prey. The bike shop has big windows, an open front door. A black guy with a skully, a white guy with a faux-hawk, an Asian girl between them, all of them laughing—a poster-perfect image. New Bushwick. Come Gentrify.

No Dr. Xu.

Did she keep up with his bike only to lose him on foot? You're slipping, Kerasha. Skinny Kerry, the more nimble spider, would never have let this happen.

But then she sees a ponytail. Two doors down from the bike shop is the Bushwick Food Co-op. The ponytail goes inside. She waits a minute before following.

One whiff of the produce and she is transported.

Goats. The food here smells like goats.

She is nine years old. Mama is kissing sobriety this month, which means Kerasha is back in school. They loaded them up on the bus this morning and drove them to the Prospect Park Zoo. The visit starts with sea lions, middles with dingoes and a red panda, and ends with goats. Ugly animals, Kerasha thinks. The only creatures in the world that smell as bad as Mama does when she's sweating off the heroin, her body cooking itself from the inside.

And this is what Kerasha smells—Mama trying to get clean, the goats just being goats—as she passes bunched kale, stinging nettles in baggies, mushrooms heaped almost to her chest.

Eyes on the prize, little Kerasha tells her. Focus on your target: Where is Dr. Xu?

The absurdity is not lost on her that she, Bushwick's peerless nightcrawler, has lost her psychiatrist in a grocery store. *Want*, think about *want*—those psychology books from Franklin often whisper to her, and today she grudgingly agrees with them. I want to lose him, she thinks. I'm afraid of what I'll learn. But unlike what happened in Dr. Xu's office, unmasking the fear here does not allow her to move through it. She is still circling aisles of cereal boxes. Compost bags, jars of organic marinara sauce . . . still no Dr. Xu.

Within, a rising sense of déjà vu, and mixed with it a swelling dread. Something like a voice asks her why this all feels so familiar.

Shut up. And this is the worst thing Dr. Xu has done to her: she's in treatment even when she's not.

You've lost someone, the voice says. You lost someone who didn't even realize you were following them. Who does this remind you of?

Stop it. Shut the fuck—

Is this a reenactment, a looping of some early childhood experience—

"Fuck you," she says aloud. "Fuck your fucking mother."

And there it is, the word is out. Sorry, Mama. I tried to leave you out of it. "Sorry," she says aloud.

"It's okay." This from a fellow shopper, a thin woman with sharp elbows. "We all have days like that." She puts a bony hand on Kerasha's arm, gives it a squeeze, and moves on.

Unsettled, itchy, Kerasha takes a moment. It's been more than five years since the warden at Franklin had Kerasha brought into his office. "I'm afraid your mother's passed," he said. It was days after Kerasha's arrival in the cage. *Passed*, Kerasha thinks. In most senses Mama had passed long ago, but at the same time, part of her never passed at all. Still with me, Kerasha thinks. Or still just ahead.

Like on the morning of Kerasha's arrest. "I'm going to be good this time," Mama said. "Still climbing. Up and up, you'll see." Then she kissed Kerry goodbye, went off for a "job interview"—and stopped at the first corner.

And just like that, Dr. Xu materializes. He's no longer wearing the khakis she last saw him in, not the crisp collared shirt, baby blue with chipped black buttons. No, somewhere behind the mushroom heap, maybe, he changed into heavy brown overalls and a coarse flannel shirt. Pulled on work gloves, thick and stained. He hauls a sloshing bucket on wheels, pushing it with the handle of a mop. And so Kerasha discovers that this odious man, whose blood and breath she had always assumed was just money and condescension, has his own kind of nightwork. She turns away. Can't bear to see him like this, can't stand that he has needs she doesn't know of. His own private mystery.

Outside the food co-op she kicks his bike. Pops two pieces of gum in her mouth and makes a promise to herself—*selves*, really. To little Kerry she swears never again to waste her craft on the ponytail. To big Kerasha she takes a blood oath to stop mind-fucking herself. No more stalking her psychiatrist, no more imagining his analysis, or assuming his postures, or spending a second in his company beyond what's ordered by the court.

A few blocks from the co-op she spits out her gum, ducks into a bodega, and buys a fresh pack. Peanut butter chocolate cups. An orange cream soda. Bag of chips. Skinny Kerasha lived on this stuff, and big Kerasha takes them more as a kind of sacrament. She repeats her oath: never again.

And then she does it again, following Dr. Xu from his office to the gym the very next day. She notes his squash-racket bag, his green water bottle, his rolled yoga mat. Never again, she tells herself. A week passes. She sticks to her promise.

But then it's murder night, and she gets the call on her drop phone from Henry.

"He's dead," he says.

Her heart freezes in her chest. "Uncle Shecky?"

"What? No, Emil." She hears him cry. "My friend."

She catches her breath. Makes sure to hide her relief when she says, "Henry, I'm so sorry." She hears low choking sounds. She gives him a moment, and takes one for herself, too. That stab of fear—the thought of something happening to Uncle Shecky—shows her how vulnerable she's become.

He says, "I need you to do something for me."

"Anything."

"Where are you?"

Funny story . . . "Around."

"Okay, I just texted you Emil's address. The cops may be going there, too, so be careful when you go in."

Be *careful*? A crooked smile. Sweet child, don't you know you're talking to the spider? "What am I looking for?"

"Grab anything connected to us," Henry says. "Like his phone, all our messaging is there. And fuck, there may be pictures of me." His voice breaks again, recovers. "And get our fucking bag, if you can find it."

"Wait, you gave him the heavy?"

Henry doesn't respond until a loud plane passes over Kerasha's head. Surprise in his voice: "Where are you?"

"What? Bad connection." She holds the phone away from her mouth. "See you back at the house." She ends the call and reads the text with Emil's address. Then she tosses the phone, per protocol, and a few seconds pass before it breaks against the street far below.

So where *is* she?

Nowhere special. Just a rooftop, you know. And ten or so feet beneath her boots, a certain psychiatrist lies sleeping.

I'll be back, she thinks at him. We're not done here.

chapter 18

Henry and Lipz are on a basketball court tucked between Towers B and C of the Moses Houses. Ending his call with Kerasha, he turns off his phone and rips it apart. His tears are drying already—he'll let out more later, but it's go time now, and his training tells him what to do.

"Give me your phone," he tells Lipz.

"Fuck no."

"I'm keeping you out of this."

"A little late for that," she says. "I saw the body. Also, you just fixed my phone. I'm not going to let you break it."

Her eyes dare him to try. He wants to, he could use the distraction. Instead he collects himself. "We were texting about where to meet."

"They're going to arrest us for texting?"

"Our texts put us near a murder. I don't want that for you, you don't want that for me."

She begins to say something, stops herself. Starts over: "For you, then." She gives him her phone.

The battery he just tosses, but the SIM card and motherboard he stomps into the asphalt. It's past midnight, which, on this basketball court, usually means music. Booze, takeout, some actual basketball.

Tonight, though, for whatever reason, it's just Henry, Lipz, and a few chest-high kids with some dice.

"We're splitting," Henry says. He gives her two hundred dollars from what's left of the make-nice money. "Don't go home. Throw some of this around."

"Henry, I don't need—"

"Be seen," he says. "Not with me."

He walks off, and his body takes over.

There's a newspaper stand on Jefferson Street. It hasn't dispensed newspapers for years, but inside, below the bottles and chip bags and cassette tapes and sullied crayon notes, beneath the false bottom, is a just-in-case bag. He empties it. A New Jersey driver's license with Henry's picture and an Americanized name of his favorite Dutch master. A thousand dollars on a Green Dot card, another two hundred in cash. Lighter fluid, a phone registered to no one, a change of clothes, matches, and a Cobra .380 pistol—a toy in Henry's large hands. Henry scans the street—clear—and strips down and changes right there. His old clothes, the ones he wore when he walked into that cold room and saw Emil's body—no, don't think about it, just keep moving—his black jeans, his hot pink T-shirt, even the boxers and socks, he stuffs everything into the newspaper stand. Sprays the lighter fluid inside, tosses in a match.

A small fire behind him, Henry heads out to restart his night. Be seen.

At the Thirsty Bear, the bartender he had that long weekend with welcomes him back and pours his usual. Henry stares at Emil's unfinished mural, that face wreathed in tentacles.

"Here, I want to show you something," the bartender says to Henry, doing something with her phone. Showing him some stupid meme. Henry looks away, uncomfortable. He remembers a night back in the spring, when he and Emil closed out the bar together. They switched from whiskey to beer (never fear!) and back again, and Emil introduced Henry to the work of Kara Walker. Henry had never heard of her, so Emil took out his phone, showed images of her work, and—

Emil's phone.

Kerasha is looking for it, but what if the police get it first? If they unlock it, if they look through it, what will they find? Cached images of Kara Walker, maybe, but also those two-headed selfies with Henry. And Henry's in the contacts list, the call log, the text threads—

The texts. The fucking texts. Henry is careful—most of the time. And when Emil went missing, Henry texted Emil's burner, per protocol, but also his personal phone. He was panicking—would've texted Emil's grandma, if he'd had the number.

His eyes return to the mural. The face seems so hideously unfinished now. The composition is childlike, the expression uncertain. And it won't *ever* be finished, he realizes. The whole mural will be painted over—fuck. Henry puts down his beer. Hands to his head. Mourning the art because he can't yet face the loss of his friend, he remembers his uncle's voice.

"I know you're smart, kid. You've got your mother's sense of street and your dad's head for numbers."

"Then why are we still doing this?" Henry was thirteen, already three years into working for his uncle, but that didn't matter. The training was never-ending.

Memory exercises: PINs, phone numbers, routing numbers, passwords, nicknames. At first it was headaches and mistakes, but over time it came to be just like putting a file in a cabinet: close it, lock it, and pull it out again when it's needed.

Getting rid of tails: Take off your hat or put one on. Ditto for your jacket, or turn it inside out. Know the stores and restaurants, which ones have back doors. Which have ground-floor bathrooms with windows you can open. Know the alleys, the fences, the bus schedules. Find a shadow and stay in it.

"Smart is no substitute for body memory," Uncle Shecky said. "When the bullets are flying, when the sirens are wailing, when there's a helicopter overhead, the hot light on you like the eye of

God—fuck knows where smart's going to be. Going gets tough, smart shits his pants. Body memory will get you in the clear. And it's this training—what we're doing now—that will get you good and programmed."

Henry never wanted to get good and programmed. Emil Scott was never good and programmed. And yet now, as Henry drinks through his second beer, his third, he admits his uncle was right. His "smart," as his uncle put it, did nothing to prevent Emil's death. Whereas his body memory—programmed under protest, but programmed just the same—has seen him through.

"Hey."

Henry turns, and here's Starr Richardson. Dressed for attention—tight black pants, low-cut white shirt tight and stark against her dark skin. She smiles at Henry, nods at the empty stool next to him. "Expecting someone?"

Henry stares at her. "You're never out like this."

"You've never looked for me." Her smile fades quickly. He wipes his eyes but it's too late. She takes his hand. "What's wrong?"

A sigh, a shake of his head. He asks if he can crash at her place.

Starr sublets a room in a crowded house. Her room: a bed, a dresser, a closet with a door that won't close. He says he'll take the floor, and she finds a clean sheet and a light blanket for him. He lies down, then she does. For a long time he listens to her listening to him. At last her breathing slows. As the night drags into morning, Henry sneezes more and more often. His eyes get itchy. Starr's cat must be here somewhere. Henry has a weirdly similar feeling about his uncle, invisible but present just the same.

Starr turns over in her sleep, makes a catlike sound as she resettles. Or maybe it's the cat. And so Henry dozes off at last, his sleep breaking on grief and open questions.

When the bedside clock shows 7:00 a.m., Henry gets up and pulls on his pants. He scribbles a note. Sketches Starr's face on the note, writes something sweet in hopes that she'll keep it. Puts the time on it, the date. Leaves it on her nightstand. *Thank you for the alibi*, he could have written. He remembers his uncle training him on this, the acceptability of a shitty alibi. "Forget 'airtight,'" Uncle Shecky said. "Legally, all you need is doubt. It just has to be reasonable." The old man's wistful smile is on Henry as he walks home, thinking back on his early lessons. Remembering the boy he'd been just yesterday.

chapter 19

Hours back, Kerasha arrives at the four-story where, per Henry's text, Emil rents half the top floor. She slips inside. Though her mind is still not quite her own, the spider rarely needs it. Her feet carry her forward. Her hands go into closets and desk drawers, and feel their way through an elm wardrobe. Her skin tells her she's not the first to search this apartment tonight.

The rooms smell of burnt coffee and overtime.

Also, on her way into the building, she heard a neighbor talking: "It's suck-ass o'clock, and these fucking cops are stomping down the stairs. And I step out into the hall to tell them what the fuck. And these guys are fat already, and now they're carrying boxes, so every footfall is like a fucking IED."

The apartment, Kerasha decides now, has been *selectively* cleaned out. If Henry's friend had a phone or a computer, if he had any paperwork at all, the police have already found it.

And yet they didn't find everything.

Once when just a little spider, as Kerry crawled down through a ground-level window into a basement apartment, she spotted something taped flat to the top of a door. A hundred-dollar bill, it turned out. Well okay, then—here's a hiding spot to look out for. She made a habit of it.

And so now in Emil's apartment, she finds two objects taped in just the same way. The first is a slip of paper. Cut like a business card, it's blank on one side, and on the other is a handwritten phone number. The second object is a driver's license. She studies the picture until she's certain. Then she pockets her two finds and heads out into the night, thinking about Henry's dead friend. Wondering how well Henry really knew him.

chapter 20

"The blues were already there," Kerasha tells Henry the next morning.

Uncle Shecky walks in with plates, asking, "Already where?"

Henry lets Kerasha's silence speak for him, too.

Plates down, Uncle Shecky sits. "Thank you for being here, thank you for being my family."

Muted sounds of eating. Henry can't touch his food. Can't stop looking at his hard-boiled egg, the color of which reminds him of Emil's skin in that HVAC room. At last he asks Kerasha, "What were the police talking about?"

"They were already gone," Kerasha says. "They'd boxed everything up."

"For the love of Jesus," Shecky says, "someone tell me what the fuck. Okay? Just what the fuck."

"But that's too fast," Henry says. He again thinks through the timing. Impossible. Even if the police found Emil the *second* Henry and Lipz left the Moses Houses, they still wouldn't have raced straight to Emil's apartment. They would have taped off the crime scene, canvased for witnesses. Stood around drinking coffee. Taken their sweet-ass time. Henry's been close to the streets a long time, he knows how this works.

And yet what he wants not to be true—what shouldn't be true—is. The police outraced Kerasha. And she didn't find Red Dog's money, and she doesn't have Emil's phone. Even that small piece of him couldn't be saved.

Henry hears an odd patter. He looks down at his plate and realizes he's crying.

"Jesus, Henry," Shecky says softly. "What's going on?"

I'm crying about some phones, he thinks.

But this is something Henry remembers from losing Mom and Dad: no one you love dies once. They die again each time you forget not to look for them. They die when their things are taken away.

A buzz, a beep—Uncle Shecky steps out of the room to take a call. When his voice is distant, Kerasha puts something on the table. "I'm sorry about your friend," she says. Henry looks up and sees she's no longer eating. She's tapping the table in front of him.

Tapping, on the table, two cards. She slides the first over. Blank.

"The cops missed this," she says. "It was taped on top of his bedroom door."

But the card, it turns out, is blank only on one side. On the other: a handwritten phone number.

And now Kerasha slides over the second card. A driver's license: Emil's face, his half-tease smirk. Only it's a Pennsylvania license, and Emil wasn't from Pennsylvania. Never lived there, as far as Henry knows, and then there's the name on the license.

The fucking name.

Henry is reminded of a lesson learned from his parents' deaths, how death moves forward and backward in time, erasing everything. Present: your special someone is gone. Future: they're never coming back. Past: you never knew them in the first place.

Hello, Charlie Gladney. So terrible to meet you.

Footsteps, Uncle Shecky coming back. Henry pockets the cards and exchanges a look with Kerasha: This is between us.

part five

the widow and her ex

chapter 21

Shecky would rather be home. Cold Guinness in hand, tenderloin in the oven, the kids at the table with him—he aches to be under his own roof. Instead he's waiting on a police report—an *incident report*, in blue-speak. He'd heard about them from Fat Boris, the family's ID printer, at an emergency meeting that day.

"I'm fucked," Shecky had said, "but how fucked?"

"Get your hands on that incident report. You'll know."

And so now Shecky wants to be home, but home is not an option.

Home, Jesus forgive him, is *dangerous*.

First the blue Impala, then the green Mustang. Next a gun on his kitchen table, and right beside it that detective's badge. Now a murder. And a quarter-million-dollar bag is in the wind, and who will be missing it? A client known to go after families first, so you can walk in on their pieces. Home should be a sanctuary, but these days he feels eyes everywhere.

Years ago Shecky did a drop in Baltimore, three million cash. A duffle bag then—many of the bills were small—but this was before you could load up Amex cards, before you could fit three million in your pocket. And the Baltimore drop was also before Henry, before Shecky had someone he could trust with a job like this. So he drove the money himself, spent as much as he had to on security, and made the drop "without incident," as he would proudly report to the client. On his way back, though, he stayed at a fleabag with actual fleas. Felt them crawling on his skin for weeks, though he never saw evidence of them outside that filthy room. And it's the same now with the police, and with Red Dog's gunmen: they're not here, and yet they're with you. Little feet, little mouths on your skin.

Right now Henry is at a sandwich shop across the street from the Eighty-Third Precinct. He's having an evening coffee with his connect Starr, trading a thousand crisps for the almighty incident report. Apparently Starr has learned the value of her position, having just taken a thousand from them yesterday. Clever girl. As for himself, well, life is all smiles for Shecky Keenan. He sits alone at the counter of a Polish greaser called Knish-Knosh. Before him is a plate with three and a half potato pierogi and two apple fritters, the one on the left halved with a fork but not yet bitten. Shecky loves food, loves eating, but tonight he can't put anything in his mouth. If his life is a ship (his supposed dad was a merchant marine, and as a child, Shecky imagined fantastical adventures for him), it's keening for the rocks.

The waitress is a slim woman with highlights and cold eyes. She refills his coffee and moves on. No how-is-everything, no hip swing—no pleasure in her work, Shecky senses. Must be around Kerasha's age. He wonders if someone's looking out for her, a father. A parole sponsor. Probably doing better with *his* charge, Shecky guesses. No detective crawling around his house.

He looks at his phone. It's been twenty-eight minutes since Henry went off to get the incident report. There are countless Henry-not-dead reasons the swap could be taking this long. Maybe Starr got stuck at her desk. Maybe Henry ducked into a bathroom stall to cry it out. Could be crouched in there, eyes closed, his big hands together—a prayer, a double fist. Shecky's seen this. Walked in on Henry one time. This was before Kerasha, but Henry was grown, and he forgot to lock the bathroom door. And Shecky came in—he had a soft step, Henry didn't even look up—and there Henry was, his long arms and legs pulled into a tight crouch. Eyes closed. A whisper: "I'm trying, Mom. But I just can't . . . I'm not good." And Shecky soft-stepped right back out, knowing too well how the dead can be great comforters. Patient listeners. They know the power of the first loss, how it's all just ripped out of you. How all later deaths will take you back.

Like me with Dannie, he thinks. *Of course* Henry will need to check in with his parents.

So Shecky understands that twenty-eight minutes—twenty-nine now—might mean nothing. Maybe the kid has to break apart before he can put himself back together. Think about Lear, a role Shecky never dared: that old bastard had to bring down the lightning before he went clear. Let the kid mourn a little, for the love of Jesus.

But Shecky never feels comfortable about Henry when he can't lay eyes on him.

He picks at a pierogi, pokes open the skin and scoops out a speck of potato. His other hand dances over his coffee mug. He is lost in his head when a tall young man strides into the restaurant, his gaze sweeping the room.

It's Henry, but there's a moment of estrangement. To Shecky this man is a surreality, a creepy stage effect. A temporary apparition, the real Henry—

Changed. Gone, Shecky knows. A new death opens up grief everywhere. Can make you mourn the living. Miss you most of all, my little Hen.

Henry's footsteps are heavy across the hardwood floor. "I got new phones out to everyone this morning. Let's go to the window."

The night he moved in, Henry cried out so often that Shecky came into his room, comforter under one arm, pillow under the other— came in and bedded down on the floor. And when he awoke, there was a little ten-year-old sleeping beside him. A beautiful thing. They were floormates for over a month, and thank Jesus Henry came into his strength. But Shecky misses those weeks when, for this small someone, he was the only person left in the world.

Still seated, Shecky whispers, "Did you get the report?"

Henry's whisper: "They think it was a mugging."

Not a whisper: "That's great!"

"Ears," Henry says, indicating people seated nearby. They go to a window table, and the waitress brings over Shecky's dinner.

"You move, you should tell me," she says to Shecky.

And your tip will be *nothing*, he thinks. But this is a joke, of course: Shecky knows a server's life, always tips well. Especially when his mood is bright. "A mugging!" he whispers. "This is amazing news."

"My friend is dead. This is the murder report." Henry drops a rolled-up stack of papers on the table. "The fuck is this amazing?"

"No, no, no. Of course. I didn't mean—I'm sorry." He is, and he waits for Henry's nod. "You're right, nothing is *amazing* here. But deliberate murder means an investigation, and with a mugging, everyone gives up."

"Not everyone." Henry flattens the papers, flips them over, and points to a yellow sticker on the back of the last page. "You seen this before?"

Shecky picks up the report. Printed on the yellow sticker: *I-Card*. Scrawled underneath that: *Det. Fung 7229*.

The report drops to the table. "Jesus fuck," Shecky says, wiping his hands on his pants. Scooching his chair back. "The fuck is I-Card?"

"I said the same thing to Starr." Henry is almost smiling, but there's no joy in it. "It means someone—a case officer—had an eye on him."

"So there was a case *before* he got himself killed?" Shecky says. "The fuck was that? I told you you're too trusting."

For fuck's sake, when will it stop? It's like the last act of an Aeschylus play—*and the kids are dead too, and—you ate them!* Only this is his family. And again Shecky is itemizing the evils—can't stop himself, his own training always to recount, to double-check, his lists. The gun on his kitchen table, the badge. The Impala, the Mustang. The frozen account, the closed account, the internal inquiry. And now the yellow sticker.

Your friend, he wants to spit at Henry. Your fucking friend. Whatever that kid meant to you, here's what he was to the cops: a giant flashing billboard—look here! look here!—pointing right at our family.

"Emil didn't *get himself killed*," Henry says at last. "This is on us. On me."

Shecky is considering his response when—chair scrape—Henry's on his feet. He's taken back the incident report, he's refolding it—he's hurrying out the door.

"Henry, where . . . ?"

A moment later, Sheckys sees him out the window. Not running from *him*, thank Jesus, but walking off after a girl.

chapter 22

"Okay, artist." Detective Kurt Fung hands the tracking phone to Emil. "Remind me how this works."

Downtown Brooklyn, a narrow alley off Bond Street, a scarred white van blocking the entrance. Outside: graffiti, cracked sidewalks, police officers dressed like vagrants. Within: Zera, Kurt, and Emil Scott—still alive, for a few more hours.

"I do my pickup," he says. "I give you the bag." His tone is very yeah-yeah-yeah, but Zera can see he's nervous.

"You give us five minutes to do our inventory," Kurt says, "we give your bag back to you."

"Not my bag," Emil says, hands up: oh, innocent me.

"Okay, jackass. We give *the* bag back to you."

"I go back to the train and finish my job. And you give me a hundred dollars."

"But you'll do it right this time." Kurt is shorter, but he's broad with muscle, and his hand lands heavy on Emil's shoulder. "Won't you."

Emil's smile is unsteady. "I always do my best."

"Of course. Always." Kurt pretends to think a moment. "Except last Tuesday. What was the problem then? Oh right, you accidentally-on-purpose turned off your phone. And the Monday before. Whoops, forgot to take pictures of the money. And then you somehow deleted the texts from your buddy." Kurt leans in. Rubs Emil's shoulder. "It's okay. I know how you're feeling. 'Hey, he's my buddy, he made me some money, I don't want him to get in trouble.' But here's the thing." Kurt leans in closer. "It's way too late for that. You're in deep with us. Everything is documented." A let's-be-friends-again smile. "And fuck *him*, man. He's the one who got you into this mess."

Emil shakes free of the detective's hand. He stuffs the tracking phone into his back pocket, his whole body a bend and a strain. Quietly: "He's my friend."

Zera's eyes are on the tracking phone in the back pocket. "That's not the right place for that."

Emil gives her a nod, which is also a playful smile. "You've got a different face," he says. "Anyone tell you that?" He waits for her to react. She doesn't. "Angles, shadows," he continues. "Everything just a little . . . haunted. You know?" His smile moves away from playful now. He wants something, she thinks, my attention, my approval—my submission. Zera has had many men look at her like this. She's unimpressed. "And your eyes are lonely." With this, he walks off to leave the alley, squeezing around the parked van.

"Watch your ass," Kurt calls.

"That's your job." Emil pats his back pocket and then he's gone.

Kurt, under his breath: "Fucking hipster."

Zera takes out the master tracking phone. The map on her screen shows a moving red dot. Emil is turning left on Schermerhorn Street, heading to the subway station. If the official MTA schedule means anything, and sometimes it does, Emil will catch the 10:47 a.m. G train back to—

"Officer Montenegro."

She looks up at Kurt, but her face is already a clear no. She's had enough "charm" for one morning.

"Are you really not going to tell me," he says, "how you got to be the queen of money laundering? Not ever?"

Her face goes from no to fuck-off, and then her phone beeps.

"We've lost the signal," she says, looking down at the screen. "He's underground."

Renaissance Java: a familiar name, but looking around, she knows she's never been here. A short line, then she's at the counter. "Large ice, six sugars," she says. Kurt's order. For herself: "Large drip. Milk." Money on the counter. Change in the tip jar. She steps back, waiting for the coffees, and checks the tracking phone. The red dot is moving again. The train is aboveground. No, the dot is zigging: Emil must already be on foot.

"Large ice? Large drip?" The barista holds up the drinks and then fits them into a cardboard tray.

Zera pockets the phone, takes the tray, and is nearly out the door when she belatedly recognizes a man—seated—she's just walked past. Thin, small, salt-and-pepper hair, a short-sleeved yellow-and-white button-down, open at the collar: it's Shecky Keenan.

Renaissance Java—*of course*. It came up in one of the intelligence reports, one of the coffee shops he's been in and out of over the past few months.

He looks different in person.

Pinned to the wall above her desk is a smeary blowup of his driver's license, enlarged to fill most of an eight-and-a-half-by-eleven piece of paper. An identical smeary blowup is attached to the draft intelligence briefing she put on her supervisor's desk last month. So yes, it's him, she's certain: she looks at his face every day. But while the smeary picture has no movement, this man is nothing but. He shifts his shoulders and winces—a slipped disk, maybe, that never got back in place. He wipes his eyes with the palms of his hands, and yawns like he hasn't slept since the cold war. And even having recognized him, she finds it hard to believe that they're the same, the smeary picture and this small man with his paper coffee cup.

Because here he's a person.

He stirs, and she comes to herself. Hurries off, wondering what's happening in her. Her tracking phone forgotten in her pocket.

She's a half block away when she gets the call.

"You got our boy?" Kurt doesn't sound full smiley, for once. Just a drop of worry, but she hears it.

"What's going on?" She takes out her tracking phone.

"Thought you could tell me."

"Stand by." The tracking phone has decided to reboot. When it's back online, she pulls up the live map. It shows a good part of Bushwick, from Flushing Avenue on the west to Gates Avenue on the east. Metropolitan Avenue to the north and Broadway to the south. And buildings are visible, and here's a parking lot, and over there's Maria Hernandez Park, where Zera met Emil for the first time.

And there's no red dot.

Zera stops walking. She looks at her unchanging screen for a long time and feels a creeping horror move through her. The red dot never comes back.

chapter 23

Outside Knish-Knosh, the day after the murder, Henry slows before he catches up with the young woman. He keeps a safe distance as she reaches the door to the Thirsty Bear. She pulls it open, and for a moment the light is full on her, and he knows he's right. It's Imani Cable, Emil's girlfriend.

Then the door is closed, and she's inside, and Henry knows he can't handle this alone.

A text to Lipz: Where you at, who you with?

Her reply, four long minutes later: Nunya.

The old joke makes him smile, his first since the HVAC room.

The HVAC room. Fuck, Henry's back there now. Emil's body, so pale, and that crater in the back of his head—

Henry shakes off the memory and, giving up on Lipz, texts Kerasha: @Thirsty Bear, need backup. He goes inside.

A small group of young men and women are gathering along the wall near the unfinished mural. Henry recognizes many of them, and one calls over to him. He finds himself in an intimate group of Emil's friends and admirers. The conversation becomes a kind of spontaneous memorial service. There's no order, no ceremony, no leadership, but almost everyone shares a story about Emil, some private memory that no one else seems to have heard before. Henry feels like an impostor. What could *he* share—the training, the fallbacks? And look what that did for him.

"He was the most generous person," Imani says. "He gave everything away. If anybody on the street asked for money, or any friend . . . Once he had this neighbor who was late on her rent . . . It was like he didn't want to hold on to the money." She's one of many who speak about Emil without even mentioning his art.

Henry shifts on his seat, can't get comfortable. Doesn't belong here. How different, his own experience with Emil, which began with cash, and ended with murder.

An hour and three tequila shots later, Henry's alone at the bar. He puts away the Charlie Gladney license, which he's been staring at for some time now, and takes out the business card Kerasha found in Emil's room. Henry looks at the blank side—still blank. Flips it, looks again at the handwritten number. 646-555-0144—he hasn't called it yet, knows he shouldn't call until he has a plan. Tequila creates a plan: fuck it, just call. He puts in the numbers, brings the phone to his ear.

"Who this?" A male voice, rough and deep. A street voice, or someone trying to sound like that.

"It's . . ." Henry has no idea. "Who are—" Click.

Fuck. Who knows if he'll get another shot at that. Never let tequila decide the plan.

This is what he's thinking when the stool beside him moves. He turns to glare at the newcomer—go away, can't you see I'm being pissy here—but then he sees who it is. Imani gives him a hateful look-over.

"Meet me outside."

Moments later, Henry is scanning the streets, looking for his backup, but of course it's pointless. Kerasha's invisible until she's not. Years before they met, he heard stories about her, the famous child thief. Dropping down into sewers, popping car trunks. He'd assumed this was grade A Bushwick shitlore, and then she moved in. He's sick of hearing his uncle say it, but he's right: she's a natural. Fuck knows how she ever got arrested. Meanwhile, here he is, wobbling over to Imani.

"It was a good memorial." He feels stupid saying this, but it's true. The stories people told. He wishes there had been something like this for Mom and Dad, instead of the bang-clang construction work that could be heard through the walls at Mom's wake. Instead of the minister at Dad's funeral, who got Dad's first name wrong.

"It was good—for a fucking memorial service," Imani says. She looks at Henry, tiny and unafraid. "So tell me how you ran him."

Fuck me. He goes for baffled: "What are you talking about?" Fails.

"You, asshole. You fucking shadow." Rapid-fire now: "Why is he dead? Why was he killed?" Her finger in his face. "That's an actual question. And you're going to answer it right now."

Henry's pulse goes from nothing to red. "You don't know me."

He backs up, she closes in. There's a stagger in his step—tequila—and determination in hers. Her voice is low and hoarse: "I've seen your face a hundred times."

She's coming at him like the wrath of an ancient god, and Henry thinks, Could *she* have done it? His body tells him yes, she's capable of anything. His back tells him he's walked into a wall. She stands before him, her head hardly as high as his chest, but he feels like the smaller one.

"The cops think he was mugged. That's bullshit. Emil had no business in that building. But you—you know something." She goes to grab him—he catches her wrists. But she pulls herself free and shoves him, and his shoulders and the back of his head hit the wall. Small person, strong push, and now she's taking a step back. Pulling out a blade.

Henry changes his angle, makes himself slim, raises his hands. The tequila means nothing, he's all body now, has been in plenty of fights. Has faced a knife and has the scars to show it. But still, he's more afraid this time. That other fight with the knife was about money, which meant the other person had a breaking point. This is something else.

"I'm Henry." He spaces out his words. "Whoever you think I am—"

"You're not a *who*, you're a *what*." She spits down at his feet. "You're a shadow. That's what he called you two, the shadow twins."

His body's ready, his head is spinning, and it's not the tequila. She's mistaken, she's confusing him with someone else. But who? "I'm not two. I don't have a twin." He's sure about this, but something about what she's saying, and the way she's saying it—it doesn't feel like crazy talk. "I'm just me, and I'm just trying to figure it out. What happened."

"Here's what didn't happen." She stabs the air. "Emil didn't get mugged. Here's what did happen: You killed him or you got him killed. You and your twin. And I'd kill you right here, except . . ." With obvious reluctance, and a shaking hand, she puts her blade away. Backs off. "Except I'm not like you."

Henry doesn't move, and still has his back to the wall long after she's left him, when Kerasha steps out from the darkness. "You did great," she says. "That could've gone a lot of bad ways." When she gets close, he can smell her lotion, and at that moment it's like he's been alone in a dark room, and she just walked in and turned on the light. Here in this alley, he's home again.

"Found this in her pocket," Kerasha says, holding up a phone. "There's something on this we want."

Henry squats down to keep himself from falling over. "Te-to-the-fucking-quila," he says, putting his hands to his head. He breathes. He doesn't throw up. He breathes. He doesn't throw up some more. He looks up at Kerasha. "Can I ask you something?"

"Take your time."

"How the fuck do you know everything?" They share a weary smile and Henry asks, "Why do we want this phone?"

chapter 24

Rewind a half hour: back in the bar, Imani is at a table with a short, muscular man. Kerasha is nearby, wrapped in shadows.

Muscle boy: "Just fucking give it to me."

"Toss your own fucking phone," Imani says.

"I did. And if the cops take yours, they'll see what we've been writing each other—"

"You've been writing me, you fucking stalker. We broke up six months ago. Get the fuck away."

Ex-boyfriend, for all his muscles and fury, gets the fuck away. Hurrying, like everyone else, right past Bushwick's invisible spider.

But what is he afraid of? What would the police find—and what does *she* get first?

Plucking the phone off Imani is easy. It also solves nothing, not right away. Gives Kerasha no lasting satisfaction. A murderer walks among them. A quarter million has vanished. Red Dog will be missing it, and Red Dog is not known for his mercy. Meanwhile, Detective 7229 has eyes on the house, and while her uncle shits himself hourly, Henry wears black, and Kerasha herself—let's face it—isn't feeling so safe. Her web is shaking, for fuck's safe.

At least with the phone, she's ahead of the hunters.

But she can't get in. The phone is in a slim case that also contains a driver's license and a credit card. Kerasha makes a mental note to shred these when she's back at her uncle's house. The urgency of the moment is the passcode. She has no idea, no guesses, no deduction. This phone will lock long before she can get into it. She brings it to Henry.

A painful admission, but he's far better with the tele-gizmos. Six years in the cage—prisoners rarely change, but phones never stop. Kerasha owns it: the noiseless spider can't do everything. And this scares her. She's barefooting up a staircase with *tacks in it*, as Mama and Langston liked to say. *Boards torn up*. Barefooting alone, usually. But tonight she takes Henry by the arm and steadies him.

"Sorry," Henry says, "tequila fingers. You'll have to do it."

"Watch the curb," she says. Left foot, right foot. If he face-plants, if he goes black, then there's no getting into the phone tonight.

"We're almost there," she says.

"Almost puking."

Out of the lot, between the brownstones, left on St. Nicholas, left on Troutman, past Smelly Terri—a homeless woman, well known in the neighborhood—and then into Alan's Happy Falafel. They walk in just like any other pair of biracial criminal cousins. Small-timers. No murder behind them.

The diner smells like cholesterol. They find a four-seater and order fries and coffee. Henry probably has a pill that could help him, but his complexion is already green. Just give him time, she tells herself. A trip to the surprisingly immaculate bathroom, and when she returns, he's slumped over the table. Kerasha indicates the plate of fries. "If you're done, we can give them to Smelly Terri."

He lifts a fry, eyes it skeptically. Lets it drop. "Fucking dog food."

Smelly Terri probably *would* eat dog food, Kerasha knows, but since coming out of the cage, Kerasha has felt a strange kinship with this woman. Has left food where Smelly Terri will find it. A blanket, once, another time a bag of clean clothes. A box of wet wipes, a case of mineral water.

Dr. Xu, no doubt, would use all this against her. Patient overidentifies with benign schizophrenic. She can see him jotting down notes

with that silver pen, arming himself for yet another report of unsatis-
factory progress: "Defective role model a possible factor in, or co-
symptom of, intractable recalcitrance."

Kerasha waves over Bashar, the night waiter.

"Nothing else?" he asks.

"Advil," Henry says.

"All out. Sorry, boss." Kerasha asks Bashar to box up the leftovers,
and he takes the plate away. Sneaks her a suggestive smile as he goes.
She looks away.

Henry now: less obviously drunk. She takes him to Sunset
Cinemas, the boarded-up movie theater on Wyckoff Street. A family
safe house. The combination lock looks rusty, but the dial spins just
fine. Counterclockwise 21, clockwise 8, counterclockwise 31, then
the trick: a firm press at the dead center.

Dead center, she thinks. How death frames the language, serves
everywhere as a point of reference. *Dead reckoning, dead wrong, dead
likeness.* Death as a completion, as an example of perfection. Dead runner: the only kind you can trust. Dead mama—a fantasy, right? Do
they *ever* go away?

Kerasha leads Henry inside the safe house and sits him on the
nappy rug. Their flashlights stand upright on the bare concrete and
project pillars of dusty light.

"Are you clear now?" she asks.

"As I'll ever be." Henry takes the phone and gets to work. This safe
house is well-tooled, which is why she chose it. While Henry screen-
taps and mumbles, Kerasha sits down. Crosses her legs, feet on
thighs—a pose Nicole the yoga embezzler told her would bring
"astro-physiological peace." Dead calm, Kerasha thinks. And Henry
is dead tired, whereas Mama is just dead—the air here is thick with
bad memories.

A half block from the safe house is the site of the stupidest, most
dangerous job Kerasha ever pulled. Mama was sober in a bad way,
shaking and sweating, puking until it came out black. Skinny Kerasha
ransacked the bodega pharmacies but Mama wouldn't touch anything but the real stuff. Wouldn't *look* at her, which wasn't unusual,

but when her eyes went yellow Kerasha understood what Mama needed. Down Cypress Avenue, left on Johnson, then on to Gardner—across the street and two doors down from Sunset Cinemas—a trio of slinging nobodies sat on lawn chairs passing a bottle. They rated women passersby with handmade scorecards, laughing big with their gold teeth. Not noticing the skinny girl, even as her hands went beneath the center lawn chair.

The glassines were greasy. She would have a hard time soaping that feeling off her skin.

Kerasha had never cooked heroin before. Never loaded a syringe, never fired to a vein. But Mama was too shaky to do it herself, so Kerasha did what she had seen. And from that day, Mama got her daily bag.

Deadfall. Dead end.

"Apple fucking 7," Henry says. He's been working at Imani's phone with a Cellebrite data extractor, a Christmas gift to the family from Fat Boris. "Same shit the cops use," Henry had told her the first time he showed her the device. "Israeli technology. Unlocks a phone like a motherfucker." But now he tosses the extractor aside.

"You can't unlock it?" Kerasha doesn't even know what's on the phone. She heard the police would want it, though, and she's desperate to stay ahead of those fuckers. To be the one in control.

Why? Are you afraid? It's Dr. Xu-in-her-head, asking stupid questions. Did I hear a break in your voice? It's okay to be afraid.

She doesn't answer.

This phone represents something, he says. Hope, maybe? That your little web will hold? But what if this hope is false? What would it mean if the web broke, and you tumbled down alone? Who would you be without your little family—what would you *do*?

"Let's go back to the house and get some sleep," she tells Henry. "You'll look at it again tomorrow."

"Tomorrow's too late." Henry lets the phone drop to his lap. "She'll notice it's gone, and she'll wipe it."

Kerasha's hope sinks fast. "She can do that remotely?"

"You can do anything remotely."

Sinking—sinking—sunk. But then an idea comes out before she's even thought it: "Even if we take out the SIM card?"

Henry sits up. "How the fuck do you know everything?"

Kerasha looks down, unsure what to do with a compliment. "I had good cellies."

Henry pushes himself to his feet, rummages around the room, and staggers back with a thin nail and an odd-looking pick. A minute later he pops open the phone and pulls out a white chip. "And we're saved," he says, but his smile is thin. "We still have to get into her messages?"

Kerasha thinks about the locker room combination locks she's opened. The doorknob locks, the sturdy deadbolts, the window latches she's had to cut or punch glass to get at. Even the cheapest locks can take labor, can take time and repeated efforts.

She tips her head to the Cellebrite device. "Try again."

Two hours later, they're in.

Girlfriend's phone, the second it's unlocked, flashes an unhappy warning: *Low Battery*. And now Kerasha's own phone is vibrating. The first message on her new phone is from Uncle Shecky: U OK? Then: LMK.

Am I? She scans the room for trouble. A shabby couch covered with a dusty cloth. Weak orange lights from their flashlights. Henry on his back, hands still on his head.

"Tequila done me dirty," he says.

Dead to the world, she thinks. Mama might've found that funny.

She texts Uncle Shecky: We ok. And though she believes this, a tiny part of her wonders. We ok: this could have been the runner's last text, his sense of reality right up until someone crushed his head. It's the nature, it's in the *definition* of unknown dangers: they come from everywhere, from nowhere. And the threats you're ready for never arrive. Let's not forget the lessons of the Franklin cafeteria, of that fateful spork fight.

Another text from her uncle: DR XU 2PM TOMRW. NO XCUSE.

Fuck. For five happy seconds she'd forgotten all about the little man. And this will be worse than her ordinary visits to Dr. Xu, which are bad enough. This is going to him with her web snapping apart. It's difficult to see herself surviving the full fifty-five minutes. Not taking him by the ponytail and slamming his face into that coffee table.

More texts from Uncle Shecky: JUST GET THRU IT. He's psychic, sometimes, but he texts like a twelve-year-old girl: I CLEAN YR ROOM. I WASH YR CLOTHES. Make that a very sweet, very thoughtful twelve-year-old girl.

Stay out, she texts back. Don't touch my shit. There's gratitude between these lines. She hopes he can feel it.

Another whimpering beep from girlfriend's phone. Another groan from Henry.

Cuz needs a bed, she thinks. A snap decision: family first. She powers down the phone so it can't be traced or wiped remotely. She hopes. She brings Henry home and waits at the top of the basement stairs, watching him stumble down to his room. He makes it without falling. An inspirational metaphor, she thinks. Wonder what Mama could do with it.

Cook it and shoot it, she thinks. Needle to vein, vein to heart. Sorry, Mama, bad joke.

In her own room, alone with girlfriend's unlocked phone, she hits the power button. Dead black. Dead nothing. Dead battery, she remembers. Tomorrow, she thinks, and she takes a book off the shelf Henry built for her. Gets into bed with it. Sometime later, book down, lights out, she's drifting off, with Mama in her head.

Goodnight balloon. In the not-yet-terrible days Mama used to read this to her. Goodnight, Detective 7229. Goodnight, Smelly Terri.

The sheets are soft and the scent is gentle lavender. Uncle Shecky did her right.

Goodnight, almost, kind-of family. Goodnight, not-Franklin.

More improvisations wear her out, but she goes down with a line from the actual book. *Goodnight nobody.*

City full of strangers, Kerasha falls into an uneasy sleep.

chapter 25

When Shecky Keenan was eight years old, his uncle Tomas went into the cage, which meant Shecky had to move back in with uncle Samuel. His only sober uncle, Samuel believed Shecky was half devil, and for transgressions such as slowness, falling and crying, looking funny, or looking crooked, Shecky was put in the wicked box, which was a closet that smelled of mildew and scat. The length of Shecky's sentence ranged from one to ten minutes, depending on the severity of his sin. But the sentence had little to do with the amount of time Shecky actually spent locked in that closet, because Uncle Samuel couldn't stay off his phone, and he would go through his parish directory (he was an angry churchgoer), and he would shout Jesus fire at whoever answered, shout till he lost all sense of time, shout till he didn't know whom he was shouting at or whether they were still on the line. And Shecky would remain in that wicked box until Dannie came for him. And she always, always came for him.

Three days after the murder, Shecky can't stop thinking about his sister.

He puts coffees, plates of toast and eggs and beans, a huge fruit bowl, a tub of honey butter, a jar of pickles, and a bottle of Tabasco on the table. He surveys the assembled with some astonishment and discomfort. Kerasha sits apart with her book, her mouth set against what he suspects is a nascent smile. Then there's his Henry with a rag-wrapped ice pack against his head. There's no telling what, if anything, he can hear through that hangover. And last, in the guest seat, there's Henry's girl, the one who sneaks in through the basement window. She has no business even being near his house, but here she is at his dining room table, half naked to show off her tattoos. Shecky doesn't like her here, doesn't like her here like this. But he can't kick her out. One of the tattoos is the same Japanese script that was inked on his sister. Shecky has forgotten a lot about Dannie, which shames him, but he's held on to the translation of this script: *The world is but a drop of dew, a drop of dew and yet—*

"And yet it means something to *us*," Dannie explained to him.

It was one of the tattoos the police used to identify her body.

This girl with Dannie's tattoo is "Lipz" to Henry, but Shecky remembers her real name is Nadina Villa Lobos. Lipz smokes at his table. No one else smokes at his table. Her whole disposition is shabby-joyous, though, and she's got more charm than you'd expect from a shelter girl with a murder rap. Killed her stepdad, Shecky remembers. Beating on her mom, so the girl just brained him. And here she is, smiling at his Henry. Looking very at home. He's never noticed this before, the ways she's like Dannie: the sense of humor, the manic energy. And he wonders how many chances she gets to sit down like this and enjoy a proper meal.

"Thank you for being here," Shecky says, sitting down. "Thank you for being my family." After the tiniest hesitation, he turns to Lipz: "Thanks for joining us." He puts on a smile.

Breakfast is over. Cigarette in her mouth, a phone in her hand, Lipz talks with her eyes on Henry: "Fuck am I looking for?" This phone was swiped off the dead runner's girlfriend and can supposedly identify or confirm who the murderer is. Shecky keeps his doubts to himself.

"Girlfriend had a jealous ex." Henry's voice is all sandpaper.

"I heard him talking," Kerasha says. "He was worried about the police."

"Sketchy as fuck," Henry says.

"So I'm typing in 'sketchy ex-boyfriend.'" Lipz wags the phone at Henry. "Nothing's coming up."

"His name's Noah. Fuck, Lipz, this is hard enough without you—"

"*I'm* making this hard? How was I supposed to guess *Noah*? Your friend's girlfriend's ex—this is common knowledge?"

Henry winces, and Shecky has to hide his smile. Dannie definitely could have said something like this. Damn this girl, she shouldn't be here, but she sure as shit is bringing him back.

At Uncle Samuel's, Dannie would sneak him out of the wicked box, and sometimes she took hits for this. Then one day Uncle Samuel had had enough of them. He beat them out of his apartment and beat them all the way to Uncle Joseph's. It was quieter there, and the kids had time for more than mere survival. Dannie sat with Shecky and his homework at the kitchen table. She taught him number and memory tricks, many of which he uses today—uses automatically, proof that Dannie lives on in the wiring of his brain. But Dannie was more than tricks, of course, and this Dannie—the whole person—is long gone.

Gone, what a gentle way of putting it. How about killed. Raped and strangled and tossed. Dog-found, coroner-carved, and evidence-photographed. Not that there was ever anyone to inculpate. The killer, faceless, ghostly. The sister, dumped into a pine casket. Shipped off to Cypress Hill Cemetery just two days after the police released her body. Shecky was already back at school—Uncle Joseph made the arrangements and didn't tell Shecky until it was all over. And so Danis Phillipa Keenan went down, buried by strangers, no one there to say who she was and that she'd been loved. Buried without family.

Now and then over the years his treasonous heart has asked him whether she even existed. No one speaks of her. He's guilty of that himself. He's shown no photographs, never mentioned her to Henry.

Her voice he recalls but also doubts. Did she really sound like that? The things he remembers her saying—are *any* not made up? Other questions he can't always answer: Did anyone ever love him? Had he ever known family?

Well hopefully the answer is here, in this room.

Henry is looking alive now, watching Lipz as she reads the text exchange aloud. Changing her voice, text by text. Kerasha is watching her, too, only she's obviously fighting back laughter. Lipz shouldn't be here, she's an outsider—but she's doing so well, with her voices, and this is turning into a family moment: the whole room has a single focus.

Imani, the girlfriend: Stop texting me.

Noah, the ex: Where's Emil?

Imani: Fuck you

Noah: You don't know where he is

Imani: Shaddup

Noah: You don't know who he's fucking with

Imani: Stop stalking him. Stop texting me. Die.

Noah: I saw him with a woman.

A pause as Lipz taps on the phone. She resumes in her own voice, turning to Henry: "She never responded to this."

Henry adjusts his ice pack. Shecky deflates a little. This texting melodrama—so simple, and so well read! And it was a very Dannie moment, but now it's over.

"So what are we saying?" Kerasha asks the table. "That the girlfriend found out Emil was cheating, and she killed him?"

"That didn't happen," Henry grumbles. "She's not like that."

"Which is exactly what makes her"—Lipz stubs out her cigarette theatrically—"our *prime suspect.*"

Henry glares at her, and Shecky understands that her tone is most unwelcome—to him. For Shecky, though, Lipz should be up for a Tony.

For the role of Dannie.

And just like that, the glee is gone, because the pain of losing her is always *right there*. Coming in, going out, every breath.

It was his eleventh birthday.

At the last minute, Uncle Joseph insisted that they celebrate with cake and pizza at the corner drunk house. Uncle Joseph called over his own crew, a few of their girlfriends and kids, and then a random neighbor and her randomer cousin.

Shecky invited Dannie.

A week earlier she had moved in with a much older boyfriend who had his own apartment down the street. Shecky still saw her daily, but he missed her every second she wasn't around. This was the period when Dannie was just beginning to get steady work as a stage manager, and that night she had a rehearsal. "I'll run it fast," she promised him. "I'll be there for you. Save me some cake." But then she didn't come, and she didn't call, and she went on not coming or calling. The party was over. Shecky still remembers the sticky floor. Remembers the too-loud music, that a pigeon somehow got into the drunk house. Remembers, also, his empty stomach: in his head Dannie had always been just about to appear. He had wanted to eat with her.

Shecky brought her slice home and put it in the refrigerator. He hated Dannie for not coming, hated that she'd promised, hated that he'd told everyone at the party she was on her way. Hated that when he'd asked Uncle Joseph to call her one last time, he'd said, "Leave that bitch alone." Hated *her* for this, because Uncle Joseph was Uncle Joseph, but Dannie was supposed to be better.

Late that night Shecky went back to the refrigerator and ate her cake. Another hour, no call, no Dannie. Bitch.

Alone again in the dark, he wrapped himself in his tattered blanket, wormed to the almost-flat part of the sofa-bed mattress, and listened to the shouts and laughter and clatter of his uncle's card game in the adjoining room. Dozing, Shecky's hatred for Dannie receded. In its place crept a wispy dream, which he would regret for the rest of his life. In the dream he stood above a beautiful, slim girl. She was pale. She was still. Struck by a car while crossing the street with an armful of gifts. And Shecky felt so light and free: his beautiful sister was dead, and this proved she hadn't forgotten his birthday after all.

The detectives came around the day after the party. They

questioned Uncle Joseph and they questioned and re-questioned, Shecky learned later, a man from Uncle Joseph's crew, who had a history of hurting girls. But because nothing came of this—no one was ever arrested, and there never was a proper funeral—Shecky didn't quite believe Dannie was forever gone until he was visited by a city social worker. It was from her that Shecky learned, very belatedly, that his beautiful, terrible dream had come true. His sister hadn't been car-crushed while carrying an armful of presents, but she really had died on her way to him. "Your sister loved you very much," the social worker explained to Shecky, having first primed him with Skittles. "She never forgot about you. I can't tell you how I know that," she added, with a quick, almost guilty look at her briefcase, "but it's true. She was going to your party." The moment Shecky started to cry, the social worker herself came apart. And when she excused herself and rushed off to find the bathroom, Shecky quieted down. Helped himself to her briefcase. Picked out a copy of Dannie's incident report. Shecky couldn't define half the words in that report, but he understood it perfectly. Dannie's death excused her, just like he'd hoped. And by the logic of a child—a logic essentially still with him, despite everything—it was his own lonely wish that killed her.

"What's next?" Henry says. Coming back to his senses, Shecky scans the room, wondering what he missed. Kerasha has formed her hands into a ball, fingertips touching fingertips. Henry's eyes are closed, but he manages a nod toward Lipz. "Keep reading."

"There's nothing to read," she says, tapping the phone. "She never responds to him—fuck. Wait. Looks like boyfriend got a new phone the next week. Here's a new thread. But it's totally one-sided."

Noah: You're better off without him.

Noah again: I'm getting you back.

Lipz lowers the phone and the kids exchange looks: Lipz to Henry, Henry to Kerasha, now all eyes on Shecky. The room is eerie and somehow electrified, and Shecky agrees with what they're not saying. The girlfriend's ex-boyfriend, what's his name—Noah—he looks bad here. *Better off without him*, and then—a body. But Shecky knows that death comes at you sideways. What's *likely* is dust under what *is*.

"This is guesswork," Henry says at last. Breaking the silence, echoing Shecky's own thoughts. "We've got to analyze this shit."

Attaboy. He's proud of the kid. The pudgy boy who used to brawl with his classmates—he'd never paused to *analyze*.

"No way it's Noah," Henry says. "Emil got snuck on a job. Carrying a bag. Did Noah just get lucky? Decides to kill him—the first time Emil's ever had a heavy?" He takes his ice pack to the kitchen. Comes back with a bag of frozen vegetables, sits and puts that to his head. "Emil's girlfriend called me a shadow. And she said he had another shadow, meaning—fuck if I know. Maybe someone followed him around? Figured out his pattern?"

Shecky blows out some breath, doesn't like the taste of his mouth. "Since when do our runners follow *patterns*?" A blade in his voice now. "Where's your head, Henry? I trained you better than that."

"We don't live in training." Henry raises his eyes. "I know everything is perfect in your ledger, but we live *here*."

The room is airless, Shecky hard-looking at Henry, Henry hard-looking back at him.

"Let's say there *was* a pattern," Henry continues, a moment later. "Could be it wasn't on our side. Could be the pattern was on the drop-off, and Red Dog's looking into how *his* guy went wrong."

Lipz snorts. "If Red Dog's guy went wrong, we'll hear about that shit fast. He puts boys *down* when they get stupid." With a kind of glee she grabs a peach from the fruit bowl. She brings it close to her mouth and then asks, looking at no one in particular, "But how long before he comes after *you*?"

A response comes from the forgotten seat: "We should look at the ledger." Kerasha nods up toward the office on the second floor. "We can make a list of all the days he did jobs for us. And if he's texting with Imani on those days, while he's out on his run for us . . ." To Henry she adds, as if apologetically: "I'm sorry. But maybe there is a pattern."

"We're *not* bringing the ledger down here." Shecky's glare directs Kerasha to Lipz, who is so very not-family. Who should never even be in the same room with the ledger, let alone present while it's read. He's about to add some choice words to this effect when Henry stirs and says, "June sixteenth. June twenty-fourth." He adjusts his bag of frozen veggies. "We don't need the ledger, I remember his days."

A half hour passes. Somewhere in the middle of it, Lipz gives the phone to Kerasha and goes to the kitchen, where—and this amazes Shecky—she starts washing dishes. Henry, meanwhile, has his head in his hands, and Kerasha is still just sitting there with the phone in her hand, scrolling and reading. Shecky can hear Lipz humming in the kitchen, can hear little splashes from the sink where she's working. This is a moment of peace. This is wasted time. The dead runner's girlfriend, her ex—this is far from helpful. He's about to restart the conversation when Kerasha, who's been going through the phone all this time, looks up at Henry: "Emil had a studio?"

Henry raises his head. "What about it?"

Lipz comes in from the kitchen, wiping her hands with a dish-cloth, and all eyes are on Kerasha when she says, "Emil went to the studio every day he did a job for us. At least that's what he wrote. Here: Heading to studio. And here: Leaving studio now."

Lipz: "Pattern—boom."

"Or it could just be a coincidence," Shecky says. "Like he washes his hands every day. That doesn't mean it's the reason he . . . you know."

Kerasha, God bless her, turns to Henry and speaks to him in a tender, low voice, as if they're the only ones in the room: "I'll go look at it with you." She puts down the girlfriend's phone. "I'll help you get in."

The hopeful-grateful look Henry gives Kerasha now is tender, rare, and potent. Shecky catches this look and feels something tight in his chest. He lifts a trembling mug. The kids are working together, he thinks, and what a beautiful thing—they'll keep each other safe.

But the next killing happens that night.

chapter 26

Suicide by patient—is this a thing? Dr. Xu obviously wants to die, obviously wants her to be his killer. Two weeks before the murder, Kerasha is tempted.

"Let's get back to the kleptomania," he says. That pen—faux fountain tip for the faux doctor—is out and uncapped and ready to memorialize recalcitrance. "How do we define it?"

Same way we did last week, homunculus.

"Stealing," she says. He likes to correct her, so she gives him every opportunity. Let him feel smart. Let him feel his treatment is shepherding a poor soul out of her dark ignorance. If he feels superior enough during these sessions, maybe next month—just maybe—he'll tell the court she's a good little girl. No recalcitrance after all, that was a misdiagnosis. Disregard previous notes to the contrary, judge. This patient doesn't need further mind-fucking.

"Kleptomania," Dr. Xu says, pocketing his pen, "is an ungovernable compulsion to steal. Not the stealing itself. This distinction is subtle, but it's important, and I want you to understand it. The compulsion is what we're getting at here. It's why you're in this room."

"That and the court order." Fuck, she wasn't supposed to say that out loud. It's just that he's talking about her as though there were something wrong with her brain. Bad chemistry, childhood traumas—she read plenty about both in the Franklin library. For her, though, stealing has always been straightforward. Skinny Kerasha did it because she was poor. With Mama and her daily bag, little Kerasha undoubtedly had "issues," but the more pressing concern was always hunger.

A few weeks ago a fishbowl full of marbles appeared on Dr. Xu's coffee table. She fixes her eyes on it, focuses on her breathing. Nicole, her yoga embezzler jail buddy, would be proud. *Let* on the inhale, *go* on the exhale. Only Kerasha's om for the ponytail is *stay* (breathe in) *the fuck out of my head* (breathe out).

Dr. Xu shifts in his chair and brings his hands together, just the fingertips. That hateful pose he studied, she's more certain than ever, from some TV psychiatrist. She's also certain he's still congratulating himself on his definition of *kleptomania*. "So what do you think is behind this"—TV psychiatrist pause—"compulsion?"

She lets the question hang a long time before saying, "You mean, why do I, like, steal?" Pained, slow consideration, then an idiot's nonanswer: this is one of her tricks for passing the time here. It lets him feel superior, which is his goal, and gets her off without having revealed anything, which is hers. Win-win, Uncle Shecky, that's how we get through this.

That and swiping a couple of marbles from the fishbowl. Her newest trick for killing time here—klepto-*what*, Dr. Xu? Easy handwork, so stupid of him to put the fishbowl next to the big tissue box.

"Do people actually cry here?" she had asked during their first meeting.

"Some do. Some cry every time they come in." Jesus fuck, her uncle would say, who'd choose this profession?

"Do you feel like crying, Kerasha?" he'd asked.

She just stared at him, which he apparently took as a heavy maybe. "Because if you ever do, now or at any point in our treatment, it would be absolutely okay."

Today, though, things are not *absolutely okay* with Dr. Xu. He's showing his frustration. "I don't mean why do you 'like, steal.'" Some movement around the nostrils. "*Like* suggests approximation. There is no approximation in my question." His eyes narrow to slits as he leans forward: "I mean why do you steal, and I mean that precisely."

Oh, so you want to get *grammatical*, Dr. Xu? The marbles send warm tingles across her palm. Don't fight him, she thinks. Keep it in your head.

Fuck my head.

"I don't, like, *steal*," she says. "I, like, *stole*. I got, like, *caught*, and I learned my, like—my fucking lesson."

"You haven't learned anything," Dr. Xu says, "if you don't understand why you did it."

"So that *is* what you want to know." She gives him an idiot's gotcha smile. "You want to know, like, why I stole."

He winces, shakes his head, and is just opening his mouth when she talks over him:

"I stole because I wanted stuff. I saw something, or heard about something, or thought there'd be something somewhere. And I fucking took it."

There, little man, happy now? She's given him something close to a real answer. Scary close, in fact, because she doesn't know why she gave it.

But the little man is never happy with her level of discomfort. Always finds a new excuse to poke, pierce, slice.

"You mentioned *want*," he says. "Maybe we can talk about where that came from."

"Where want came from?" Pause, question the question, pause. But the trick isn't working this time. Somewhere inside her, a vague unease is hardening into a mass. It's like when she hears a police siren. It's never for her, she knows, never because of her.

Except when it is.

And that's how she feels sitting before this fishbowl full of marbles, with this little man and his ponytail. He may not know what he's doing, but sometimes even little men can blunder in the right direction. Her brain hurts just above the left temple. Too tired to think sensibly, she catches herself wondering whether his incompetency might give him an advantage over her. Before today she was thinking grandmaster chess, ten steps ahead, but his moves have been beyond logic. Motivated, really, only by a desire to make her hate herself.

Come on, Kerasha, her inner Uncle Shecky texts, just get thru it. In minutes you'll walk away from this fishbowl of marbles, and in a half hour you'll be back in the bosom of your almost-family. Back on your web. In your dreams tonight you can wrap him in filaments and put your fangs in him. You can watch as the venom liquefies his organs, and he'll die terribly in your dream. Here, though, you've got to just let him be.

"You remind me of a patient I once had."

Kerasha hates this story already. Whoever this cunty patient was, if she even existed, Kerasha is not like her. And how would Dr. Xu know what Kerasha is like? Before today she's never given him real answers, just like he's never asked her real questions. Dogshit for dogshit—that's their pact.

"And this patient used to take things." This patient never was, she's certain now. "She could be visiting her aunt, and she'd take washcloths. She could be at her job—she was a metalworker—and she took tools. She could even be—and this is just another example—at a doctor's office. And even there she'd find something to take."

An odd vibration. It comes in at her palms, it fills the room, and then the air is electrified.

No, not the whole room. Just the pocket of her jeans. The marbles are humming. She squeezes them and thinks, He doesn't know. He can't. This I-once-had-a-patient is nothing, is a nonperson. Is not Kerasha fucking Brown. And Dr. Xu's ponytail confirms this.

The little man drums his fingertips, smiling to himself. Relishing a memory, it looks like. Bringing to mind the first innocent, healthy patient he drove to suicide.

Kerasha feels sick. Her hand on the marbles is limp, her skin on the glass tingly.

He doesn't know. He can't.

"This patient—let's call her Kay, though that's not her real name." That's no one's name, that's a fucking letter. And it happens to be the first letter of my name, you little bitch. How stupid you must think I am. "Kay once put it like this: I don't take *what* I want, I take *because* I want. Or words to that effect."

Words to fuck your mother, but Kerasha says nothing.

She keeps her hand in her pocket and the marbles in her hand. She squeezes as if she means to crush them to powder.

Dr. Xu leans forward, separates his fingertips, and holds his hands palms-up toward her. Another studied pose: the humble monk sharing his bowl of rice.

"That's for you to think on." He points to his wrist, though there's no watch. "We're done for today."

This is the first time a session ran out without her noticing it, without her counting down the seconds. This is also the first time she walks out with a question fluttering around her head like a dirty bat. And it's not exactly Dr. Xu's bat, but it's one he let in.

She's never wanted glass marbles in her life; why are two in her pocket?

A terrible awareness cracks open in her. Turning from it, she's nine years old again, she's on the rooftop of Tower B of the Moses Houses. Safe at last from Mama and her needles, she watches the sun rise over downtown Brooklyn. The rugged skyline. The red warming to yellow.

part six

Not a day passes, not a minute or second without a corpse.

—WALT WHITMAN

chapter 27

Emil Scott's art studio is an attic apartment about a block from where he was killed. It is three days after the murder when Henry takes in the canvas-lined walls, the sharply slanted ceiling. Wood boards on cinderblocks serve as shelves for paints, scratch paper, and brushes. The smell here is toxic, the floor a Jackson Pollack. Holy ground, Henry thinks.

Stepping in, he touches the low ceiling. Emil was even taller than Henry, he must have had to squat to work here. Strange, to think of Emil Scott, poised and comfortable wherever Henry saw him, laboring here. Bent over. But Emil was slinging powder when they met, Henry remembers, and running cash when he was killed. Emil's paintings and murals may have sold, but this converted attic must have been all he could afford.

Henry is still processing this when one of the works catches his breath. Smeared across a three-by-five-foot canvas are two gray-black figures, multi-armed and wretchedly twisted. The figures grapple and yet somehow face away from each other, and the violence of the image brings Henry back to Tiger's room. He remembers Lipz with her red keys, sawing lines into Tiger's scalp. And then Henry comes back to what he's looking at. And it hits him. "Jesus fuck," he says, "one of those is me."

Kerasha looks from the canvas to Henry and back again. Her face a question mark.

"Emil's girlfriend said he was being *run*," Henry says. "She talked about 'shadow twins,' and she said I was one of them."

Kerasha looks long at the canvas. "The one on the left has weird hands," she says quietly. Fingers twisted like corkscrews, and stretched long—Henry sees it now too. "But otherwise . . ." Kerasha shakes her head and turns back to Henry with an expression of something like pity. "I'm sorry," she says, "but they could be anyone."

Henry feels a weight in his chest. She doesn't get it. And once again within him is a surge of feeling—more than a feeling, it's an idea, an emanation, an expression of his whole mixed-up truth. He goes to a standing pipe. Leans against it, crosses his arms.

Kerasha, meanwhile, has crossed the room and opened a file cabinet. She didn't even hesitate, it seems to Henry, before yanking out Emil's drawers and rummaging through his things. This famous thief, the family *natural*, is at work here; and okay, fine, she's doing exactly what they came for. But he wishes she weren't chewing gum. Fucking disrespectful.

Henry turns away, goes to the opposite wall. Has himself a sulk. The feeling burns off when he discovers more shadow twins. Some of the renderings are mounted canvases, others just sketches laid flat on the floor. In the middle of everything is a stool. Henry wonders if this was part of Emil's process, to entomb himself in a project. To keep himself from seeing out.

Henry lowers himself onto the stool. He pictures Emil working here, leaning over the canvases. Using sticks of willow charcoal, shading and then scraping and smoothing with a scrap of moist cloth. Henry breathes in primer, waxes, ash. Sees wood shavings from hand-sharpened pencils. Henry puts down the charcoal stick and picks up a spray diffuser. Sniffs it, puts that down, too. And after a quick glance at Kerasha, who thankfully still has her back to him, he closes his eyes. Loses himself in the feeling that Emil is really here—on this stool, alive.

Sometime later, Henry opens his eyes and sees the sketchbook.

It's sandwiched between two bare canvases, so at first just a corner of the sketchbook protrudes. But Henry recognizes the cover, the distinct teal flower pattern. Emil carried these sketchbooks everywhere, used them for "mathing and trapping," as he called it: "mathing" problems of perspective; "trapping" faces and other details he spotted throughout the day. Henry picks up the sketchbook and, for a moment, just holds it. Back at the Thirsty Bear is a mural Emil won't complete; in this sketchbook are works he won't start. The unfinished life of an artist isn't in the bones or on the gravestone, Henry thinks, it's in these pages.

Henry opens the sketchbook, and the first face he sees is a woman's. A little boyish, the nose somehow off, a long forehead—but while the face could have been sketched by anyone, Emil's art is unmistakable in the hands. The fingers are bent, the wrists twisted, the effect entirely monstrous and, at the same time, affecting. What happened to those hands, who did this to her, what kind of person is she? But how can Henry guess? The face looks unfinished: tiny lines for eyes and ears, no mouth, nothing else. But is the *sketch* unfinished, Henry wonders, or was what's missing—the incompleteness— something Emil saw in the woman? Henry turns more pages.

New faces, many Henry recognizes: Jay Dyer and other Bushwick artists. Imani, the bartender at the Thirsty Bear, Imani again. Smelly Terri, and then a few people who spoke at that impromptu memorial service. Emil always sketched people he actually saw, Henry remembers: "Real places, real people—always start with what you see." Emil pushed Henry hard this way. Called Henry out—gently but clearly enough—for *trying* to be imaginative. "You can plan composition, but you can't plan weird. Just do what you see, and your hand will get weird on its own."

And Emil's hand does get weird. Here's the woman again, only now she casts a shadow, and three sketches later she's *all* shadow, and then there's a second shadow, and Henry knows this is him, knows this is what he was to Emil: not a person, not a substance, but an absence.

Henry's crying when he smells lavender and bubble gum. He

looks up. Kerasha is before him with another of Emil's sketchbooks, turning the pages. Behold the family natural, Henry thinks again, the consummate professional, always working, always finding. No, not *another*, he realizes—the same sketchbook. His own hands are empty. She swiped it, but when, how the fuck?

"He wrote the date on the first page," she says. "He started drawing this woman in April."

The same month he and Emil met. Henry thinks back to that first opening where they sniffed each other out, the criminal artist, the artist criminal. He feels heartsick, he is dizzy, and then a scrap of paper slips out of the sketchbook. It lazes toward the floor; Kerasha plucks it from the air. Studies it, her face thoughtful.

"The name of the killer?" Henry asks. LMAO, thank you, I'll be here all night.

But when Kerasha doesn't immediately answer, Henry—always the fool—begins to hope. "What is it?"

Kerasha turns over the scrap. Studies the back. "Cha-Ching Money Services, receipt for money order, eight hundred cash. Dated"—she turns it back over and reads off the date. "That mean anything to you?"

"That was his last run—the last one he finished. Also . . ." Thoughts turning, another alarm going off in his head. Cha-Ching is a splotch on New Utrecht Ave. Henry knows it well. It's a pain to get to, no good trains or buses, but Henry used to be a regular there, bringing bags of cash for his uncle. Now Henry sends his own runners there. "Fuck. That's where Emil was supposed to make his big drop."

"But he never got there, right?" Kerasha asks, following Henry out of the studio. "I mean, you found his body in that room."

"Fuck do I know." He shakes his head, going down the stairs. "He could have been brought there."

chapter 28

"You don't know someone," Uncle Shecky says, "till get your nose up their money." Henry is fourteen years old. "Where's it come from? Who's paying them to do what they do? To be who they are?" Henry is fifteen, he is eighteen. "Who's in control?" Henry is twenty-one. "You don't know anything until you smell that money."

Three days after the murder, dusk, Henry stands outside Cha-Ching Money Services. He takes in his city. The reek of diesel from the nearby Luk station. A blinking, hissing streetlight, the long shadow from the parked semi and its double trailer. He's safe out here, where he can't smell the money. Where he can't learn, from the records in this building, whether Emil completed his last run, like a good boy. Or whether—

He doesn't know how to follow his suspicion. Can't sense the shape of it. But it's there in him, just beneath the surface, and he's afraid of what'll happen if it manifests. Who his friend will turn out to be. So let's stay out here forever.

And then a dark sedan approaches, slows, and panther-creeps toward him. Is this badge 7229, he wonders, or is this a gun with a clipful of you-owe-me's from Red Dog? The latter Henry almost wouldn't mind. To die out here, not knowing the truth about his friend, but also not having given up on his search, is darkly seductive. Then the car passes and Henry lets out his breath.

Sorry, Emil. But you're gone, I'm here, and privacy is for the living.

He steps to the door.

Inside Cha-Ching the night clerk empties her waste bin into a larger garbage container. "Everything is recorded," she says. She hasn't looked up.

Henry looks around. He and the clerk are the only people in the room, but she's speaking as if they're in the middle of a conversation. The bluish lights and the muted goth-disco beat add to the sense that he's on ayahuasca.

"Cameras are everywhere," she says. "Your face is already on tape."

"This is a friendly visit," Henry says.

"The vault has a time lock," she says. "I couldn't open it if I wanted to."

At last, she looks up. He doesn't recognize her from his drop-off days. She's sixty-something, got a wattle on her neck. His heart goes out to her. Old lady on a night shift—she doesn't want to be here either.

Henry approaches, grabs a deposit ticket on his way. There's a cup of pens—he takes one, sketches Emil, and brings the sketch to the counter. "You seen this guy?"

The woman squints at the picture. There's a moment of unmistakable recognition—she looks up suddenly at Henry—but then she's shaking her head. "Sorry. Not ringing any bells."

"Emil wasn't a *bell*," Henry says. Heat from his fist moves up his arm. From his arm to his shoulder, from his neck to his heart. He catches himself. Lowers his voice and looks down. "He was my friend."

The woman's hand drops. "Was?" At last she looks Henry straight in the face. "What happened to him?"

They're in the break room, and on the far wall is a vault door. "I wasn't lying before," says the clerk. "There's a time lock." An ancient percolator shakes and then there's a pop. The woman, who's introduced herself as Priscilla, fills two mugs. "Irish or Mexican?"

"Both."

"You're a bold one." She tops off his mug with whiskey and tequila, hers with just whiskey. "Your friend was a sweetie," she says. "The winos, the heads, they all knew he was soft. They saw him coming up, and they'd all gather around. He had a dollar for everyone. Or a smile if he didn't have anything. Wasn't afraid to say hello or shake a hand. And some of those guys . . ." She shudders. "I wouldn't touch them. But your friend was kind."

"Did he ever come here with anyone?" Henry asks. "Maybe a woman with messed-up hands?"

Priscilla shakes her head. "Just himself." They're quiet together until at last the vault door lets out a thunk. Priscilla looks up at the clock. "Unlocked," she says. "We have a half hour."

A key, a combination, a press of her palm against a scanner. The door opens. Inside are files, loose and in boxes. She seems to know her way, so Henry lets her disappear into the stacks. His eyes wander. He scans the labels. AARON to ARONSON. KESSLER to KOSARIN. And how many of these are runners, Henry wonders, moving money for others, helping them stay hidden? And were any of *them* run so badly—that they got killed?

"Found him," Priscilla says. She opens a folder as she approaches and takes out a thin stack of transaction slips. "What date are you looking for?"

Henry takes out his wallet. "How much for the whole file?"

In the break room, Henry spreads out the transaction slips. Puts them in chronological order, then flips through them, creating in his mind a partial history. April 15: $1,500 went into a Chase account belonging to an imaginary nonprofit. On April 22, $500 became a money order payable to Furnace Maintenance LLC—a shell company Henry knows well, because he set it up himself. And everything flows as it should by the system Uncle Shecky designed years ago—until late

June. This was Emil's last completed run, and on this slip is a big red X.

Henry stares at the red slashes. Holds it up for the clerk: "What happened here?"

Priscilla walks over, squints as she puts on her glasses. She flips it over and looks at its backside. "The transfer got returned."

"What?"

"They sent the money back."

"Who the fuck returns money?"

She takes the slip into the vault. Comes back a minute later with a folded letter. "It went through, initially," she says. "So there weren't any problems with the routing number, or the account. Then a week or two go by, and we get this."

She hands him the letter. Henry reads: "We regret to inform you that your account with Capital One is closed effective immediately due to receipt of subpoena(s) and/or suspension warrant(s) from law enforcement."

Henry folds up the letter, nods his thanks to Priscilla, and calmly walks the fuck out. He can already hear his uncle's reaction: Come on, Hen—law enforcement? (Told you your boy wasn't cut out for this shit. An *artist*, for fuck's sake, what were you thinking? Of course he screwed something up. And the bank noticed, and they shut down our pass-through, but fuck the pass-through. Do you know who else noticed? The street. Bet your life on it, kid, the street smelled weakness—smelled the big money bag you put on him—and hunted him down.)

Uncle Shecky won't have to say these words. A look and everything will be understood between them. Just one look, and Henry will be nothing. He can't face his uncle like this. He thinks about his Cobra, and how easy it would be to take it in his hand, and put the barrel into his mouth.

But will he have to?

There's no dishonor in having a problem. No dishonor even in making a mistake, not if you own it. The way out, the way to survive this fucking summer, is to go to his uncle with everything worked out.

And I *will* work this out.

Only right now Henry doesn't want to be alone.

He's with Lipz in the basement, passing time like an old married couple—apart together. Lipz is on his bed, reading, while Henry sits at his draftsman's desk. There's a 2B pencil in his hand, but it hasn't moved in some time. Henry is in a memory.

A month earlier, Henry showed Emil a painting he'd made in high school. It was of Lipz, and one of his last completed works, the centerpiece of the portfolio that brought in those rejection letters. "Give it to me real," Henry said. "What do you think?" Emil looked long at the painting, brought his big nose right up against the canvas. Henry's breath was shallow, his ears warm, the taste of salt on his tongue. And even before Emil turned to him, Henry knew it was hopeless. He was a fixer's muscle, nothing more.

Emil's smile was unforgivably mischievous. "You've got a certain . . ." But then he must have caught something in Henry's expression, intuited that additional criticism, or even a tease, would be cruel. Emil's smile changed and he didn't complete the thought.

"Come on, man," Henry said. "Just fucking say it." If humiliation must come, it should decimate. "What do you think?"

Emil's answer was to turn Henry away from the three-year-old failure. To point at a space on the wall where nothing hung. "How about there?" Emil asked. "What are you going to make there?"

That night Emil retaught Henry brushwork from scratch. At one point Henry became so frustrated he snapped his stippler in half and stabbed the canvas. Put two fingers into the fabric, ripped it open, and then smashed up the frame. Emil waited for him to catch his breath and then said: "We're going to the Greif."

The Greif, a boutique gallery in downtown Brooklyn, was not open at eleven o'clock on a Monday night. But Emil had a friendly ex—an *old encounter*, he called her—who could let him in at any hour. She wanted to join them and chat; Emil told her to wait outside. To Henry he said, "I want you to feel something."

He led Henry to an abstract of reds and blues. "Be right back." Emil walked off, and Henry had a premonition that he was falling into a prank. That Emil wouldn't return, would leave him alone in this strange space. Then, one by one, the lights went out. Henry was gripped by excitement, by raw fear. Anything could happen here. He heard *ti-tap ti-tap*s, Emil's hard-soled shoes on the naked concrete. Then Emil was beside him. The smell of sweat and kush. The voice. "No color now. No composition, just texture," Emil said. "This is how I learned."

Emil took Henry's hand—no man except his father had ever touched Henry like this—and skimmed Henry's fingertips along the canvas. "He used a Filbert here," Emil said. "And over by the edge he used the liner brush. A stippler's somewhere in the middle—where is it—here."

Henry felt the different textures, guided by that rough hand.

He's still trembling when Lipz calls out to him from the bed. "Hey. I have something to tell you."

Henry turns, not enough so she can see his face.

"I told Red Dog what you said. How Tiger got cuffed, and the police they let him go. Like right away. And I told Red Dog you thought that was kinda sketch."

Henry turns a little more.

"Red Dog had a guy look into it."

Henry turns the rest of the way. "And?"

"And what do you think." She sniffs. "It doesn't look good." Lipz is one of the hardest people Henry knows, but even she has her moments. "I mean, Tiger's a bitch, but . . ." Another sniff. "You ever wish you didn't know something?"

chapter 29

The following morning, the close of breakfast. Second coffees are steaming on the table when Shecky puts before Kerasha the grand project that had him awake all night: countersurveillance.

Lacey Atkinson is Shecky's across-the-backyard neighbor. The Atkinson house has an extra story over Shecky's, and directly below the southeast window is a cable switchbox. A surveillance camera mounted on this switchbox will have a clear view of their shared yard. Swiveled 40 degrees clockwise, the camera will cover the alley between Shecky's house and the brownstone next door. Swiveled 120 degrees counterclockwise from the starting point, it will cover the street corner where his block adjoins Maria Hernandez Park. Now nudge it up, just a few degrees. The camera will cover a full quarter block of Hart Street between Bushwick Avenue and Evergreen.

"Do you understand what I'm saying?" Shecky leans in toward Kerasha and gives the table a hard tap. "We have a way of watching our watcher."

Shecky takes out and holds up, with some pride, his eraser-smeared diagrams. Last night he penciled angles and calculations on sketch paper he'd rescued from the recycling bin; traces of Henry's hesitant drawings can still be seen around Shecky's own work.

"Pretty clever, right?" he says, when it becomes clear that Kerasha won't say it herself. "Not bad for a law school dropout."

Kerasha meets his eyes, her expression somewhere between amused and annoyed, and Shecky fears he's being dismissed. Does she pick up on his fear? Pity him? Who can say. But whatever the reason, her little smile vanishes, and now she's giving his diagrams a slow second look.

A shrug. "Yeah, maybe." She reopens her book.

Shecky is stung but unfazed. His next step is to see his backyard neighbor. Lacey is a widow, barely seventy but already half past senile. Seventy is an age that would have terrified Shecky just five years ago. Now he accepts that it's part of his own continuum, if he's lucky, a few steps ahead but on the same path. You build your life and then watch it fall apart. That or you die early, and those are the options.

He chats up Lacey and gives a plausible pretext for putting up a ladder against the back of her house. "That damn switchbox," he says. "It's giving me all kinds of grief."

Lacey looks confused but says, "Do what you do."

Shecky tries not to notice that she's forgotten her pants again. Averting his eyes, relieved to be putting some distance between himself and those knobby legs, he prays his own dying will have more dignity. Hopes that whenever his reckoning comes, he won't be so completely alone.

As he reaches his back porch, his business cell vibrates, the screen flashing a *P*. He steps inside his house to take the call. "Cousin?" The conversation is quick and coded.

"I got the letter from Aunt Maria," Vasya says. Meaning: The Paradise Club acknowledges receipt of this month's transfers.

"And how's she holding up with the arthritis?" Shecky asks. Meaning: Did you get all the money?

"Just fine, thank you," Vasya says. "Truth is, we don't bother to count it, half the time."

He dropped the code—Shecky hears this like the roll of distant thunder.

"You always come through for us," Vasya continues.

Fucking reckless, Vasya. This isn't an improv show, just say the goddamn lines. Shecky wonders what's going on with Vasya, what he's not saying, but a phone call is no place for that kind of conversation. He hangs up feeling unsettled. The code is for *you*, Shecky wants to remind Vasya. I don't just value my partners—I actually care about them. Maybe more than I should. And this mounted camera—it's for you, too. My security enables yours—

And with this he reenters his house.

"Kerasha? Henry?" Gone, he already knows, recognizing the lonely-house smell. Feeling within himself the rise of that old black panic.

On his dining room table he unboxes and assembles the surveillance camera he picked up yesterday. A half hour passes in numb focus, and then the green "ready" light flashes twice. Needing only his ladder now, Shecky returns to the kitchen, opens the basement door, and is still holding the knob when he feels a powerful, rough hand close over his wrist.

"Not a sound," the man says. Shecky doesn't speak as he's turned around by the wrist. His back now to the staircase, he has an uncanny sense that he's already been pushed, is already falling backward. The man is a kid, though, maybe a few years older than Henry. Not quite as tall, but more muscular, and with wide, powerful shoulders. Red pants. A wifebeater, huge arms. His head is heavily bandaged, and Shecky remembers the old rule about wounded beasts.

"Not a sound," the man says again, now digging his nails into Shecky's wrist, "listen to her first."

"Oh, just fucking let him go," a familiar voice says. "What's he going to do, call the police?"

Shecky shouldn't have been surprised, but he is—he's horrified—that *her* turns out to be Henry's worst and craziest friend. And now her army boots are clumping across his linoleum floor. "Hi again," she says. "Remember me?"

Shecky feels something flare up inside him. "Of course I remember you." He could spit. "I fucking fed you. And if you're looking for Henry—"

"This isn't about Henry."

"—he's not—"

"This is about you."

Shecky concentrates on his breathing, the way he does on stage. His wrist hurts more, then it hurts less, as his hand pulses and grows numb. His frustration is beyond. He's in his own kitchen, he's near an old-fashioned landline phone—he's near his fucking knives—but he can't move an inch. Two against one might as well be a million against one. The only question is how much they'd hurt him before he'd hit the floor for the last time.

"Actually . . ." Lipz looks half amused and half sad as she studies his face. "This isn't about you either. This is about two hundred and fifty thousand things that aren't you."

At last the big guy lets go.

Shecky massages his wrist. It hurts more as the feeling comes back. He thinks, absurdly, about his ledger, about whether he'll be able to code and log new entries.

"Look at me," Lipz says. "Listen to me. Henry's my boy. I love him, and I'll love him till I have to kill him. And I even love *you*, in a fucked-up kind of way. That breakfast here. That meant a lot to me. Especially because I know damn well you don't want me near your fucking house." Shecky almost protests, but he sees the I-fucking-dare-you look in her eyes. "I'm saying love," she continues. "You're hearing love. I'm *feeling* love. But love wouldn't stop me, wouldn't slow me down, if I needed to cut you to get my money back. Or cut Henry. Here's how it works."

She hops on the kitchen counter, her army boots banging against the cabinet.

"The lost money—Red Dog says it's on me. He says I brought you in, I vouched for you, I put my name on you guys."

Shecky feels a tightness in his chest. "*You* brought us Red Dog?" He'd assumed Henry's connect was someone sane and responsible.

Someone who didn't have a murder on their rap sheet. "Fucking Henry—"

"I know, right? Because where's *my* cut?" Lipz kicks cabinets in a marching rhythm. "There's no justice in Brooklyn. Bag's gone missing. And I didn't touch it, but my name's on it. So what do you think? Am I going to let that go?"

Shecky watches her boots scuff the doors of his kitchen cabinets. Can't take it. "That's all between you and Red Dog," he blurts out. "I can't help you. You need to leave."

And now she leaps off the counter. And she's holding, Shecky notices too late, one of the same steak knives he took stock of just moments ago. She brings the knife close to his nose. "Red Dog trusted you with his money. You were supposed to clean it. You fucking lost it. Red Dog says it's on me? Fuck no, I'm putting it on you. I . . ." She turns suddenly, throws the knife into the sink, and puts her hands to her head. "Fuck! You think I *like* this?"

He backs away.

"My name is all I got," she says, catching her breath. "And there's nothing I wouldn't do to you—to Henry—to get my name back." She comes closer, so close he can feel her breath on him. "I know you understand me."

"I can't get your boss his money," he says, holding himself back with great effort, "I can't *do my business* with you up in my face like this."

She studies him and he knows she will cut him. But then she just nods to the big guy, and at last both of them are out the door.

Shecky Keenan is alone in his kitchen, shaking. And then all at once the shaking is over and he's up and he's holding his diagrams. The security camera is more than a clever idea, it's a necessity—he can't have gangsters surprising him in his own kitchen. This is his *home*, the people he loves live here. He will protect it.

Diagrams into pocket, ladder to the backyard. He raises the ladder, leans it against Lacey's house—carefully, carefully—so as not to leave marks on Lacey's yellow paint. Do what you do, he tells himself, his bad ankles screaming as he ascends. The switchbox is directly above him now; he should have positioned the ladder a foot farther to the right. Never mind, he'll reach above, he'll grope. He unclips the camera from his belt. A few screws, a double-sided adhesive pad, and it's ready to be mounted.

But when Shecky reaches over to press the camera against the switchbox's flat top, his hand brushes up against a solid object. Something is already on the switchbox. Groping, he feels the sticky crumble of some animal in decay. Another shot of adrenaline hits him when he feels a metal bowl flanked by small glass panels. He can't detach it. Can't figure out what it is.

Shecky descends (damn the ankles), shifts the ladder, climbs back up (now the left knee is screaming), and then he sees it, compact and metal and blinking. It's a pole camera, already installed just where he told Kerasha it should be. Only it's not here to watch over the family. It's looking down on it.

A police camera.

They got here first, they picked his exact spot, and Jesus knows how long this blue eye has been facing his home. What has it seen? Henry with his girls, Shecky moving files in his office, Kerasha slipping in and out at odd hours. It's horrifying, what he doesn't know, the evidence they could already have. He feels utterly defeated.

And yet there's also a kind of validation in this. He worked through the night guesstimating his property lines, considering every angle for the camera, practical or impractical, every possible height for mounting. He sketched until his forearms were gray with smeared graphite, and though this morning Kerasha doubted him ("yeah, maybe"), and though in truth he'd doubted himself, his math was right after all.

Thump.

The unexpected pleasure he's taking in his own defeat is kicked aside as his ladder inches across the ground, then sways. *Thump.* Shecky grips the switchbox. The ladder begins to fall away from the house. He fumbles at it with his feet, trying to kick it back into place. *Thump.*

"Hey there," she says. *Thump.* "Hey again."

Shecky hugs the switchbox with both arms. Tries to use his feet to bring the ladder back against the house.

Thump. The ladder swings to the side this time, and while Shecky's feet become tangled in the second-to-topmost rung, he manages to grab a drainpipe with his left hand. Immediately he feels it bend under his weight.

Thump. The ladder bounces against Lacey's painted wall, scratching a wide, dirty rust mark.

Shecky catches another corner with both hands. Half hanging at an odd angle, he's looking down, and Lipz is smiling up at him. Eyes red, cheeks wet. There's no muscleman this time. Shecky understands, fully now, that she's the one to fear.

"Hi there," she says, bringing her heavy army boot against the bottom rung. "Just wanted to remind you I'm serious."

She stomps—

Thump.

Shecky tries to answer but manages only a noise. The ladder sways, tilts. Shecky grips Lacey's window ledge, grabs the bracket of a window AC unit. Feels it slide out of position.

"Just don't forget me," she says, smiling and crying up at him, stomping and kicking his ladder again and again. *Thump, thump, thump.* "Don't forget my name."

Shecky hooks his arm over one of the AC brackets, wraps his foot around the side rail of the ladder, and feels himself swaying toward and then away from the house. He's still hanging against the house when he realizes Lipz has walked off. He's been dismissed, he supposes, and is at liberty to drop at his leisure. His heart racing, he considers his peril, his powerlessness, and most of all his humiliation before the police, who must have been watching this whole time.

chapter 30

The day Emil Scott goes missing, Zera returns to the alley on Bond Street between Livingston and Schermerhorn. She's done this walk before, she's been doing it all afternoon; and yes, she's doing it again now.

She squeezes between the brown brick wall and the place where the van was parked when he left the alley. She holds her tracking phone and matches, as closely as she can, the footsteps of her missing informant. Out of the alley. Left on Bond Street, right on Schermerhorn, she walks down the steps to the subway platform. Her badge in its leather case hangs from the chain around her neck. Her service gun is strapped against her hip. Also strapped: her Taser. Eyes are on her, she feels them, as she waits on the platform. At last the train. She boards. Her hands disappear under her crossed arms. She looks left to right to left again, and again, without letting her eyes find anyone. Or be found.

Aboveground, she reactivates her tracking phone and pulls up her informant's movement history from the morning. She follows the red dot—where it *was*, not where it *is*—past a Lebanese restaurant, past a pawnshop. Past a narrow alley between two brownstones.

No.

She backsteps.

She goes into the alley and here are the dumpsters and garbage cans she already searched this afternoon. She pictures her informant as she saw him at the van. As she saw him at that picnic bench, where she met him back in the spring. And then she pictures him here. She sees him picking up a bag of money. She sees him, in another scenario, arriving here but then changing course. Sensing that something wasn't right. Nothing unusual here, jobs get messy all the time, he's not her first informant. But he is, she acknowledges, her first to disappear.

Emil Scott has always been different, she reflects. Part of every informant's job when they come with the money bag to the police is to brief her and Kurt on every detail—"however insignificant," Zera tells them—while the officers count and take pictures of the cash. Emil's accounts have always been extraordinary, such a flood of odd details. Zera remembers how, despite herself, she came to marvel at his visual memory. And eventually to share in his excitement about the strange things he saw, and to look forward to the sketches he brought.

Which, of course, she has always carefully photographed and vouchered.

Resuming her walk, she takes out her phone. Pulls up pictures of his sketches: a battered shoebox beneath a car, a cat beside the shoebox, one eye open. A pilly sweater, one arm still crossed over a pile of cash. Zera's other informants seem determined to see little and remember less, erasing the world as they move through it. Whereas Emil, in his own way—in *her* way, really—keeps his lights on.

But are his on now?

Zera is on Myrtle Avenue, about a quarter block from where it hits Stockholm Street. She has stopped walking. She taps and taps at her tracking phone, zooming in and out, adjusting the settings. At last she reaches the final point of precision. The red dot on the screen covers thirty feet in every direction from where she stands now. On the ground this is not a vast area. The flat ground, however, is not the only space Zera must reckon with. The red dot is not a circle, she was trained to remember, but a pillar, and extending up, in this instance, to the roofs of at least three four-story buildings. Dropping below-ground into basements, sewers, cable lines, and gas tunnels. Thirty feet, in three dimensions, might as well be an ocean, and the lost tracking phone is not much bigger than a pair of credit cards, one stacked on top of the other.

Credit cards. *Money.*

"Money." She's remembering herself in the precinct training room, standing at the whiteboard. Talking to a couple dozen uniformed police officers, half of them asleep, about the Human Trafficking Task Force. "If we can catch the moneymen," she told them, "they can take us to the monsters."

And if we can get them, Zera feels rather than hears these last words, then maybe it wasn't for nothing. Katja, Sveta . . . maybe the next girl will be okay. Maybe you can be, too.

Her phone buzzes, a call from her supervisor. He'll want her back at the precinct, she knows, but she's not ready to give up just yet. Her informant, her initiative, her responsibility. She silences her phone.

Eyes moving: the street, the sidewalk, the curb. A manhole, a McDonald's cup, other loose cups, paper bags, plastic bags. A sub-way grate. A storm drain. Rubble and loose chunks of concrete at a collapsed stretch of the curb. The informant's tracking phone can be anywhere. So she looks everywhere, picking, poking, digging. Using and wearing out three pairs of rubber gloves. And then the sky turns orange, and she at last accepts an unacceptable fact. The phone was here and now it isn't. She takes off her gloves. Turns a slow circle.

Passersby, snippets of conversation, storefronts, placards, and advertisements—not English, not any of the half-dozen languages she picked up at the Paradise House—not *human*, it seems to her. She is a speck windblown toward the vanishing point. She is, unexpect-edly, back at Golubovci airport.

She was nineteen years old (maybe), at last on her way out of Montenegro, and she was dazzled almost to the point of blindness. The candy racks, the cigarette packs, the neon lights outside the café and the duty-free shop, the harsh overhead lights of the airport itself.

And then there was the noise from the intercom, and the gate-check staff shouting instructions at the passengers, the passengers shouting back—strangers yelling at strangers, families cursing among themselves.

"This must be so exciting for you!" The nonprofit that brought Zera to the United States had sent, to be her shepherd, an aggressively chipper young woman. Zera can no longer remember her name. She can, however, recall the specific feeling she had at that noisy airport. She did not feel saved. What she felt was annihilation. Away, at last, from the Paradise House, she was no one's captive, no one's warm body. Away, at last—she was no one at all. And for her this absence was, in its own surprising way, a threat, and it was unlike anything she'd faced in the Paradise House.

Now she stands on Myrtle Avenue near Stockholm Street. There's a weight on her hip that represents her power to kill. There's a badge pinned to her chest that announces her power to cage. And neither can alter a bitter truth. Through her whole life outside the Paradise House, she's looked for a way to undo what had happened within it. Emil was her chance.

A train rumbles beneath her feet. The informant's tracking phone could be down on those tracks, right next to his body.

She thinks back on how she managed Emil, and compares this with how the men at the Paradise House managed *her*. And this much she has to say for those well-dressed men: they'd never have let her get killed.

She was worth too much to them.

chapter 31

Kerry is nine years old, and she crawls down the Tower C fire escape. It's Christmas Eve. It's not a particularly cold winter, has hardly been Christmassy at all, but that afternoon it rained, and then the damp abruptly froze over. There's an ice slick over the corrugated metal. Every step is unsteady, every inch a pop or a crunch. She moves slowly. Stops when she comes to laughter. On the other side of a frosted window, beyond the spider plant and succulents and cactus that line the windowsill, a family exchanges gifts. Two ties for the daddy. A small silver box for the mommy—Kerasha can't make out what's inside. And for the kids, the boxes are stacked high and deep, green ribbons for the older girl, red for the toddler. Hours pass. The family is gone. Shivering, Kerasha pries open the latch with a loose key she'd found a few days ago. She moves aside the spider plant and succulents and cactus and climbs inside. She goes straight to the gifts the girls left behind. Her hands shiver still as she takes the one that made her heart ache, a beautiful illustrated *His Dark Materials* boxed set. One touch and a warmth spreads through her hands and then all over her body. *I see*, she thinks, *I want, I take, I have.* And so on her ninth Christmas she attains something Mama never will, knowledge that life does not exist only to grind you down. It's there to be taken.

And why am I remembering this now, she asks herself, why here? For that Christmas has bobbed up from deep memory at the residence of her psychiatrist. Which, by the way, she's in the process of burglarizing.

The runner's body is four days cold.

The six-story condo development on Parkside is new and understated, with tan bricks and tall windows. A doorman sits out front, a retired blue, Kerasha can tell. He has the girth, the drinker's eyes, the narrow and truncated forehead. She catches all this on a walk-by. Sees a large coffee cup in front of him, another in the overstuffed trash can. He'll have to pee, she thinks. She could just wait him out, there's obviously no backup. But there's a camera right outside the main entrance. She spots it on her second walk-by, positioned low and center, where the residents can see it. *They're* who it's there for, she realizes. The camera is the same as the potted ficus and the classic movie posters. It's background. It's comfort.

Still, a camera is a camera, and for Kerasha Brown, there are always better options.

At a bodega a few blocks away she buys a pack of cigarettes, though she doesn't smoke, and a candy bar, not her brand. Better to leave false leads, Kerasha taught herself long ago, than none at all; the only safe blue is the one who thinks he's onto something.

Alongside Dr. Xu's apartment complex on its north side is a street lined with gleaming new streetlights. Skinny Kerasha would have shimmied up one of these. Waited for a lull in foot and street traffic, and then leapt from the crossbar to one of the second-floor balconies. Skinny Kerasha is not here tonight. Too tired for that Catwoman shit, Kerasha has hardly slept since Henry's runner turned up dead. It's a lazy, humid afternoon, and she feels old.

When did this happen to me?

A question Mama used to ask when she was on one of her comedowns.

Fuck. These are the worst moments in life. Worse than the arrest, worse than the two days she spent in solitary after the spork fight. She can hear the groans of her spirit friends Whitman and Saint Augustine, but fuck *them*, dead white assholes. The worst moments are recognition.

Having ruled out the north side of the apartment complex, Kerasha walks along a quiet residential block. Opposite the new apartment Dr. Xu lives in is old Brooklyn: two- and three-family housing, blue and yellow paint, stained and crumbling, probably bought a generation ago for fifty thousand and now each worth half a million. No purchase here for a patient spider; just witnesses. She moves on. At the corner two stroller moms catch up while their dogs, strapped to the carriages, snap at each other. The moms hating each other, Kerasha guesses, just as much. Passing them, she unsnaps the leashes.

Good luck, guys.

Amid the snarls and cries of the dogfight, Kerasha enters Dr. Xu's complex through the service entrance. No camera here, of course. The door is already wedged open with a loose block of wood, and Kerasha finds herself steps behind two deliverymen hauling a couch. Both of them wearing back-support belts; both of them black, and she wonders if the three of them are the only ones in the building. Wonders why she bothered casing the front door when there was a colored entrance. Skinny Kerasha would have come straight here.

You're rusty, girl.

Inside at last. The place is hers. She leaves a wrapper and a cigarette and hits the stairs.

On the floor outside room 8A is a bouquet of flowers in a glass vase stained purple. She picks it up, a perfect cover story should she run into someone: Who, sweet innocent me? I'm just the delivery girl.

She finds Dr. Xu's apartment by following the stink of condescension. And by knowing the apartment number, which she got from a piece of personal mail she found in his office. The vase she sets outside a neighbor's door, along with another wrapper and another cigarette.

Shake it, girl, skinny Kerasha says. Here's the one place you can't drag ass.

There are two locks, one of them a dead bolt, neither taking more than a minute to open. Inside, door closed, her heart races. Her fingertips tingle. What Mama felt, she supposes, the moment she pushed the plunger. A foretaste of the rush; delicious anticipation.

Easy, K. Skin warm, breath shallow, she realizes she's become aroused. Desire? Huh. She wonders what she'll do with it.

A chirp.

Really, Dr. Xu, a fucking alarm?

She glides across the dining room, the eight-seat table shimmering in the near dark. *He polishes*, she thinks. Of course he does.

Already her hands on it: the alarm is an NERS-F154, newer, prettier than the F150, but really the same toy she mastered when she was fourteen. She pulls down the front flap. Uses a safety pin to release the plastic panel. It *wants* to be deactivated, she thinks, all the NERS models are the same. Uses the safety pin again on the reset switch. The panel snaps back into place, ditto the front panel, and boom, the alarm is silent. Flashes green, reads ARMED AND READY! She gives the alarm a pat. Moves on.

The apartment is tasteful, modern, and bland. She is somehow both unsurprised and disappointed. These are the private quarters of Andrew Xu, distinguished doctor of mind rape. Where are the chains? The strange smells, the jarred fetuses—the child in the leather mask, chained to the oven—where the fuck is she?

The reality is Dr. Xu lives in an Ikea showroom. Lives amid birch and other cream-colored woods. Framed black-and-white photographs, mostly trains or train stations. And then she spots his bookshelves—flypaper to Kerasha. The top shelves are all paperback thrillers: with creased spines, these are the books he actually read. The next two shelves are pristine hardcovers, mostly nonfiction. The trophy-wife books, she thinks, what you buy to be seen with. The bottom shelves, about knee- and then ankle-high, are big volumes, art books that someone, she decides, regifted to him. Textbooks from med school, must be twenty years out of date. But also on this shelf is a slender volume she immediately recognizes, *An Unquiet Mind*. She stole this same book from Human Relations on Flushing Avenue just days ago. Unsettled, she moves to the bathroom.

Above the sink is a mounted toothbrush holder, identical to the one in the upstairs bathroom of her uncle's house. The lonesome toothbrush here is unexpectedly affecting. Even she, a spider defined by her solitude, has someone to share a bathroom with. A life for Dr. Xu comes into view. Quiet mornings, blue nights. Alone, except at his office. Alone, except when a patient sits across from him, sharing pain over a bowl of marbles.

Kerasha is uneasy and confused. This isn't why she came here. But now into his medicine cabinet.

Nail clippers. Sleeping pills and multivitamins. Baking soda toothpaste. Shaving cream for sensitive skin, contact lens solution for sensitive eyes. Every loose object she rotates 180 degrees. He will come home to this, his privacy fingered. What he's tried with her, she's doing to him.

In the kitchen walk-in pantry she finds cases of wine stacked four high. Still sealed, she notices. Dusty. Printed labels on the water-stained cardboard: MERLOT OF THE MONTH CLUB. The labels are addressed to Dr. and Mrs. Andrew Xu.

Unhappy girl, Kerasha thinks, but at least you got away. Thank your stars, Mrs. No Longer Xu. There's no court order dragging *you* back.

Again unease, again confusion. This is not what she came for, but already her hands are at work, opening drawers. Turning forks upside down, swapping teaspoons and tablespoons. She loosens the paper towel roll and rigs it to fall when he touches it. Then she moves to the bedroom.

On the nightstand is another book, Jhumpa Lahiri, and she hates that Dr. Xu has turned out to be a genuine reader. She moves his bookmark back several pages. Petty, she knows, but there's an exquisite frisson just the same—the tiny shiver moves all the way through her.

Outside, curbside, she wonders what happened, why it feels like she was the one who got dirtied. Wonders, also, why she didn't go further. She could go back and unscrew a lightbulb. Breathe on his mirror. Trace the seams of his pillow with her fingertips, with her lips.

But she won't go back, she promises herself. And she won't ever visit when he's inside.

part seven

the snitch in effigy

chapter 32

There's no good seating at Catania Bakery on Harman Street, so Henry and Starr take their pastry bag curbside. Starr opens the bag, gets to work, and speaks through mouthfuls of food.

"Everything's awful," Starr says, her face flushed. "I can't even describe . . ." But she does describe, in great detail, the expensive dying of her cat Banana. The lump on her neck, the credit card Starr used to cover the bill. The new lump found on her "belly-welly," her fur getting oily. Banana too sick to lick herself clean.

Henry finds this more than a little disgusting. He puts down his coffee.

"So then Dr. Hirsh is like, 'We have to think about what's best for Banana.' And I'm like, What the hell does that mean? But I know."

Henry nods. Banana is important to Starr, Starr is important to him, so this is just one of those moments when he has to nod and say he's sorry.

"But it's worse," she says. "So finally, I'm like, okay. I'll do it." Starr blows her nose into her napkin. "And then it's over, and I'm like a wreck. And I'm on my way out of the clinic, and the witch at the front desk"—another nose blow—"she's like, excuse me, Ms. Richardson? And I thought she was going to say how sorry she was, and I was already opening up my arms to take a hug. Because I needed it. But she gives me a bill!"

And so Henry learns that the cost of feline euthanasia, at least at Camp Happy Paws, is eighty-five dollars. "That's awful," he says. He waits a respectful moment and then says, "Your text said something about—"

"So I call my sister," Starr says, having blown her nose over Henry's question. "And she's a total bitch. And I ask for some money, and she's like, 'Wait, you paid? You could've gotten money for this. Fucking post it on Craigslist. *Somebody* would pay to kill a cat.'"

Henry slides closer to Starr. He rubs her back, waiting for her to stop crying. Noting, now that he's close to her, that she is wearing a black bra under her white shirt. His body tells him this is a very good combination for her. His body asks him if, under different circumstances, he might want to complicate their friendship. He tells his body to shut the fuck up. She's in pain, stupid. Just be there for her.

His phone buzzes. His hand goes for it, but he fights the impulse. Allows his friend to have her cry. Sometime later, Starr is coming back to herself again, and she manages a sly smile. "So you know how you asked me to look out for a woman with weird hands?"

Henry sits up straight. "You found her?"

"She kind of fell into my lap." She takes out her phone. "So the on-duty sergeant sends me out on a doughnut run. And I get the doughnuts, and I'm heading to the conference room. And on my way, I pass this office. And boom—she's in there."

"This is for real?"

"Check it out." She holds up her phone for Henry. On-screen: a voice recorder app.

"You didn't."

"I totally did! Listen."

Henry tries.

But apparently the phone mic is a joke, and the noise from Harman Street is a motherfucker. So they go back into Catania Bakery, go past the counters, the ovens, and a baker who gives Henry a thumbs-up. Now he and Starr are alone together in the bathroom. Door closed, knob lock engaged—black bra, white shirt—but here's Starr, handing over the phone. Then her smile breaks open—she's obviously proud of herself—and she reaches over and taps the phone.

Silence.

"Shoot," Starr says. "I think I . . . I thought . . ."

"It's okay," Henry says. He would forgive much more, being this close to her, and his heart is racing and sinking at the same time. "What did you hear?"

Starr grumbles at her phone as she puts it back into her pocket. "Not a lot, but the cop with the hands is Officer Montenegro. I looked her up—she's a field intelligence officer cross-designated to work in the Human Trafficking Task Force."

"English, please."

"She reads all the reports that come through the precinct. She's supposed to spot trends and make connections."

Montenegro—Henry kicks the name around in his head. Nada. "She wasn't on Emil's incident report."

"I know, I double-checked that too," Starr says, taking out her phone again just to scowl at it.

"So how's she connected?"

"The short answer is, I don't know. But when I passed by, she was talking with this detective. And I heard her say the name Emil Scott, and I was like, whuuuuuh?"

Someone walks past the bathroom, pushing something on squeaky wheels. They wait for the squeaker to pass, then Henry says, "These fucking ranks. Is the detective more or less scary than a field intelligence officer?"

"Well, she scares *me* more," Starr says, "but he's homicide. Total hotshot. That's the first thing I wanted to tell you. I don't remember the guy's name, but he's not usually at the station."

Henry has mixed feelings about this. He remembers what his uncle said, about how with a mugging everyone gives up, but an intentional murder means an investigation. So while this homicide detective is bad for the family, could he maybe somehow be good for Emil?

"Any chance the homicide guy was there about a different case?"

"Possible. The detective could've been there for more than one reason. But the name I heard was Emil Scott." Okay, very bad for the family—Henry accepts this now. The cops are paying more attention.

"And then I heard this other name," Starr says, "a woman's name. Something like Veh—" A banging at the bathroom door. When it stops, Starr finishes her thought in a whisper: "Seh-something. I don't remember."

"Could that be the cop with the hands?"

Starr shakes her head. "*Her* first name is Zera—seriously, that's a name. But Geh was another victim."

Another round of banging. From outside: "Get out of there!"

Henry bangs back on the door. "Just a fucking minute!" With more civility, to Starr: "A victim of what?"

"I couldn't hear everything," Starr says. "But one thing Montenegro said—"

Outside: "Get the fuck out of there!"

"—another homicide, another blunt instrument to the back of the head."

chapter 33

"A partner is coming," Uncle Shecky says in the dining room that afternoon.

Kerasha looks up from the padlock. Deceptively simple-looking, the Konnekt 1501: chrome plating, Russia-red spin dial, Cyrillic characters stamped on the back. A knockoff of the Master Lock 1500D, the Konnekt 1501 is made in Irkutsk and should be a joke. And yet six years ago Kerasha fell to the Konnekt 1501—locked in a utility closet, challenged and flustered and ultimately defeated by this silly twist of metal—and that was when they finally caught her. This is the Dr. Xu of padlocks, she decides: it defeats you not by cunning, but by its faults.

Uncle Shecky is chewing pink bubble gum. A piece from her own pack, by the look and smell of it. He probably grabbed the gum from nerves, didn't even realize he was doing it. May not be totally aware it's in his mouth now. Poor Uncle Shecky. This partner must be important. She asks if he wants her to leave.

"What? Leave? No. Kerasha, this is your home."

He's asked her to leave before, but she says nothing and waits for him to continue. "Vasya's an old, old friend." He nods as though someone else is speaking, and his response to himself is agitated agreement. "Okay, he's not a saint. And the Paradise Club—as I understand it—it's a kind of gentlemen's club. I don't know, I've never gone inside." He shudders. Probably did go there at least once. "But Vasya's among the trusted. And when I told him about the watchman, he was as concerned as if it were his own family getting peeped. He actually said that, just like his own family. He said he'd take care of everything. And listen, Kerasha, about that watchman . . ." His fingers, Kerasha notices, are dancing over each other. There's a tremor in his voice, a shamed look-away every few seconds.

He wants so badly to be the one protecting us, Kerasha thinks. But now he's asking for my help with something. Poor, sweet Uncle Shecky. He may be the least underworldly underworlder she's ever met. So what does he want? A break-in, she suspects. A grab. A listen.

"Vasya's among the trusted," Uncle Shecky repeats. "He's a partner with partners of his own, and he's trying to get help for us. He doesn't deserve to come under this *thing*." Uncle Shecky points at the window, and indicating the pole cam mounted atop the cable switchbox, he delivers a line that could come from Tennyson: "This is the eye that never closes."

"And you want me to close it."

"I want you *safe*," he says, just as he collapses into a chair. He rubs his chin with the backs of his hands, left and then right. "Everything I do comes from that."

Kerasha presses her hook pick against the Konnekt and pulls on the ring. The padlock doesn't give. Konnekt 2, Kerasha 0. She gets to her feet.

"I'll pluck the eye for you, Uncle Shecky."

"Jesus fuck, I got you so twisted up in this," he says. "Your poor mother, what would she say?"

Got my meds? Unfunny, but Kerasha is in no position to turn away defense mechanisms. When memory tosses your devil back at you, a bitter smile can be your only friend. She pictures Mama's smile, that forced, side-cracked grin she adopted after Kerasha became her supplier. The half-hopeful, half-shamed look she had when Kerasha walked in the door. Kerasha took to leaving Mama's daily bag in a sugar bowl on the kitchen table, slipping in and out just to avoid that look.

"I swore to her grave I'd look after you," Uncle Shecky says. "And now look what I'm doing. Sending you out into—wait a sec. Speaking of danger."

Kerasha stops at the doorway.

"Henry's crazy friend, the one who was here the other morning. She came back."

Kerasha nods, having already smelled Lipz's cigarette fug in the kitchen. Having seen the boot prints on the floor. She'd been wondering when Uncle Shecky was going to fill her in.

"I haven't said anything to Henry yet," Uncle Shecky says. "Haven't decided what to do about her. She wants Red Dog's money, and that's a fair ask. But she's also a legitimate psychopath." Uncle Shecky gets up, goes to the window. "Watch out for her."

Kerasha gets her backpack and heads out. She walks around the block and buys a new pack of bubble gum. Continues through a rubble lot, doubles back across Lacey Atkinson's yard, and spots the old lady through a window. Kerasha pops a disappointed bubble. She had hoped to slip into the house. Wanted this to be an easy job.

Can't go through, skinny Kerasha coaches her, gotta go over.

She comes to the alley where the cats fuck. The fire escape hangs off yellow-splashed bricks. She moves a battered folding chair beneath it, climbs up, and grips the coarse, rusty metal. Pull-ups used to be like breaths. Now she strains, grunts, and all but herniates herself before she can kick the chair away. Hurt but alive, she's on the first landing. Catching her breath. Looking down at the chair as ugly memories come at her.

In her years at Franklin there were four suicides. Two were inmates on kitchen duty. Each shotgunned a half bottle of lye, one just a week after the other. The second was an "apparent copycat suicide," the warden explained over the intercom. Kerasha hated this, found it offensive. If the *method* of self-destruction was sometimes borrowed, the *act* was always personal. Ask any junkie. Ask her daughter.

The third suicide slit her wrists with glass.

"Where'd she get the glass?" everyone wanted to know, as though the death were beside the point.

Kerasha is remembering the final suicide as she slips through an open window. Moves through a grimy apartment and then enters a cigarette-butt-littered hall. Gets into a utility closet, climbs a ladder to the roof. The final suicide took place in Franklin's movie room. The lights weren't even dimmed for the movies—for the "inmates' own safety," as the warden liked to remind them—but it wasn't until the credits were rolling that someone noticed. In the back of the room, while everyone else had been watching *Pitch Perfect 2*, one of the inmates had managed to hang herself in perfect silence. Kerasha remembers how she marveled at the chair on the floor, that it had landed noiselessly on a towel. What tradecraft.

From the roof she looks down and sees a grill, wooden lawn furniture, an empty hammock lazing in the breeze. Sees irregular potato-garden rows, and in them the blue rubber ball she placed there herself before heading up. Her marker.

She positions herself so that the blue ball is directly below her line of sight. Beneath her now, though obscured by a drainpipe, is the pole camera. She opens her backpack and takes out a coil of rope and loops it around and around the TV satellite dish. She descends. At her feet now is a slender concrete ledge splattered with bird shit. A few inches beneath it: a steel box with a glass half-dome. This is it, the will, the force, to do her family harm.

Well *I* have a will, little box. *I* am a force. Dr. Xu, if you're watching from inside my head, please take out that silver pen. Scribble this, Dr. Xu: this recalcitrant patient has fate caught in her web.

From the back pocket of her jeans she takes out a garbage bag with drawstrings. She nets the pole cam. Pulls the drawstrings taut, and just like that, she's blinded the watcher.

How do you like that, little box? World gone dark—welcome to my Brooklyn.

Out with the power socket wrench, out with the wire cutters. The pole cam, detached from the switchbox, looks like a dead crab, the kind Mama's last and worst man used to eat at their kitchen table. Cracking the legs with his fingers, spitting bits of shell on the floor.

Kerasha climbs down. Reaches ground level, where, as she passes through the alley, a scent brings her all the way back. It's acrid and chemical and sweet. It's nutmeg and it's vinegar, and it's that inimitable, uncategorizable something extra—she turns slowly, unable not to, but already knows what she'll see.

This is the vinegar-and-mud smell of shit-grade heroin.

The smell of her childhood, and Mama, whom she half expects to see.

Only Kerasha's spider eyes take in no one and nobody. She is alone in this alley.

But the smell must come from *somewhere*—currents and breezes, of course that's the explanation. And yet to Kerasha at this moment, the smell seems to emanate from the dark material of the universe itself. Nowhere, everywhere, it's inside and out. She doesn't need Dr. Xu to explain this.

It's in *her*.

She sprints from the alley, skinny Kerry coaching her: Eyes on your feet, big strides, you're riding through a tunnel, darkness all around, eyes on your feet, eyes on your feet . . .

But when her concentration slips, she catches sight of a basement window. And though the angle is bad, the glass smeared and grass-covered, somehow, through a slant of an angle of a crack, she sees her.

A girl, couldn't be more than twelve. Cross-legged on the floor. Putting a needle in her arm. And this girl Kerasha sees through the impossible slant of the angle of the crack—she looks up at just that moment. And when she meets Kerasha's gaze, she pushes in the plunger, and it's almost a physical blow to Kerasha, the face of this girl.

Little Kerry, I know you.

chapter 34

Crazy texts come that day, and the first are from Lipz. Go hardware, she writes. Get fire exting.

WTF? he writes back. Uncertain whether this is code or a relapse. She's been off the hard stuff for years, but this is cray-cray, even by Lipz standards.

Red Dog rising, she writes. Don't die.

At first Henry is just annoyed: Lipz is no stranger to the panic button. Then she in-boxes him a picture of a burning mattress.

Going dark now, she writes. Love you.

Henry's chest contracts. Red Dog rising? *Love you*? He's still feeling out a response when his other phones—the runner phones—all start screaming. Calls, texts, photos, videos, variations on a common theme: scorched car. Garbage can ablaze. Crack house blackened.

What this shit? one of his runners writes. You know?

Henry re-texts this exact message, using a fresh burner, to the number from the card Kerasha found on Emil's door. The message goes through, but 646-555-0144, whoever it is, never responds.

Henry climbs through the attic skylight of his uncle's house and surveys Brooklyn from the roof. Gray sky over Bushwick, here and there a spot of fire. *Draw this*, his inner Emil tells him. His phone vibrates, a new image has arrived: a shopping cart—burning, of course—a big woman stands beside it. Her dead-eyed look brings Henry back. He is seven and before him is Mom's casket. He is ten and he's taken the bus to Dad's psych ward for his weekly visit, and the orderly, without looking up from her phone, says Dad "went" two days prior and is already at the funeral home, "waiting for whatever." This dead-eyed woman and her burning shopping cart—Smelly Terri, Henry recognizes her now—has the look of someone from whom all has been taken. Draw her, Emil says. These are your people.

Henry climbs down. Hasn't found a pencil when a voice from behind says, "Go down into the basement."

Uncle Shecky, arriving home with his own phones bleeping, has become a different man. A blur of movement, a field commander rising up under fire. He opens doors, opens windows. Pulls down curtains, turns on the sink, fills a bucket, takes it somewhere, limps back. "Henry, do you know where the generator is?"

"Y-yes." Almost a stammer. Henry is unused to seeing his uncle like this. "Behind my weight bench."

"Get it," Uncle Shecky says, tightening his belt. "Check the valve, make sure it's all the way closed. Then lift with your knees, and get that thing out of our house."

Adrenaline and muscle and nothing else, Henry sprints downstairs, pulls up the tank. Forgets to check the valve—a splash of propane, and droplets land on a long-forgotten canvas. A painting Henry began in high school, and it's been sitting here, unfinished, for years. *Starlight Friend*, he was going to call it. It shows Lipz when she was a cokehead, Lipz the way she looked when the powder was just kicking in, and she's twirling like a little girl. Her outstretched arms, her open-mouthed smile—but now the propane has bled the colors.

It hurts him, to see Lipz disfigured like this. He checks his phone, activates WeChat, the messaging app he uses just for her. Gone dark still. No, worse, gone dark *yesterday*. The messages he'd been reading, he now sees, were all sent almost twenty hours ago. WeChat apparently chose today to fuck with him. Mental math: the time between now and Lipz's messages, twenty hours. The time between the messages and the bakery bathroom, where Starr played that recording for him: seven hours. The time between the bakery bathroom and the meeting Starr had recorded: no fucking idea. So drop the math and face the thought. Messages from Lipz, silence since then, and sometime *during this silence—*

A second murder, the one Starr told him about: another crushed head.

Henry humps the dripping tank upstairs and out the front door and down the block. In Maria Hernandez Park he stashes the tank behind a pair of bent trees. A deflated kickball underfoot, Henry catches his breath. The air is gritty. His hands are oily, his eyes sting. Red Dog rising, Lipz wrote. And Brooklyn is burning, and Lipz dropped the L bomb, and is there still a girl he can love back?

In the house, the television is blaring. A local newscaster stands before a burning car and says, "Still no explanation." Turning, Henry almost trips over Uncle Shecky. "Thank Jesus," Uncle Shecky says. "You're safe."

"*You* sent me out," Henry points out. He goes to the kitchen, washes the propane off his hands, and comes back wiping them with a dishcloth. "Lipz thinks it's Red Dog. And she's missing, by the way."

Uncle Shecky opens his mouth to say something. Closes it. Shaking his head, he rubs his forearms as if trying to warm his hands. "We can't rule out the possibility," he says at last, "that this whole show is about *us*." Then he limp-marches off.

Henry follows, watching his uncle pull out the oven and secure the gas line. "Us how?"

"Right now every firehouse is empty," Uncle Shecky says. "Every patrol car is out."

"And Red Dog *wants* attention?"

"He's directing it." Uncle Shecky pushes the oven back, takes the dishcloth from Henry, and wipes his hands. "This is the kind of chaos that could cover a murder."

Or three, Henry thinks. Two hundred and fifty thousand dollars doesn't die alone. Lost money means lost lives, and then a question hits him like a punch: "Where's Kerasha?"

Uncle Shecky shakes his head.

"Fuhhhhk," Henry says. "This could mean—" He stops himself. Sees the pain and worry on his uncle's face, and takes the fear out of his voice. "Kerasha looks after herself. I'm sure she's okay."

"She's a person," Uncle Shecky says. "We're all vulnerable."

Henry nods. He goes into the basement and gets his gun.

The Cobra .380 is small and light. It holds five bullets, and has enough firepower to fluff a pillow. It's all he has. He double-checks that it's loaded, puts it in his pocket, and finds his uncle in the up-stairs office, standing over his coded ledger.

"Uncle Shecky?"

His uncle turns a page in his ledger. "I'm here."

"There's something I haven't told you." Henry swallows. "I spoke to Starr." Another swallow. "She said there was another murder."

Uncle Shecky closes the ledger. His body trembles as he turns to face Henry head-on. "She said *what*?"

"A second murder, maybe connected to the first. The name—" Henry tries again to keep the fear out of his voice. Fails. "Someone whose name sounds like *Seh*. But she wasn't sure."

His uncle pales. "Could it have been *Keh*?" Swaying a little, he puts his hand to the wall. "It was a girl?"

"I was worried it was Lipz," Henry says quickly. "She still hasn't written me back. And she knew about the fires, and she said Red Dog was behind them. I didn't think . . . I mean, I thought . . ." Henry looks down. "I didn't think about Kerasha."

Uncle Shecky straightens. He picks up the ledger, walks to Henry, and cracks the great book across his face.

Henry finds himself on the floor. More shocked than hurt, he looks up at his uncle. Who's still holding the book. And Henry sees Uncle Shecky large again, the man who appeared out of nowhere and took him in. Who held Henry when he was small and had no one.

A dead echoing moment, as if after a gunshot. Henry to self: Did that—did he—am I?

There's no answer, but there's a hot pain on his cheek that feels like a scratch. And he's still on the floor.

"Hey."

From the hall, a new voice. Henry pushes up, stands, and turns, and here's Kerasha, slipping past him. She walks to Uncle Shecky, takes the ledger from his hands, carries it to his desk, and sets it down. Then she turns back to Henry. "You okay?"

Henry touches his cheek, checks his hand. "Yeah." No blood.

She turns to her uncle. "You?"

Uncle Shecky doesn't answer. Seems more stunned than anyone, and his silence stretches on until Kerasha says, "Someone's on the porch."

A race down the stairs, Henry with a clear lead.

"It's just Vasya," Shecky calls out from behind. Sounding a little winded.

"You don't know that."

"He's coming over. We have a meeting."

"Red Dog is killing tonight," Henry says, shouting back over his shoulder from the bottom of the staircase. "We could be next."

"Why would he do that?"

Henry stops and turns. "I can think of two hundred and fifty thousand reasons."

Uncle Shecky catches up, breathing hard. "And how will he get his money back," he says, bending over, putting his hands on his knees, "if he kills us."

"So let me explain that to him," Henry says. "He's my client, and it was my runner. This is on me." He lowers his voice, puts his hands together as if pleading. "This is how you trained me. You have to let me do this."

When Uncle Shecky shakes his head no, Henry turns from him anyway. Goes to the door.

Memories from his own training. *Put your left foot just before the jamb*—Uncle Shecky taught him this. Henry's fourteen again, and he's sixteen, and it's last month. "You can't stop them from breaking down the door," Uncle Shecky said once, "but you can stop them from kicking it into your face." The training is long over; the training is inside him. "Stand perpendicular to the door, like you're boxing it." Henry won't put his eye anywhere near the peephole. Right hand to the gun, left hand on the knob.

"Henry, wait," Uncle Shecky says, but Henry pulls open the door, and Lipz is already tumbling into the house.

A crushing embrace. Relief, exasperation. Henry pushes Lipz away and looks her over. No bruises, no fear. But her eyes are bloodshot and wet, and her hands are black with ashes.

"The *fuck*," Uncle Shecky says.

Before Uncle Shecky can get out another word, Henry takes Lipz to the porch, closes the door behind him, and gives her a second hug. "You're okay."

"It was Tiger," she says. "Red Dog hacked him up and burned the pieces. Because of us." She backs up to the rail of the porch, leans against it, head in her hands. "Tiger got out too quick. You thought it, I told it."

Henry takes this in. Street justice is always ugly, but he's never heard of someone getting dropped like this. Red Dog kills when he has to, but efficiently—a blade in the back, a bullet from the shadows. But this is beyond business, beyond assassination—this is a blood-soaked rite.

Not your problem, he tells himself. Remember what's important: Kerasha is alive, Lipz is alive.

But there's no stopping Lipz, no way not to hear how her hated and beloved mostly-ex was hunted down. Spread out in small parts around the neighborhood. No way not to take in that Tiger was burned—bit by bit—with notice to all the witnesses:

This is what happens to snitches.

part eight

the trusted partner

chapter 35

Just before nine o'clock that night, Shecky Keenan receives a text. It's on a partner phone, the one he uses exclusively with Vasya, whom Shecky had been expecting at the house for some time. He's canceling, Shecky thinks, he's done with my emergencies, he's found another fixer. But the text tells him to step out of the house. So this will be a walk-and-talk, Shecky supposes. Not a terrible idea, considering the blue Impala, the green Mustang, the detective's badge, the I-Card, the pole camera Kerasha cut down. The closed and frozen accounts, the internal inquiry. The fires. Vasya's caution protects me too, Shecky thinks. Hope to Jesus this is a sign of trust.

Stepping out into another humid night, he hears a honk from a sedan idling a few doors down. A livery cab, judging by its make and condition. Shecky hesitates, wishing his affairs were less disordered, worrying about the kids. Uncertain whether he will live through the night.

A driver steps out, a heavyset man in a crisp white shirt. "Good evening, sir. You're Vasya's friend?"

I hope so.

He gets into the back, which smells of some lemony cleaning solution. There's a briefcase on the seat. Shecky buckles himself in and doesn't touch it.

Behind the driver's seat, on a glass panel, blue stickers indicate that the cab is licensed by the city's Taxi and Limousine Commission. Maybe this is real. Maybe I won't die after all. Vasya is just avoiding the house, an understandable precaution under the circumstances. But Shecky can't relax about the driver until the car pulls up to a curb. Until he sees that they've parked outside Knish-Knosh, the same greaser where he and Henry had looked over the incident report.

The driver comes around and opens the door for Shecky. "It's all paid for," he says, when Shecky offers money. Shecky nonetheless gives him a five-dollar bill and is turning toward the greaser when the driver, standing behind him now, says, "Just a minute, sir." Shecky half expects a gunshot, a numb, deaf moment before he feels he's been hit. This is how it happens, he's heard. But there's no shot and here's the driver with his crisp shirt, pushing the briefcase at him.

"That isn't mine," Shecky says.

The driver just smiles, and Shecky, at a loss, gives him another five-dollar bill. When the cab at last drives off, Shecky has the briefcase in hand.

Just inside the diner, a yellowish, suited man with polished shoes inspects the pie racks. Even from behind Shecky can recognize Vasya by his head, which is small and bald and unusually round. Vasya carries himself like a man who buys what he wants and pays cash. Shecky's relief at seeing his longtime partner is considerable. This is no hatchet man come to fire him, no gun sent to end things. And yet his relief doesn't last long. Vasya turns and his smile is chilling.

They are seated and given menus. Beers are poured for them before Shecky can even concentrate on the menu. Vasya, meanwhile, is becoming unnervingly irreverent and casual; deliberately—perversely, even—he steers the conversation straight at the most unsettling topics.

"What's happening to our city?" Vasya asks. "The death of a young artist. Murder and fires. A burnt arm found next to a hydrant. The papers say it could be a gang war, but can you believe them?"

Shecky attempts his own smile. He feels queasy and regrets the fried pierogi he just ordered. Wonders if it's too late to get something easier on the stomach.

"Gang wars can end," Vasya says, lowering his voice, "but mugging will never go away. This is just my opinion, but who *doesn't* want to knock someone down? At least once in a while, right? The feeling you must get, standing over a body, able to take anything from it, or do anything to it—such power. It must be like a narcotic."

Shecky says nothing.

The food arrives: shish kabob for Vasya, the fried pierogi for Shecky. "Speaking of narcotics. There's a new device, I don't know if you've heard of it. They say it's very effective with opioids." Vasya slices a square of spiced lamb. "It administers a precise dose—and that can be calibrated—but it can be administered anywhere, by anyone. No rubber band around the arm, no foil or spoon, no slapping for a vein. You just press the little device to the body, and pop! The little needle goes in and out. There's no mess. You use the device once, and then you throw it away. It's the same technology as the EpiPen, only—on the street, at least—they're calling it the FeniPen. Because it was originally designed to administer fentanyl. Isn't that clever?"

Vasya eats heartily. Shecky feels like he's in a play he never got the lines for, but who knows, he could be putting on a decent show. This is something he's learned at the Watts Community Theater: his best work comes when he takes his mind off what he's doing.

"I see you have your briefcase," Vasya says sometime later, wiping his mouth.

"*My* briefcase?" Shecky says. "I wasn't sure."

"Open it up, look inside," Vasya says. "Everything that was in that garbage bag—it's all there for you. We kept nothing for ourselves, after paying our contractor. Ten percent, industry standard."

Really, Shecky thinks, there's a standard for *this*?

Vasya signals for a second beer. "To be honest, my first impulse was to cover the expenses myself, out of my own pocket. From a private family account. But I know you too well. You would have been offended. I could almost hear your words: 'This is my mess. I'll pay the cleaning bill.' What do you think, does that sound like you? Minus the accent, of course."

Say *thank you*, Shecky coaches himself. Come on, just say the lines, give your audience the old humble-grovel. But before Shecky can say anything, the waitress is there with Vasya's beer. She puts it down, looks at Shecky's plate, and asks if anything is wrong with the pierogi.

"It's fine," Shecky says.

"I forget, you always dine with your family," Vasya says. "I appreciate your keeping me company." He looks up at the waitress. "Two espressos, please," he says, absently tapping his lapel pin. "And you can take these plates—we're done."

The sense of dread gives way to light-headedness. How surreal, this moment. Shecky has always liked Vasya. Has considered, for a long time now, asking him to a meal just like this. No talk of transactions, just two gray men exchanging life notes over a couple of beers. But look at him. His suit, his shoes, his smile, the ease of his movements—and the talk is of opioids and murder. This man is *not* my type, Shecky wants to tell someone. I'm not like him, I know better, I know what happens when a life is taken.

But you're still sitting here.

And he's still sitting there for the shift change at Knish-Knosh, when the waitress who brought their food is replaced by the slim and cold-eyed woman Shecky has seen here before. And this waitress takes one look at Vasya, freezes, and runs back to the kitchen. And she never comes back, and the bill is delivered by a busboy. No explanation.

Minutes later Shecky and Vasya are at the register, splitting the bill and then shaking hands. It's over, Shecky thinks. I've got the lost money, minus "expenses." I made it.

"You don't have to thank me," Vasya says, leaving Shecky to wonder whether he unthinkingly said *thanks*, or whether Vasya is excusing him. "And what is gratitude between men like us? We're so tangled," he continues, as they step outside. "Whether we like it or not, we're all accountable for each other's sins."

They shake hands again, and Shecky feels that all of Brooklyn has collapsed under the weight of these words. Accountable for each other's sins—is it possible? Getting into the cab, giving his address, sinking into his seat, Shecky can't keep his thoughts away from it. Vasya was speaking grandly, just beer talk—but what if he's right? Could I be accountable for the acts of my partners? And what about Henry? Is he accountable for *my* sins? Is he already being punished for them?

No, that's nonsense, there was no sin here. Not by me. I can't be blamed for what I don't do, what I can't stop, what I don't even know is happening.

But what about all the work you put into not knowing? (Dannie's eyes are narrowed, her arms crossed.) What about what you taught Henry: you never know someone till you've got your nose up their money. How about *yours*? Where does it come from? Respect for a client's privacy—such a show of class. But also—such a convenience. How long can you keep turning away?

He remembers the slim, cold-eyed waitress, the expression on her face when she recognized Vasya. He thinks of Kerasha, who must be around the same age. She, too, could be working the night shift, he thinks, if life had dealt her another hand. She, too, could have reason to fear a man like Vasya.

And he calls Kerasha because he aches to hear her safe, calls her because *she* doesn't call, calls because he somehow knows, even in the absence of evidence, that his beautiful niece is in danger.

chapter 36

"Is this a medical emergency?"

The woman speaks as though through a mouthful of sticky taffy, and Kerasha is sympathetic. Taffy-mouth works for Dr. Andrew Xu, answering his after-hours line. Paid horribly, Kerasha is certain, to listen to all the people the little man has fucked up, to make sense of their crazy talk and then pass on their messages. Life has treated this woman badly, so what if a mouthful of taffy helps her get through it. There are worse things she could do to herself.

"Ma'am? Are you there?"

Another point in this woman's favor: she asks valid questions. *Is this a medical emergency? Am* I here? Or am I in that basement room putting a needle in my arm? That girl had more than a likeness—she had a sameness. *I acknowledge the duplicates of myself,* Uncle Walt sings to her. He will be her audio guide today, not exactly leading, but traveling with her.

It was just hours ago that Kerasha saw her sameness with the needle. Okay, a needle, what-evskies, nothing to tweet about. This is Brooklyn, after all: the streets are paved with syringes. But this wasn't some faceless skell looking up from that basement window, and this was no one's mama. Those eyes, that defiance, that shame—Kerasha knows them well. Remembers what she was ten years ago, the girl the world looked past.

Well *I* saw her, Kerasha thinks now about her sameness. I saw the needle in her arm, and I watched her push the plunger. Jesus fuck, what's happening to me?

"Ma'am?" Kerasha hears a muted cluck, as though the woman is using her tongue to dislodge the taffy from her molars.

What could be happening: time travel, unlikely. Stress-induced hallucination, quite possible. Schizophrenia, not out of the question. But is this a medical emergency? Kerasha gives the only answer she can, and isn't sure she actually says it aloud: "I'm calling to acknowledge the duplicates of myself."

This sounds like something Henry might say. He saw his duplicates all over the dead runner's studio, and it took an outside perspective, hers, to spot differences. To help him differentiate between *self* and *other*. (Thank you, Johari window; thank you, Franklin library psychology section.) Now she needs this same help for herself, but fuck knows why she picked Dr. Xu.

I didn't pick him, she thinks, eager to forgive herself. Her hand grabbed the phone, her fingers did the dialing. *She* never memorized Dr. Xu's after-hours emergency number, but what was left in her of little Kerry—*ever unreeling*, Uncle Walt whispers, *ceaselessly musing*—must've seen it somewhere. See, want, take—it's not me making this call. She hangs up and tosses her phone.

As she climbs down from the roof of Dr. Xu's office, self-disgust bubbles up, burns and fouls her mouth. Really, Kay—*him*? That TV-shrink posture, the coffee table, that ponytail, those dusty boxes of merlot, the fucking bowl of marbles, that lonesome toothbrush—*he's* the one you call?

Uncle Walt passes the mic to guest speakers. First, herself: I don't take *what* I want, I take *because* I want.

Next, ponytail himself: But where do you think that comes from—your want?

She hates not knowing. Fears, at the same time, answers that peep out from the dark.

"There's more to you than you're telling me," Dr. Xu said to her once. This was their very first meeting, but already he was unleashing the full power of his condescension. "And that's to be expected. Resistance is part of therapy. But I am beginning to question," he continued, putting his hands into a ball, "whether there's more to you than you're telling yourself."

Kerasha checks her surroundings. Is startled to discover, as Uncle Walt put it, where she has wandered in her vision. The streets of Bushwick reek of burnt rubber and plastic, of dirty chemical fires. The snitch barbecue, Kerasha remembers. Red Dog's work.

So Brooklyn has a new forever stink, she thinks. An air stain, Mama might call it.

She passes a man with broad shoulders and hairy arms and scars on his face. Wisps of short hairs cover his shirt. He smells of pomade. A barber, probably. But he moves like a hunter, starting and stopping. Watching, listening, looking for someone. Another spider with fangs, she intuits, dangerous. She puts space between them. Shoves him out of mind, because something worse is coming at her, the numbness that precedes the itch. Kerasha slaps her arms.

"Get the blood flowing." This is from Nicole the yoga embezzler, Kerasha's old cellie. "Always be feeling, even if it's pain." Pain to choke off the itch, to quiet the ponytail's voice. Stinging pain to stop his questions, and then comes actual pain, when she stumbles over a bottle, one of those giant malts Mama's last and worst boyfriend used to drink. Trips and falls and scrapes her palms on the asphalt. Road burn. The streetlight shows black granules in the red wet circles cut into her flesh. My dirty little stigmata, she thinks. She can already hear the homily from Sister Xenia, the mother superior at Sisters of Mercy. At the halfway house where Kerasha spent the first month of her probation, she heard a lot about God's will. If Sister Xenia saw her cut hands now, she'd undoubtedly call them "a blessing."

More like a humbling, Kerasha thinks. How did this happen? She stumbled—she, the noiseless patient spider. She who sees hair clippings, who cuts down pole cams. Only when there's a giant bottle of malt liquor on the sidewalk, somehow she doesn't see it. She falls right over it, because her brain blotted it out.

She had—what's the term—a negative hallucination. More words are coming back to her from the Franklin library psychology section, which consisted of five books. A negative hallucination is not seeing something right in front of you. A hallucination of an absence.

She had no idea this was still in her head, which puts it in the same family as Dr. Xu's after-hours emergency number. The thought of this number plops her down into another imagined session with the bowl of marbles. Doctor: Why didn't you see the bottle? Patient: Want. Exhibit A, her run-in with Dr. Xu's file cabinet. She recalls and re-experiences her humiliation when she realized she wanted not to see what was in the cabinet. When she realized she was afraid.

Want, that dirty old bastard, hid the bottle of malt liquor. I wanted not to see it.

Dr. Xu, ever insatiable, ever ponytailed, asks why.

Another insultingly obvious question, and she doesn't need a medical degree to answer it. The bottle signifies the beast, Mama's worst and last boyfriend. Signifies the one who straightened out little Kerry's family history, who explained that Mama took up pain pills, and later heroin, after Kerasha was born. Does *after* mean *because*? Kerasha now proposes an addendum for the *Dictionary of American Regional English*, Bushwick edition: *after* is a sometimes synonym for *it's all my fucking fault. After* means I did this to her, I'm the one who made her sick. Fuck you to hell, *after*. Kerasha would take anything to get away from that monster. Negative hallucinations, road burn— whatever it took for her to *get thru* that guilt. Whatever was strong enough to cast *after* into the dark.

Ahead is a messenger bike: duct tape on the handlebars, electric tape on the basket. The fence the bike is chained to is wobbly, and she pries it open using the lock itself as a wedge. This city is made for thieves, she thinks. She mounts and pedals hard. With the wind in her hair and on her face and chest, she knows she's moving and yet feels she's stuck. Feels like she's biking through the mouth of Dr. Xu's answering service, pedaling over taffy teeth.

"Open all senses," Nicole used to tell her, "and not just your own. See from my eyes. Listen as that chair." Kerasha never did listen as a chair, but she forces herself to notice the people she's biking past. Not just to rely on the instincts and peripheral vision of skinny Kerry, but to use the full mind of her current big self. Her city is suddenly peopled. Here's a pair of squat hard-hat men, both drunk, it looks like, but still wearing their reflective work vests. Here's a little old woman with a bent back and a walker. Kerasha wonders about the back, how long it's been curved like this. Whether the woman can go an hour without thinking about it and, if so, what mindfulness technique she uses. Give me the right teacher, Kerasha thinks, and I'll disciple myself like a motherfucker. Pedal, pedal, Uncle Walt narrating once more:

> Wandering and confused. . . . lost to myself. . . .
> Pausing and gazing and bending and stopping.

Skateboarders, shirtless potbellied men, a pair of bike cops each with a foot-long hero. What's this, Camp Happy Paws? Looks like a pet store. New to Kerasha, who remembers the refrigerator repair shop that used to be here. A city can change in six years. Can a person? Hope to Jesus, Uncle Shecky would say. This is one of the few points where he, Saint Augustine, and Sister Xenia would all agree, and of course June Jordan has something to say about this: *My name is my own my own my own.*

Kerasha wipes out. One minute pedaling away on her stolen bike, the next airborne, then skidding across the asphalt, she rolls until she stops, and now she lies still, except that she's shaking. Her brain, like a pair of doctor's hands, moves up and down her body. Where does it hurt, and is anything ripped or broken, and are you going to get up from this or has the next *you* already taken shape—the old you just another corpse.

"Are you okay?"

Okay enough to raise her eyes, and here's that girl again: dirty, kindly, a touch shy, a heap of sly. The girl Kerasha saw through the basement window, with the needle. Here I am, she thinks. Little me.

A time blur. She must have remounted the bike, because in a moment of clarity she catches herself leaning it against a fence behind Hank's Fit Rite Tires, a holdout in Bushwick's shrinking industrial section. A hangout for kids, Kerasha remembers, the kind who aren't given bikes, who wouldn't just leave one lying around. Little Kerry spent some time in this lot but hasn't visited since before Franklin. Little has changed: the familiar smell of oil, the same Teen Titan faces spray-painted on the concrete-block wall. The hum of traffic. Kerasha can just make out the overpass over the twin auto-body shops across the street.

She wonders whether she came here straight, or whether she zigzagged like the good little thief she used to be. She wonders whether the good little thief and the basement girl are the same, and whether the "are you okay?" girl is just another specter. *I am the history of the rejection of who I am.*

"I'm trying, Dr. Xu," she says. The words come out and rouse her, and she is suddenly outside Dr. Xu's office building. By the orange-gray glow of the streetlights, the squat, wide complex is unexpectedly beautiful.

Her hand pulls out a fresh burner phone. Her fingers once again dial the emergency after-hours number.

"Yes, this is a medical emergency," she says. No taffy mouth on the line this time, it's a human energy bomb, a woman with an accent Kerasha can't place.

"Please hold!" This woman is shouting at midnight, joyous, and she sounds amazing for someone screening calls from crazies. Medicated, Kerasha decides, another patient, probably, working off her community-service obligation. All too relatable, until Kerasha sees through the dirty trick. Realizes that this poor patient is being forced to participate in someone else's mind fuck, getting thru it by becoming complicit.

Not for me, Kerasha thinks. I'll just stick to my own meltdown, thank you very much. Got plenty of voices already, my own wrong way to do things.

"This is Dr. Brown." Reserved and cautious, she sounds, and Kerasha pictures a heavyset black woman with salt-and-pepper hair. Pictures herself, but older, and realizes this woman is another of her psychiatrist's absurd inventions, the other half of Kay. This "doctor" has my last name, asshole. Was I not supposed to notice?

Reluctantly, Kerasha admits to herself that this anger is just a front. What she really feels is disappointment. She called and he didn't answer. He was supposed to get on the phone, he was supposed to ask if she was okay. "Guess it's just us, Kerry," Mama used to say, usually in the wake of a breakup. "You and me against the darkness." And now I'm grown, and it's *still* Mama and me and the darkness.

"I need Dr. Xu," Kerasha hears herself saying. Hating herself for it.

A sigh from Dr. Brown, or whatever her real name is. "Dr. Xu is not on call." No doubt this is the hundredth time she's had to explain this tonight. But this is the first time you're explaining it to *me*, bitch—how about some compassion? Dr. Brown talks through a yawn: "Please describe your emergency."

"I can't get away from myself," Kerasha says. Or maybe she just thinks this. The phone is off. It is in her hand, her trusty fingers having done her work for her once more. Another blur. The skyline changes as she runs east against the night. She catches a street kid's frightened look. Scared of *me*, Kerasha realizes, and then she's here and gone and here again, now in the thick stink of Smelly Terri. Minutes later she sees the big woman, slow-pushing her new shopping cart. Shaking a sleepy maraca. Kerasha wonders whether, rather than the reserved and cautious Dr. Brown, her future self might be Smelly Kerry. No strain to the imagination here, just another woman with a shopping cart and a forgotten history.

Kerasha moves past the old warehouses, some empty, some dens for skells. A few are getting the loft treatment—she visited one recently, when she took the gun and the badge from the detective's nightstand—but all these buildings are crumbling inside, all are soft in the bones. And beyond the warehouses are the Moses towers.

The lock on the service door off Lafayette Street is still broken. The stairwell takes her to the basement, where the grate to the boiler room is still loose. Skinny Kerry probably had no trouble slipping in, but big Kerasha can hardly fit through it. Somehow she twists and pushes and squeezes into the air shaft. The windowsills, from floor to roof, are quality stone, and Kerasha steps and pulls and swings her way to the top, knocking down, as she goes, little tokens of family life. Plants, mostly, but also clay vases, dolls, and action figures. People make and collect art, even here, Kerasha knows better than to be surprised. But she's moved, despite herself, by a drawing fingered into the dust of an unwashed window. A figure of a girl reaching for a breakaway balloon. The bend of the string shows wind, and the girl's just standing there with her arm up. She's not chasing the balloon, Kerasha knows. She's saying goodbye.

On the roof of Tower C, Kerasha catches her breath. Counts down from fifty-four, and wonders if Nicole, the yoga embezzler, wherever she is now, is feeling a happy twinge. See, Nikki? I listened. *Let* on the inhale, *go* on the exhale. Sister Xenia would call this prayer, and Saint Augustine and Malcolm X speak from experience: however you sin, even if you enjoy it, God is there for you. God will wait.

But Kerasha doesn't think *she* can.

Let, inhale, *go*, exhale.

Of all her advisers, it's Nicole she trusts. With oxygen comes perspective. Looking out across Brooklyn, she sees an expanse of dingy potential. Countless windows to open, countless doors. Over the course of her lifetime, however long it may run, she will never run out of places to break into. Pausing and gazing, invading—

Evading.

Her breath stops.

I don't take *what* I want, I take *because* I want.

And where does it come from, this want?

A wet, shaking chill comes over her. Her sense of dingy potential, absolute five seconds ago, now shivers small and ugly in the shadow of something massive. Again she slaps her arms. Get the blood flowing. Always be feeling, even if it's pain. Anything to *get thru* that shadow. Once more Kerasha beholds the winking yellow lights of Brooklyn. Beholds, also, the luminous citadel of Manhattan. These are the stars by which she navigated her childhood. They tell her she's home now. Her long night's journey has ended.

Sanctuary, she thinks, this vast rooftop her private domain. No one else has set foot up here, as far as she knows, not since the last layer of waterproof coating was brushed over it. With no badges, no skells, no wardens, and no Mama, this is the one place no one can hurt her.

"Bullshit."

Kerasha sinks. Her breath—her precious, counted breath—is all gone now.

All is gone.

"This isn't the place you come to be *alone*." The voice is familiar, so soft, so light. And such power it has over her, Kerasha can't raise her eyes to face it.

Which may just be her least-bad strategy. "Eyes on your feet, girl-friend," Nicole used to say. "Ground yourself—the literal ground, our angry earth. Put your pain in perspective, girlfriend, and say *thank you*, angry earth. You hold us up, day after shitty day." Evasion after shitty evasion.

Kerasha's feet have never held such a fascination for her. Look at them, those laces, taut and carefully knotted. You can tell a real thief, she thinks humorlessly, because she doesn't trip over her own feet.

"Smile," Nicole used to say. "The brain belongs to the body, not the other way around. Studies have been all up in this shit. A fake smile actually gets you partway to happy. 'Fake it till you make it'— that comes from a false assumption. Faking *is* making it. Deep shit, right?"

Kerasha pushes her mouth into a smile. This does nothing for her happiness, but she doesn't want to disappoint Nicole, even if it's just Nicole-in-her-head. So she raises her eyes from her feet and fixes them on the skinny, dirty girl who shares this dark night with her. Covered by the same starless mass, lit ugly by the same winking lights, the girl holds up a bucket. She gives it a good shake, and the rattle is of a churning mass of tiny metal bits.

"Our bucket was right where we left it," the girl says. She indicates a nook under the tower's secondary heat vent. The angle of the overhang and an imperfection in the roof rust have protected the bucket from years of wind and rain. I acknowledge this duplicate of myself, Kerasha thinks. A new personal low: she wishes Dr. Xu not only would answer her calls, but could be here with her on this roof. So what if he looked toward the bucket girl and sees only the naked air. The point is Kerasha shows progress. Please, good doctor, take out that pen: this patient's hallucinations have gone from negative to positive.

The bucket rattles again. This time the girl not only shakes it but holds it up and tilts the rim toward Kerasha, daring her to peek inside. "Aren't you curious? Aren't you *itchy*?"

Kerasha again forces a smile, the way Nicole taught her, but the neurons don't fire. Never did. Fake happy never could cross over.

What's real is the acrid smell of vinegar and metal and burnt tar, and that inimitable something-something. The bucket is directly under her nose now. The girl is before her, reeking, unwashed. "There's more to you than you're telling me," she whispers, "but what I want you to think about is what you're not telling yourself."

Then the girl is gone, and Kerasha holds the bucket in her own two hands. Even alone, even in darkness, there's no sanctuary. True history: this spot on the roof of Tower C isn't where little Kerry came to get her head right.

It's where she came to get high.

Double yourself, one last whisper from Uncle Walt, *and receive me darkness*.

Then the bucket drops, and there's a sweet, silver tinkle as a hundred dirty needles spill out around her feet.

chapter 37

That night, in the second-floor office of a narrow house in Brooklyn, the door is locked, the blinds drawn, and a blackout curtain is pulled down and secured to the wall with Velcro strips. Shecky, unshaven and looking especially thin, sits on the floor and opens a briefcase. The snap locks are faulty, he notices. The Paradise Club obviously doesn't want this back.

And no wonder. Inside the briefcase, in place of the Paradise Club's usual crisp white-and-blue currency bands, are crumpled tens and fives. A handful of Jacksons, an occasional Grant. The bills are stained and faded, and Shecky can identify a few counterfeits by sight. Nature of the business, counterfeits mixing in. He'd identify more by touch, he knows, but right now he's wearing nitrile gloves. A line from somewhere: "A pure hand needs no glove to cover it." Well whoever wrote that obviously never smelled narco money. Was never near the oils and powders, the raw human filth. Shecky breathes through his mouth, but he's not ungrateful. It's the foulness of this money, along with the prevalence of counterfeits, that justifies the 10 percent fee Shecky charges clients like Red Dog. Whereas with his mom-and-pop-shop clients, he keeps only 5.

Shecky sorts and bands the bills, counting as he goes. The soundtrack to *Futurity* plays from his phone and helps keep his mind off the stink. Ten dollars, twenty, five, five . . . He doesn't need a tally sheet to see columns in his head. Tens, twenties, ones, more ones, all make tick marks that flow to subtotals, which in turn swell to a grand total: $225,000. After putting the money back inside, Shecky can barely get the briefcase to close. The lock doesn't catch until he puts his whole body against it.

Simple math: $250,000 lost in a black garbage bag, $225,000 in this battered briefcase, means $25,000 the Paradise Club is keeping to "cover expenses," as Vasya put it.

Twenty-five thousand. So that's what it costs now to get rid of a problem.

He shakes his head, thinking about Henry's friend, as he recloses the battered briefcase.

The storage unit he rents under a Delaware-incorporated LLC is on a side street off Broadway. The padlock is difficult to open with shaking hands, but at last Shecky gets into it. He turns on his hurricane lamp, and his heart clenches and for a moment seems to stop. He comes here every month, always has papers or drives to pick up or drop off, yet every visit is charged. Each object, aside from his active business documents, touches on some mistake, some loss, some alternate version of himself he can no longer see. Here are vacuum cleaners left over from when teenaged Shecky would scavenge from streets and dumps, repair and reassemble what he could, and resell them so that he could pay Uncle Joseph for his "monthly keep." Here are the textbooks he bought used for his two semesters at Brooklyn Law, back when Uncle Joseph still wanted him to be the "family Jew." Next, participation trophies from high school swimming. Shecky guesses no one else kept theirs, or had so little to keep.

He puts the briefcase on the wobbly desk, another relic from his law school days. Turns to the immense file cabinet right next to the desk—this is where he keeps the files he can't throw away yet. He unlocks and efficiently empties the cabinet, creating neat stacks of files and drives on the desk. He has to move the briefcase closer to the edge of the desk as more and more files come out. Amazing how much this cabinet can hold. Some of the files he knows by sight, from the color and thickness of the folder. Some he's touched just this past week. Business only, the stuff in this cabinet, though right now what he needs is handwritten on a card taped *beneath* it.

Twenty-five thousand dollars went to Vasya's contractor, which means twenty-five thousand dollars must be found for Red Dog—and found quickly. Henry's crazy friend made a terribly strong case for that. In a sense it's as though, having snuck into the house, she's never left it: he can still feel those ladder kicks. Removing the last files from the cabinet, Shecky decides he'll waive his usual fee for Red Dog. The full month of secured transfers—on the house. Painful, to let go of money like that, but appropriate under the circumstances. He goes further. Entertains the option of permanently reducing his rate for the client. A full one percent? Two? But hold up, old man, stop right there: you can't make business decisions with shaking hands. Haven't you learned?

Shecky coughs into the crook of his arm. Has half a mind to throw himself into the East River, only there's a money problem to be worked out. For the kids.

Twenty-five thousand dollars—Shecky doesn't have it just lying around the house. While the fixer manages many bags of cash, he doesn't keep much of it. Most of the money returns to the client, and then there are operational expenses. Burner phones, burner computers, the runners, the transaction surcharges, Kerasha's legal fees—everything adds up, and forty-eight thousand dollars would have to come out of the house. A reverse mortgage, if only it were in his name. And so Shecky will have to tap the family's emergency reserves. Secured by private-client banks—the fixers' fixers, you can't imagine better—these accounts have no documented connection to Shecky Keenan, Henry Vek, or Kerasha Brown. Instead they belong to a paper family, the identifications of whom are handwritten on the index card taped beneath the cabinet.

Which Shecky, at this moment, is not strong enough to lift.

He curses himself. You do everything online. You use your

computer for every client. You have your protocols, your IP spoofers, and your anonymized cloud accounts. You regularly swap out old laptops and phones—so why, for *emergency* money, are you depending on an *index card*? There's exactly one reason you can't access your accounts right now: you.

His hands are shaking. He can't lift the cabinet, even though it's empty, even though he tries and tries, the metal biting into his skin, and even though he's clenching his core—the cabinet is unimpressed. It hasn't gotten heavier, he knows, but age has unmanned him. The miseries of this past week. And so he calls Henry and then waits at his old desk, lost in a thoughtless fog. Drumming his fingers not far from the briefcase stuffed with dirties.

The door opens with a bang, as if kicked. "The fuck are we doing here?" Henry storms in and looks around.

We, for Shecky, is the operative word. Trailing Henry is that girl.

"We," Shecky whispers, "is you and me. She can't be here."

"*She*," Lipz says, before Henry can get out a syllable, "is getting her name back. Where's my money?"

Henry looks from her to Shecky and back again. "Am I missing something?"

"Your uncle and I had a little chat," Lipz says. "He didn't tell you?"

"She came into the house." Shecky tries to keep the anger out of his voice. Fails. "She told me *she's* our connect to the client." With a hardening look at Henry: "Something I should have heard from *you*."

"You talked without me?" Henry looks fit to break something. "The two of you—alone?" Hopefully the something will be Lipz. "Behind my back? The fuck is that?"

Lipz shrugs. "Business."

"You don't know a goddamn thing about business," Shecky says. "Neither of you." To Henry: "Our storage unit isn't for friends. It's not for clients, and it's certainly not for her."

Lipz lights a cigarette. "Rude."

"You've put the whole family at risk," Shecky says to Henry. "We'll have to find a new unit now. She's a problem, she shouldn't be here."

"Okay, but she's my problem," Henry says. "And my partner. You called me here, she was with me—we're here. So let's get through this, okay? I can handle her."

Lipz ashes on the floor. "Since when?"

"Partner?" Shecky looks from Henry to Lipz and back again. "You're together now?"

"Define *together*," Lipz says, taking a long pull on her cigarette. Then flicking it, and pulling out a gun.

Her eyes are on Shecky, who is frozen—can't breathe—but her gun is on Henry.

No, no, *no!* Not him—

"You've always been a bitch to me," she tells Shecky. "But this isn't personal. This is about you being bad at your job."

Shecky straightens. His panic scatters, and out from the mist comes a violent determination. "You touch my boy, and I will fucking end you."

She rolls her eyes. Mouths a word Shecky is pretty sure is *whatevuh*. "You lost the money. You. This is your operation. Take responsibility, get me the money, or I'll hit you where you're soft."

"You selfish, sloppy addict." Henry takes a step closer to Lipz—*closer to the gun*—and now he stands between Shecky and death. "This is too crazy, even for you. You're using again." Panic comes back and hits Shecky like a cold bolt to the chest. This must be what it feels like to have a heart attack. He tries to maneuver himself in front of Henry but is immediately overpowered—is lifted and set down a few feet back.

A snort from Lipz. "You guys are too cute."

"This is selfish bullshit," Henry spits at Lipz. "I'm not twelve-stepping with you a second time. We're done. You get that? You and me are fucking—"

"The money," Lipz says to Shecky, leaning to speak around Henry.

Shecky is shaking. He puts a hand on the desk, and it wobbles. There's a gun taped to the back of this desk, but how to grab it, pull off the tape, and turn and use it—it's impossible. She could empty her weapon twice.

"You'll get the money," Shecky says. A low growl. "I'm working on it."

"That doesn't sound like a plan."

"The plan is we're getting a loan. From another client."

The announcement visibly jolts Henry, who turns to look at him. "Since when?"

Shecky speaks past him. "The loan will square things for us. Please, for fuck's sake." His eyes on the gun, his voice cracking. "Put it down."

Lipz looks at Shecky a long time. Then she smiles, points the gun at her own head, and pulls the trigger.

Click.

A long, dark quiet, then a roar from Henry: "Fuuuuck!"

Shecky opens his eyes. Hadn't realized he'd closed them. He breathes but can't catch any air.

"A loan!" Lipz is smiling as she pockets the gun. Heads for the door. "We can be friends again, I love it. So glad I stopped by."

"And now you're getting the fuck out," Shecky says. He slams the door behind her, then turns his full anger on Henry.

"I should've guessed the gun was empty," Henry says to Shecky, reaching around Shecky to bolt the door. "That wasn't real."

"Then why are you locking the door." Shecky is still catching his breath, still trying to get some warmth back into his body. The kicks to his ladder, the gun pointed at Henry. "That girl is dangerous. Get rid of her, we'll all live longer." He's about to say something else but sees Henry's shaking now, too, coming off the adrenaline. And Shecky once again feels he's with the little boy Henry was, the small person who slept on the floor beside him. Shecky touches Henry's shoulder. Indicates the file cabinet: "Come on, help me lift this."

"Wait, what you said about the loan." Henry nods them away from the door, and the two move to the far side of the storage unit. Low voice: "Total bullshit?"

"We've already got the money." Lower voice: "It's in that briefcase."

"Holy fuck." He looks back to the door. Soft-shoes to the brief-case, touches it. Then seems to catch himself. "Wait. Can't we just give this to Lipz?"

"She's not our client," Shecky says. "And we get no commission for losing cash and then giving it back. We're going to treat this like a normal job. We'll get the money into the machine, and it'll hit Red Dog's offshores by tomorrow."

Henry nods, backs away from the briefcase. "Who're we borrow-ing from?"

"Our friend at the Paradise Club. He got us most of the way there."

"Most of the way?" Once again he looks back at the door. "Red Dog's not going to be okay with that."

"That's why I called you here." Shecky, growing impatient, again points Henry to the file cabinet. "I need your help lifting this up. There's a card taped to the bottom."

"A card?"

"An index card. With the details for our emergency accounts. The PINs, the names I used. Give me a hand, will you? My fucking knees."

Henry blinks. "We have emergency accounts?"

"Of course we do." Impatience heating up now. "I set them up when you moved in. Got a couple in Luxembourg, a new one in Singapore. Quiet countries. No wars, no problems. And there's a new account for Kerasha. So come on, help me."

Henry looks at the cabinet, then back at Shecky. "You never told me."

"And you're fucking welcome for that." He takes a step closer, a glow in his eyes reflected from the hurricane lamp. "Some things are better not knowing. When the cops come at you with questions, and you say I don't know—it's better if you really don't know. But we don't live in the better, right? Your friend went out and got himself killed. And my knees are fucked, and I can't lift this thing up anymore. Last month I could, but tonight—just fucking help me."

But Henry is backing away from him. His face is in shadows, his voice a low, steady growl. "Emil didn't get himself anything'd. He was murdered."

"Okay, fine, it was murder." Shecky is so done with this shit. "But sometimes murder gets invited."

"Excuse you?" Henry's voice is raised, and Shecky sharpens his own.

"Tell the truth. Your *friend*. Was he a good runner? Did he follow the rules? Did he check in when he said he would—always? Did he hand over his receipts—all of them? Every time? Was he discreet?" He's been approaching this whole time, and now he's right up in Henry's face. "Would you have given him a big carry—would you have even kept him on—if he wasn't your friend?"

Henry says nothing for a long time, but there's a soft sound from some quiet, pushed-back corner of his chest—it's either a little cry or a no. Then the kid goes to the cabinet. And finally—fucking finally—he squats, lifts, leans the big metal piece against the wall, and paws the card off the bottom.

Shecky watches his nephew admiringly. Regretfully. "Thanks, Hen," he says, taking the card. Feeling a little sick inside. "Listen. I'm sorry about what you're going through. It's just—"

A thud and then a shuffling sound.

The cabinet, dropped rather than repositioned, has decided to release a drawer. And the drawer hits the desk, and one of the file stacks tumbles down. Loose papers drift, clipped and rubber-banded packets hit the floor. And in Shecky's rush to save another file from sliding off the desk, he knocks down the briefcase. It manages a little bounce before it breaks open, and despite Shecky's sorting and rubber-banding, filthy cash spills out across the floor.

The room is silent except for the quickening of Shecky's heart. And Henry's looking at the money, looking at him. And Henry may be muddy-headed sometimes, and he's certainly too soft and trusting with his friends. But the kid is neck-deep in the business, and here's something Henry has known since he was a boy: money from the Paradise Club has never looked like this.

Across a frozen, never-ending moment, Shecky feels Henry's eyes on him, waiting for an explanation.

chapter 38

"Think, you junkie cunt. Where is it? *Think*."

While Mama paces, Kerry Brown, twelve years old, sits out on the fire escape. She peeks in only when, judging by Mama's footsteps, she won't be spotted. Mama walks the kitchen, pausing to turn out cupboards, to scratch herself, to scream at the walls and laugh. "Come out, come out, olly-olly-oxy!" She's not looking for Kerry, of course. She's looking for the yellow-white powder in the little glass vial, which Kerry has in the palm of her hand. On TV, people hold crucifixes this way. They close their eyes and pray with their hands to their mouths, and Kerry wants to say something to the vial. But how do you pray to a yellow-white powder? What do you ask for, and what do you promise?

"I'm so sorry," Mama says, but not to Kerry. Never to Kerry. "I hid you and forgot where. You know how my mind is now. A staggered, tripped boy, a shod-toe. I'll remember once you're in my blood. That's the irony, right? The old lady needs her glasses to find her glasses. And *this* lady just needs her meds, and she put them . . . Where? Think, cunt, think. Stupid, stupid, stupid."

Hearing sickening, rhythmic thuds, Kerry risks another peek. Mama is beating the word *stupid* into her head, punching the sides of her skull, hitting the same two points again and again, as though those were the places where her memories went to hide. Kerry can't watch this for long. Fire escape to top floor, top floor to hall, hall to airshaft, airshaft to roof. She arrives at her secret spot. Here, and nowhere else, she is safe. Here she turns over the ways she is wicked. Mama wants something. Kerry has it, but she's not letting go. Mama is in pain. Kerry can make it go away, as she has so many times before, but this time she won't. And Mama doesn't suspect her, blames herself, not her Kerry, for the lost medicine.

Well look at your twelve-year-old now, Mama. Heading up to try a little medicine myself.

Kerry has a sterile syringe, swiped this morning from Krupa Pharmacy. A lighter from the bodega, a spoon from Peter Luger— she went all the way into Williamsburg yesterday just to palm something quality. Only the best for a first kiss.

Hello, darkness. It's been a long time coming.

Five years later the police find her unconscious in the supply closet of Krupa Pharmacy, having somehow—in a kind of anti-miracle— locked herself inside with a Konnekt padlock. Scattered around her are the sterile syringes she came for. Also with her is a backpack stuffed with bags of heroin, a half kilo's worth, yanked from her dealer's supplier. This is enough to put her in the cage for three years, and qualifies her for a sentence extension when she is caught after escaping the prison.

It's almost a week after the murder, Kerasha is twenty-three years old. She walks to the corner of Weirfield and Evergreen and spots the same old dealer on the same old stoop—no, it's not the *same* kid, they never last. Not that she was ever a regular customer. She was always more of a taker than a buyer. But this new dealer has the same sleepy look as the old dealer. And he gives her the same leer, and the transaction is smooth, like he's been expecting her all this time. It feels good to pay for it.

As for the powder, she hasn't tasted it in years, but it's a once-and-always lover, knows just where to touch her. But first there's pleasure in anticipation, in the slow walk to the bus stop. The twin vials make a single lump in her pocket, not much bigger than a marble.

Are you listening, ponytail? You got that silver pen ready?

Here's the truth about the almighty want. It doesn't come from Mama or her daily bag. It doesn't come from me supplying her, and it doesn't even come from *after*. Not from hunger, not from picking and stealing, not from the filaments that never landed, the web that never held, not from being the girl the world looked past. The want came simply, and came only, from the heroin. It's my first and faithful; life is the substitute, not the other way around.

On the roof of the Moses Houses' Tower C, Kerasha, once a famous child thief, now a graduate of the Franklin Institute of Those Who Failed Even at Crime, puts the needle in her arm. She feels the burn move up her neck, then the prickle, then the quiet.

Let on the inhale, *go* on the exhale.

Hello, darkness. Feels good to be home.

chapter 39

"It wasn't loaded," Lipz says.

"I didn't know that." Henry is driving them back from the Gowanus storage unit. "That could have gone sideways fast. If I'd had my gun—"

"Yeah, yeah. You would've killed me." She rolls down the window. Spits. "I've been through worse."

A honk, and Henry changes lanes. He's driving too fast, he knows, but his foot wants to go straight through the floorboard. Their borrowed van belongs to a former runner, now a roofer, and the interior smells like lung disease. Henry has half a mind to eject Lipz from this van, and maybe run her over with it, but he needs answers.

"So you and my uncle got together," he says, "and neither of you fucking told me?"

She's uncharacteristically silent. He looks over. She's giving him boo-hoo eyes. Speaking in a boo-hoo voice: "And are you . . . *sad*?"

"I'm angry." He gives her what he wants to be an angry look, but which he knows, in fact, is really just . . . *sad*. "I don't know that we're going to get past this."

"It's not like I had a choice. Your uncle controls the money. He makes the decisions." She spits again and then rolls the window back up. "You made that perfectly clear when we were talking about my cut."

"But I'm the one who's fixing everything!" Again, Henry hears the sad little boy in his voice. Doesn't like it, so he slows himself down. Deepens his voice. "Talk to your boss. He can check his off-shores tomorrow. So no more pointing your gun at anyone, okay? Including yourself. You'd better not be using again."

"I'm not." She gives him a long, steady look before turning back to the window. "But if I were high right now, I'd say exactly the same thing."

Henry takes the van around a double-parked taxi. "Your boss got his money, you got your name. Everyone's happy." He slows, changes lanes to pass a wide-load truck, speeds up again. Glances over at Lipz, who's still looking out the window. Henry asks, "Aren't you happy?"

She turns back to him, but only for a moment. "We're not built for that."

Dawn, they're parked at a Mobil station. A knock at the window. Henry rolls it down: it's his regular Thursday guy.

"Everything okay, boss?"

"Getting there." Henry hands over the briefcase. "The slips are inside. Wait for my text. Then it's a rush job, okay? Double pay, but fucking do it right."

"No problem, boss." Thursday makes to go, but then he takes a second look at Lipz, who's now sleeping in the front passenger seat. "Cute."

Henry starts the van. "Don't let her hear you say that."

At long last, the Moses Houses. Henry circles two times before finding a parking spot. He texts the roofer, puts two twenties in the glove compartment, and helps Lipz out of her seat.

"Where's the money?" she asks, talking through a yawn.

"On its way." He checks his phone, pockets it. "All I need is unsecured Wi-Fi."

"So come on up with me." There's a dare in her smile. "We can do it in my bedroom."

Lipz lives with her aunt, a charter school administrator who likes to explain why poverty is a lifestyle choice. To Henry, Aunt Mercedes is the ultimate fake-respectable don't-give-a-fucker. Also, her apartment always reeks of patchouli.

"This is Henry," Lipz says to her aunt, as she leads Henry through the kitchen. "We're going to my room. We're going to fuck."

Lipz's announcement is, of course, performance: Henry and Aunt Mercedes have known and hated each other for years. This morning Aunt Mercedes is in her usual seat at the kitchen table, painting her nails, a phone tucked between her shoulder and her ear. Her scowl is nasty, but Lipz just blows her a kiss. Leads Henry to her bedroom, pushes open the door and disappears inside. Henry stops in her doorway. "I need ten minutes."

"You're not even a little turned on?"

"By myself. I'm getting your name back."

She pulls off her socks and comes to him barefoot. "Henry, Henry, Henry. You really are the sweetest." She takes his hand. Tender touch, quiet voice: "Fuck this up and I burn your house down." Then she's pulling him down to her, and her close, close whisper is almost a kiss. "You've got to get out of this." Even closer: "You're still good."

It all starts with a text: Tammy in?

Henry's first message is to a morning teller at a Western Union in downtown Brooklyn. For months he's paid this teller fifty dollars per response, whether or not the response helps him. This morning it does.

Tammy in, is the response. There's no Tammy, of course, but the teller is available. Hallelujah, Henry writes back. He switches phones and dispatches his Thursday guy. The briefcase is on its way. Just a half hour later, Henry gets Thursday's confirmation: Touchdown. The money has been delivered. An anxious minute passes, two, then Henry receives the sister text from Not-Tammy. A string of letters and numbers, which Henry decodes by hand. He double-checks the number, then takes a deep breath—not one dirty dollar is missing.

From Western Union the money speeds to Apple Bank. From there to Mexico, from Mexico to Lagos to the Moon, the money scatters across the dark, but soon enough it will converge on Red Dog's account in Sint Maarten. Henry cracks his knuckles. Feels a familiar ease spreading across his universe. He's hearing now, for the first time since Emil's death, the steady whirr of the family money machine.

Can you hear it too, Uncle Shecky? We're up and running again.

But now the easy feeling takes a gray turn. Henry thinks about how things have been for him and Uncle Shecky. He sees them in their upstairs office, where the ledger came down hard. He sees them in the storage unit, where the cash spilled out of the briefcase, and that scared look on his uncle's face.

"This is a loan from a friend," Uncle Shecky said then. "I was in no position to ask where the money came from, and neither are you."

Another beep, Henry checks his phone. A message on WhatsApp, a happy dog emoji. This is from the burner account Henry just set up for his uncle, and it means, simply, that everything is done. The coffee shop magic worked, and the money is already on its way to Sint Maarten. It's almost official: Lipz has her name back.

Henry holds the moment. Lifts the bedside lamp and, minding the cord, walks the small room. On the wall opposite Lipz's bed is a window facing an air shaft. On the sill are loose coins, a box of tissues, the books *Flash Boys* and *The Best Bad Things* (Lipz has always been a reader), a stack of DVDs (and an unapologetic porn hound), a box cutter, and—

No.

Tiger's wallet. Henry recognizes it by the silver chain, the fake claw marks burned into the leather.

How could she have kept this? Tiger was murdered. Red Dog was behind it, of course, but the actual killer, as far as Henry knows, hasn't been ID'd. If the cops walk in right now—and fuck knows they could have a thousand reasons to toss Lipz's room—they will have questions. Like how did this end up on her windowsill? Like what does she know about the murder?

And what *does* she know?

Henry goes through the wallet. He puts the cash under Lipz's pillow, but down the air shaft: receipts, money order tickets, business cards. He stops at a tiny photograph of a baby. Jesus, could Tiger have had a daughter? Answer: of course he could have a daughter. Henry shakes it off and keeps going. More down the air shaft: a half-dozen battered credit cards, all obviously recoded—the embossed numbers nearly flat, the names scraped off. Henry is about to toss the wallet itself when he sees something poking out. He reopens the wallet. Pulls out a driver's license.

The picture is of Tiger, but the name . . . Henry searches his memory for Tiger's government name—what was it, Daquan something— but Daquan something isn't the point. The point is that while the name on this license is bullshit, the style of it is sickeningly familiar. The point is that this bullshit license bears the seal of the state of Pennsylvania, and it looks a hell of a lot like the license that belonged to a nonperson called Charlie Gladney.

And then there's the little card just behind the license. Side A: blank. Side B: a handwritten phone number.

646-555-0144.

Henry takes out his own wallet, checks the number on the card Kerasha found on the top of Emil's door. The same. Henry's stomach turns, and there's a tremor in his hand as he takes out his phone and dials.

"Who this?"

This voice—a man's, cold and very low—Henry still can't place it. But if he can get the motherfucker talking, whoever he is, if Henry can just keep him on the line—

"I have your money," Henry says, to bait the man. "Where can we meet?"

Immediately he hears the click. Damn. Reckless with anger, he shoots a text at the mystery number: I know what you did.

No response.

Henry's follow-up text: I'll find you.

Nothing.

Henry is motionless for a long time, except his fingers, which still tremble. Two dead men, one phone number in common—so whose is it? But now his own phone is buzzing.

"You're not going to believe this," Starr says. "Remember that other murder? The one the detective was talking about?"

"Oh fuck. Wait a sec." Henry lowers the phone. Doesn't want Lipz to hear any part of this conversation, and doesn't trust her not to be listening in. He goes to the door, opens it, and hears Lipz and her aunt cursing each other out in Spanish. Henry closes the door, plants his foot behind it, and says "Okay, go ahead. What about the second murder?"

"It was actually the first. I got the incident report. She died like three years ago." She stops, and Henry hears background voices, but quickly muffled, as if Starr covered the phone with her hand. A moment later he hears her draw in her breath. "Okay, I'm back."

Henry cracks the door again. In the kitchen, Lipz's hand is raised—no, it's coming down—no, it *came* down. Her aunt's mug flies off the table.

Henry recloses the door. "Let me guess," he says to Starr. "They never caught the guy."

"Worse than that," Starr says. "Blunt instrument, back of the head. The full case file boxed off and shipped off to deep storage."

Henry ends the call feeling more than a little heartsick. Emil's case will never be solved—not by police. And Henry feels a different kind of sickness wondering how many other "blunt instrument, back of the head" murder files might be collecting dust in that storage site.

He slips out of Lipz's bedroom and past the kitchen, where Lipz and her aunt are now breaking plates. The noise gives him cover. He makes it out unnoticed. On the walk home, he thinks about what Lipz said—that he could still get out of this. That he was good. He's surprised to realize that he believes the same about her. The evidence in Lipz's favor may be scant, but fuck it. The heart knows what it knows.

Lipz is on his mind as he ascends the steps to the little house on Hart Street, and later that night, her murder will close out the summer.

chapter 40

Three years earlier, Zera is called in late at night to identify a corpse. Another uniformed officer and a detective are waiting for her at the dumpster. The detective is unusually tall, and his badge hangs from a chain around his thick neck. He coughs into his arm as she approaches. Turns his head to spit. "Officer Montenegro?"

"Yes, sir." Standing at attention before him, she recognizes this detective as Daniel Bilardello, who is well known and must be filling in for someone tonight. Jane Doe IDs are not prime assignments.

The detective pulls on gloves and kneels before the long black bag. He unzips it far enough to reveal a head. "Give me some light."

The uniformed officer takes a flashlight off his belt. Clicks it on, shines it on the face of the Jane Doe.

A mild nausea catches Zera by surprise. Months can go by without anything like this coming up in her.

Bilardello asks, "That your informant?"

"Yes, sir." There's no doubt it's Sveta Lvov, the woman with the Paradise Club tattoo. For about a year Sveta has served as an occasional informant for the department, but she's never testified, never given information on her own masters. Always been afraid. Technically, Sveta isn't Zera's informant: Zera is still just a uniformed officer, but she gets pulled into meetings to serve as translator. Zera knows this face well. "What happened?"

"Officially, presumed a mugging." Detective Bilardello removes his gloves. "Unofficially, of course it's a mugging. No purse, no wallet, no phone. Also, the back of her head is crushed."

Zera puts on her own gloves. "Mind if I . . . ?" She squats, the flashlight cuts the dark, and a moment later she's shuddering. The light shows a casserole of hair, skull, and brain.

Rising back up, she sees the detective's narrowed eyes. "You're new to this."

She doesn't answer.

"This is pretty common, okay? Prostitutes are easy targets. Half of them are high, they work in the dark. And it's not unusual for a prostitute—I'm assuming she's a prostitute—"

"Yes, sir."

"It's not unusual for a prostitute to end a night with a purse full of cash."

Zera nods, but she remembers how the man at the Paradise House never let any of his girls handle money. Payments at the front door, no tips allowed. She asks, "Did you find the weapon?"

Bilardello's smile is not friendly. "Are you the detective here?"

Zera waits. He'll talk, he's a man, he can't not explain himself. And he's right to suspect her—she's suspecting him right back. He's blowing off this case.

"This is pretty common," the detective repeats. Zera had been counting in her head. The detective's capacity for his own silence: less than ten seconds. "Some fucking homeless psycho, right? A junkie. He sees a girl, he sees her purse. He picks up his wrench. And these guys all have something—a wrench, a bat, a pipe. It's survival, right? And he comes up on the girl, and he bashes her head. Takes the purse, keeps the wrench. Now your turn. Why does he keep the wrench?"

Zera pretends to think. Still knows how to pump the male ego, when it serves her. One, two, three—"He doesn't want to leave prints."

"He doesn't want to lose the wrench." A cruel smile. "You're over-thinking this. You have to understand, with junkies and whores, it's a different life. Almost a different species, you understand me?"

Zera crosses her arms over her chest and tucks her hands underneath.

She knocks on the office door. The answer is a cough. She opens the door and steps inside. Three days after the death of Emil Scott, Zera approaches Detective Bilardello. This isn't his regular office, he's here on some assignment, but he's already created a smell here: cigarette ashes left wet. Meat put out in sunlight. Bilardello, almost skeletal now, is bent awkwardly over his keyboard, and when he turns to her, the snarl on the left side of his face looks permanent. Zera has heard about the lung cancer, but he must've caught a stroke as well. Yet here he is, working through his dying. Zera, who herself has nothing to stay home for, feels bolstered. He may be a man, but he's her kind of worker, and he'll help her if he can.

She raises her badge, which now, like his, hangs around her neck from a chain lanyard. "Zera Montenegro, field intelligence officer. I'm also with the Human Trafficking Task Force, working on assignment with Detective Fung."

"Good luck with *that* assignment." A wolf's smile, but only half his mouth. "How's he enjoying the rubber room?" Zera doesn't smile back. The rubber room is where cop careers go to die. Kurt's been on an "administrative assignment" since he reported the disappearance of his badge and service weapon. Zera doesn't miss him personally, but his reassignment has been an operational setback. As a detective, and as the lead case officer, he had access to records she can't get at any-more. The live-feed from the camera covering Shecky Keenan's house, for example. This is precisely the time she should be watching it.

"Detective Bilardello," she says, "I am requesting your assistance."

The wolf's smile gets uglier now. "Of course you are." He fixes his right eye on her. She feels his half gaze moving across her body, slip-ping over her twisted hands, her chest, then back to her hands. "That dead prostitute," he says. "You ID'd her down on Sixty-Third. Name was . . ." Uneven blink. "Sveta Lvov."

"Yes, sir." She holds up two case files. "She's half of why I'm here."

She's bolstered by his remembering her—his brain is still working—but when she tries to give him the files, he won't touch them. Just stares at her with the one working eye. "I heard about your informant. It's a tough break, but you need to talk to the case officer."

"He won't return my calls."

They stare at each other, then their words overlap.

"Both blunt-object homicides," Zera says.

"We get one a week."

"Back of the head—"

"And that's just in Brooklyn."

"No murder weapon recovered."

"This kind of death is fairly common for a prostitute."

"He wasn't a prostitute," Zera says sharply. "He was working for me."

Bilardello puts out a smile that's also a fuck-you. "You're not the cause of everything."

Zera, surprised by her own emotion, composes herself. "The Paradise Club is a human-trafficking network that brings in and sells girls. Sveta Lvov was one of those girls. Emil Scott . . ." She hesitates, then rushes: "Both victims were connected to the Paradise Club, they were both informants, and they both died the same way."

"And they probably both liked french fries," the detective says. "Did they die because of the french fries?"

"French fries are not a criminal enterprise," Zera says. "The Paradise Club is."

The detective's smile changes shape. "Fair point. But here's the problem." Less contempt now. "And you already know this—I heard your hesitation." He coughs into a tissue. "Scott and the Paradise Club. Can you *prove* the connection?"

She keeps her eyes on him. Doesn't move.

"You're overthinking this." He tosses his tissue, gets another. "We all want explanations. Everyone wants a story about what causes what. We want to think things are understood and under control. Let me tell you. Things are not understood. Things are not under control." A new cough. "Take a step back. Look at the cases like an outsider. A prostitute is killed. A guy with a bag of cash is killed. Both are informants. What else could you expect for them? Think about the kind of person who becomes an informant. Or an artist. Or a whore. And here's another thing I want you to think about."

He turns back to his desk. Picks up a file. "This is Alan Nguyen. Breadwinner for his family. Gunned down for the eighty bucks in his pocket." He puts down this file, picks up another. "This is Margery Omahen. Schoolteacher, killed for no fucking reason anyone can think of. And look at this. And this. And this." He indicates a stack of files. "How much time do you think I've got for a couple of people who—I'll say it—weren't even people?"

That evening Zera calls the precinct and, by a phone trick she figured out by accident one day, she skips to her supervisor's voicemail without actually ringing his line. "This is Officer Montenegro," she says. "I am reporting from the field for the duration of my tour in connection with the Human Trafficking Task Force." In truth, her tour ended hours ago. Also long since ended: her faith in the Human Trafficking Task Force. But she keeps moving, remembering Katja. Not that Katja can be *saved*—it was over for her the moment she came into the Paradise House. But there's another Katja out there, and another Sveta, too.

And maybe another me.

She remembers the smell in Bilardello's office. She'll prove him wrong.

Badge against her chest, gun against her hip, she interviews an MTA station agent at the Hoyt-Schermerhorn subway stop. She's been re-tracing Emil Scott's last movements. This was where he went dark.

"Are there any blind spots," she asks the station agent, "any places not covered by the security cameras?"

The man smiles without humor. "How much time do you have?"

There are cameras at the turnstiles and cameras pointing into and out from the station agent's booth. There are cameras near the storage and utilities closets. There are cameras looking down each side of the platform, and more by the elevators and emergency exits.

The places where there *aren't* cameras: innumerable.

"There's a joke among the transit cops," the station agent says. "You want to hide in this station, all you have to do is stand still or move."

Sometime later she is on the platform, arms crossed over her chest, struggling to collect herself. Several days past real sleep, her senses are unreliable. But down on the tracks, just a few yards into the tunnel, there's a blind spot she hasn't shined her light on yet. It's just a little enclave, a place where track workers store tools and loose parts. A place where homeless people, the station agent informed her, were once known to camp out. This is a place where someone or something could disappear for a long time. Zera has her flashlight in hand. She could shine it from the platform, or she could hop down and walk a few paces. The station agent has his eye on her. He'll hold the train if he has to, and it's still six minutes away. She walks to the very edge of the platform, where it meets the wall of the tunnel. Her thumb on the button, she raises her flashlight.

And hesitates. This nook is her last unturned stone. After she looks inside, she has nothing. And it's already over: there's no reason to think this nook has anything to do with anything, no reason for Emil Scott to have even set foot on *this* platform. But to have one last not-known thing—it's her hope. And when her light goes on, her hope goes away.

Her heart is heavy when her phone, which has been buzzing indifferently for hours, bleats as if to announce a hurricane.

"Officer Montenegro, repeat, Officer Montenegro."

She recognizes the voice of her supervisor, recognizes the tone. Knows how his calm can be a kind of sheath.

She raises the phone to her mouth. "I'm here."

"And where is *here*?"

"Sir, my initiative—"

"Where are you?"

"I've been canvassing for witnesses. I've been looking at video evidence, testing whether the presumed mugging of my informant may be—"

"Listen to my words, officer. I'm coming to you. Now. Where are you. Right now."

Zera feels herself afloat. Feels the hours she's worked in solitude, off the books, without a supervisor, without food. A vague memory returns, the sensation of manacles on her wrists. This decides it for her—*I'm done.* Zera does not tell her supervisor where she is. She names, instead, her preference for where she'll be fired—and goes there.

Her soon-to-be-former supervisor is an apple-shaped man, his thick arms now crossed over his huge chest. "You were absent without leave for four days," he says. "I've already filed my disciplinary report."

"My informant—"

"Not your concern."

"His murder—"

"Not your concern. Listen to me carefully, Officer Montenegro. The hooker project, the money-laundering bullshit—that was your case, if you can call it that. If there was even a crime there." She begins to say something about murder, but he raises his hand like a stop signal. He makes her feel his silence and then he says, "You're done."

Hours later, Renaissance Java. She was the first one here—she waited outside for it to open. And now she sits with a coffee facing an empty chair. Shecky Keenan isn't here, of course. Why would he be, why today at five o'clock in the morning. And soon he's not even the one she's thinking of, not the person she's picturing seated across from her.

Katja, a dead-eyed nineteen-year-old, sniffs at Zera through the smoke of her burning cigarette. I told you, lights *off,* she says, pointing at her head. The first law of survival at the Paradise House.

I wanted to, Zera thinks back at her. I couldn't.

Okay, so your lights are still on. Katja crosses her arms. Did you really think that would make a difference?

part nine

behind god's back

chapter 41

Shecky walks to DeKalb Avenue, where he catches the B38 bus. He exits at Fulton Street, kills a quarter hour at the Court Street Barnes & Noble, then buys two coffees—one espresso, one small black—on his way to the Hoyt-Schermerhorn subway stop. His waiter days again come back to him: holding both coffees, he swipes his MetroCard and descends to the platform. On the scarred bench he settles and watches trains come and go. Vasya arrives on the minute, dressed, as ever, in a beautiful suit and shining shoes. The Hello Kitty pin on his lapel.

"It's perfect," Vasya says, after a sip from the espresso. "You remembered. Excellent customer service." The phrase is strange, coming from him. His mood strange, too, it seems to Shecky. They're here on unpleasant business.

"We try to keep the client happy," Shecky says. He wants to match Vasya's tone but hears his own falseness: "But I guess I'm the client today."

"Nonsense, we're past that. You've been saying this for years." He elbows Shecky gently. "We're partners."

Shecky's stomach has been cooking acid all day, but now it boils up. He tries to settle himself, but there's no getting away from it: Vasya has become physically repulsive to him. The strange lighting on the platform is at once over-bright and inadequate. Vasya's forehead seems to glow, while his face beneath the eyes is all shadows. An odd and specific fear comes at Shecky, that Vasya will bite him, will snap off the tip of his nose. Shecky's organs are misfiring, most of all his heart: he can feel his pulse moving through him, can hear his own slow, angry heartbeat—as he catches Vasya watching a girl walk by. Tapping his lapel pin.

The Paradise Club, Dannie whispers to him—don't play dumb, you know what they do.

"Thank you for seeing me," Shecky says. He called this meeting, but he wants it over and forgotten—and Shecky can be good at forgetting—even before it's begun. Vasya, meanwhile, seems extravagantly unhurried. He brushes off the pants of his beautiful suit and finishes his espresso. He stretches and smiles, watching the girl till she's gone. Then his eyes sweep the platform, looking for who's next.

"What a summer," Vasya says at last. "That artist who died—so tragic. I saw that notice in the *Post*. Who knows, maybe he'll be the next Van Gogh. The starving genius laboring in obscurity, the early death, his value discovered when it's all too late. Every generation needs this story, yes?"

Shecky also saw the notice in the *Post*. It was just a thumbnail, the kind families pay for, and there were identical notices in the *Daily News* and the *Times*. There was also a one-paragraph obit in some sloppy art magazine Shecky had never heard of—Henry had left a copy on the dining room table. No cause of death was printed, only that the artist had "died suddenly." It was the same on Twitter and Facebook, except there, someone had added a link to Nar-Anon. Nowhere was there mention of Shecky's family, thank Jesus, nor of any money lost or found. Best of all, there was no reference to an active police investigation. Henry's friend may have been a disaster as a runner, but he sure did know how to die.

More acid in the stomach. Shecky hates that he's down here on the ugly subway platform, hates that he bought an espresso for this man. Hates how Vasya's acting, like they're old friends with a lifetime of understanding between them. Like they're the same kind of man. Of course Shecky thought this himself, but that was before the summer turned red. Before he had that miserable dinner and saw the waitress run off. I'm *not* like him, he wants to tell Dannie, we're different men. But Shecky has a sudden, crazy fear that when the next train arrives, Dannie will step off it, and she'll see Shecky with Vasya, and he'll have to answer to her.

I'm not like him, I'm not his partner.

Then why do you take his money?

The gas station takes his money. The grocery store takes his money. Are *they* complicit?

"Let's get to business," Shecky says. His tone is more commanding than he intended, but he wants this conversation to move. He needs to be out of this space where the trains never stop. Where Dannie will see the man he's with—

And the man you are, she whispers.

Shecky clears his throat. "We have another problem."

"How unlucky for you," Vasya says, turning to him with a smile. "What's his name?"

Shecky shakes his head no, afraid to open his mouth. One spoken word and he'll be clutching his stomach, crying out from the acid. Vasya's presence is beyond repulsive to him now, and worst of all is the childlike, unaffected happy manner of Vasya's speech. There's no mistaking his pleasure in just sitting here beside him, the two of them talking together, stretching out the time.

As if they were family.

Another girl, another tap of the pin. And Shecky looks—really looks, for the first time—and sees that the little cat has a pink ribbon, and in the center of the ribbon is a tiny glass dot. A hidden camera— Shecky would bet his life on it.

Everything he sees revolts him. Vasya watching the girls, sneaking pictures of them. The litter on the tracks, the graffiti on the walls, an unwashed schizoid, two teens play-pushing each other near the platform's edge. A phrase he used to hear from his uncle Samuel comes unexpectedly back to him: *behind God's back.* In Uncle Samuel's house, this meant only somewhere unimaginably far off—but for Shecky, in these words, there's a weight and a darkness.

And Vasya's still smiling, and Shecky's supposed to smile back, supposed to be in on the jokes. A dead runner, young girls on the subway—hilarious! But Shecky isn't enjoying any of this. And his stomach, his head, they're both pulsing, and the rhythm is that of a slowing heart. Something terrible is happening inside him. Neither kid showed for breakfast this morning, and here he is, behind God's back, having coffee with the devil. And *I'm* accountable for *his* sins, Shecky reminds himself. This is my partner.

Shecky turns to look Vasya in the eye and say he's had enough, he's calling it off, but instead he's remembering the three texts he received early this morning.

I KNOW.

One minute later: I'll tell him.

Another minute: $$$

The messages were from a number Shecky didn't recognize, but he had no doubt who sent them.

"Everything is up to you," Vasya is saying. "It's the same as last time. You can give me a name, or you just give me the details. But you have to tell me how to find him."

Shecky takes a deep breath. "Not a him." Another breath. "And tell your guy to do it different this time. It can't go down the same way."

Late afternoon, Shecky Keenan leaves the subway and finds a quiet bench where he can sit in the sun and let his stomach figure itself out. He checks his phones for messages from the kids—none, of course. He watches pigeons and counts breezes, and the hours pass, and though the shadows move under a reddening sky, the name he gave to Vasya is still foul in his mouth.

chapter 42

His first date in a lifetime—Andrew Xu does not do well.

During appetizers he somehow brings up his divorce. Yes, it was just this past spring, and yes, Andrew was married, and yes, he was married to a woman. His date, Kevin, a tall white man, was selected for Andrew by an app called BlindLove. ("Sky-High Confidence— you'll have a great time!") Kevin makes no effort to hide his discomfort, and when the waitress talks about dessert, he interrupts, already taking out his wallet: "Just the check. Separate bills."

It's before nine o'clock on a Saturday night, and Andrew is once again lying sideways on his couch, watching a movie on his laptop. Tonight it's *Fireworks Wednesday*, another of his wife's favorites. My ex-wife, he reminds himself. Years pass before ten o'clock, the hour he promised his psychiatrist he'd wait for. At last he takes his Silenor and gets into bed. *My* bed, he reminds himself, forcing himself not to save a place for her. To lie in the center.

Darkness now, chemical and perfect.

Sometime later: awareness that his sleep is breaking up. That he is not alone.

"Wandering and confused," she mumbles, "lost to myself."

He recognizes his patient by her lavender scent, and knows

immediately she's been here for some time. The nightstand lamp is on. A beautiful young woman sits under the yellow-orange light of his bedroom. She sits in his bedside armchair, her bare feet on his ottoman, her hair casting giant shadows. Her eyes, always so quick in his office, are now closed. Kerasha has never come to him like this.

"So here's me again," she says, "ever unreeling. Ever unreeled." A pause. He feels the Silenor pulling him back down and decides this is all just a chemical dream, but then she changes her voice and asks, "Where did you get smacked?"

This new voice is whiny, nasal, and pedantic. And familiar. She's asking my questions, he realizes. She's doing our session.

"Oh, you know, just here and there," she says, answering in her own voice. Playful and coy, at ease as she never is in his office. "I take my hits at the library, in front of the TV, with a burger, in the cage. I don't make a show of it—it's just like popping gum. No drooling, not for me, no slant-standing. I'm my own girl."

His disorientation gives way to pity, which almost immediately is drowned in disgust. She's nothing but sickness now. He wants her out of his bedroom. Hates that her bare feet have been on his honeymoon rug, the one he and his wife picked up in that dusty bazaar in Cappadocia.

My ex-wife.

It takes all his self-control not to scream Kerasha out of his apartment. To remember that she is his patient and he her doctor. She's more than her sickness, he coaches himself. Sickness is what brought her here, sickness is what you signed up for.

And with these and other mantras of his profession, he calms himself. The residual Silenor doesn't hurt.

"So how do you do it?" she asks herself, again in that nasal voice.

My nasal voice, he reminds himself.

"Just follow the rules," she says, answering in her own voice. "They're pretty basic. Just ask any twelve-year-old."

A longer silence this time. He hates himself for his disgust and impatience. Twelve years old, he thinks, that must be when she started. He tries to remember the mental health file he received from Corrections: they documented addiction, but did they have that detail? But really, what does it matter. Whatever the age was, she's a patient. She needs help. He wants to sit up and take her hand, which he's never done with a patient before, but has heard from colleagues isn't always inappropriate. He wants to be closer to her, but this is his bedroom, and it's 2:04 a.m., and he can't rule out the possibility that she has come here to hurt him.

"So tell me about these rules," she says as him, bringing her hands together in a manner his wife—ex-wife—used to mock.

"Rules are simple," she answers. "Shoot the muscle, never a vein. Don't chase it, don't top it off. Just taste it and ride it out."

"That's it?" she asks herself.

"Don't look at me like that," she answers, now using a third voice, low and brittle. "It's no big whatever, Kerry. It's just heroin."

The mother, he thinks.

"Diamorphine," she continues. "Developed as a medicine. A prescribed analgesic. Comes from a plant, you can get it organic." The mother's voice trails off.

Kerasha is slouched in his chair looking down at her hands. Her whole body—the curve of her shoulders, the drop of her head—emanates an old and terrible misery. Slowly, quietly, he lifts his sheet and light blanket. Sits up, shifts his legs over the edge of the bed. Presses the soles of his feet down on the honeymoon mat, and stands before her.

"Filament, filament, filament," she says quietly. Herself again, only smaller.

Into the silence he thinks, This is the moment. Another step on his honeymoon rug—the distance is nothing, he's almost surprised by how easy this is—and, standing before her, he reaches for her hand. "I'm glad we're finally talking about this," he says.

When she looks up, the hatred in her eyes is so fierce it drives him back. Her face is ancient and has ancient power. "An addict is someone who tries to quit," she says, as he stumbles back against the bed. "I am the leavings of many deaths."

And with this her throat scrapes over itself, emitting a sound like an engine grinding over slipped gears. She crumples, and her knees are on his honeymoon rug when warm vomit splashes his ankles.

chapter 43

"And that's how they found her," Starr is saying. "Henry, I'm so, so sorry."

He lowers the phone. Looks up at the basement window Lipz used to climb in through.

Starr's voice, from a great distance: "Henry? Hen?"

He lets the phone drop.

Where you at? Who you with?

Nunya.

He backsteps until he feels the bed behind him, then turns and sees the mud on his sheets.

The funeral is held the following week. Red-bricked and newly painted, Saint Thomas Aquinas is Aunt Mercedes's church, and though none in the congregation had a thought for Lipz when she was alive, her death has the place packed. As Henry enters, happy children dart before him. He sees Aunt Mercedes laughing near the votive candle rack, her eyes moving triumphantly down the line of condolers. Henry pushes his way to the basement-floor women's room, where Starr is, as promised, waiting for him.

"Hurry," she says, pulling him into the bathroom—this is their second bathroom meeting this summer. "Everyone and their mom is trying to get in here. I keep saying the toilet's broken." After closing the door and turning the lock, she lets out a long breath. "I'm so sorry. I want to help. Let me help you. I'm trying."

"I know. Thank you." Henry touches her arm. "So that cop with the hands." Back to business. "Did you find out anything?"

"You asked me to dig." Starr takes out her phone. "I dug." A few clicks. "Officer Montenegro. First name: Zera. Assignment: field intelligence officer. That's old news, but check it—*special* assignment: Human Trafficking Task Force." She stops reading, lowers her phone. "Field intelligence, human trafficking. Something's weird here."

"Besides her hands?"

"The homicides. What's she doing with them?"

Henry frowns. "*Human* trafficking?"

"Prostitutes," Starr says. "Trafficking usually means brought in from overseas. Vietnam, Russia, Poland, Albania. Most of them are drugged, tricked, or kidnapped."

Henry frowns, thinking of the Paradise Club. Remembering a rumor he heard years ago. Something about a girl who disappeared, and the Paradise Club needing to move extra money that month.

"Speaking of human trafficking," Starr says, tapping again on her phone. "Here. Detective Fung is Detective Kurt Fung, badge 7229. That's the number you asked about." Off Henry's nod, she continues: "He *was* assigned to human trafficking, too, but he's on admin leave. Which means he screwed up." She looks up from her phone. "The rumor is he lost his gun. *And* his badge. So now he's moving files."

"Okay, back to the other cop," Henry says. "Zera whatever-the-fuck. What's she got to do with anything?"

"I asked around." More clicking. "First off, everyone's scared of her. She's *intense*. Works nonstop, never smiles. Here." She holds up her phone and shows a stolen snapshot—terrible angle, horrible lighting—of a pale and angular woman. The woman is in uniform, her hair is chopped short, and it could be the angle or the blur, but some kind of chill seems to be coming off her. Henry remembers Emil's studio—the shadow twins—and tries to match this woman to the second shadow. It's possible.

"Question," Henry says. "That case Emil was tied to, the one on that yellow sticker."

"The I-Card."

"Was weird cop working on it?"

"I'd have to check, but . . ." Starr thinks for a moment. "There's a case management system, but that's internal. I'd have to go back to the precinct, and I'm not on duty until Monday."

"Okay, but *someone's* on duty." He can picture Uncle Shecky shaking his head no, don't bring in an outsider, but fuck it. "Can you phone a friend?"

Starr smiles. "Carmen." She pushes buttons. "Huh." Pockets her phone. "No signal. Come outside with me?"

Henry nods but then feels a tug inside him. "Let's meet there in ten." A deep breath. "Some unfinished business upstairs."

Henry pushes his way to the coffin. It seems so small and so insignificant, just a little box beneath the grand altar, so far below the stained-glass windows that rainbow up to the belfry. He smells incense and heavy perfume, and everywhere—everywhere—there's laughter. The closer Henry gets to Lipz's coffin, the smaller it seems to become, and now he's beside it, wondering whether he can just slip it into his pocket. Take her away from this terrible place, and keep her with him forever. Overdose. Seriously, Lipz? You did this? Fuck. A dark and massive grief is taking hold of him when someone grabs his wrist.

His body, in motion, can do its own fighting. His left hand grabs a pew, keeps him from being yanked to the floor. His right is a raised fist, but then he sees who holds him, a stranger with grieving eyes. Seated.

"Been looking for you for days. Bring it in." The stranger releases his grip on Henry's wrist, then rises from the pew and pulls Henry into a back-slapping hug. The man, withdrawing, wipes his eyes with a black pocket square and looks Henry up and down. "People saying you're asking questions." His voice is deep and low. "You watching yourself?"

The man is slim but imposing with a close-to-the-skull haircut. His suit is immaculate, and it looks tailored to his compact body. He has the air of a holy elder, though Henry puts him in his late twenties.

"Who are you?" Henry says.

His smile is sly. "You don't know who you know." He extends a hand. "Chancellor."

Chancellor. It takes Henry a moment. Chancellor *Tomlin*, the signatory on the Sint Maarten account. Holy fuck.

Moments later, Henry is on a stone bench in a secluded vestry, looking at Lipz's casket from a different angle. Beside him sits Red Dog, the real thing, and nearby are his four children playing with crayons, Legos, and plastic police cars.

"What you just said," Henry says. "Watching myself." He pauses. To watch *himself*—he feels a profound possibility in this. And there's a surge of hope blended with fear, and it's one of those beautiful, dangerous feelings, and it's in him, so close to the surface. And so he asks, "How?"

"How what?"

"How do I watch myself?"

"Start with looking at *that*." Red Dog indicates the casket. "Makes you think, doesn't it? Who you are, what you do. Something like this happens, one of your people goes, you know you're due for a reckoning." He turns back to Henry. Lowers his voice. "You feel me?"

Henry nods.

"A few years ago I didn't give a fuck. About anything. Everything was business. But now." Red Dog indicates the children. "I got to think about the place I'm making for them." The child with the police cars crashes two of them together. "Harder," Red Dog tells the kid, then turns to Henry with a serious expression. "You watch out. It'll happen to you. You'll wake up one day and you'll look around, and you're twenty-six years old, and you've got four kids, and you're asking yourself, What the fuck am I?" Eyes back to the casket. "They're saying she OD'd. I don't know, man. If she did and it was my product—that weighs heavy. Tell you what, though. We're due for a reckoning."

A long quiet, then a change in the air. Henry turns to see Red Dog has been watching him, his expression sensitive and penetrating.

"She talked about you." Red Dog leans in. "She showed me pictures, two of you when you were kids. She said some heavy shit."

"She could be pretty smart," Henry says, "when she wasn't totally fucking crazy."

"She said the same thing about you. She said . . ." He collects his memories, and then speaks fast and with force: "She said you're smarter than you want to be. She said you feel things more than other people do. You're sensitive."

Henry lets out his breath. He'd held it, unknowingly, through the whole pronouncement. He sits in thoughtful silence, sensing that the person he is, the person he has been for years, is just a breath and a blink from transformation.

"She was my people," Red Dog says, "you were hers. You and me are brothers now. You need something, you come to me."

Henry sees the clarity in Red Dog's eyes. The sincerity. He moves in closer and asks, "I need to ask you about Tiger."

Red Dog immediately backs away. "Never heard of it."

Henry opens his mouth to respond but hasn't managed a word before—

"Crayons!"

One of the children has rematerialized. She has her father's commanding glare, and she waves a fistful of crayons at Henry. Streaks of orange and blue cover her dress, her small fingers, and her plump face. "Crayons," she tells Henry again, "draw." Henry looks down on her and, for a fraught and exhausted moment, can't say whether she is a child or a woodland creature. And before Red Dog can shoo her off, she's pressed her crayons, warm and sticky, into Henry's hand.

When she's gone, Red Dog scans the room. "The fuck is your game," he says, "throwing that word at me."

"All due respect," Henry says. "This is just me talking. We're here, right? For the same reason." He nods toward the casket, and Red Dog follows his eyes. When his expression softens, Henry asks, "How did you know he was . . . ?"

A snitch.

Red Dog rolls back his shoulders. Closes his eyes and moves his head, stretching his neck. "It's just business," he says. "I've got records. I fucking checked them."

He shakes Red Dog's hand and walks off to the clatter of Legos. He spots Starr back at the church entrance; she's waving him over.

Pushing and wending his way to Starr, Henry gets caught in a current of smiling mourners, and this current carries him to a mounted photograph of Lipz. The image is distorted, her face barely recognizable from the blocky pixels. But standing tall next to it is Aunt Mercedes, glowing before the crowd gathered around her, unable to disguise how much she's enjoying the attention. "The sink was full of hair," she shouts, her smile open and toothy. "And I was livid. I mean, this was the morning of my job interview at Bright Horizons, and I was already running late." At first Henry thinks she's telling the story of when Lipz, then eleven years old, shaved stripes into her head—thinks Aunt Mercedes is getting the story wrong. Then he realizes she's telling some other story, not talking about Lipz at all. More strange feelings, and that sense of a great and terrible loss, move within him. He hurries to Starr.

Outside: cool, quiet.

"I spoke to Carmen," Starr says, waving her phone. "Good news. She's on duty. She's alone at the main desk." She pauses as someone passes between them to enter the church. Then she says, in a different tone, "She wants to talk to you."

Henry makes a face. "She wants money."

"Would you trust her if she didn't?" Starr taps the screen and hands over the phone.

And then the phone is in his hand and the number is on the screen and Henry hears the first pulse of the call going through. He also sees a number lit up on the screen—646-555-0100—and just below are the words *Precinct Front Desk*.

Henry lowers the phone and extends his arm to its full length, as if to get the screen as far from his face as possible. "What. The *jizz*. Is THAT!?"

Starr moves to his side. "Henry, what are you . . . ?"

A tinny voice from the phone: "Eighty-Third Precinct. Hello?" A pause. "Starr?"

Starr takes the phone from Henry before he can drop it. He's fumbling for his wallet, taking out the two businesses cards. He backs up so he's in the full light from the church entrance, and here are the cards. One side, blank. Flip them over, the same handwritten number: 646-555-0144.

Starr's voice, a thousand miles away: "Henry, what's going on?"

Henry thinks: Fuck if *I* know. But here's Starr's hand on his arm, and here's her worried look, and it hits him: Who better to ask?

"Do cops ever make fake IDs?"

She looks puzzled. "Like for undercovers?"

"Like for an informant." The word was bitter out of his mouth, but now it's out and there's no swallowing it back. "You ever hear anything like that?"

She shakes her head. "I don't know how that would make sense. I know some informants get paid, but it's all cash, and that's pretty straightforward. I can't think of any reason why—" Her expression changes. "The visitor logs."

With her firm no, Henry had felt a flicker of hope. Maybe he could drop his suspicions and go back to loving his friend. But now comes this wave of nausea. "What visitor logs?"

"Everyone who comes to the precinct signs in at the front desk," Starr explains. "I work there sometimes. And there's this old-school clipboard, and you write your name and show your ID."

Henry tries to fill in the blanks. Can't. "The informant shows a fake ID at the *precinct*?"

Starr shrugs. "I'm just thinking aloud. The visitor log is kind of out in the open. If I'm an informant, I don't want *nobody* seeing my name and wondering what I was doing at the precinct. Also—hey, where are you going?"

Henry moves and thinks as if through a dream, only dimly aware that Starr is keeping up with him.

chapter 44

They stop at the Thirsty Bear, and when Starr nudges him, he looks up and there, still, is Emil's unfinished mural. "They haven't painted it over," she says.

"Yet."

"Maybe they'll keep it."

They sit at the bar. The bartender brings their drinks without asking. "How long have you been coming here?" he asks. "Regular?"

"Since Banana got cancer." She drums her fingers on her glass. "I left him alone every few nights. For a few hours. On purpose. I had to get myself ready for, you know."

"Surviving." Then he asks, "Have you ever been betrayed?"

Nothing in the conversation has touched on this, but she's not thrown, and there's only a short, bitter laugh before she says, "Oh yeah. There's a list." Then she looks him over carefully before asking, "You want to talk about it?"

"I wasn't, like, cheated on," Henry says quickly. "Not by a woman. Never."

She turns her wineglass. "But your friend."

There's a heavy weight Henry must push inside himself. At last he raises his hand, points his finger at the unfinished mural. "He made that." But Henry's not thinking about the mural. He's calling up all the little warning signs he's tried to ignore. The yellow sticker on Emil's incident report. The Pennsylvania driver's license. The card taped to the top of Emil's door, and that same card in Tiger's wallet. And Tiger had a Pennsylvania license, and he got killed as a snitch, and the number on the cards was NYPD.

"He made that painting," Starr says carefully, "but—he did something else?"

Henry sits on his hands. "I think but I don't know. But this is the pisser: Uncle Shecky was right." He draws in his breath. "Fucking Emil. I never should have brought him in. And fuck me, thinking I had everything under control. And I *still* don't know."

Starr taps her glass. "And you can't sit on suspicion."

"Because it doesn't feel right. This wasn't the guy I knew. He taught me things. On his own time, not just for money. He *cared*. And now I'm just spinning. Can't sit still, can't sleep. I keep thinking there's an explanation, or a coincidence—some way to make it okay. I mean, does it *have* to be the worst-case scenario? And here's what's making me crazy. I've got this hunch, okay? That I can go back to the house—like right now—and open up the records. And I can piece it all together, and I'll know what's what."

Starr fishes out Henry's hand from under him. "But you won't be able to unknow it."

Henry turns to her. "He was my friend."

"Okay, he meant something to you." She gives his hand another squeeze. "But you don't have to have only one feeling about him. You can miss him *and* be mad at him. No one's perfect."

"Yeah, but here's the thing about imperfection." There's a break in the bar music, and over the fragile quiet he says, "Flaws, mistakes, whatever you've got—I need to know who I'm with."

He feels embarrassed, holding hands at this fuck-and-run bar. But his hand is still in hers when she says, "So go find out."

In the upstairs office, Henry unlocks his uncle's desk, pulls open the top drawer, and stops at the sight of his gun. He locked it in the drawer the morning after Tiger got killed. Hasn't thought much about it since then. Now he takes it out. Feels the weight, the shape, the dense mass of it. He looks it over, squeezes the grip, tests the safety, on off, off on. A breeze rattles the blinds: the window is open. His fascination breaks with a shudder, and he pushes the gun down into the front right pocket of his jeans. Closes the window, smooths the blinds. Another shudder. The gun doesn't belong in this office. He'll find a better place for it tonight. He turns off the overhead light, adjusts the gun in his pocket, and goes back to the desk. Settles into the chair, flips on the lamp. The desk is covered with laptops and phones. More are in the drawers, he knows, along with charities' registration filings, wills, tax records, power of attorney papers, deeds, credit reports, notary stamps, certified corporate records, and keys to safety deposit boxes. Money moves in the dark, and this room is where much of the darkness is created. Over the past year Henry has come to work in this office almost as much as his uncle does. This is their hub for the daily flow of money and information. Foggy-headed, Henry moves aside the ledger. Picks, absently, through the papers. Soloway Equities, the Toohey Group, the Brecher Foundation. He wonders if these names are purposely false or just seem so to him. The chits and crypt sheets Henry keeps for his runners, the equivalents Uncle Shecky has for the clients—all records listing *living* people are destroyed or stored off-site. The families, nonprofits, LLCs, and trusts here are all just transactional conveniences. Like Emil, Henry thinks bitterly. Like me.

The drawers closed, the computers locked or shut down, he reaches absently for the gun but instead feels something small and semisoft, like a tube of wax. Puzzled, he digs it out of his pocket—a black Crayola crayon. He fishes out another crayon, this one purple, and remembers the kids at Lipz's funeral. Remembers the little girl who brought over the crayons while he was talking to Red Dog. That was another life, he thinks. That was less than twelve hours ago. And the pistol is in his *right* pocket.

Henry puts the crayons on the desk, sets the pistol beside them, and checks his phone: 3:16 a.m. He removes his shoes and pads to his uncle's bedroom. Doesn't want to wake him. Kinda wants to talk to him. But the room is empty, the bed unmade. No one keeps regular hours in this house, but it's rare for his uncle to be out like this. Henry catches himself feeling relieved. Why? Pushing the feeling down, steeling himself, he returns to the office. The gun going once more into his pocket, he sits back at the desk and takes out paper and lets loose the black and purple crayons. He hardly glances down, pays no attention to what his hands are doing. His gaze is drawn instead to the wall behind the desk, which is covered with framed playbills from his uncle's productions. Though Henry stopped going years ago, he remembers well the mixture of amazement and discomfort he felt whenever he saw his uncle on stage. Who *was* this man, and who knew he had *that* inside him? The productions were always so cheap and sloppy, but his uncle went all out. The shouting lawyer in *A View from a Bridge*, the suicide dad in *August: Osage County*, the idiot teacher in *The Seagull*. The different roles, the accents, the ways he moved. The strangers he could become, when he wanted to. And maybe Emil was a little like that, too.

Henry's crayons keep working. He hardly looks at them, but the playbills, which he's sat before a hundred times, hold a new and un-expected fascination for him. It's as though they've been behind a curtain and now here they are. They're nothing like the glossy book-lets from the Broadway shows Henry went to with his uncle years ago. These are cheap printouts, folded and stapled. And yet here they are in real frames.

He hears a noise and his thoughts blow away. He looks down at what his crayons have made and recognizes his uncle's face, narrow and with frightened eyes. An unhappy smile as Henry looks at the bent line he's made for his uncle's mouth. "You never know someone," he says for his uncle, "till you get your nose up their money."

Your turn, Emil. What've you got for me?

Henry grabs a sheet of scrap paper, a pencil. He flips through the pages of the ledger, goes back to summer, back to the day of Emil's first carry. He focuses on the left side of the open book: the runner logs. Everything here is in black ink, and this is Henry's own handwriting. Henry's pencil moves over the scrap paper with no hesitation. He copies dates and figures, and in less than fifteen minutes, he's written out a complete schedule of Emil's pickups and deposits. These transactions have always been documented, but they've never been itemized like this—all of Emil's work for the family is now in one place, a single timeline, the records not intermingled with those of other runners. Henry looks down Emil's list. Here's $4,998 from Benny the roofer, and there's a $4,998 confirmed wire through MoneyGram. Here's $813 from Chabad House, and there's a $813 confirmed money order through a Duane Reade in Williamsburg. And so on. Emil's whole short career as a runner: he never pinched a dollar.

It's done, Henry checked it, but he takes a second look at the schedule he's drafted. There's still a large space on the right side of the page. Something's missing. He's traced money *moving through* Emil—but hasn't confirmed that the money made its way back to the clients. Hasn't looked at records from the family's transactional accounts. This is Uncle's Shecky's side of the business, but Henry's helped with it, and he understands how it works. The money goes through these accounts—usually at least two—before it goes back to the client. Henry flips ahead a few pages in the ledger. Focuses on the right-side pages. Here the ink is blue, rather than black, and the handwriting his uncle's, rather than his own. Henry completes his schedule more carefully now. Because this is his uncle's work, he can't decode everything on autopilot. Several times, he wonders if he's getting things wrong. He thinks he might be wrong, it's quite possible he is wrong, only—

He's not wrong. There's a pattern.

Emil didn't skim. Most runners do, sooner or later, whining to Henry that their $500 bag had only $450 in it. Or it must've been that Payomatic teller with the red hair: she's got the quick hands and the side game, everyone knows about *her*. Henry's heard every weak-ass excuse. His fists know what to do with them. But this wasn't Emil. Whether by wire transfers, money orders, or good old-fashioned cash deposits, the money he picked up went into the system. All of it, every time. Emil *was* different, as Henry had reassured Uncle Shecky. He did his job.

But he was also doing something else. Internal inquiry, account closed, account frozen—starting this summer, two to four weeks after nearly every transaction Emil touched, something bad happened to a family account. Subpoena. Court order. Service from law enforcement. There can be no doubt now—

Come *on*, kid, fucking own it. There hasn't been real doubt for some time. The police weren't watching your boy. They were steering him.

"You fucking tool," he says aloud. But at least half his anger is toward himself. If Emil was a tool, Henry was one of the people who'd used him. Henry had promised he'd go to his uncle after he had everything worked out. So here it is, the thing he worked out: his friend was a rat. And Henry had put a load of cash on him, made him a moving target, gotten him killed, and put the whole family in danger.

Henry opens the window. Breathes in the night, returns to the desk. A dead minute passes.

Then a summer breeze comes in, and like a ghost hand, it turns a page of the ledger. Opens it to a loose sheet of paper.

Henry picks it up. Blue ink, no cross-outs or corrections. Every seven has a midline, every zero a slash, and there's no dollar sign anywhere. Uncle Shecky's hand.

And the numbers are the same as Henry's.

His hands shaking, Henry puts his uncle's schedule next to his own. Every digit is the same, the fucking layout is the same, and why wouldn't it be? It was Uncle Shecky who taught Henry how to do this.

Uncle Shecky who checked the records first, and saw Emil for what he was.

Poison.

And a new kind of rage is moving Henry now, a fury with red intent, and he's on his feet, his hands shaking as he shreds the schedules. He's ripping up time, he's ripping out mistakes, he's ripping apart not only the dead snitch but the man who had him murdered. Henry remembers his uncle's face, that guilty-surprised expression when the money spilled out of the briefcase. And his uncle's meetings

with Vasya, and it's so obvious now—how could he have missed it?—
there was no loan from the Paradise Club, only a return. Pleasure
doing business, here's the money we found on the guy we killed for you.
So let's give it up for the trusted partner, and mad props for Uncle
Shecky. Old man cuts a loose end like a motherfucker.

Careful what you teach, old man.

Henry picks up the gun.

chapter 45

Five nights back, Shecky can still feel the oil from Vasya's goodbye handshake when he accepts that he can no longer look away from what he's accountable for. He will stop nothing in motion, but he will see what he is and know what he does. Still out in the dusk, still on that bench with the pigeons, he uses a new burner to call Vasya. "Have your contractor find me in Maria Hernandez Park," he says. "I will personally lead him to the 'problem.'"

"You, there on the spot?" Vasya is sputtering. "It's a terrible risk. Think about—"

"Me being there eliminates all risk," Shecky says. He regrets that they're barely keeping to their code-speak. There are moments, though, when a misunderstanding is more dangerous than a wiretap. "What if your contractor finds the wrong person? I'll make sure he doesn't. And don't worry—she won't be spooked if she sees me. She'll think I'm bringing her money. And another—"

"Enough, enough!" Vasya's voice, usually slick as his hand oil, is now a squeak. In the ringing quiet that follows this, Shecky catches his breath, and supposes his partner is doing the same. "You're right," Vasya says at last. "You trust me, I trust the contractor, and so now I will trust you two together."

After blanking and dumping the new phone, Shecky stops at

Hava Java, washes up in the bathroom, and gets a light coffee to go. He takes out his old phone and responds to the messages he received this morning:

Meet me tonight, he writes. I'll make things right for you.

About damn time, she shoots back.

He sends the where and the when. She agrees immediately, and apparently without suspicion. Funny, how the mind works. She's a smart girl, obviously—she figured *him* out. Henry and Kerasha didn't, but they have their love to blind them. But *her* love—her name—is at stake, and she can't see past it. She probably thinks this is the beginning of a partnership between equals.

And then it's nighttime. He checks for messages from the kids: nada and nada, surprise surprise. Then he heads out to watch a murder.

At a bodega near the southeast entrance to Maria Hernandez Park, Shecky stocks up on snacks and magazines. A bag of pretzels, two bottles of pomegranate seltzer, a baggie of loose-leaf tobacco and some papers—fucking heck, why not—and, carrying all this in a black plastic bag, he takes a slow stroll around the park. At long last, the rendezvous.

A fug of infused marijuana, the muttered words "fucking dick-rider," draw him to a secluded gazebo. The pillared marble structure is built like a Greek temple—a site of sacrifice, how perfect—and though he tries to remember some choice lines from *Antigone*, that part of his brain is walled off.

He gets close enough to see Lipz settling on a bench, smoking and doing something on her phone. He finds a bench for himself—nearby, but secluded—and shoots a text to the contractor: *Arrival*.

He rolls a cigarette and lights it on his first match, despite the breeze and his being out of practice. He lets it slow-burn in his hand. This bench is creaky old wood, not like the stone benches in the gazebo, and every shift of his weight seems to announce him to the night. He wonders how many lonesome hours he's spent waiting in the quiet like this—he, who fears a silent house above all else. He draws on the cigarette, and twelve years roll back.

It's the summer of hope, less than thirty-six hours before Henry is to move in with him. Shecky Keenan scrubs the house, giving it the whole floor-to-wall vinegar rubdown. He takes a rag to the corners and counters and windows and even the slats of the venetians. Before 4:00 a.m., his excitement too big to be roofed, he rushes out into the still-black morning. He actually jogged. Forty-six years old, bony and breathless, wrecked ankles, but here he is, bopping up and down under the street lamps. He passes slouched junkies, flattened drunks—Brooklyn lawn furniture, Dannie used to call them. This morning she's a happy spirit. Parkside, he ascends a little hill, and come sunup, the world is for him.

At the park's northwest entrance he finds bustle and light. Three trucks are already here, another is pulling in. Two women crouch on the asphalt and line up poles thick as standpipes. Adjustments, readjustments, then they fasten the connectors. Light rope ties the poles to waterproofed canvas. Men appear, and the five-person team secure and pull from different corners. The morning's first vendor tent rises up: Bushwick's weekly farmers market is alive. The bread man stacks loaves while his partner uses a thick marker to write prices on index cards. Teams, most consisting of unshaven men and pixie-cut women, open crates. Shecky walks among them, inspecting the cucumbers, the tomatoes. The peaches are heaped chest-high. Across the way is Katti the Fish Girl—years later, he will partner with her and help her open a storefront on Howard Place—and she's layering ice over pink, gray, and yellow fillets. Full daylight now. He recognizes hake, swordfish, and cod. Katti closes the cooler she just emptied and opens another. Now out with the scallops, out with bluefish, gutted and cleaned but otherwise whole. Eyeballs still in place.

"Too early for a sale?" Shecky asks.

"Never too early to take a buck," Katti says, changing to a new pair of rubber gloves. She's a young woman with an easy smile but hard, mercantile eyes. "What's your fish?"

He points to a stack of orange fish, wide and thick-bodied. "Those got a name?" Like the bluefish, these fish are gutted but whole.

"Porgy. Good eye, these are the best I've got today. Look at you," she adds, as if now addressing the fish directly, "selling yourselves before the market opens."

"Hard to cook?"

"Can you turn on an oven?"

Shecky smiles. "Just figured it out last month." And reading cookbooks, for the first time in his life. Testing out recipes, even went into Manhattan for a class. He'll be cooking for two now, and he wants to do it right.

"Here's what I do." Katti leans toward him and lowers her voice, as if she were taking him into her confidence. "There're eight hundred ways to cook the thing, but I say keep it simple. Porgy isn't the kind of fish you need to hide under a layer of seasoning. Just add salt and pepper."

"Butter?"

"Of course. And it goes in the oven at three-fifty. Just put a fork in it after ten minutes. If it goes in easy, you're done."

"You *bake* it?"

"The oven does the baking. I have a glass of wine."

Shecky thinks the porgy is the most beautiful thing he's ever seen. "This is it," he says. This big-eyed fish will welcome his nephew home. And the moment the fish is bagged and double-bagged, he feels the weight of it. His nephew is coming to *live* with him—a boy, entrusted to him, will share his meals and his roof. Will ensure that his life will always be peopled and that his house will never again be quiet. Shecky feels as if awakening from a sleep he was unaware of. Gone, at last, are the battles with the city's Department of Youth and Children Services—a bureau created and staffed by mis-wired robots. Gone, at last, are Henry's Florida aunts, who never wanted the boy at all, but fought him for a piece of Alessandro and Molly's tiny trust.

All that scheming drama is nothing now. Hear this, Brooklyn, take a look at this fucking fish.

I got a family.

It's been more than a decade since he brought home that fish. Years since he last saw the boy who couldn't sleep alone, or even the eager adolescent Shecky took into his business. And here Shecky sits on a park bench at two in the morning, losing another night's sleep for the kid—who doesn't even know, and mustn't ever learn, what's being done for him.

Shecky's cigarette burns forgotten in his hand. His mind drifts down the streets surrounding the park, and he tries to picture the gray and indefinite figure of the man he's waiting for. Did he stop at an ATM on the way here, like an everyday normal person on his way to work, maybe the Bank of America on Knickerbocker.

The Bank of America on Knickerbocker.

It was at this branch, Shecky remembers with a sinking feeling, that luck first turned against the family. Shecky remembers the notices from various banks. Remembers the headaches and night sweats, and the *losses* he took, developing new channels for his clients' money. And leaning forward on his park bench now, putting a hand to his forehead, Shecky remembers that miserable night he holed up in his office, reviewing his ledger. Scheduling out the closing and freezing of his accounts, and determining that the point of inception, the event that started everything, was a cash deposit at the Bank of America on Knickerbocker. So who made that deposit? Shecky put his records side-by-side with Henry's. It was obvious. One runner, and no other, had touched each of the closed accounts. Shecky sat back, crossed his arms, and smiled. He felt as though a great cleansing wind had blown through his life, carrying away his doubts and confusion. All was clear now: the banks were backing away because of the cops, and the cops were coming close because of the runner.

He picked up the phone.

He put it down.

A warning bell was ringing in his head. He'd been hearing it for a while now, even before he'd finished his timeline. Of all the runners, of all the people it could be—why did it have to be this one? "He's an artist," Henry had said, with a small, almost embarrassed smile, the first time he told Shecky about Emil Scott. Henry had looked so hesitant, so vulnerable. "Do you think . . . sometime . . . maybe he could come by for dinner?"

But now Shecky had the phone in his hand. He *had* to make this call. This was a non-choice, but still he hesitated.

For a moment.

"We have a personnel problem," he told Vasya. A hard stillness grew cold in his chest. "Just one person."

And the problem was gone within twenty-four hours.

Dimly, as if coming out of a dream, Shecky becomes aware of approaching footsteps. He tosses what's left of his cigarette. He stands up from the bench and shakes the outstretched gloved hand.

"Where is he?" the man asks.

"*She*," Shecky says, "is over in the gazebo."

The surprise on the man's face is unmistakable. The contractor had come to kill a man. The floppy pretext Shecky invented for being here in person was justified after all. If Shecky weren't here, this man would now go off and murder—who knows? Shecky forces himself to take a good look at the man, a large and strange creature who seems to be studying him in turn. He wears a backpack slung over one shoulder. Shecky's heard just a few words but thinks he's picked up on an Eastern European accent. A whiff of pomade gives Shecky his second startle of the night: he knows this man. It's the barber they call Matt.

"Well then," Shecky says, "no point in . . ." He nods toward the gazebo.

Matt smiles, showing his big teeth. "She won't feel a thing." Already unzipping a side pocket of his backpack, he walks to the gazebo, unhurriedly but directly.

Enough already, Dannie says—once again the big sister who got him out of the wicked box. Who came for him always. You've heard me say this to the players, but you don't have to rip your heart out. You've faced what you've done. You've owned this already. Leave.

But Shecky's hands are shaking and he can't roll a second cigarette. Then the match won't light, and then, Jesus fuck, this is *too much*, he can't just—

Shecky charges the gazebo and arrives in time to see Lipz sitting on the bench, illuminated by the ghastly streetlights, looking around expectantly—looking for *him*. And the barber called Matt stands behind and over her, raising a small tube as if it's a dagger.

"Wait," Shecky says, though later he won't be certain he said it loudly enough, or even that he said it at all.

Matt presses the tube into the girl's arm and immediately smashes the base of the tube with the palm of his other hand. She lets out a squeak, then a cry, as he backs away. The tube spinning on the ground, her cry becomes a roar, and her body convulses, and she kicks herself off the bench and hits the stone floor hard with a terrible sound. And her screams continue, and Shecky turns away but makes himself look back, and she writhes so violently her body seems to bounce off the stone floor. Matt, meanwhile, is smiling. He's putting the tube back into his pocket. His flat, broad face shows bemused, if mild, surprise as the girl roars and bangs herself against the ground, arcing her back, her feet pushing her up and turning her round and over. She moves as though her flesh is in flames, and she thrashes and then—and this horrifies Shecky more than anything that has already come—she sits upright. A peaceful slump. Her back is to Shecky, so he can't know what her face shows or what she's looking at, but for a few seconds she's silent, and then her body falls forward and stops moving. A half minute passes.

And Shecky is aghast at how crude this all is. A fake OD—surely there must be more to the plan than *this*? The Paradise Club, with their crisp cash and their shining shoes—with their hired assassin and his special weapon—surely there will be some final masterstroke? There must be, or else Detective 7229 will piece it together. Could he really believe the two deaths, both connected to the family, are coincidental?

But then Shecky sees the calm, self-satisfied look on Matt's face as he gives Shecky a lazy wave and walks off. And Shecky remembers that this is Brooklyn, where the police don't dig any deeper than they have to. They sure as fuck didn't for Dannie. Shecky remembers all too well the totality of *that* investigation: a few door knocks, a collective shrug, and then off with the files to deep storage.

So here's a very convenient truth, for Shecky, about Detective 7229. He isn't piecing together shit. He'll take what he's given.

And now Shecky can see the whole investigation play out. An addict is found dead with something in her blood—another OD, cursory investigation, file closed. The partners of Shecky Keenan may be sloppy, but he operates in a world where sloppy is good enough.

Shecky stands over the girl and for a long time keeps his eyes on what he's done.

"I'm so sorry," he says. For a moment, he is.

chapter 46

There are three people Henry feels like killing right now. The first is already dead, the second expected any minute. And the third sits at his uncle's desk, his heart heavy with doubt and hurt.

A sound from downstairs.

Henry Vek closes the ledger, rises with the gun, and goes to the door. He listens. Another sound brings him into the hall.

His body hot and cold, his mind clear, he waits for his uncle's voice. Can already almost see the small, nervous face peering up at him from the bottom of the stairwell. Henry raises the gun with shaking hands.

No one's in the stairwell.

Thank God.

No, no, be strong. Two shots—one out, one in, just like breath—then it's over.

Henry switches the gun to his left hand. He stomps to announce himself. Flips off the safety and puts his finger on the trigger. There's something wrong with his eyes—fuck, now he's crying—but he feels so light and free. See, Uncle Shecky? I met the problem head-on. I worked it out all by myself—just like you—and now I'm completing the solution. Stomp, stomp, he descends, and at last a shadow falls over the bottom step. He squeezes the trigger. Squeezes harder, digs his palm into the grip, but it's not enough, the trigger bends but doesn't catch until—

He's at the bottom step. He's caught up with the shadow and discovered it's his own.

Please God, say he's not home.

Turning the corner, he switches his gun back to his right hand, wipes his palm against his jeans, and is just getting a new, dry hold on the grip when he sees that the dining room table is set. A full family breakfast.

The gun lowers.

Before Henry are three plates, three mugs, three sets of silver on cloth napkins. On bowls and plates are eggs and toast, bacon and fruit. Henry touches the toast: still warm.

Uncle Shecky must have just walked out of the room, Henry thinks. I've been couch-surfing for days, Kerasha has been MIA fuck knows how long, but here's our breakfast, just the way we like it. The Tabasco bottle is near Kerasha's plate, the rhubarb jam closer to mine. Never mind that Uncle Shecky must have come home drunk off his ass, for him to have whipped up this meal at stupid o'clock in the morning. He never—never—gives up on us. Even after all this shit, he wants us to walk in the door and know there'll always be a place for us here.

Our home. Henry wipes his eyes. He was watching over us.

Like he always has.

Henry sets the gun on the table and walks out the door.

part ten

the living

chapter 47

One hour earlier, as Henry waits, quiet and motionless in the upstairs office, Kerasha slips into the house.

Her web just isn't right. Henry's bed is made, which means he's been a long time gone and Uncle Shecky couldn't help himself. Uncle Shecky's bed, meanwhile, is rumpled, as if squeezed all over by angry, frightened fists. There's no Guinness in the fridge, there are bags of recyclables in the yard, and the reek of summer garbage is especially foul. Uncle Shecky must have missed their Department of Sanitation pickup date, but none of this so unnerves her as the quiet. This is a ghost house, she thinks. This is no place for the living.

Fuck no, not *my* web.

Her nausea in remission, she gets to work. The rotting garbage and bags of recyclables she puts in front of Lacey Atkinson's house— sanitation is due to pick up on that block tomorrow morning. After washing her hands, she makes her uncle's bed and messes up Henry's. Quiet movements, she feels like an intruder. But it's the house that's all wrong. How do we fix it? Back on the ground floor she mops, as her uncle does, with vinegar and water. She makes a fresh solution and douses a rag to wipe down the kitchen and then the dining room, which she considers the center of her web: the filaments here hold the whole thing together.

She sniffs, she looks, she listens. Nothing *extra* is here, she decides, after checking for bugs, both insect and electronic; what's wrong is that something is missing. She moves to the kitchen. Finds eggs, a half stick of butter, a can of coffee, a frozen whole-wheat semolina loaf, a bottle of Tabasco, and a few dirty onions and potatoes, which, when washed, turn out to be perfectly fryable. Back of the fridge, sausage and bacon—they pass the smell test, so she gets them going in the skillet. She takes out a big pan and finds the percolator. Fires up the stove and measures the coffee and water. She chops the onions and potatoes, drops a hunk of butter into the pan, and uses her knife to scrape the potatoes and onions from the cutting board to the pan. She tilts the pan and, with a big wooden spoon, rolls everything over and under the butter. The potatoes crisped, she cracks the eggs over them, and then checks the sausage and bacon—hissing and popping. And so, in motion and in how she absently whistles, she becomes her uncle; this is his daily breakfast routine, which has amazed and frightened and warmed her from morning one.

The percolator shakes and the house smells as it ought to. She lays out three plates and three sets of silverware, polishing the tongs of a not-quite-clean fork with the hem of her not-at-all-clean shirt. Now Kerasha summons her inner barista: straight black for Uncle Shecky, cream and sugar for herself, just cream for Henry. *Thank you for being here, thank you for being my family.* Breakfast for three, and nobody's here to eat it.

The clock tells her it is 3:00 a.m. Her body turns against itself, her skin itchy, nausea like a churning ocean.

She goes to her room. Bumps into a bookshelf, but it holds steady—Henry did her right. She's sweating but she covers herself with a heavy blanket. Hot and cold, she smells her own foul body and hears the rattle of her teeth. It will pass, she insists to herself. All I am is here now.

Jesus fuck, her inner Uncle Shecky asks, when did you turn into Nicole?

But I *am* here now. And the now is powerful. It's not Dr. Xu's apartment or the taxi he put her in. The now annihilates all that. The past happened, the now says, but this is something else.

A hazy head. Saint Augustine crawls into bed with her. His lecherous hands search her, find the spot on her arm where the needle went in.

"Listen," he says, "like your very parole depends on it." He smells like malt and his voice is the beast's, the worst and last boyfriend who taught her about *after*. "Philistines ask me, What was your 'God' doing *before* he created the universe? Why was he wasting all that empty time? I tell them, time is part of the universe God created. There is no before. Now, young lady"—he squeezes Kerasha's hand—"take that to your life. Your God. Your first true moment is right now. God has renewed you. Your time has just started." He strokes her cheek and his eyes are Mama's, his voice gentle like hers was. "Do you feel me?"

She does and she doesn't. Ten hours later, she finds herself sitting in front of a bowl of marbles, wondering how there can be no before when last night is a mark on her arm.

"So I'm guessing last night will have some part in my evaluation," she says. Although technically, she adds in her head, last night we weren't in session.

"We can talk about the evaluation later," Dr. Xu says. His hands move over each other, not quite finding the ball. "How are you feeling?"

Like sunshine, Kerasha thinks. No sweats, just a little dry mouth. She'd been clean a long spell before last night, but she still remembers how it works. Just give her a ginger ale and some dragon-fried rice, and she'll be the perkiest little spider in Brooklyn.

We wear the mask that grins and lies.

"Eh." She shrugs. "Not bad, for a relapse."

"But . . ." Dr. Xu's mouth hangs open, his eyes expectant, then hurt. It's hard to see him like this, acting so human. At last he asks, "Was it different this time?"

"I was ashamed." It takes her a moment to accept that these words came out of her, that the ponytail wasn't pulling some trick of ventriloquism. Another moment to accept that not only are these words hers, but they're true. Before last night she had never been with someone when the sickness hit.

"So what changed?" The way he squirms, along with the delicacy of his voice, further unsettles her. "Why this time," he continues, when she doesn't answer, "didn't you do it alone?"

She risks a glance and is amazed to see that his eyes are kind. The *fuck*, her inner Henry says. Where's the condescension? Then the obvious answer hits her. Last night she crossed a line that can't be uncrossed. She went into his home, for fuck's sake, puked on his floor. He can be a human to her now because they're breaking up.

"So who's my new shrink?" That's right, motherfucker, you don't cry goodbye to this spider—*I'm* losing *you*.

"Do you want a new psychiatrist?" he asks.

"Obvi." Here you go again, Dr. Ponytail, you and your fucking want. But want here provides a convenient answer to a question that's been troubling her. Yes, of course, she wants to lose him—why else did she show up at his apartment, smacked?

Dr. Xu presses his fingertips together and makes a ball with his hands. It's about time, she thinks. No more pretending to care, Dr. Xu. You're back to your true self: a man-shaped wad of condescension.

But then it occurs to her, and for the first time, that this ball gesture may not be an affectation picked up from some TV shrink. It may be a way for the man to summon patience, and not to hop up on his coffee table and shout bullshit.

He asks, "So what are we going to do about the heroin problem?" The directness of the question makes her shiver.

"There's no heroin problem," she says. How about we talk about the heroin *solution*. Seriously, *using* is the operative word—using has always been a choice, has always been something she could control. The rules are simple. Shoot to the muscle, not a vein. Don't top it off, just ride it out, and never increase the dose. Just keep your head right, and no more locking yourself into supply closets. No more getting caught.

"So what happened last night?"

The heroin was cheap and dirty, she thinks. I didn't follow the rules. I was off it too long, then I started at the old dose, and it was impure.

"Don't you fucking look at me like that," she says.

His knowing nod, the tiny flare of his nostrils, and the dance of his fingertips against each other—she can't take it. She stands and, for some reason, grabs a fistful of marbles, spilling a few to rattle and roll off the coffee table. "Don't you fucking look at me like that," she says again. More loose marbles bounce off the coffee table. A few slip through her fingers and patter on the floor.

"How am I looking at you?"

"Like I'm some junkie in denial."

Dr. Xu says nothing.

"Do you think I'm in denial?" She hates the scratch in her voice.

"These are the right questions," he says, checking his nonexistent watch. "And we still have time. But I want to make sure you have a chance to talk about what you brought with you today."

"What I *brought*?"

Just like old times, she thinks, my old question-the-question defense. What is this, week one? Jesus fuck, Kerry, you were in his bedroom last night. You puked on his rug, and he put his hand on your back. What you *brought*, Kerry, he's asking, and he has a right to.

In the fog of her anger, she forgot about the bucket.

She sinks back to the couch. Shame—how it had surprised her when she mentioned it to him, and how quickly she chased it back in the dark. She's ashamed again now. He wants to see what you brought, she tells herself, and you brought it for a reason. Reluctantly, moving as if with all her muscles stretched or torn, she reaches under the coffee table and pulls up the bucket. Deny *this*, motherfucker, she tells herself, and she looks down and makes herself see the syringes.

"These are my dog tags," she finally says.

"Can you explain that?"

"If anyone finds me," she says, "this tells them who I belong to."

The doctor's smile, if it's there at all, is tiny. Get on with it, he's probably thinking, show it to me. And why not? He already knows. Her hands trembling, the needles tinkling, Kerasha pushes the bucket across the coffee table. It scrapes across the table and leaves a streak of rust. This streak on the coffee table shames her even more than what happened last night.

At last the bucket is before Dr. Xu. He picks it up nonchalantly, as if to show it's just a dirty metal thing and has no power. The moment he peers inside, however, he makes a sound and thrusts the bucket back at her, nearly spilling the needles. For a terrible few seconds his fear and disgust are naked before her. And when he is placid again, she decides she likes him more for the lapse.

"Let's talk about why you carry that around," Dr. Xu says, pushing himself back into his seat and wiping his hands on his pants. "Are you trying to take ownership of what's in there?"

"I don't know who owns who," she says. "This helps me remember." She shoots a look at her own imaginary watch. "Is it time?"

He gives her a look as though he wants to ask a question—Do you *want* it to be time?—but then stops himself. His expression changing, his mouth growing small, he shifts uncomfortably in his seat and looks at his hands as he says, "I cleared out my next appointment."

This leaves her breathless.

"We need time," he continues, "to discuss your evaluation."

A roaring wave of nausea. Black and purple spots. The sound of a cell door scraping across the concrete floor. The smell of the mildewed mattress, the banging of the radiator pipes in winter, the cracked toilet that, when flushed, splashes up and wets the cell floor. Motherfucker, she thinks. Dr. Ponytail saw me out, cleaned up my puke, and then called Franklin to reserve a spot for me. *Of course* he wrote her evaluation. This is how it works: you're judged at your moment of failure. The room shakes gently. Just the passing J train, she supposes, but then her vision blurs around the edges. The one point of focus is the pinched space above his nose and between his eyes.

"I don't think I can handle this." She hates her tiny, little girl's voice, hates her tiny, little girl's weakness. Just a month out of the halfway house—how did I get so soft? Clean sheets smelling of lavender, giant breakfasts with real-meat bacon and cream-and-sugar coffees; Uncle Shecky and his *get thru it* texts, big Henry and his girls and his tantrums. Dirty, silly Brooklyn, which she's studied so carefully over this month, falling in love from rooftops and shadows.

Dr. Xu goes to his desk, unlocks a drawer, and takes out printed pages, a thin, stapled packet. He places the evaluation on the coffee table.

Kerasha can't look at it. Her eyes lock on the tiny hook where the handle catches the base of her bucket.

"You don't have to read it," Dr. Xu says. "In this room, you're in control."

Get thru it, Kerry, she tells herself, you've been through worse.

Been through? Her inner Mama shakes the bucket at her. You've *done* worse than read something ugly about yourself. That evaluation is pages, and words got nothing on a bucket of needles. Which you added to *last night*.

Her hands shake as she reads. Kerasha has always been a fast reader, and her retention is strong and comprehension immediate— but she has to go over each paragraph several times before she can make sense of it. And yet here and there individual words flare up: *Recalcitrant. Combative.* Words, phrases: *Willfully overlooks documented facts. Wall of denial. Self-destructive behavior patterns, including—*

And at last she's on the final page, and only here finds the words that heat and bend the air: "The patient has made remarkable progress, and continued outpatient treatment is expected to facilitate further social reintegration and recovery."

Minutes pass, then Kerasha places the evaluation on the coffee table. Covers, not realizing it, the rust stain left by her bucket. Her eyes fix on the bowl of marbles as she says, "You didn't mention the throwing up."

There's a silence until she raises her eyes. "Sometimes there's a gap," Dr. Xu says, "between the court's requirements and the patient's."

She studies the space just above his nose. Scans his receding hair-line, his slender fingers, his tiny mouth. There is no warmth coming from him, but for the first time she sees his restraint as a type of kindness. She asks, "I'm not going back in the cage?"

"I'm not recommending that."

She picks up the evaluation again, turning pages but reading nothing except the last sentence. She feels the burn on her chin once more. It's a draft, she reminds herself. The evaluation won't be filed until next month. Nothing to get excited about, she still has time to fuck things up. And yet she's given herself goose bumps again, and feels preternaturally sensitive to the fabric of the couch she sits on, its softness; to the floor beneath her shoes, the gentle push of the rug, and the hardness beneath. And more than ever she feels *spatially* sensitive, physically tuned into her position in the world. Here she is on the top floor of a three-story cinder-block-and-glass commercial building, and beneath it is the foundation, stone and concrete and steel, and beneath that, past whatever rubble and human detritus has been crushed and mixed together—down below is the earth. *Her* earth, the same as Mama's, Uncle Shecky's, and the little man's—here it is, here it's always been, touching her all this time. She's held up by a fucking planet. And whatever mistakes she's made and will make, whatever defects she will patch over or succumb to, there's space here for her little life.

"Are you surprised?" Dr. Xu asks. It takes her a moment to understand that he's still talking about the evaluation, that he wasn't privy to her lofty thoughts, which embarrass her now, and which she will never discuss. "Did you expect something else from this session?" His plain, narrow face is toying with a smile.

She finds nothing funny in any of this, including the grace he's shown her. "Last night I shot heroin and broke into your apartment," she says. "I didn't expect us to be talking about hope."

"Relapse is part of recovery." Back to pedant mode, before he softens: "But it's not the only part." One last look at his watch-less wrist and he says, "Now it's time. But to your point," he continues, looking up, and now his smile is big and warm, "of course there's hope. I wouldn't be here if I didn't believe in your recovery."

And neither would I.

Fuck, am I really here because I believe in therapy?

No, not belief. Hope. And there's a wonder and a joy in this, and in learning that there's still hope.

She leaves the office by the front door and takes the bus like a normal person. She walks in the sunlight and drinks a half-dozen ginger ales over the course of the day, and then her stomach is right and her head is sleepy but clear. Under a reddening sky she walks to her uncle's house, which she hasn't been back to since she laid out that breakfast early this morning. This feels right, coming home now. She'll have a good dinner tonight, and her bedsheets will be clean and smell of lavender. The smell of a charcoal barbecue she passes, two kids chasing a third on a bike, a sweaty couple repainting an old truck—my city, she thinks, my web. She crosses the street, turns a corner, and smiles at the sight of her uncle's house. Upstairs, on the bookshelf Henry built for her, is her copy of June Jordan's *Directed by Desire*, and already her head is full of it: the scent of the paper, the dog-eared page where "Poem About My Rights" begins, the shape of the text on this page:

I am not wrong: Wrong is not my name

After a good dinner she'll fall asleep with this book, and she's smiling as she walks up the cracked porch steps, feeling tired but at peace with how everything is.

But she's not quite at the door when she feels the itch.

Midnight, she's been wandering for hours. One step ahead of a second relapse—not this time, fucker. What, you don't know about the spider? I run, I hide, I know every nook and shadow. I *won't* let you catch me, not again, I've got family. I am *more* than the history of the rejection of—

Blasting its horn, a flatbed guns a yellow light and nearly runs her over. Coughing dust, hurrying to the curb, she checks herself for injury: scraped knees below her dirty shorts. The spot on her arm still sore from the previous night.

Kerasha comes to her senses. She is holding a bucket, and she is not where she ought to be.

The corner of Himrod Street and Cypress Avenue is almost a mile from her uncle's house but just four blocks past the Moses Houses. What is this, she thinks, a test? Haven't I failed enough already? She looks down at her bucket. The closest streetlight blinking orange, it's too dark to see the needles, but she's knows they're in there, knows they're dirty with her blood. And here I am, four blocks past the Moses Houses—why would a legacy junkie be here, except to score?

Reassurance comes, unexpectedly, from little Kerry. The child thief, still alive in big Kerasha's head, makes her point with emphasis: yes, you're almost a mile from Uncle Shecky's house, but you're four blocks *past* the Moses Houses. In your broken-headed ramble, Kerry explains, you walked along the fence of the Moses Houses and directly before its towers, and then got yourself a full quarter mile past all the slingers and ball boys and gawkers. Look at the linen supply store, look at that boarded-up Shell station, you know these places. While you were fleeing a second relapse, your feet took you to Sisters of Mercy.

How curious.

The halfway house holds no happy memories for her. She passed her long days here reading Saint Augustine, dodging group meetings. It's hardly come to mind since she left, and mostly she remembers the smell of untreated skin disease. The chapel seat she occupied, the pasty eggs, the sawdust biscuits. The near-perfect silence she kept, which no one seemed to notice. And yet apparently this loose-bricked church has quietly held its place in some dusty corner of her heart, and has now taken control of her feet. Why did it call her here?

Outside the front door is a small congregation of smokers—the methadone crowd, she remembers. They'd been using the real stuff off and on in the cage, just like she did, and now they're jittering it out with the snake oil, too raw to sleep. Though never in this crowd herself, she had her own sleepless nights, and she used to watch the smokers from her dorm window. Counting the tiny lights and puffs to pass the time. Their minder this morning is a white woman, Sister Kimberly, and Kerasha is surprised to see her pull on her own cigarette. Good for you, she thinks, mixing in with the sinners. Then it occurs to her that any one of the sisters here could have once been a resident.

When Sister Kimberly flicks her spent cigarette into a shadow, Kerasha realizes that dawn is coming, and she hears a whisper from Sophocles: *Whatever escapes the night*, he says somewhere, *the light of day will ravage*. This is from one of the plays she read at her uncle's house, she doesn't remember which—any paragraph from one could have been sniped out and pasted into another; but the line has a special resonance now, and she takes it as a personal warning. Last night she miraculously carried her itch straight past the Moses Houses. Sunup imminent, reckoning overdue, it's time to take shelter.

The front door to Sisters of Mercy has two locks, she remembers, only one of which is ever used. But this lock is an old Italian model, and she'll need a drill to get through it. She'd have to wait out the smokers, but she can't risk that, not with the Sophocles warning. Her hour of need is now.

Her spider instincts taking over, Kerasha drops the bucket she's been carrying. Barely registers the tinkle of the needles inside.

Fence to ledge, ledge to gutter—which bends under her weight— roof to utility window, which no one ever thought to bar, and which is barely wide enough for her ass. Down on the chapel floor, here among the pews and stacked Bibles, Kerasha is hit by that old half-way smell. Here live the lost and the sick, here the surrendered and the broken.

My peeps.

Just outside the chapel is the corridor that leads to the dormitory rooms. A mumbler brushes past her, materializing and then just as quickly dematerializing in the foul air. In theory this woman is here to *transition*, as the authorities call it, but what exactly is this woman transitioning to? It's a sick joke, though the same could be said for a career thief who doubles as a legacy junkie.

The corridor silent, Kerasha quickly reaches the door to the cramped, slope-floored room she shared when she herself was transitioning here. She pauses. Her left hand feels empty. She looks at it and remembers the bucket she left behind.

The door to her old room is locked, per protocol—too many trysts and fights among the *pilgrims*, as Sister Xenia called them—but the lock doesn't last. Who's in my bed tonight, Kerasha wonders as she opens the door. Who's the new me, and what's *she* running from? Stepping lightly, she enters. Morning comes red through the barred, curtainless window. There are four twin beds, and the only empty one, she notices right away, is her own.

Was mine, she reminds herself. But then Saint Augustine whispers about God creating a new now, and Nicole tells her to trust her body, and at this moment—at this now—her body is sleepy.

The mattress has a dip on the left side, just where she left it. This dip reminds her of all that made her unhappy here. She closes her eyes, knowing she'll be unhappy here again, and falls asleep tasting the breakfast they'll serve: the pasty eggs, the sawdust biscuits. The coffee will be burnt, she knows, because nothing here comes with love.

You have to find that in yourself.

chapter 48

"Think about what you're doing," Dannie once told a player, consoling him after a production failed even by community theater standards. "You're standing in borrowed clothes. You're speaking made-up words in a made-up voice. So what if the theater is half empty. You're dreaming the ridiculous dream. Every ticket stub is a blessing."

Kerasha's daily calls, mostly around five o'clock, are more than ticket stubs. They're more than he got when she slept under his roof, and more than he's getting from Henry. But it's hard to bless *every* ticket stub when the truth is he's alone again.

"Give them time," he hears from Fat Boris, a frequent coffee buddy. "They'll come back to you."

"Your mouth to God's ears." He smiles as if he's joking.

Every five o'clock Kerasha asks about food. "What are you eating?" "How did you make it?" "Which pan did you use for the sauce?" Apparently the food at the halfway house is cockroach paste, and so far each of his care packages has been returned to him. The sisters with their rules. "What's on the stove?" she asks when she calls early. At first his answers are fabrications. His niece is in recovery, he's learned, she doesn't need to hear that he's living on Guinness. But after just a week of bullshitting about mutton and potatoes, hake and chips, cabbage stew and a curried steak, he heads out to Katti the Fish Girl. Reinvests in his fridge and larder.

He schedules his days around the five o'clock calls. He puts her on speakerphone, sets the phone in the center of the table, and lets his mouth loose as he eats. It's like they're having dinner again. What he wouldn't give for a speakerphone dinner with Henry.

"What's on your plate?" becomes Kerasha's leading question in their new routine.

His closing question hasn't changed: "When are you coming home?"

"Not today," she says. "I'm sorry, Uncle Shecky." Once she tells him she's "taking things one breath at a time." He snorts, thinking this is a joke, that she must be mocking the twelve-steppers. But then she talks about someone named Nicole, and Shecky loses the thread.

"And how are the sisters," he asks. "Still on and on with the Jesus?"

"They just want me to keep my options open," she says. Her tone is surprisingly respectful.

The weekends are full workdays, but Tuesdays and Wednesdays are slow, and Shecky often has a cocktail with his backyard neighbor Lacey, who lately has been mistaking him for her long-dead brother-in-law. Her mind is clear about her estrangement from and resentment of her own children, though, and she becomes heated when he talks about Henry.

"Never calls? Come on."

"Never."

"Once a month?"

"He was here and then he wasn't. And I've got friends who've seen him around," he adds quickly, off her alarmed expression. "Nothing bad has happened to him—he's not in a cast or anything." The bad thing happened to *me*, Shecky adds in his head.

"He's an ingrate, that's the problem," Lacey says, splashing wine as she refills their glasses. "You made a home for him. A *life*." Shecky tries to wave this off, but Lacey can't be stopped: "You taught him your trade, and you looked the other way when he brought around those trashy girls." She sounds ten years younger today, and Shecky becomes uncomfortable with the effect her words are having on him. The pride and indignation they're stirring up. "You gave him everything and now he's run off. Listen to me, David: maybe it's time to see that as a blessing."

He gives her a warm two-handed handshake, wondering who David is, but seeing real heat and loyalty in Lacey's watery eyes.

Errands. There's no Impala these days, no Mustang, that whole watcher business gone and, weirdly, a little missed. In the evening he sinks into Kerasha's armchair and sips Jameson and reads an investment magazine until he dozes. After the ten o'clock news, which for the third week running features nothing on the summer's murders, he heads up the creaking stairs, pausing every few steps, listening, without realizing it, for footsteps, for a car, for some hint that one of the kids is coming home.

On his way to his bedroom he stops at Kerasha's, which for years had been Henry's. A dangerous detour, he knows, but he can't help himself. On the wicker rocking chair that was Henry's mother's is the gray hooded sweatshirt Kerasha arrived in. The desk is carved inside out—Henry's penknife graffiti, all mushroom clouds and broken-necked bunnies and crossed swords. On the bookshelf are slim poetry chapbooks, bookended by glow-in-the-dark skulls Shecky bought for Henry the exact day—of course this was how it played out—the kid declared Halloween "bullshit." Shecky sits on the bed but feels like an intruder. In this room lives his hope that the kids really did have some kind of life in this house, that they knew family, with him and with each other, and that from time to time each of them must feel there's something to come back for. Such a fragile hope, he might break it with a sigh. He closes the door gently behind him.

"Here's the thing about those kids," Lacey Atkinson had said. They were nearly at the bottom of the bottle by this point, and most of her anger had burned off. "You loved them enough to make a home for them. And you thought that was the hard part. But take it from this old lady. I had three little bastards who grew up to be three big bastards, and I'm telling you, *that's not the hard part.*" And she fixed her watery eyes on him, and she leaned forward in her lawn chair, as if wanting to make sure she could see on his face that he was paying attention and would understand her. "Loving them *here* is nothing."

The hard part, she doesn't have to say, is loving them gone.

He shuts himself up in his room and, standing alone in the dark of his empty house, he throws up a prayer to whoever's listening. Just now and then, he thinks, just now and then—please let them—

The phone.

Out the door, across the hall, down the stairs, into the dining room. And at last he gets the phone to his ear, and the silence just before the words is a beautiful terror.

"Henry?"

Only it's Fat Boris, calling to ask if Shecky heard about Vasya.

Shecky catches his breath. "What happened to Vasya?"

"So they found him down by the subway track, in this fucking enclave?" Fat Boris says it like a question. "Someone handcuffed him to a pole. He broke his wrists, trying to pull out. But he didn't get himself out, and it was five days before someone found him. And he was dehydrated like a fucking castaway. And his wrists were all cut up from the cuffs, you know. Infected and shit. So you know what they had to do? People talk about going hands-free, but this is too much."

And when Shecky asks who did it, Fat Boris lets out a grunt that sounds like a laugh. "You think he's talking about this? They've got him in a white room over at Bellevue. But the cop I spoke to said whoever did it? Not a trace. Absolute professional."

chapter 49

Zera remains in her position at the precinct for less than a week after Nadina Villa Lobos is officially written off as an overdose, and her small part of the Human Trafficking Task Force is "consolidated" into oblivion. Zera's application for a transfer is accepted with suspicious efficiency. As if someone has been looking out for it.

In the records department she's given no long-term assignments, and her short-term projects take up only a few hours each workday. Day after day, she arrives minutes before her shift begins and clocks out seconds after it ends. The hours of her outside life are countless and quiet. She sleeps, or rather lies unmoving, on her bed, from sundown to sunup. No memories chase her. Her blood runs slow and cool.

And yet her lights are still on, and below this dark, gentle quiet, her soul is asking questions.

Is there another way to keep faith with Katja? Instead of going after the men, could she help the girls?

Zera was born of evil and had known evil all her life. She escaped evil, and then she turned herself around and faced it again. But this isn't her whole story, she reminds herself now. However brutal her early days, however quiet and cool her blood runs now, she's known kindness. Like that nonprofit that brought her out of Montenegro:

maybe she owes them help, even more than she owes the Paradise men further revenge.

Late September she submits her resignation. There are exit interviews and paperwork, but there's no discussion, official or even just conversational, of why she's leaving the department. She empties her locker: change of clothes, bar of soap, toothbrush and toothpaste. A cracked Hello Kitty lapel pin. It's a cool evening and there's still some blue in the sky when she walks out of One Police Plaza for the last time. She has no badge now, no gun, uniform, or supervisor. She also has no schedule. Everywhere forgotten, nowhere expected, she has disappeared, in one sense, but to herself she has just arrived.

Exiting the subway, then continuing on her long walk back to her studio apartment in Greenpoint, she works out a budget in her head. She has lived simply, and for years she's banked most of her police officer's salary. For a full year, longer even, she can get by on her savings. She can even go to the actually charitable charity as a volunteer.

Waiting at an intersection for traffic to pass, she considers a cover letter for her application, and falters. The words and phrases come quickly, and as quickly she rejects them. Who is this *me* I'm putting forward? Onetime beneficiary, no. Victim, no. Zera Montenegro—also no.

Who will I be—she asks herself the whole question for the first time—who will I be when I am more than what was done to me?

Zera stops short. Before her is Sweet n' Bitty, the pie shop she's walked past for years. An invitation: scents of cinnamon, of honey and toasted nuts, of fruits baked in brown sugar. She watches her reflection move and grow large on the glass door, and then she is inside.

The shop sells more than just pies, she discovers. On a stool overlooking the kitchen, she watches one of the line cooks use his thumb to scrape avocado out of its shell. "Rhubarb-apple pie," she says when her server appears, the word *rhubarb* new to her tongue. "Coffee."

A wall-mounted television screen. A video, almost silent: a man with a mole. A grocery store. A credit card. She watches the video absently at first, then confusion draws her in, and finally, without warning, she's utterly lost from herself.

It's an episode of *Mr. Bean*, she'll later learn.

Zera is sitting on a stool in Sweet n' Bitty, watching *Mr. Bean* with her whole being, when she's startled by a close sound, a clackety-snuffle so loud and strange, she rocks back in her stool. What *was* that sound? So close she almost felt it. And she looks around, and the server is smiling at her, and so is a woman on a nearby stool. And Zera realizes that this sound has come from herself.

That was me. I laughed.

She is still warm from her laugh when her coffee and pie are set before her. Her hand shakes a little as she picks up her fork. That was me, she tells herself again. More firmly now: that was me. This *is* me.

My lights are still on, she thinks, feeling warm inside. Feeling strong.

My lights are still on, and this is what I sound like.

chapter 50

Not long after he walks out of the little house on Hart Street for the last time, Henry settles into a convenient and often unclothed cohabitation with Starr. Her preferred positions—and she teaches him more than one—all have her facing the mirror. "I like to see myself happy," she tells him once in an afterglow.

Through an old client, Henry finds a job at a T-Mobile store. He takes to the work and quickly establishes himself as a kind of wizard with burner phones. New clients for the store include dealers, gangsters, adulterers, attorneys, and political operatives. The store's owners note the revenue spike, welcome the cash payments, and promote Henry to night manager.

"These are really good," Starr says to Henry one morning. She's paused with her coffee at the kitchen table, where Henry's been working with charcoal pencils and Crayola crayons. Sketching hands, eyes, and faces on a big sheet of butcher paper.

Henry pauses. Comes down from his cloud and considers his own work with some skepticism. To him everything before him looks bloodless and mathematical, but what-fucking-ever. He's given up on making something good, and is enjoying the freedom—as Emil always told him he would—of creating without giving a fuck. Now Henry looks up. Starr's expression is peculiar, and Henry at first isn't sure what to make of it. Then she shifts her feet, and Henry under-stands there's something she's excited to tell him.

"So I was walking by Pauper's Palette," she begins, and explains that the art-supply store is at last opening its top floor as an exhibit space. The first installation will be called "New Hands," and it'll showcase art by day-jobbing nobodies who've never sold anywhere. Who try, nonetheless, to express something, and put it out there, and find a name for themselves. "You should submit something."

That night Henry again snakes the toilet. "Fuck you, Louis," he says, referring to their largest and most disgusting housemate. "Fuck you, Louis," he says again as they pass in the hall. Once more in the kitchen, Henry mixes a drink, chews an edible, and sits down with his laptop to complete the online submission form.

The rejection arrives the following morning.

Henry sulks and tells Starr nothing of what's happened. A week passes, and then, nearly the exact moment he's forgotten about Pauper's Palette, Henry receives a second email. "Dear Henry," he reads, "Although we were not able to find a place for your work in our inaugural 'New Hands' installation, our judges were impressed by your 'Content and Intent' description." Reading on, Henry is amazed to learn that the bullshit he dashed off for the online submission form has secured him an invitation to "contribute content" to the installa-tion. This almost sounds like they want his art after all, but through further emails he learns that they want him to create the installation's handouts. These are to include "Content and Intent" paragraphs on the chosen works and thumbnail biographies for the chosen artists. Henry himself, of course, is not among the chosen.

"They've got balls," Henry says, oven mitts on, lifting a sausage and mushroom pizza out of the oven.

"But you submitted! That's amazing!" Starr rushes over to kiss him.

"Careful, it's hot."

"I'm so proud of you."

"But what they're asking me to do." He puts down the pizza and takes off his mitts. "It's bullshit, right?"

"It's a way in." She returns to her seat, still glowing. "Can I read what you wrote?"

The "New Hands" installation opening begins at nine o'clock, which means no one arrives before ten. Henry drags Starr by the hand and shoves a way for them through the line. Inside she releases his hand. "You're squeezing too hard."

"Sorry. Antsy."

"Antsy is okay. Hand-crushing? Not so much."

He moves from exhibit to exhibit, examining each of the paintings and sculptures inch by inch, looking for answers. Why this, why that—and not his own? Of course he performed this same exercise when writing the installation's handouts. Now, however, he's seeing many of the works in person for the first time. The broken Rubik's cube, the splash of paste on dirty cardboard. His feelings swing, every ten feet, between outrage at having been ranked below the garbage, and a sense of humbling. Here and there is genuine talent.

"Where are your handouts?" Starr asks.

Henry detaches himself from a legitimately amazing abstract oil painting. His handouts? He forgot to look.

Sometime later, Starr gives Henry a kiss before heading off for the bathroom. He watches her back and feels something warm come up in him as he wanders the exhibition. He stops before an easel he didn't notice before. The fuck? There's no way this painting was here a minute ago, no way he could've walked past it without noticing. This painting shouldn't be here. This fucking painting—is his.

It's *Starlight Friend*, the portrait of Lipz he began in high school. The one Kerasha always liked.

"Hey." A familiar voice, low for a woman. He turns and there she is.

"You stole my painting *into* the installation?"

Her little smile is back, and Henry is moved almost to tears. Kerasha nods toward a fire door. "You got a minute?"

Stairwell, Henry and Kerasha alone.

"So I got your message about the show," she says. "Obviously."

"And are you . . ."

"Clean, eight weeks." A big smile. "Thank you for the books. And thank you, thank you for the calls."

"And your church place," he says. "Are you *out* out?"

"Just for a few hours." She looks him over. "How about you? Surviving?"

"Better than that, but . . ." He goes to the corner, puts his back to one side of it, and crosses his arms over his chest. "So there's the girl, who's amazing, and the job, and it's fine. But I've still got this feeling like—I'm nobody. And it'd be different if I could say it right. Or paint it. Or at least do some fucking thing about it."

"Really." She walks to Henry's corner. Puts her back to the other side of it, so she and Henry are close but not looking right at each other. "So you think if you're not painting, or saying something with words, you don't matter?" He looks up at her, and she lowers her voice, and her eyes are on him steady. "I've watched a lot of people," she says. "And I've watched you, and here's something you maybe don't know about yourself. You're always doing things for the people you care about. Like always. So listen to me. Your feelings? They're coming out loud and clear. And for the people in your life? For me?" She nudges him with an elbow. "You matter like a motherfucker."

Henry breaks eye contact. This is too much. And while he wants to take it in, he pushes away from it. Then he tries again. I matter. Is this possible? And it's a lot, and it's tempting, and it's impossible—

And it's family.

Henry makes himself look up. "We're family," he says. "For the rest. Wherever you been, whatever you do—" He puts up an open hand. "You're not alone."

A long quiet. Her eyes are on his hand, on him, on his hand again. She's scared. And for a moment Henry can almost feel something of a past he knows so little of. And then he watches her release it.

Kerasha straightens up and takes his hand. "I'm not alone." And though her smile is uncertain, her grip is strong.

That night in the kitchen, Henry sits awake through the dark hours. His conversation with Kerasha has loosened something in him, and he thinks about Starr, asleep in the bed they've been sharing. He thinks about Kerasha, probably awake with one of her books. Then he thinks about the little house on Hart Street, the man inside. And how scared he must have been, when Henry first came into his life. A little kid—how can you protect him, when you know the devil and keep his books? Henry can't imagine what his uncle felt, not really, but he's trying.

Questions and questions, as Henry sits at the kitchen table, holding his phone.

Acknowledgments

With thanks to—
my mother, who taught me to read
my father, who told me stories
my brother, who got me to write mine down
and Jen, Max, and Faye, who woke up the heart I write from.

This story became a book because of many people. The writers Abigail Beshkin and Victoria Fullard were true creative partners. Anne Stameshkin championed the story even before she read it. Jenni Ferrari-Adler is the ultimate swashbuckling adventure-agent: she rescued the book from a lunatic (me), guided it safely on a perilous journey (revisions), and delivered it into good hands (Daphne's). Jenni also gave the book its name. Daphne Durham is an editor whose awesomeness is so unbelievable I actually thought at first she wasn't real. I still sometimes have my doubts, but Daphne's edits and insights have been *beyond*. Thanks, also, to Jenni's Union Literary team, including Taylor Curtin, Shaun Dolan, and Sally Wofford-Girand, and to Daphne's MCD / Farrar, Straus and Giroux team, including the mighty Lydia Zoells, Sara Birmingham, Janine Barlow, Tyler Comrie, Rodrigo Corral, Abby Kagan, Maureen Klier, Sean McDonald, Alex Merto, Lauren Roberts, and Jeff Seroy. I am also grateful to Jiah Shin at Creative Artists Agency for championing this story in television.

Other early readers, supporters, and advisors have included Mike Attebery, Mikael Awake, Mike Brecher, Katrina Carrasco, Harlan Coben, Jay Dyer, Rob Hart, Liz Keenan, Josh Kendall, Karyn Marcus, Kimberly McCreight, Jenny

Milchman, Madeline Miller, Gigi Pandian, Katie Petrachonis, Alex Rehm, John Scopelleti, Jeff Soloway, Clare Toohey, Patricia Voda, Greg Wands, and Ruiyan Xu.

Additional life support while writing this book came from the following people and, in many cases, their whole families: Mike Strausz and the JC: Seth Kessler, Aaron Kobernick, David Parzen, Matt Rochkind, and Dan Zimmerman. The LaSpinas and Chiofalos. Meredith, Z, O, and E Selfon, the Hirshenson family, Leon Sompolinsky & Lauren Leimbach, Barbara Michalak Reilly, John Paul Reilly, John Michael Reilly, Jill, J, and C Reilly, and the Sloane family. Chad Benson & Sarah Robb, Emily Bradford, Angel LaPorte, Osaretin Omoigui, Karla Nappi, Ben Ross, Willie Schaeffer, Felice Sontupe, Paul Strocko, Laura Utrata and Bill Vasilopoulos, John Weber, and Meredith Weil.

These lists are incomplete. Forgive me.